LESSONS IN LIFE

JULIE HOUSTON

Boldwood

First published in Great Britain in 2025 by Boldwood Books Ltd.

Copyright © Julie Houston, 2025

Cover Design by Alice Moore Design

Cover Images: Shutterstock

The moral right of Julie Houston to be identified as the author of this work has been asserted in accordance with the Copyright, Designs and Patents Act 1988.

All rights reserved. No part of this book may be reproduced in any form or by any electronic or mechanical means, including information storage and retrieval systems, without written permission from the author, except for the use of brief quotations in a book review. This book is a work of fiction and, except in the case of historical fact, any resemblance to actual persons, living or dead, is purely coincidental.

Every effort has been made to obtain the necessary permissions with reference to copyright material, both illustrative and quoted. We apologise for any omissions in this respect and will be pleased to make the appropriate acknowledgements in any future edition.

A CIP catalogue record for this book is available from the British Library.

Paperback ISBN 978-1-83561-016-9

Large Print ISBN 978-1-83561-017-6

Hardback ISBN 978-1-83561-015-2

Ebook ISBN 978-1-83561-018-3

Kindle ISBN 978-1-83561-019-0

Audio CD ISBN 978-1-83561-010-7

MP3 CD ISBN 978-1-83561-011-4

Digital audio download ISBN 978-1-83561-012-1

This book is printed on certified sustainable paper. Boldwood Books is dedicated to putting sustainability at the heart of our business. For more information please visit https://www.boldwoodbooks.com/about-us/sustainability/

Boldwood Books Ltd, 23 Bowerdean Street, London, SW6 3TN

www.boldwoodbooks.com

To the Kalkan Chicks: Clare, Jilly and Vicky. Long may we drink rosé in the sunshine.

PROLOGUE
JANUARY 1964, MIRPUR, PAKISTAN

Junayd

'I'm not going there, *Ammi*. I'm really not.' Fifteen-year-old Junayd Sattar turned to face his mother. He pointed the old-fashioned Kodak 35 in her direction, knowing his memory of her was likely to fade if he was to do as she was now pleading, while knowing a photo would not.

'But your father insists, Junayd. Allah only knows, I don't want to lose you and your brothers as well as your father, but you can't stay here. I can't stay here much longer either with your sisters, but there is the opportunity for *you* to go to England. The British government is inviting you – begging you to go to work there. It is a rich country – you will go to school there for a few years and then work hard and make money. And what an opportunity, Junayd, what a great thing it will be to join your *abba* and your uncles and make us all so proud. Once you are given a great education, you can maybe go to Oxford or Cambridge and become a doctor? Or, if not, you could make your fortune working in the grand textile mills they have over there, and then have money to bring back here and we will all go and live in Lahore...'

Junayd turned away from his mother and walked to the open door of the family's simple three rooms, welcoming the arrival of the warm winter rain now falling gently onto the acres and acres of farmland and allotments of his village of Tangdew and the chessboard of surrounding villages, laid out like a painting in front of him. Beautiful land, his native land, *his* land, which would soon be covered over by the black fathomless depths of the Mangla Dam. Here, where the Jhelum River met the heavily forested foothills of the Pir Panjal mountains, billions of gallons of water would be driven in to devour the haze of colour in front of him – shades of mauve, ochre and green – while he and his family were driven out.

Junayd raised his beloved camera once again, clicking for posterity his homeland that would soon be no more.

1

JANUARY 2024, BEDDINGFIELD, WEST YORKSHIRE

Robyn

'Robyn, no, no, stay. Stay in my *lurve nest*.' Fabian's arm snaked seductively round my middle, his hands warm, searching, inviting as I started to move from the bed.

'Oh God, if only.' I eased my body back towards him, wanting nothing more than to remain. I was torn between tittering at the daft expression he'd just come out with, responding to this heavenly man's hands or jumping out of said *lurve nest*, aka Fabian's bed, in his sister Jemima's apartment in Harrogate. Glancing at my phone on the bedside table, I took the third option, horrible though it was, and headed for the shower.

'Well, at least let me in there with you,' Fabian called. 'I don't recall christening that shower yet.'

'Fabian,' I yelled over the Niagara Falls explosion of icy water that had me screeching like a banshee, 'it's almost 6 a.m. and it's... hell, it's... freezing... I've to be in school by eight thirty... Oh, I can't stand this... any longer... were you timing me...? Did I manage the full minute...?' I stabbed at the temperature control, letting out a moan of pure ecstasy as warmth replaced the cold and my numb fingers started to return to life.

'You're such a drama queen.' Fabian was at the basin now, cleaning his teeth.

'Drama *teacher*.' I grinned, pulling at the white towel around Fabian's hips, eager as always to get a final glimpse of his toned buttocks to see me through the days ahead without his actual presence.

'But it's the first day of the new term. No kids in, you said. What's the hurry?'

'You know what that road out of Leeds is like on a Monday morning. And,' I added primly, 'I'm a professional. The kids might not actually be in school, but I can't turn up to the morning's staff meeting in last night's little black dress and ridiculous heels.' I rubbed at my right leg. It had just about recovered from the ACL accident that had brought me back to Yorkshire from my time in musical theatre in London, but did still give me some gyp, especially after subjecting it to several hours in my one and only pair of heels.

'Give that headteacher of yours a hard-on if you did.' Fabian *would* persist in bringing up the fact that Mason Donoghue – the rather gorgeous and charismatic head of St Mede's – and I had had a bit of a fling last term. Not overly professional of either of us but, *as far as I knew*, we'd been discreet, it had lasted only a few weeks and both of us had been aware that we'd sought each other out when the person we both really wanted to be with was unavailable.

'Right, I'm off,' I said, once I'd towelled myself dry and pulled on jeans and a jumper. 'Got to go home and get changed before school. All my files are there too. What are you up to?'

'Oh, the usual.'

'The usual?'

'Cooking, cleaning, shopping. Walking Boris on The Stray. A man's work is never done...'

'Do you miss it?'

'What?'

'You know what.' I went to put my arms around this man I'd adored since first setting eyes on him defending in the Central Criminal Court in London eight months earlier. I'd taken myself along to Courtroom 4 hoping to find a woman barrister I could emulate for the part in a TV drama I'd been up for later that week. I hadn't got the part, but had ended up losing my heart to Fabian Mansfield Carrington KC, son of Roland Carrington, Lord Chief Justice of England and Wales.

'Hmm, sometimes. You know...' Fabian broke off, nuzzling at my neck. I batted him away, simultaneously looking at my watch, but knowing I needed to understand what Fabian was thinking.

'Oh, Fabian, it was your life. All you'd worked for.' I held my breath. Was Fabian trying to tell me he wanted to go back to London? Back to the beautiful family-owned apartment overlooking Green Park? Back to his roots in Marlow in Buckinghamshire? Back to his burgeoning career in the Old Bailey? 'Am *I* the one stopping you returning south? I'll come back with you, if that's what you want?' I took his hand. 'Really.'

'What and tear you away from St Mede's, that most prestigious of educational establishments in the whole of West Yorkshire?'

'Don't scoff,' I snapped crossly.

'Robyn,' Fabian said calmly as if talking to an argumentative child, 'it's a sink school, struggling to survive with a headteacher who'll be off the minute something else comes up. The kids are bloody hard work and the staff are fed up. I bet half the teachers will have rung in sick with Covid or flu or some other made-up complaint when the doors are actually opened to the kids again in the morning.'

'So, *do you* want to go back?' I felt my heart sink a little.

'I didn't say that, Robyn. The work was making me ill, you know that. Dealing with the flak from defending the Soho Slasher while trying to live up to the Carrington name...' Fabian broke off and I knew he was still fighting his demons. All the Carrington family, including his misogynistic and racist half-brother, Julius, with whom I'd had several run-ins, were well known in London's legal world and were blaming me for Fabian's defection from his chosen profession. 'It's just that I'm at a bit of a loss with what to do with myself. It's fine when Jemima's here – which isn't very often – and you're here, which, now that the new term's begun, will be even less. There's only so much helping out at food banks or giving free legal advice to those on the streets who can't afford it. So, yes, I do miss striding around a court, bantering with the CPS, irritating the judge – as I so often did – in charge of the proceedings.'

'OK, what about your dream?'

'Which one? Since last night, all my dreams now feature you in that black basque and suspenders you had hidden under your dress.'

'Hidden?' I laughed, remembering Fabian propelling me from our table at the black-tie do we'd been invited to by Fabian's lovely younger sister who'd been up for some business award and outside into the freezing January evening. 'Well, you certainly found them.' I laughed, slightly embarrassed, recalling Fabian's hands slowly inching up my black-stockinged legs, my back arched against the cold Yorkshire stone of the grand building on the outskirts of Leeds. The cry of release, muffled by Fabian's hand, as he brought me – as he always did – to an explosive climax. 'Your restaurant dream?' I insisted, even though I knew, by staying to talk some more, I was going to end up stuck in traffic on the M62.

'Oh, just a dream.' Fabian smiled sadly. 'What do *I* know about starting up an eating establishment when there are restaurants going to the wall on a daily basis?'

'What do *you* know about food? Fabian, food is your life...'

'Don't be daft. *You're* my life.'

'...and don't forget you came third in the Christmas Yorkshire TopChef competition. Still not sure how you wormed your way into that one, having only been resident in Yorkshire for a couple of months at the time.'

'But beaten by your sister.' Fabian laughed. 'Now, she *is* good. Jess is a natural.'

'So are you,' I soothed. 'You know more about what to do with a Jerusalem artichoke than I do with a bag of cheese and onion crisps. Right, I really am off.'

'People can't afford to eat out any more.' Fabian sighed, pulling me towards him again, unwilling, I knew, to let me go.

'Unless you're in London? Where all the dosh is? Are you saying, Fabian, that London's the place you'd want to have a restaurant?'

'God no...' Fabian paused. 'I don't know. I don't know *what* I want. Apart from you, Robyn.' He smiled, reaching for my coat buttons and fastening me up as he might a child before taking Boris's collar to prevent him following me out into the still-dark January morning. 'Go on, off you go, ignore me, it's just a miserable Monday in January and I'm not used to having no structure to my day. And, I'm missing you already.'

* * *

As I drove the thirty miles back to my mum's place in Beddingfield, the pretty village in West Yorkshire where I'd grown up and where Mum still lived in the small cottage next to my big sister, Jess, I knew Fabian and I had some serious decision-making to do. Shortly after I'd met him, he'd taken on the defence of Rupert Henderson-Smith, possibly London's most prolific rapist and murderer to date. Henderson-Smith, an ex-Etonian whose family moved in the same social circles as Fabian's parents, had been dubbed the Soho Slasher for his predilection for slaughtering young women in the Soho area where I'd been living at the time. The relief I'd felt when Henderson-Smith was finally arrested and charged, and women like myself were able to walk the streets safely once more, turned to anger when, without telling me, Fabian colluded with his family to take on the notorious case. The subsequent hate and trolling, as well as verbal and physical attacks directed at Fabian outside his London apartment and chambers by women's groups, had him leaving the case, his profession and his family. He'd fled north to recover from the onslaught, moving in with Jemima, house-sitting and dog-sitting when Jemima flew off around Europe in her role as financial advisor to a large American company.

I swore when the traffic in front started to slow down as I neared the junction for the M62, rear lights blinking and turning red as the cars came to a standstill. I really was going to be late and Mason wouldn't be happy. He could be as sharp-tongued and demanding of his staff as he was of the five hundred kids in his care. I saw a gap in the traffic and went for it.

* * *

'You're going to be late, Robyn.' Mum was already switching on the kettle.

'I know, I know, I know.' I headed for my room – the tiny box room with its single bed I'd moved into on my return from London back in September.

'Is your knee giving you trouble again?' Mum called after me. 'You were limping slightly just then.'

'Wearing high heels when I shouldn't,' I called back down the stairs. Jeans, sweater, trainers, that was all I needed for a teachers-only day.

Ten minutes later I grabbed at the toast and marmalade Mum had prepared for me. 'What're you up to?'

'Well, actually, I'm going up to Hudson House with Jess.'

'Oh?' I turned to Mum, draining my cup of coffee and swallowing before ramming in the remains of the toast. 'You reckon you're ready for an old folks home, then?'

'I didn't hear a word of that,' Mum tutted. 'Don't speak with your mouth full.' Mum might have brought up the three of us – Jess, me and fifteen-year-old Sorrel – for the majority of our childhoods as a single mum, but she'd constantly insisted on good manners throughout.

'I know, I know.' I grinned in her direction. '"I didn't bring you up by hand" to have you speaking with your mouth full,' I added, misquoting Mrs Gargery to the recalcitrant Pip in *Great Expectations*, as the three of us always did when Mum got uppity. 'So, why are you off to Hudson House if not to bag a bed up there?'

'I'm feeling so much better these days now that Matt has got me onto this new medication. There's little to be done out in the garden this time of year – which is where I'd rather be – so I'm going to do a bit of volunteering, you know, *chatting and patting* as Jess calls it up at the home.'

Matt Spencer was Mum's new consultant at the local hospital where she'd ended up back in the autumn after a particularly frightening attack of acute porphyria, the chronic, possibly inherited, ailment she'd had to deal with most of her adult life. He'd not only got her up and running again and on some new drugs that appeared to be keeping her in remission, but seemed also to be giving her a new lease of life. And, I acknowledged, wishing I'd time for another coffee, this lovely, rather shy consultant had fallen in love with Jess into the bargain, and, for that, we all loved him back.

'Oh, I thought you must be turning yourself in up there.' I laughed, reaching for my car keys and school bag.

'Robyn, I'm fifty-four years old.' Mum sniffed. 'I'm ready for a bit of life after spending all these years bringing you three up while waiting for your dad to show his face.'

'Not sure you're going to find any life in God's Waiting Room,' I chortled. 'And,' I added, 'you're getting very bolshie these days, you know.' It was rare for Mum to criticise Jayden, our Jamaican-heritage reggae-singing dad with whom she'd run off, leaving her adoptive parents somewhere in Sheffield, intent on no return. *Somewhere in Sheffield* was about all we knew of these grandparents of ours because that was all we'd ever been told about the couple who'd adopted Mum as a tiny baby. It had been only very recently that Jayden, with his morbid fear of educational establishments brought about after being excluded from the many he'd been sent to, had let on that Mum had actually attended St Mark's just outside Sheffield, one of the top public schools in the country. Jess and I had grilled Mum after this revelation, but all she'd say was that it was all in the past and that was where it was going to stay.

'So, good, you're doing a bit of volunteering. Get you out and about. A chance to meet new people rather than always waiting in, hoping Jayden's going to drop by.'

Mum snorted derisively. 'You'll have me doing armchair aerobics next and getting excited when I throw a one in a game of Beetle.'

'Bit ageist that, Mum. Listen, if you've so much time on your hands, you can always come and help the wardrobe department with this production of *Grease* we're putting on at Easter.'

Mum's eyes lit up. 'Ooh, yes, I'll do that. I'm not bad with a needle.'

'Except we don't actually have a wardrobe yet. And certainly, no props or outfits to go in it.'

* * *

'You're late, Ms Allen.' Mason Donoghue was obviously in one of his moods. Probably his wife, to whom he'd recently returned after a fairly lengthy separation, giving him earache again. 'Right,' he went on as I slid into the vacant seat next to Petra Waters, the deputy head sitting to Mason's left. 'Can we crack on? We've a lot to discuss and, I'm afraid, it's not all pleasant.'

Petra shifted her feet, appearing unsure where to put them next.

'Unpleasant?' I whispered, pulling a face. 'What's that all about?' Then, as Petra massaged her six-months-pregnant abdomen, I asked, 'You OK?'

Mason broke off from speaking, glaring over his spectacles in our direction.

'Wind,' she reassured me, moving slightly once more. 'One big burp and I'd be fine, but don't think that would go down too well, do you?'

'Why's Mason glaring at us? Doesn't he understand pregnant women have special needs?'

'You shouldn't be sitting there. That chair's for Melanie Potter. You'll have to shift once she arrives.'

'Who?'

'Shh...'

'Any relation to Harry? Is she a wizard?'

Petra tittered. 'No, chair of governors. Once Mason's given us the third degree, she's coming into the meeting to talk to us.'

'What about?'

Petra raised her eyebrows in my direction but said nothing more, settling back while Mason went through the usual litany of directives: timetabling, staff lateness, staff dress – he didn't want to see anyone without a tie...

'I don't own a tie,' I whispered and Petra laughed, turning it into a cough as Mason glanced our way once more.

'So,' Mason went on, 'I'm planning a series of team breakfasts in my office: I want each subject department, the administration team, the caretakers and kitchen staff to join me in turn...'

'He's not asking us to share our Rice Krispies with Caretaker Ken?' I pulled a face in Petra's direction.

'Now,' Mason said, obviously back in his stride, 'since September I've observed at least one of all of your lessons and I'll be starting the cycle once again from next week. I'm not there to judge...'

I found myself switching off from Mason's pep talk, conjuring up, instead, lovely pictures of Fabian in his tux and black tie at Jemima's do the previous evening. The mere thought of ever losing him again, as I had when we'd fallen out over his unpleasant family and Fabian's decision to defend the Soho Slasher, was enough to have my pulse race in anguish.

'Excuse me...'

'Robyn...' Petra was nudging me none too gently and I looked up from my lovely reverie to find the entire staff staring at me and a tall, raw-boned woman, perhaps in her fifties, hovering meaningfully at my side.

'Oh, sorry, sorry.' I jumped up, removing myself, overflowing bag and files to the vacant chair at the back of the staffroom in order that Melanie Potter could claim her rightful place at the front with the senior leadership team.

'I know Mason wanted me here this morning,' Ms Potter was saying, 'to support him as regards a couple of things that have arisen over the Christmas break. As Chair of Governors, I need you to know that one of St Mede's pupils was very badly hurt in a knife attack last night. It will be on the local news this evening and both myself and Mason have been asked to comment.'

'One of our kids?' Jo Cooper, Head of History, spoke the question that was on all our lips.

'Joel Sinclair.' Mason nodded, visibly upset.

'Joel?' I briefly closed my eyes. Joel Sinclair, one of the most talented dancers I'd come across in years, with the potential to go far were he allowed to do just that by the OCG of drug dealers his family was a part of. Joel Sinclair, the lovely, exceptionally bright kid who'd rescued me from the notorious Year 9 class on my very first morning here at St Mede's. Joel Sinclair, my little sister Sorrel's best friend.

I realised Melanie and Mason had moved on. Already moved on from something *so awful*? Was there worse to come?

There apparently was.

'...And this terrible incident, which unfortunately happened late last night on the edge of the school playing fields – I'm assuming you all came in through the main gate and didn't see the police cordons – will do absolutely nothing to help what we're about to tell you now.'

Ms Potter paused, and there was a collective holding of breath as the entire staff focused on what the chair of governors was about to say.

'In a nutshell, the local authority is determined to go ahead with what they've been wanting to do for years.'

'What? Close us down?' Dave Mallinson, Head of English, asked.

'Knock us down,' Mason put in dryly. 'Apparently Frozen has had its eye on the site for years. Melanie and I were in a meeting yesterday and the local council can't wait to wash its hands of us. The Sattar brothers are determined to go ahead with their plans.'

'The Sattar brothers?' Molly Burkinshaw, the young maths teacher who was even newer to St Mede's than me, turned in my direction.

'Local businessmen,' I whispered. 'They're intent on world domination when it comes to their frozen fishfingers and sweetcorn.'

'Blimey.' Molly blew out a long sigh.

'Blimey indeed,' I replied.

2

The full staff meeting, followed by departmental meetings, seemed to go on for ever. I found myself having to straddle both the English department meeting, run by Dave Mallinson, an old-timer whom I liked enormously, as well as the girls' PE department under whose directive my role as dance teacher unfortunately sat. Unfortunately, because Colleen McCartney, Head of PE, and I didn't always see eye to eye. Colleen's ideas for teaching dance were at odds with my own: she appeared to actually teach as little of it as possible, wanting instead to get the kids out cross-country running or on the netball courts. The cross-country running invariably ended up with the older girls hunkered down behind the hedge at the boundary of the school premises, reaching for their phones and vapes to get them through the sixty-minute session. I was convinced Colleen was totally aware of what was going on, but at least they were out of Colleen's hair – and her gym – and she wasn't being confronted with bolshie adolescents refusing to shin up ropes or go in goal on the hockey pitch.

I spent the compulsory twenty minutes with Colleen and the two ECT PE teachers, outlining my plans for the spring term before escaping down to the drama studio in the very bowels of the school. Expecting it to be as freezing down there as it usually was – and especially after the two weeks' Christmas break – I was pleasantly surprised to find it warm and actually fairly inviting. I'd spent a lot of time at the end of last term ensuring the studio was as welcoming as possible. Not only for the kids in my dance and drama classes, but also for the mums who'd asked if they could come along to the contemporary dance, as well as the Zumba and Sh'bam sessions I'd started running at their request.

'You responsible for this?' I asked as Mason appeared at my side.

'For what?'

'Putting the heat on. You usually say your budget won't stretch to it.' I raised an eye in his direction thinking, as I always did, that, had Fabian not reappeared in my life and Mason's wife not returned to his, there would probably still be something ongoing between us.

'Yep.'

'Good of you.'

'I don't want to lose you.'

'Lose me?'

'Now that your barrister bloke has come to reclaim you I'm half expecting you to hand in your notice and be heading back to your old life in London with him.'

'Possibly on the cards.' I nodded, recalling the conversation with Fabian that morning. 'And,' I added, 'if you remember I'm here at St Mede's on a supply basis. I don't have to give you *any* notice.'

Mason looked worried. 'I'd forgotten that. Right, we need to get you onto contract.'

'No, we don't,' I warned. 'I like the freedom supply work gives me. Means I can be up and off at the drop of a hat.'

'I'll have a word with Melanie Potter re an actual contract,' Mason said, ignoring what I was saying. 'And are you? Thinking of going? You wouldn't leave us when we're in the middle of rehearsals for *Grease*?' Mason put a hand on my arm, stroking it gently, and I gave it, and then its owner, a warning glance.

'No, of course not. I wouldn't do that to the kids when they've been working so hard.' I looked pointedly at Mason's hand where it continued to rest on my arm, and eventually he sighed, removing it. 'The thing is, Robyn, what you and I had…'

'What you and I had?' I actually laughed at that. 'Mason, we had a bit of a fling.'

'Oh, surely it was more than a bit of a fling?'

'A bit of a fling,' I repeated firmly. 'And both of us always worried that Petra and the rest of the staff would cotton on to what was going on. Does your wife *know* what went on?'

'Does your barrister?' Mason came right back at me.

'No. Although, to be honest, it really is nothing to do with him who I was with when we weren't together.'

'Exactly.' Mason nodded. 'Nothing to do with my wife either. She and I were separated at the time.'

We stood our ground, both of us slightly embarrassed where this conversation appeared to be taking us, and it was something of a relief when Petra appeared at the door.

'You two OK?' Always suspicious that something was going on between the pair of us, Petra narrowed her eyes slightly. 'Police are here, Mason. Want to talk to you about Joel.'

Joel. Goodness, in all this skirting round each other, I realised Mason and I hadn't discussed Joel Sinclair.

'Does your Sorrel know anything?' Petra asked, folding her

arms and leaning against the doorframe. 'She and Joel are pretty close, aren't they?'

I nodded. 'He's her best mate although, to be honest, Mum's none too happy that they're friends. His family has one hell of a reputation. And my dad, who deigned to call in on Boxing Day, actually tried coming the heavy father with her. Which is a bit of a laugh, seeing he was never really there for any of us when we were growing up.'

'He's getting quite a name for himself, your dad.' Mason, always a fan of Jayden's reggae-based music, waxed lyrical about the man as he always did. 'Heard him being interviewed on Radio 4 the other morning.'

'Let's hope Sorrel gets the place at Susan Yates Theatre School,' Petra said, ignoring Mason's fanboying of my dad. 'Get her out of Joel's way.'

'I like Joel.' I frowned. 'He's a good kid. Bright. He just wants to dance, but he's in too deep with his dad's lot.'

'I think it's got bigger now than simply his dad's mates,' Mason said.

Petra shook her head. 'Surely the Youth Justice Service and his defence team will make sure he's afforded some protection? You know, now that he's in hospital? Isn't that what being on a court order means? To rehabilitate?'

'Look, the pair of you—' Mason turned back to us '—keep this to yourself. I don't want the world and his wife knowing – these people that Joel's got himself involved with are, apparently, highly organised. It's not a two-bit village affair, you know. There's a network that's spread across Yorkshire, into Manchester and down to Birmingham and London, factions within this network fighting for their position as top dog. They have kids like Joel starting "work" in the morning after being handed a backpack of drugs, a burner phone, a bike and a knife, all of which are handed back at the end of the "shift".'

We both stared at Mason, and Petra put a hand to her growing bump as if to protect her unborn child from what was going on in a world it would be introduced to in just a few months' time.

'Joel rarely opens up to me,' Mason went on, 'but I had a chat with him on the last day of term and he said, "Mr Donoghue, what's the alternative? My dad's in prison and is being coerced in there just as much as I am out here. I have to think about my dad, and my mum and my little sister."'

'Oh, poor Joel,' I said. 'And all he wants to do is sit his GCSEs and then get into dance as a career. Fat chance of that while he's being controlled like this.'

'My biggest concern,' Mason went on, 'is that it's actually easier for kids like Joel to ultimately accept their lot rather than get themselves out of it. To become hardened to it all and end up simply working their way up the career-criminal ladder. Joel's very bright; it could easily become his profession. And, if it does, he'll probably end up very rich: the bosses of these types of criminal gangs are millionaires,' he added.

'Or very dead,' I said bleakly. 'I need to get Sorrel away from him, don't I?'

* * *

'How was your first day back?' Jess, head in a recipe book, didn't look up as I walked into her kitchen. She was back from a shift at Hudson House and, as per usual, up to her ears creating fabulous food.

'A bit disconcerting, to be honest.'

'Oh?' Jess was obviously too intent on scanning the page in front of her to take in what I was saying.

When she didn't respond further, I said, 'Didn't think you needed cookery books?'

'I don't really. Just checking whether Delia adds vinegar to her meringues. Never convinced it's the best thing to do.'

'Where's Lola?'

'In bed.'

'Oh?'

'She's been with Dean all day,' Jess went on. 'Had a McDonald's and been to the cinema with him; probably eaten too much junk food.'

'You OK with that?'

'What, her knocking back burgers and chocolate milkshake? No, not really...' She stopped. 'Oh, you mean her spending time with Dean? Of course; he's her dad.' Jess glanced across at me. 'She says she wants him to come back home. That *he* wants to come back home.'

'Forget that.' I almost laughed. 'When you've got the lovely consultant in your bed and your life?'

'I know, I know... it's just...'

'Just what?' I moved over to the kitchen unit where Jess was working, pinching a couple of blueberries intended for the so far non-existent meringues. 'Don't tell me you're even *thinking* of having that tosser back.'

'Dean's Lola's dad.'

'Now you're behaving like Mum always did with Jayden. Letting him back in when he'd tired of wherever he'd been. And with whoever he'd been with.'

Ignoring the criticism, Jess finally gave me her full attention. 'Disconcerting?'

'Sorry?'

'You said the day had been disconcerting. I thought it was teachers-only day today? It was at Lola's school. Hence Lola being with Dean.'

'It was.'

'So, how come disconcerting?' she asked once again. 'You suddenly realised you've still got the hots for Mason Donoghue?' Jess, only half listening, carried on perusing recipes. Mason's granny, Denise, was in Jess's care up at Hudson House and Jess, along with Mum, thought Mason quite marvellous. I knew the pair of them still weren't convinced that Fabian, after our big fallout in London four months earlier, was the right man for me.

'No!' I tutted crossly. 'For heaven's sake, Jess. No, two things announced in the staff meeting this morning: Joel Sinclair's been attacked—'

'Joel Sinclair? That friend of Sorrel's? Her boyfriend? If he is her boyfriend? What do you mean *attacked*?' That news finally had Jess relegating Delia into second place.

'Rival drug gang probably. It'll be on TV on tonight's *Focus North*. Where *is* Sorrel? She was in bed when I left this morning and wasn't next door when I got home.'

'*I* don't know,' Jess said somewhat irritably. 'She's almost sixteen, about to leave home if she wins the place at the Susan Yates place in London. She'll be out and about with her mates somewhere.'

'She doesn't have that many friends,' I reminded Jess. 'Spends most of her time with Joel.'

'Maybe she's up at the hospital visiting.'

'Don't think that'd be allowed, do you? You know, with all the police stuff going on. Sorrel won't be able to just swan onto the ward with a bunch of grapes. Joel's already got a conviction and on a pretty tough youth court order...'

'A court order?' Jess frowned, but continued separating eggs, carefully weighing the whites in a bowl.

'For possession with intent to supply,' I said.

'You seem to know a lot about it.' Jess gave me her full attention again.

'Well, yes, I do. With Joel being friendly with Sorrel, Mason keeps me in the loop with what's going on.'

'Best thing for Sorrel is to make sure she gets this place in London. Get her away from someone involved in all this. Especially if now he's been attacked.' Jess reached for a bag of sugar but suddenly stared in my direction. 'And, at least Sorrel wasn't with him last night when he was hurt.'

'She was round here with you, wasn't she? Another maths session with you and Matt?' We were all helping to get Sorrel's maths grades up: the Susan Yates Theatre School was as intent on academic strength as on their demand for exceptional talent in the creative arts.

'You said there were two disconcerting things?' Jess looked up again. 'Mum's OK, isn't she?'

'Hasn't she been with you up at Hudson House? She said she was going to.'

Jess nodded. 'She's been with me most of the afternoon. I actually left her there, chatting away to the old men. They took one look at her and were like bees round a honeypot. We forget – or at least I do sometimes when I just see her as our mum – what a stunning-looking woman she is. You know, with her gardening gloves on, or when she's not been too well and having to rest on the sofa, I forget how gorgeous she is. She was having a great time; says she wants to come up on a regular basis. Give her some confidence about applying for some part-time work.'

'Really? Oh, well, that's good. She was so much happier when she had that little job in the gift shop and café in the village. I've never understood why she hasn't done the degree course she's always wanted to do. She did get her A levels, although she never told us she had until recently. For some reason she's always liked us to believe she'd run off with Jayden at sixteen or seventeen rather than waiting until the minute she'd done her A levels.'

'You know why,' Jess said mildly. 'Didn't want us delving into that posh public school she went to. Didn't want us to find out more about those adoptive parents of hers. And she was never able to enrol on any degree course as a mature student for the same reason she couldn't commit to other things she wanted to do. She's always been so aware of the bloody awful condition she inherited.'

'Suppose.' I looked round for the tin that was always full of Jess's home-made biscuits.

'So?' Jess stopped what she was doing, turning her full attention on me.

'So?'

'The disconcerting thing, apart from this friend of Sorrel's being set upon?'

'St Mede's is in danger of being closed down.'

'It's always had a stay of execution over its head, has that place. It was on the point of either falling down, or being closed down, when we were kids at Beddingfield Comp. You know, when the St Mede's lot would ambush us on the school bus?'

I nodded, remembering. We'd always been up for a tussle with the rival school in the next village.

'And, anyway, why's that of concern to *you*?' Jess asked, giving me one of her looks. 'You hated the place when you started there in September. I thought you'd be out of there as soon as you could? Heading back to London with Fabian?'

I was beginning to realise that although she'd now met Fabian and said she approved of him, Jess seemed unable to talk about him without some little derogatory dig, without an air of slight disparagement. I knew it was probably only Jess in full-on protective mode, but also knew it had been a major coup when Jess had beaten him into third place just before Christmas, when they'd both got into the finals of the Yorkshire Christmas TopChef competition.

'Possibly.' I nodded. 'You're right. If Fabian heads back south, I'll be going with him.'

'So, you're thinking of packing up and leaving us all again, are you?' Despite Jess's apparent flippant comments re my returning to London, I knew she'd hate me leaving Beddingfield again. Especially as Sorrel would possibly be on the point of leaving too.

'I hate only seeing Fabian for snatched weekends,' I said. I was already missing him, felt depressed at the thought of my lonely single bed next door at Mum's place. On the couple of occasions he'd stayed over with me at Mum's cottage, we'd had to bunk down together in the single bed. We'd both been uneasy, embarrassed even, at finding ourselves having to revert to the status of teenagers, knowing Mum was in her room across the landing and Sorrel able to hear any cries of passion through the thin wall separating her bedroom from the tiny box room we were in. To be fair, Mum had offered up her bed, but I'd no intention of turfing her out. As a result, as soon as Christmas was over (both Fabian and his sister, Jemima, had dutifully returned to the bosom of the Carrington family for the festive season) I'd gone to stay with Fabian in Harrogate but, with a new term about to start, that was no longer possible.

It really was time to move on.

'Actually,' Jess was now saying, 'you're not the only one to have had some disconcerting news today.'

'Oh? What's up? You pregnant?' I laughed in Jess's direction at the very idea.

'Yes.'

'What?' My head shot up in shock. 'You and Dr Matt are having a baby?' A little part of me felt a flicker of envy. Why, I'd no idea. I wasn't yet thirty and the last thing I wanted was a baby.

'No, of course not, you moron.' Jess was grinning. 'There's a rumour going round the staff that the Richardsons, who own Hudson House, are ready to sell up.'

'Oh?' I stared. 'What do you mean?'

'What d'you *think* I mean? John and Ruth Richardson have had enough and want out. Mind you, they've not said a word to me about it so probably just a rumour. You know, tittle tattle and gossip are rife in care homes.'

'As in any institution,' I said. 'So as a going concern?'

'Well, yes, I suppose so. I hope so anyway. Otherwise, that's my job and everyone else's at Hudson House up the swanny. I heard Bex, one of the staff, talking. She clammed up when she knew I was behind her so I had a word with Brenda in the kitchen – she's always my grass – who tells me everything that's going on. Someone called Kamran Sattar apparently.'

'One of the Sattar brothers?'

'Never heard of the Sattar brothers. Should I have? Are they famous?' Jess asked.

'Frozen? The Sattar brothers who own the frozen-food factory on Willow Lane where you worked at one point? Of course you've heard of them!'

'Oh, *them*?' Jess, about to turn on her Kenwood to whisk egg whites, stopped in her tracks. 'Blimey, are they taking over the whole village?'

'Well, apparently, they're after St Mede's,' I said. 'Want the place pulled down so they can buy the land from the council and expand Frozen. The council will think all their Christmases have come at once. A good price for the site, a surfeit of new jobs for those who want them and, best of all, the closing down of the local education authority's biggest headache.'

'They can't want the Hudson House site as well, then, surely?' Jess stared. 'I really assumed it was being sold as a going concern. All the guests able to stay and not have to be found places for. Well, that really has ruined my day. Thank you very much, Robyn.'

3

LISA

Thank goodness for Matt Spencer. *Dr* Matt Spencer. Of course, it was de rigueur to call consultants *Mr*, but Lisa had never understood the logic behind this little anomaly. Why go through all that medical training to gain the coveted title, only to discard it once the professional ladder had been climbed? And Matt, at only thirty-five, must be one of the youngest neurological consultants specialising in rare conditions like her own. But again, Lisa thought as she locked her cottage door and headed down the garden path to her car, *thank goodness* for the man. He'd arrived on the Green Lea wing of the town's hospital just before she'd been rushed in with the worst attack yet of the horrible condition she'd been burdened with, and which had ruined her life.

Or was it Jayden who'd done that? Had Jayden Allen – Jess, Robyn and Sorrel's father – done more to keep her in the situation in which she'd found herself after running away from home as soon as she could, than the porphyria? She'd willingly slipped away with Jayden (indeed, she'd instigated the flight) leaving her parents in that stultifying house in Sheffield, never to return. But no, she couldn't blame Jayden entirely for keeping her here in

Beddingfield for the past thirty years or so. With two toddlers and then, when the older girls had been in their early teens, a third pregnancy, she'd just got on with being a single mum, bringing them up the best she could. Because, with no family to fall back on, no siblings, aunts or uncles around, nor any professional career training, there was little else she could do.

And at least Jayden, constantly touring the UK, Europe and then the world, had never kept her short of money. There'd always been cash in her current account, the mortgage and bills paid on time. Jayden might, more often than not, have been physically absent from the beautiful Yorkshire village of Beddingfield, much more into his music – and presumably his other women – than the daily responsibility of his growing family, but she'd never had to worry about money. She'd been *a kept woman*, or, she argued silently, eschewing the unpleasant phrase with all the connotations that went with it, rather a full-time stay-at-home mum.

She'd always been there for her girls on their return from school and during school holidays. Except when the symptoms had manifested themselves. When the appalling, panic-inducing seizures had taken hold of her body and she'd had to ring neighbours for help. And when, on a couple of occasions – and here, Lisa closed her eyes, remembering her precious girls screaming in the hands of social services – they had been temporarily taken into care when she was hospitalised and Jayden couldn't be contacted.

Much easier now to keep in touch of course, but there'd been many occasions when trying to keep her little ship with its precious cargo afloat and sailing in the right direction had threatened to overwhelm her. Then Matt, like a knight on a white charger – OK, a consultant in a white coat – had managed her condition in a way no other medical expert had before. New ideas, new drugs, new thinking about how to deal with what was an extremely rare condition.

Her biggest worry these days was no longer for herself but for her girls. She'd finally got Matt to admit that yes, porphyria could be inherited, one or both parents passing along a genetic mutation to their child, but, as Matt had also told her, although porphyria couldn't be cured, medicines and certain lifestyle changes would certainly help to manage it.

And so far, neither Robyn, nor Jess, nor Sorrel had shown any disposition to the condition, which usually manifested itself in a first attack between the ages of fifteen and forty-five. Did one ever stop worrying about one's children, even when they were into their thirties? There was Jess, in a relationship with the wonderful Matt who clearly adored her, and yet Lisa knew her eldest daughter was wavering about her husband and, let's face it, Dean Butterworth was as much a waste of space as Jayden Allen.

Lisa was spreading her wings. She felt physically and mentally better than she had for years. There was life out there and she was going for it in a way she hadn't since running away from home a few weeks after her eighteenth birthday. With A levels finished, she'd packed a bag and left, not thinking of the consequences, desperate just to be with Jayden and away from Adrian and Karen Foley, the headteacher and his wife who'd adopted her when she was just a few weeks old. She'd followed Jayden wherever he went. She was his woman, sometimes staying at the odorous flat in Harehills in Leeds, but usually accompanying him and his band around the country and Europe. She'd adored those days and nights on the road, leaving behind the horrible years spent first in Surrey, before moving with the Foleys up to South Yorkshire. Adrian Foley had taken on the headship of the most prestigious public school in Sheffield where she, from the age of nine, was also enrolled. And look where *that* had led Adrian Foley. Was it any wonder she'd left when she could, without a backwards glance at *Father*? Or, come to that, *Mother*.

Visiting at Hudson House was just the first step in her determination to change her life. Lisa stared at her reflection in the rear-view mirror, rather startled to see, now that she'd experimented with a new blusher and lipstick, the attractive olive-skinned and chiselled face of her younger days. The face presumably inherited from her Indian-born birth mother and English father. Or was it the other way round? She'd never been able to find out, the Foleys refusing to tell her the truth about her actual heritage. Maybe they hadn't known themselves? Maybe she was a total foundling, and no one had any idea at all where she'd come from? Abandoned on the doorstep of a church? Or a mosque? What was her heritage? Certainly, the Foleys had never answered her questions truthfully, changing their story – her story – at whim. She'd never forgive them for the way they'd brought her up, refusing to tell her who she was. Where she'd come from.

Lisa shook her head slightly to dispel the thoughts and images of her childhood with the Foleys and smiled, thankful that Robyn had finally got round to buying herself the little runaround she needed to get her and Sorrel to school in Little Micklethwaite, as well as up to Harrogate to see this new man of hers.

This had left Lisa free to take her car back and do what *she* wanted. She'd enjoyed being with these old folks so much yesterday up at Hudson House, she was on her way back up there again now. Jess had laughed at her enthusiasm, said she'd soon be put off if she had to wipe a few bottoms and brush food-impacted dentures, but Lisa was more than willing to give it a go. Who knew? She might even end up with a job up there. Jess was constantly complaining of being short-staffed.

Lisa turned the radio back to Radio 4 from where Sorrel had been listening to Radio 1, put the car into gear and set off.

* * *

'Mum? Oh, I didn't think you were serious when you said you were coming back. We didn't put you off, then?' Jess, in the middle of trying to persuade Joe that going out into the garden in just his underpants and one slipper was not a good idea, was hovering at the heavy oak front door when Lisa arrived. 'I don't want you overdoing things, Mum.' Jess frowned. 'Don't forget how poorly you were just four months ago.'

'Matt says it's good for me to get out and about. And I feel absolutely fine.'

'She's looking *more* than fine.' Joe leered in her direction and Lisa laughed. 'She's a grand girl, this friend of yours, Jess.'

'I'm Lisa, Joe. Hello, how are you? We met yesterday. Do you remember?'

'Remember, love? I've had an 'ard-on ever since you left.' Joe fumbled suggestively at his boxers and Jess tutted.

'Don't go encouraging him, Mum.'

'She's a grand-looking woman is this one,' Joe repeated. 'D'you know her, Jess, love? Have you met her before? Shall I introduce you to her?'

'Lisa's my mum, Joe,' Jess repeated and smiled, patting the old man's arm while attempting to steer him back to his room for the rest of his clothes. 'I told you that yesterday.'

'Oh, no, I don't think that's right.' Joe frowned, rubbing his hand across his grizzled grey chin. 'Think you've got that wrong. I think she's your sister.'

Lisa laughed again and Jess, catching sight of one of the male care assistants, beckoned him over. 'Would you take Joe up to his room, Azir? Help him shower, shave and dress. I just want a word with my mother here.'

Lisa followed Jess down the red-carpeted corridor where fragrant bowls of early-blooming hyacinth were in competition with the scent of beeswax drifting off the highly polished sideboard.

'Right, Mum,' Jess said once she'd closed the door on her office. 'What's happening with Sorrel?'

'What do you mean what's happening with her?' Lisa felt a tremor of anxiety. Guilt even. Was there something going on with her youngest daughter again? Something she didn't know about, but should? Lisa closed her eyes slightly, remembering the recalcitrant and mutinous Sorrel of six months ago when she'd been constantly called into Beddingfield High to be bombarded with more of Sorrel's misdemeanours and her eventual expulsion.

Lisa turned to Jess, who appeared accusatory. Sometimes – in fact quite a lot of the time – Lisa wondered just who was the actual mother and who the daughter. Jess had always appeared older than her years, looking out for Robyn and then Sorrel when Lisa had had to take to her bed once again, and for that she was sorry. Had Lisa's condition robbed Jess of her youth? Kept her from university? Had it been Lisa's fault that her eldest daughter had remained in the village with that waste of space Dean Butterworth when she should have been off, spreading her wings? She'd been such a clever girl at school, studying for A levels in maths and sciences just as Lisa herself had done in sixth form at St Mark's in Sheffield. And yet Jess hadn't taken up the offered place at Newcastle University and then, pregnant at just nineteen or so with Lola, she and Dean had bought the Hollises' cottage next door when it came up for sale. Now Jess had spent the last few years trying to make ends meet by working at this care home instead of doing what she really dreamed of doing –

running her own catering business. Having said that, Jess was now in charge here at Hudson House, Lisa thought proudly. She'd seen the way the younger care assistants deferred to her. Knew that Jess ran a tight ship for the owners, who left more and more of the day-to-day running of the place to her, not putting in much of an appearance at all these days.

'Mum, when Robyn arrived home from school yesterday, Sorrel wasn't in.'

'Sorrel is sixteen next month. I know she should be getting in some early nights if she's going to do her best at this audition in London, but she's been a different girl lately. She's really buckled down to her schoolwork. You know that. Look how she's doing in maths with you and Matt.' Lisa snorted somewhat disparagingly. 'Dean would never have had the brainpower to help Sorrel with quadratic equations.'

Ignoring Lisa's dig at her absent husband while attempting to big up Matt, Jess tutted. 'You do know Joel was set on the night before last?'

'Yes, of course I do. It was the main story on *Focus North* last night. And it was all Robyn could talk about once she was back from St Mede's yesterday afternoon. But you know, while I've said all along that the Sinclairs are a bad lot, Robyn appears to really like Joel. When I raised doubts about him, she said to give him a chance; not tar him with the same brush as his notorious family. Sorrel tells me they're just mates. Nothing more.'

'She does always say that, yes, I know.' Jess folded her arms. 'But, Mum, either way, the last thing she should be doing is always hanging around with him.'

'They said exactly the same thing about me and your father.' Lisa found herself suddenly changing her tune with regards her youngest daughter's friendship with Joel Sinclair. You shouldn't judge a sixteen-year-old by his family. Look at how judgmental the Foleys had been the one time they'd met Jayden. And it was only the once: she'd been warned never to bring that 'scruffy, druggy half-caste into our family home ever again'. So, instead, she'd *left* the family home. Gladly, willingly. Never to return.

Goodness, how times had changed in the thirty years since. No one, but especially educated and professional people like Adrian and Karen Foley, would ever dare speak of someone in such degrading and racist language.

'Yes, and we still do,' Jess was saying, bringing Lisa back to the present.

'Still do what?'

'Say exactly the same about you and Jayden. Robyn and I've been telling you for years to get Jayden out of your life.'

'Jess, I may have spent too many years waiting for your dad to come back to us, but at the end of the day he's provided for us when I've been unable to work. I've not had to chase him through the Child Support Agency for money. Right, enough of me and your father. What can I do to help here today?'

Jess smiled. 'I never for one minute thought you'd be back again, Mum. Thought one day here would be enough to put you off for life.' She paused, thinking. 'So, you could shadow Bex if you want. She's just finishing off breakfasts at the moment. Don't forget, you will need to check with the residents before you go into their rooms...'

'Of course.' Jess did have a tendency to treat her as some sort of bumbling halfwit.

'Their dignity and safety are the first things you should be considering. Oh, hang on, Denise looks like she needs something. Denise is Mason's granny, Mum.'

'Ah, I was hoping to meet her yesterday. You know how much I like Mason.'

'He's back with his wife, Mum. Don't get your hopes up.'

'One should always have hope.' Lisa grinned, heading for the breakfast room. 'Look at Pandora.'

'Would you mind helping to serve hot drinks, Lisa?' Bex, Lisa could see, was torn between wanting to show this 'helper' that she, herself, was in control of breakfasts, while being seen to defer to her boss's mum. 'We're very late this morning. It's already after ten and we're still at the toast and marmalade stage.'

'Of course.' Lisa smiled. 'Just show me the best way to go about it, would you, Bex?'

Lisa spent the next fifteen minutes pouring tea and coffee at the ten tables of four occupants, passing over jugs of cold milk and bowls of sugar while making small talk and steadying cups in shaking hands back onto saucers.

'Ah.' A beautifully turned-out woman pointed a red-varnished talon in Lisa's direction. 'Someone new. Lovely! Someone to have a decent conversation with round here instead of being thrust in front of the box to watch *Homes Under the Hammer*.' She sniffed disdainfully at the elderly man next to her who was dribbling tea down his front. 'Oh, for heaven's sake...'

'What do you want to chat about, Christine?' Lisa asked cheerfully.

'Oh, the state of the economy, Brexit, you know...'

'No one here to do that with you?'

'All gone to the fecking turf club,' Christine said crossly. She manoeuvred her wheelchair at speed away from the table, winked at Lisa and, *Telegraph* to hand, made her way from the breakfast room.

'We seem to have lost one,' Bex was saying, frowning.

'Out the front door again?' Lisa asked. 'Shall I go and look?'

'Possibly. It's Eloise up on Daffodil level.'

'Sorry, I don't think I know who you mean. Did I meet her yesterday, I wonder?'

'Possibly not,' Bex said. 'She's only been with us since just before Christmas and has been getting very distressed when we've tried to persuade her out of her room to join the others at mealtimes or for activity sessions.'

'What does she look like?'

'She's only in her early seventies, blonde hair, tall. She looks a bit like Grace Kelly, apparently.'

'I'm surprised you know who Grace Kelly is, at your age.' Lisa grinned.

'I don't really. It was Glenys, sitting over there—' Bex indicated with an egg-smeared fork one of the residents on the far table who was laughing at something her neighbour was saying '—who said it. I haven't a clue who this Grace Kelly is.'

'*Was.*' Lisa smiled. 'She's dead now. And does she? Look like Grace Kelly, I mean? Goodness. What on earth is she doing here if she looks like Grace Kelly and is only in her early seventies?'

'Dementia, I'm afraid. Which can strike at any age.'

'Can it?' Lisa recalled how she'd popped up to her bedroom only that morning but, when she got there, couldn't for the life of her remember what she'd gone there for. That was a bit worrying. Don't say she was a contender for early onset dementia when she was feeling so well after years of dreading an episode of the porphyria.

'She's still being assessed as to which wing she should really be on,' Bex was saying. 'Her husband wants her on the dementia wing for specialist care. If you can't find her, Lisa, you'll need to tell Jess.'

'OK, no problem, I'll pop upstairs first and see if she's up there.' Lisa patted the arm of Lilian, the silver-haired ninety-five-year-old who'd clutched at her sleeve all the while she'd been at her table, and moved away towards the entrance. Then she took the flight of swirly-patterned-carpeted stairs to the second floor, which had been divided into en suite bedrooms. This had been a magnificent house at one time. Built, Jess had told her, as so many of these northern mansions were, for the entitled owners of the industrial woollen mills for which West Yorkshire had become so renowned. Lisa walked quickly, stopping at each bedroom door to read the names of the residents until she finally saw the one labelled Eloise. She hesitated, not wanting to intrude on someone's personal space, especially if they hadn't felt like joining the others for breakfast, but eventually tapped lightly on the cream-painted door.

'Eloise?' she called softly, pushing open the door.

The room was empty, the bed neatly made.

4

'Have you seen Jess?' Lisa walked quickly down the stairs towards Jess's office, stopping to speak to one of the carers once she saw the door ahead of her firmly closed.

'She said we weren't to disturb her.' The girl, who couldn't have been much older than Sorrel and in the process of propelling two snow-white-haired residents towards the lounge, nodded importantly. 'Got visitors.'

'This early?' Lisa, glancing at her watch, realised it was later than she'd thought. 'I can't find Eloise, and Bex said I should tell Jess.'

'Have you looked in the garden? Would you mind? I've got my hands full at the moment. It's bingo in ten minutes and there's always a fight to get the best seats. You can't miss her: she's very beautiful.'

'I heard.' Lisa smiled back. 'Shall I go out the front door?'

'That'll just take you onto the drive. She's more likely to be out the back. That's where she was yesterday.' The girl – Stephie, according to her badge – pointed a finger down the hall towards the kitchens as the two women in her care tugged impatiently at her sleeve. 'Servants' and tradesman's entrance originally – leads out to the gardens. Try going up through the old orchard and vegetable gardens. It's a bit of a hike, but she seems to like going out there for some reason.'

'Thanks.'

The cold January air hit her as soon as she opened the back door, but came as something of a relief after the overheated, cloying atmosphere of the inside of Hudson House. Lisa let out a little involuntary 'Oh' of surprise when she saw just how big the grounds were. Although, on closer inspection, not overly well kept. Not well kept at all.

'Too much damned ivy,' Lisa muttered, her expert gardener's eye noting the leafless stems of climbing roses struggling to survive in the ivy's unrelenting march forwards.

Summer seemed such a long way off and Lisa sighed as she clasped her frozen hands into two fists to bring back some heat into them. She needed to crack on if this Eloise was out here. She must be freezing, especially having not eaten breakfast. But which way to go? Who'd have thought Jess's care home was situated in the midst of such a glorious garden? Certainly, as far as she could recall, Jess had never mentioned how spectacular Hudson House's gardens were. Or, she saw, must have been in their heyday, years ago.

Lisa took the now overgrown path through a large orchard to her right, stopping every couple of seconds to take in and admire the different types of fruit tree, before exiting through the clearing ahead of her.

'Oh?' Lisa acknowledged the second surprise of the garden as she continued to search for the Grace Kelly lookalike. There, to her left, was a building. Well, not really a building, she acknowledged, but some sort of summer house.

Despite its size and apparent neglect, the summer house was

quite stunning, its pale classical lines giving a heads up to an obvious Grecian influence. Recalling the Classics A level Adrian Foley – himself a Cambridge graduate of the subject – had made her take alongside maths and sciences, Lisa was easily able to identify the Doric fluted columns set into white marble. Blimey, this was a bit different from the Yorkshire stone of the main house. In fact, bloody daft; incongruous even. Who the hell had wanted a replica of the White House in their Beddingfield back garden? She wouldn't have been surprised to have seen the Stars and Stripes unfurling merrily into the grey snow-laden sky. Fascinated, Lisa hurried towards it, slipping slightly on the wet grass as she did so, forgetting for a few seconds that she was here on another mission.

She walked up a couple of white marbled steps, green, wet and exceedingly slippery with lichen, old autumn leaves and dirt that the years had accumulated there. Icy drizzle was starting to fall.

Peering through the filthy cracked windows, shivering slightly as the icy drizzle caught in her hair and neck, Lisa knew she needed to return to the main house. Eloise didn't appear to be out here in the garden. She was just about to turn and make her way back inside, hoping that the missing woman had made her way to the dining room to salvage what, if anything, was left of breakfast, when a small movement inside the summer house made her turn her face towards it. A tall, upright and unmistakably elegant woman dressed in a brown skirt and fawn sweater was leaning against the far wall, her eyes closed, arms wrapped around herself but not, Lisa saw, in what she'd first assumed to be a protective stance. Rather, as though she were in a passionate embrace.

Eloise presumably.

Lisa made her way round to the huge double doors and let

herself in but hesitated, not wanting to frighten the woman. 'Eloise. Eloise?' she called gently. 'Hello, I'm Lisa. You've missed breakfast. Why don't you come back inside with me now? You must be freezing out here without a coat.' When she didn't reply, Lisa moved towards her, gently taking her arm.

Startled, the woman moved back slightly, staring at Lisa as if woken from a deep sleep.

'Eloise?' Lisa said again.

'I'm sorry, I don't hear too well.' The woman's voice was educated with no hint of the West Yorkshire accent that most round here spoke with. Lisa herself had not fully acquired the northern flattened vowels, having been brought up in Surrey until she was nine and then corrected at every turn by Adrian and Karen Foley if she ever dared to say *bath* with its shortened 'a' rather than *barth* with the elongated vowel.

'I'm sorry, I disturbed you.' Lisa said speaking loudly while making sure the woman could see her lips moving. 'Look, it's sleeting now. We need to get back inside.'

'Just a moment.' Eloise fumbled at her skirt with numb hands, seemingly looking for pockets. 'I don't seem to have brought my hearing aids with me,' she said finally, almost accusingly, as though it were possibly Lisa's fault that she was without them.

'I bet you're hungry,' Lisa mouthed.

'I'm rarely hungry.' Eloise raised an eyebrow. 'Especially now that he's brought me back here of all places.'

'Brought you *back*?' Lisa smiled, not understanding.

'I'm not staying. You do realise that?' Eloise glared at Lisa.

'Come on, why don't we get a coffee?'

'The filthy stuff they *call* coffee, you mean? Once I'm released, I'll order some from Fortnum's.'

'It's not a prison, Eloise.'

'I think you'll find it is. Are you new? One of the warders? You're not wearing the uniform.'

'I'm Lisa. I'm actually Jess's mum.'

'Jess?' Eloise followed Lisa as she made for the door. 'Who is Jess?'

'She's in charge round here,' Lisa said proudly. 'This is only the second time I've been allowed to visit. Well, not visit as such; I'm actually volunteering. To be honest, I'm hoping there might be some work for me here.'

'There's always work in prisons like this. Crying out for staff, I believe.'

'I don't think, Eloise, that if this was a prison, there'd be gardens like this one.' Lisa paused, thinking aloud. 'I wonder if they'd let me work in it?'

'You'll have to ask Mummy...'

'Jess d'you mean?' They'd come back through the rose garden and Lisa opened the kitchen door, grateful now for the rush of warmth from within.

'...she does most of the hiring and firing although Daddy, typically, always thinks it's his job to take on new staff.'

'Right.'

'Oh, Eloise, there you are. We've been searching the whole house for you.' Bex was in the kitchen as they walked through, loading a trolley with teacups and the huge institutional aluminium tea and coffee pots.

'Shall I make Eloise some toast?' Lisa asked. 'She missed breakfast.'

'Would you like that, Eloise?' Bex said, not looking at her.

'She hasn't got her hearing aids in,' Lisa explained when Eloise didn't answer.

'Again? Where've you put them this time, Eloise?' Bex asked. 'We spent a good hour looking for them yesterday, didn't we? If you'd like to help serve morning coffee, Lisa, that would be great. I'll make Eloise some toast but she'll need to eat it in here or the others will all want toast instead of biscuits. Or think it's tomorrow already and breakfast time again.' Bex laughed at this. 'Come on, Eloise, let's go up to your room first and see if we can find those hearing aids of yours.'

* * *

Lisa spent the next hour helping Stephie and Azir with tea and coffee before taking the trolley back to the kitchen and stacking the huge dishwasher so that the kitchen staff could get on with lunch preparations. She should have volunteered to do this years ago, Lisa thought, relishing being useful.

Over the past few years, once her girls were at school, she'd had several little part-time jobs and loved them all. She'd been taken on a couple of days a week at the tourist shop and café in the village, which had been utterly perfect for her, fitting in around the girls' schooling and Robyn's and then Sorrel's dance and theatre sessions. Beddingfield, having won Best Yorkshire Village 2018, was still dining out on its win, visitors stopping off to roam its streets and beautiful countryside as well as buying souvenirs and the now famous Beddingfield Brownies.

And then, as per usual, just when she'd really thought she was making a difference to Beddingfield, the village she loved so much, her condition had had her back in bed with fatigue or, more frighteningly, returned to hospital once again with seizures, leaving Jess to take care of Sorrel, and the employment given to someone else.

As if reading Lisa's thoughts, Jess appeared at her side as she continued to load the dishwasher. 'Mum, you're doing too much,'

Jess warned. 'You do this, think you're OK and then wham, you're back in bed again.'

'Jess,' Lisa said, ignoring the concern in Jess's voice as well as the suggestion that she leave just when she was enjoying herself, 'I'd like to work in the garden.'

'OK, go home, then. But have a rest first.' Jess frowned. 'I can't imagine what there is to do in your garden in January.'

'No, this one.'

'This one what?' Jess was irritable.

'This *garden*.'

'Mum, we have gardeners here.'

'Well, they're not doing a very good job.'

'Tell me about it.' Jess shook her head. 'We can never get them here and when they do put in an appearance, they spend time drinking coffee and chatting up the staff. Anyway—' She broke off. 'We shan't be needing them much longer...' Jess's face crumpled.

'What?' Lisa reached out a hand to this eldest daughter of hers who rarely showed her feelings, but just got on with what life threw at her. 'Jess, what is it?'

'The place is being sold.'

'What? *This* place?' Lisa exhaled the breath she'd been holding in.

'Hmm. Mum, what am I going to do? I've a mortgage to pay, a ten-year-old who already eats for England...'

'Well, that's because you feed her such delicious stuff...'

'Mum, don't be facile,' Jess said crossly. 'I really can't be arsed going through all the rigmarole of signing on and looking for a new job.'

'But surely, whoever's bought the place will want to keep you on? You particularly. The staff respect you and the residents love you.'

'Not convinced,' Jess said somewhat mulishly. 'Anyway, they're knocking the place down.'

'The new owners are? Oh, Jess.'

'I've just had John and Ruth Richardson in...'

'The new owners?'

'No, no, they own the place *now*. Have done for the last twenty years or so. I think Covid and then a whole load of new health and safety regulations have finally made their minds up for them. Running care homes these days is not only hard work but sometimes just not viable. Anyway, they're off to Benidorm to retire.'

'Well, more fool them,' Lisa said, pulling a face. 'Costa del Sol when you could be here in Yorkshire and out in that glorious garden?' She nodded towards the grounds beyond the kitchen window. 'What will happen to all the residents?'

'Their families will have to find other care homes for them.'

'And what about those who have no family?'

'Mum, I don't know. I just don't know.' Jess pulled a tired hand through her dark curls.

'So, who's bought it? Have there not been loads of people coming to look round it? Didn't the Richardsons have the good manners to inform you first? Did you have no idea?' Lisa found herself becoming crosser and crosser on Jess's behalf.

'The Sattar brothers,' Jess said crossly. 'You know, the Frozen lot?'

Lisa stared. 'Oh, the brothers who're after St Mede's? Robyn was telling me all about them over tea last night. What do they want? World domination?'

'Well, village domination at least.' Jess managed a small smile. 'Not the end of the world for me, Mum, whereas for the residents here, it *will* be the end of their little world. Oh bugger. Pass those biscuits, Mum. I need carbs.'

5

ROBYN

I'd assumed that now I'd been at St Mede's for a whole term and had established myself with both the staff and the kids, the teaching itself would be easier. Easier than in those hellish first weeks when I'd had to constantly tighten the reins and crack the whip in order to keep control of the hard-work kids in my care. I left Sorrel – who'd been unusually quiet during the fifteen-minute car journey into school – at the main entrance and immediately made my way down to the drama studio to prepare for lessons. As I headed back out into the school grounds, taking a shortcut from the basement to the staffroom for the coffee I couldn't start the day without, I offered up thanks to that great teacher in the sky that I didn't, as a supply teacher, have a tutor group of my own to prepare and be responsible for. This fact alone generally gave me another ten to fifteen minutes at the start of each day: time to catch up with the seemingly never-ending marking and planning, once the rest of the staff had departed for their registration groups.

I was shaking icy raindrops from my mass of black curls and

debating whether I actually had time for coffee when Mason popped his head round the door.

'Ah, found you.' Mason came into the staffroom, closing the door behind him.

'I wasn't hiding.' I pulled a face. 'Oh, all right then, I was. You looking for me?' I narrowed my eyes slightly, anticipating yet more work being chucked in my direction. 'What?'

'Celia Logan's not in. And…' Mason frowned. '…won't be in for some time, I'm afraid.'

'Oh?' My heart sank; I knew what was coming. 'Escaped, has she?'

'Broken pelvis. She was air-ambulanced off Courcheval 850 at the end of the day on Saturday. A snowboarder took her out. She was only able to contact me here at school once you'd all left yesterday or I could have let you know what I've had to come up with, at the meeting itself. Mind you, I had enough on my plate to deal with what with Joel, the police, the press and then the bloody Sattar brothers.'

'Right.' I cursed under my breath.

'So, I'd like you to step in as form teacher for her class for the foreseeable future, Robyn. Could you get along there now? Pronto? There's no one with them.'

'Are you saying I've to be… to be *mother* to the worst class in the school? Year 9CL are now officially my responsibility? Oh, I don't think so, Mason. In fact, I *know* not so. Come on, I'm still in my ECT years. They'll eat me alive.'

Mason laughed. 'Their *mother*? I've never heard the role of a form tutor equated to mothering. No,' he cajoled, 'you'll be their form teacher, their mentor and confidante. They'll come to you when they can't cope, when they're upset, worried, frightened of their world and what it throws at them…'

'They're just as likely to be throwing stuff *at me*. And, they know more about the world than I do. You should hear what they get up to once school is out. Actually, when they're still in school, to be honest.' I knew I was gabbling, playing for time, but I couldn't stop. Once I stopped talking, Mason would find a way in and I'd be doomed. Doomed to be 9CL's form teacher for eternity. 'And who do *I* go to when *I'm* feeling upset, worried and bloody frightened?'

'You know you can always come to me, Robyn. My door's always open to you...'

Ignoring the suggestive look in Mason's beguiling brown eyes – the look that had seduced me into his bed only a couple of months earlier – I tutted, but carried on in the same vein. 'Frightened like I am now, Mason, at the very thought of facing them every morning for registration? At least when I take them just once a week for their drama session, I know, a bit like visiting the dentist, or... or... Christmas or... or... having a smear test I won't be having to put myself through it again for a while.'

'While we're at it, Robyn, and I confirmed this with Melanie Potter yesterday, we'd like to offer you the position of drama and English teacher on a proper contract. Keeping you on here on a supply basis is bloody expensive, to be honest. I'll get all the papers to sign over to you asap...'

'Mason, I told you yesterday, no. I need to be able to be up and off if Fabian decides he wants to be back in London for his work.'

'I thought he'd run *away* from London? Left his responsibilities when it all got too much for him?'

'Mason, leave it out. Please? OK, OK, I'll go and register 9CL now, but it's a one-off. You need someone with more experience.'

'Lovely. I knew you'd be up for it. Just give myself or Petra a shout if there are any problems. Assembly in ten minutes. You're going to be late if you don't go now.'

Glaring at Mason, I gathered my laptop and bag and headed for the door, pausing to turn before I left the room. 'I need to talk to you about Joel, Mason. What's going on? I can't get anything out of Sorrel. Says she knows nothing.'

'I assumed *you'd* know more, what with Sorrel being Joel's mate. I need coffee. I've assembly in ten minutes and I can't face a new term and a new assembly – with all the usual rubbish preaching about New Year resolutions – without caffeine.'

'Do I hear some cynicism creeping in?'

Ignoring me, Mason switched on the kettle before reaching for the instant coffee and, knowing myself dismissed, I headed unwillingly along G corridor and up the stairs to the notorious 9CL's tutor room, where it was obvious from the raucous noise coming from behind the closed classroom door the thirteen-year-olds were already tuned up to give it all they'd got. I took a deep breath and went in.

'Hello, miss, did you have a good Christmas?' Lacey Mosley gave me a welcoming wave before continuing with the French plait she was constructing on Sienna Walker's blonde head.

Well, at least I was being acknowledged rather than ignored. Maybe, after a term here, I was at last being given some credence.

'I did, thank you. Right, OK, seats, all of you. Now. Quick registration and then it's down to the hall for full, first-morning-back-to-school assembly.' I moved to the computer on Celia Logan's desk, quickly logging into SIMS, the online registration app, and started calling names...

'Miss.'

'Yep.'

'Yeah.'

'Miss.'

'Where's Miss Logan, miss?'

'I'm afraid she's been taken out by a snowboarder in France.'

Glancing at the clock on the wall, I tried to gallop on with the roll call. 'Charlie?'

'Miss.'

'A snowboarder? She's going out with a snowboarder? I thought she was going out with a copper.' Willow Jenkinson pulled a face. 'She's always telling us if we don't behave, she's going to bring her boyfriend in to sort us all out…'

'No, you moron, "taken out"—' Keira Jackson air-quoted the words '—as in an accident. She was going skiing over New Year. She told us that. Does that mean she'll be off for a bit, miss?'

'Well…' I started, but was interrupted before I could finish.

'Ooh, Kai, you love Miss Logan. What you gonna do without her? Kai luuuurrrrvves Miss Logan, miss.'

'Eff off, you daft bitch.' Kai Vickerman, red-faced, threw a large rubber in Daisy Slater's direction, catching the corner of her eye. Turning in fury, Daisy launched herself at Kai, pulling at his school blazer. 'Oy, ger off, Slater. Keep yer bloody hands to yourself. Me mum'll go ape if I tear this blazer again.'

'OK, OK, OK. Enough.' Hell, I could already hear my voice rising an octave and took a deep calming breath. '*Enough*, I said. OK. Right, make sure you have everything in your bags for the day ahead. Assembly! Now!'

Fifteen minutes into the new school term and I already had a headache.

* * *

By the end of lunchtime, I'd had enough.

The first rehearsal I'd planned for the forthcoming production of *Grease* came to nothing when the heating in the drama studio – prone to sulking at the best of times – finally gave up the ghost.

'Aw, miss, it's freezing down here,' Isla Boothroyd complained, hiding her numb hands up her navy school jumper. 'I hate winter. I hate January. It's ages off until we can go on holiday again and we've got our mocks soon. My dad says I should be concentrating on revising in the library rather than doing this.'

'I haven't even looked at my books over the holiday,' Noah Dyson scoffed. He kicked a screwed-up paper towel across the studio, shouting, 'Goal,' when it hit the wastepaper bin.

'I've gone off the whole thing anyhow,' Lucy Earnshaw put in, picking up her bag and voting with her feet. 'I'm hungry. We have to go on last sitting when we have these rehearsals and there's never anything left apart from a few manky chicken nuggets. And, after seeing that poor turkey with all those gibletty things up its bum on Christmas Day, I'm now a vegetarian. In fact, I'm a vegan.'

'You had sausage and chips for your tea at our house last night,' Isla accused.

'Oh, I thought they were veggie sausages. Your dad said they were,' Lucy came back at her mate, equally accusing.

'And your Sorrel's not here, is she, miss? I bet she's already got the place she's after at that posh drama school in London. Then we'll have no Sandy. *Grease* without Sandy? Well, that'll just be bloody rubbish, won't it?' Sienna Walker sniffed and looked at the others.

'Stop, stop, stop!' I put up a hand as latecomers to the rehearsal drifted in. 'Listen: a) if Sorrel does get a place at the Susan Yates school, it won't be until after Easter, maybe not even until September and, on both accounts, we'll have put on the performance by then and b) you're late,' I snapped in the new arrivals' direction. 'Look, actors and dancers need punctuality and discipline if they're to get anywhere—'

'My dad says what I need is my GCSEs if I want to be a vet,'

Isla interrupted once more. 'He says fannying around, thinking I can sing and dance just because you were once on the stage in London, miss, isn't going to help *me*.'

'A vet?' I stared. The usual response to what these kids were going to do with their lives once they left St Mede's was more often than not: 'gel nails, miss'; 'footballer, for Man U, miss'; 'have a kid, miss, and then they'll have to give me a flat'. As well as the equally disconcerting: 'Go and work for Andrew Tate, miss, and be an influencer like him.'

'OK, OK!' I put up my hands once more. 'I know where you're coming from. It's always hard getting back into things when you've had a two-week break and, you're right, it's too cold down here to stay and rehearse.' I glanced across at Jobsworth Ken, the caretaker, who'd just arrived, along with the usual air of martyrdom that always accompanied him like a bad smell. He was now making his way gloomily to the room where the school's heating and lighting daily creaked and groaned into life like an arthritic octogenarian.

'Right, it's up and running again,' Ken sniffed a few minutes later when he reappeared with an oily rag and a black greasy streak down one side of his usually immaculate brown overalls. 'But it'll be a good hour or so before it begins to warm up.' He shook his head. 'Best thing for this place is if the Sattars do get hold of it and raze it to the ground.'

For heaven's sake! I threw the caretaker a furious warning glance. The last thing I needed was the kids getting wind of what was possibly just a rumour.

'Is the school closing down, miss?' Fatima Khan pulled a face. 'Are they *pulling it down*?'

'Oh, right, then, no point in hanging round here in the freezing cold if there's going to be nowhere to put on *Grease*. I'm off for me dinner while there's some left. I'm starving.' Daisy

Slater picked up her bag, reached for her phone and headed for the door and sustenance.

'Hang on, hang on, let's get a few things sorted...' I held up a hand once more while looking out of the window where great gobstoppers of snow were beginning to fall from a mustard-yellow sky.

'Whoo, it's snowing!' Twenty pairs of adolescent feet rushed over to the window, falling over their owners in the rush to get a good view.

'Oh, come on, you lot!' I called. 'You've all seen snow before.'

'Not for years, we haven't, miss,' Ollie Metcalf shouted excitedly over his shoulder. 'You never heard of climate change?'

'OK, it's too cold to rehearse this lunchtime and we've wasted the opportunity anyway. Go and get your lunch.'

'Where *is* your Sorrel?' Isla asked.

I was wondering the same thing.

6

By the time the final bell to end the school day sounded, I realised I'd spent the whole time on a roller coaster of highs and lows. Despite the unwanted promotion to 9CL's form teacher and the *Grease* rehearsal that had come to nothing, I'd had a lovely session with the Year 7s introducing them to Michael Morpurgo's *War Horse*, which they'd lapped up and which had led to much debate, particularly from Lena Boyd who'd said she'd shoot anyone who tried to take away *her* horse to make it fight.

'You've a horse?' I'd asked.

'Well, he's a pony. I show him.'

'Show him what?' Billy Caldwell had asked, which had made me laugh and kept me going through the rest of the day.

'Where are you? What are you up to?' I fished my phone from my bag and was straight onto Fabian before the last of my Year 11 GCSE English group had even left the classroom. 'I've had enough already! I'm bloody freezing, I'm a lousy teacher and the *Grease* production seems to be falling apart around my ears. After just one day back with *these* kids, at *this* school, I need you. Right now!'

'Come over, then.' Fabian finally managed to get a word in. 'Come on! This minute! Shake the chalk dust from your hair and get in your car. If you leave now, you might just miss the rush hour on the M62.'

I couldn't think of anything I wanted more than spending the evening – the whole night – the rest of my life – with this heavenly man who was, unfortunately, up in Harrogate, a good thirty miles away.

'It's snowing here and I've no idea what the Honda's like in snow. If it's anything like me, it'll be rubbish.' I'd kept one wary eye on the weather all afternoon, while the kids – particularly the younger ones – in all my classes had kept both of theirs constantly towards the huge paned windows, instead of on me, itching to get out onto what remained of St Mede's playing fields. 'Oh, I *can't*, Fabian.' I closed my eyes, remembering I had a meeting and knowing the impracticality of leaving everything up in the air and driving – skidding – up to North Yorkshire just for the night. 'I've a planning meeting with the English department...' I looked at my watch '...which started five minutes ago. And, I need to sort out what Sorrel's up to. She's got this audition in London and I said I'd go through routines with her, but she suddenly doesn't seem as enthusiastic as she was and, to be honest, I don't know where she is and—'

'Robyn, Robyn, can you just stop talking for two minutes? Can you hear this?'

'What?' I stopped gabbling, straining to hear.

'My car keys jingling. I'm on my way.'

'Oh, *really*? Oh, *Fabian*.'

'Yep, there's no snow here. Do what you have to do there and I'll be at your mum's by six thirty.'

'And stay the night? *Stay with me*,' I sang, belting out the words of Shakespears Sister, almost light-headed with joy that

Fabian was on his way to be with me. I closed my eyes, altering the lyrics to fit the moment, while using the whiteboard rubber as microphone, letting the tension of the day out in glorious song.

'You all right, miss?' Whippety Snicket, aka Blane Higson, the fourteen-year-old with whom I'd had various run-ins the previous term, had come to find me, as he often did now that we were mates. Of sorts.

'Never better, Blane. You? You weren't in registration this morning. You know I'm taking over from Ms Logan as your form tutor for a while?' I smiled then started laughing at being caught mid-song. I realised I could cope with anything now that Fabian was coming over. 'Hang on.' I replaced the board rubber and spoke once more into my phone. 'Right, see you when you get here.' I ended the call, giving all my attention to the scrawny kid now slumped onto one of the hard wooden, graffitied chairs. He needed a haircut and, despite it being only the first day back, the collar of his white school shirt was grubby.

'Did you have a good Christmas?'

Blane shrugged his shoulders.

'What does that mean?' I asked gently, moving nearer to him. 'Did your brothers come home?'

'I told you, miss, they've gone. Can't cope with me mum and what she gets up to.'

'So, was it just you and your mum for Christmas Day?' My heart went out to him, and I instinctively put out a hand to his bent head, withdrawing it before making contact. You couldn't touch a kid these days without it being misconstrued.

'Yeah, summat like that.'

'So, who did the cooking, then?' Bloody stupid question, that, Robyn, I chastised myself. He'd probably had beans on toast on

Christmas Day while his mum saw to her heroin addiction by working the streets down in Midhope town centre.

'The meeting, Ms Allen?' Dave Mallinson, Head of English, popped his head round the door. 'We're all waiting for you. You should be off home now, Blane.'

'Coming.' I hesitated, unwilling to leave Blane when he so obviously needed someone to talk to. Once Dave had set off back down the corridor to the staffroom, I turned back to the kid who was now yawning but making little attempt to move. 'What's up, Blane? Tell me.'

'They're after me.' Blane's head was bent into his frayed shirt collar, his words muffled.

'Who's after you?' Disregarding protocol re no physical contact (unless it was in order to restrain a pupil) I put out a hand to Blane's arm.

'It's nowt, miss.'

'Blane, it's obviously *something*.'

'Nah, it's fine. I'm getting off home.' And with that, he stood, kept his head down and left the classroom.

Hell, something else to worry about. I gathered my bags and laptop and headed for the staffroom.

* * *

'I'll cook,' Jess said. 'If Fabian's coming over.'

'Don't be silly, you've been working all day up at Hudson House.' I frowned.

'You don't get it, do you?' Jess shook her head in my direction. 'Cooking, for me, is relaxation. Bring Fabian round about seven.'

I laughed at that. 'You just want to show off how much better a cook you are than he is.'

'She *does*, Aunty Robyn.' Ten-year-old Lola grinned. 'She

pretends she doesn't show off about her cooking, but she does, you know. And ever since she beat Fabian in that Christmas cooking competition, she's been wanting to show off again. You know, show him it wasn't just a... what's the word?' Lola pulled a face. 'Fluke, that's it. Wants to show him how good she *really* is.'

Jess went pink and was about to defend herself when, instead, she tutted as the kitchen door opened. 'Well, just look what the wind's blown in.'

'Grandpa!' Lola threw herself into Jayden's arms and he put down his bag, swinging her round.

'You obviously think you're staying.' Jess nodded towards his overnight case.

'I've come to see you all.' Jayden grinned his usual infectious gap-toothed smile that had beguiled women and broken hearts throughout his life. 'Should have been flying into Newcastle this afternoon – got a gig up there tomorrow evening – but the plane was diverted – bad weather apparently – so we flew into Manchester. Bit worried about the snow, to be honest, although the rest of the band have carried on straight up to the North East. So, great opportunity to pop in and see my family.'

Jess snorted slightly but turned it into a cough as Lola continued to hug Jayden.

'And, bonus,' Jayden continued, 'I finally get to meet this man of yours, Robyn. I hear he's coming over. You've kept him under wraps long enough.'

'Mum knows you're here, does she?' I asked.

'Yes, I've been round there for the last hour. Had a cup of tea with her. She says I can't stay there.' Jayden's words held an air of surprise. '*No room at the inn*, she says. Have to say, girls, your mum's looking fantastic. She looks so much better than when I saw her last month. This consultant of yours, Matt, is it, Jess? Obviously knows what he's doing.'

'He does,' Jess said pointedly.

'She's a fine-looking woman is your mum,' Jayden said, sitting down and making himself comfortable. 'You know, she could be your big sister rather than your mum. Hmm, a bit strange, that,' he went on, almost to himself, 'her saying I can't stay round there.'

I glanced across at Jess, exchanging looks: this must be the first time ever Mum had turned Jayden away.

'She's finally, after all these years, seeing some sense, Jayden,' Jess said curtly. 'So, I suppose you're wanting my box room here, then, for the night?'

'Well, I can always book into the Premier Inn down in town or The Green Dragon in the village.'

'Good, do that, then,' Jess suggested. 'Means I don't have to change the sheets in the morning.'

'No,' Lola pleaded. 'Let Grandpa stay. *I'll* change the sheets if you're too busy. So, how many's that for tea? I'll go and lay the table and have a go at the poinsettia napkin folding I've been practising.' Lola counted on her fingers: 'Grandpa and Granny; Aunty Robyn and Fabian; Mum, me, Matt and Sorrel. Shall I get out the best cutlery, Mum?'

'Matt's on duty at the hospital, Lola,' Jess said, 'so just lay for seven. And, seeing there's so many of us...'

'Look, Jess, forget me and Fabian coming round,' I protested, feeling guilty at putting her to all this work.

'...I'm giving Jayden a shopping list.' Jess scribbled a few things on a pad of paper, tearing it off with a flourish. 'Here you go, Jayden, earn your keep. You know where the Co-op is. And, I hear your latest tour is a sell-out. So, a couple of really good bottles of wine, please?'

* * *

'I really didn't want to turf your mum out of her bed.' Fabian turned with a frown once Mum had put on her coat and gone next door to Jess. 'Particularly as you said she was so ill with one of her attacks when you had to return from London back in September. Mind you, she's looking great at the moment. What's she on?'

'Well, for the first time since she met him, Mum appears to not want Jayden around. Or at least not in her bed. So, giving up her bed for us means she's not tempted to fall into it with him again. I know, I know, it's a very weird relationship they have. Nothing, of course, like your family, all doing things the correct and traditional way. Anyway, Matt Spencer has prescribed her a monthly shot of something called hemin, which limits her body's production of porphyrins. So, thank goodness for Matt and his team. The medication is really stabilising her condition and letting her get on with life. Even starting again with her life?' I gave a little laugh. 'With what she thinks she's missed. I sat with Mum for a good couple of hours last night and we talked like we've *never* done before. I've always been afraid to face up to what Mum's had to put up with since being diagnosed when she was in her thirties. Been a bit cowardly, I suppose – frightened that it's an inherited condition and that she could pass it on to Jess, Sorrel and me.'

'That why you never mentioned it in London?'

I nodded, slightly ashamed. 'I didn't want you running for the hills. You know, being landed with someone who might eventually find themselves showing signs of it.'

'And you think I'd have left you for that reason? You can't have a very high opinion of me, Robyn.'

'Fabian, I had a friend at university whose fiancé gave up on her when she went down with long-term ME. And another girl at uni who was in a relationship with someone who was a haemophiliac. She really loved him but, with his having an inherited genetic disorder, her parents went on at her non-stop about the possibility that any children they might have could either be haemophiliacs or carriers of the condition. Until they broke up.'

'I'd never heard of acute porphyria before,' Fabian said.

'No, it's very, very rare. Apparently, a cousin of Queen Elizabeth had it and, because he was descended from King George III – you know, the mad king? – they're now hypothesising that his madness may have been due to an undiagnosed family history of porphyria.'

'Right?'

'Oh, hell, Fabian, I can see in your eyes you're suddenly frightened you might end up with someone talking incessantly and foaming at the mouth...'

'Well, you do talk a lot, Robyn.' Fabian bent to kiss my mouth. 'Sometimes, the only way to shut you up is by kissing you.' He moved his mouth to my neck, licking my collarbone.

'I can still talk when you're doing that, you know,' I muttered, closing my eyes as the wonderful warmth of his soft mouth descended further and a warm hand reached inside my shirt.

'Jesus.' Fabian shot back in alarm. 'Something's watching us.'

'Something? Or someone? Is Sorrel back?' I turned my head. 'Oh, it's only Roger.'

'Forgot about the bloody rabbit.' Fabian continued to look wary when all I wanted was for him to carry on with those magical hands and mouth of his. 'You must be the only family with a rabbit instead of a dog or cat. He's actually glaring at me,' Fabian went on.

'He's very possessive. Probably thinks you shouldn't have your hands on me.' I reached for him once more. 'But *I* don't think that at all...'

With Roger, now in obvious protective mode, moving in on Fabian, I went to fetch wine and glasses from the kitchen. 'The problem is,' I called from the fridge, 'with my mum being adopted at birth, there's no way of knowing if her condition *is* inherited. It's a bit weird – Mum's never really been able to venture far or over-extend herself. But now, with her refusal to let Jayden just swan back in as he always expects to do, I wouldn't be surprised if she's finally ready to move on. Come on, a glass of wine here for Dutch courage and then I'll take you round to meet the famous reggae singer himself.'

7

'Hi, Fabian, come on in and make yourself at home.' Jess, obviously flustered at cooking for a fellow cooking enthusiast, batted Lola away from the shabby chintz-covered armchair at one end of her tiny kitchen.

'Something smells good.' Fabian, walking over to Jess and the stove, appeared equally nervous at being surrounded for the first time by the Allen women en masse, and I felt for him. 'What are you cooking? Oh, fabulous,' he enthused, handing over an upmarket bottle of Malbec. 'Is that sea bass? And with razor clams? I've never quite mastered the intricacies of how to cook those.' The pair of them immediately went into a huddle over ingredients and cooking know-how and I smiled, delighted that Jess wasn't going to be arsy as she sometimes could be when unsure of herself.

'Hello.' Jayden, who'd been upstairs obviously settling himself into Jess's tiny box room, appeared in the kitchen. 'Good to meet you at last. Fabian, isn't it?'

'You know it is, Jayden.' I tutted, taking in my dad's unshaven face and dreadlocked hair, his jeans and grubby trainers. Goodness, what a contrast to Fabian's father, Roland Carrington, Lord Chief Justice.

'Hi.' Fabian held out a hand, realised it was still attached to the wooden spoon he'd automatically picked up, and laughed. 'Pleased to meet you, Jayden.'

'D'you think you could all take yourselves next door?' Jess frowned, her face red. 'I can't concentrate when the whole of my kitchen's filled with bodies.'

'Next door?' Mum and I both pulled a face. 'We've just come from round there.'

'No,' Jess tutted. 'Next *room*. The sitting room. Lola, hand these round,' she instructed, passing over a plate of perfectly arranged tiny Brie and prosciutto shortbreads. 'We're going to be ready to eat in fifteen minutes.'

'Mum, where's Sorrel?' I asked, following Lola, who was intent on ushering the others into the sitting room where a log fire burned brightly. 'Oh, she's here now.'

We all turned to face Sorrel, who stood in the kitchen doorway, wrapped up in a black puffer coat but still in the navy St Mede's school uniform.

'I waited for you after school,' I said, 'but you weren't answering your phone and then I had to go to a meeting.'

'Robyn, just because you're teaching at my school doesn't mean you have to be my minder. I'm more than capable of getting the bus home. Which I did today.'

'You're freezing, darling.' Mum moved towards Sorrel, who was shivering. 'Come on through, by the fire. Come and get warm. Your dad's here.'

'Blimey, what did we do to deserve another visit from *him* so soon after Christmas?'

'He's in the sitting room, talking to Fabian.'

'Fabian's here?' Sorrel asked, her head turning. 'Where is he?'

'Who? Dad?'

'No,' she snapped, impatiently. 'Fabian.'

'In the sitting room talking to Dad,' I said once more.

'Good.'

'Why d'you want to talk to Fabian?' I smiled at Sorrel, pleased that she appeared to be showing an interest in him.

Without another word, and without taking off her coat, Sorrel headed for the sitting room, Mum and I following behind.

'Fabian, are you still soliciting?'

Jayden laughed loudly at that. 'Think you've got the wrong word there, sweetheart.' He leaned over to give Sorrel a welcoming hug and kiss, but she brushed him off irritably and went to stand in front of Fabian, whom she'd met on the one occasion, just before Christmas, when I'd finally introduced him to my family.

'Are you?' Sorrel demanded.

'Hello, Sorrel. How lovely to see you again.' Fabian, always polite and friendly, smiled down at her from his six-foot-two height. 'You OK? What's the matter?'

'Are you still doing what you did in London?' Sorrel spoke quickly, her words tumbling out at speed. 'I mean, we know all about how you were going to defend the Soho Slasher. I saw you on TV.'

'Not any more, no.' Fabian's tone was kind, but firm. 'I left London to get away from all that.'

'Oh? Not to be near me, then?' I went to refill Fabian's glass before turning to my little sister. 'What's up, Sorrel?'

'I want Fabian to defend Joel.' She folded her arms almost defiantly as she waited for his response.

'Sorrel!' I put out a hand. 'Fabian's a barrister. He's not a solicitor. And he's... well, he's... resting at the moment. You know like when I was working at Graphite in Mayfair when I didn't have a part at the theatre?'

'Fabian's having a bit of a rest,' Lola put in sagely. 'He's very tired. Here, have one of these, Sorrel.' Lola thrust the plate of hors d'oeuvres in Sorrel's direction.

But Sorrel, ignoring both me and her ten-year-old niece, moved closer to Fabian and continued to speak in a low, urgent voice.

'Fabian, my friend Joel's coming out of hospital at some point.'

'Well, that's good, Sorrel...' I began, but Sorrel shook her head impatiently at me.

'Joel's being discharged soon, but I'm not sure when. I've just been up to the hospital...'

'In this snow?' Mum interrupted.

'It's nearly gone, Mum, and the bus goes straight from outside school down to Midhope and the hospital.'

'But...' Mum put out a hand, her face etched with concern.

'They wouldn't let me see him, but I managed to have a word with one of the nurses. She said she thinks he's being remanded. Or was it bailed? I can't remember which.' Sorrel turned to Fabian. 'What does that mean? That he's going to prison?'

'Not necessarily.' Fabian's voice was gentle. 'The thing is, Sorrel, from what Robyn's told me about Joel, he was already on a court order because he'd been caught pushing drugs previously.'

'Only because that lot he's with made him,' Sorrel snapped. 'His dad's in prison and they've told Joel if he doesn't do as they say, his dad will be hurt in there and then they'll come after his mum and his little sister. She's only thirteen.'

'Was he found with drugs on him again?' Fabian asked pointedly. 'When he's already on what appears an intense court order for the same offence? Presumably, when the police found him after the knife attack, he had drugs on him? A burner phone? A lot of money on him?'

Sorrel shrugged, but didn't take her eyes from Fabian.

'You're to have nothing more to do with this boy, Sorrel,' Jayden interrupted crossly. 'Just get yourself off to London to the Susan Yates audition and don't get involved. Move on. I don't want you having any contact with him from now on. D'you hear?'

'So where do you get your stuff from?' Sorrel rounded on Jayden, her eyes blazing. 'For every young drug pusher, there's someone like you buying the stuff. Supply and demand, Jayden? And don't come the heavy father with me at this late stage. It's amazing we three have turned out so well, considering who our father is.'

'Sorrel!' Mum warned but, whereas in the past she would have defended Jayden to the hilt, she merely raised an eye in his direction and said nothing more.

'A bit of weed every now and again.' Jayden had the grace to look embarrassed. 'Medicinal. *Never* any hard stuff,' he protested.

Ignoring him, Sorrel turned back to Fabian. 'So, what does remand mean for a sixteen-year-old?'

'Not necessarily prison.' Fabian smiled. 'At worst he could be remanded to a youth detention centre – round here, usually somewhere like Wetherby. But it's quite possible he'll be remanded to the local authority.'

'What does that mean?' Jayden and I spoke as one.

'Well, the principle is that everyone is entitled to bail, but sometimes it's just too risky to allow bail. You know, a youth like Joel could continue to offend. But the main reason I would imagine he's been refused bail is for his own protection. If he's being manipulated and coerced by this gang that he's found himself in—'

'I'm sorry,' Jayden interrupted, 'no one just finds themselves in a drug gang. He must have sought out these people.'

'Oh, you know *nothing*.' Sorrel almost spat the words. 'They found *him*, Jayden. Through his dad.'

'So,' Fabian continued, 'a child, like Joel—'

'He's not a child,' Sorrel protested hotly.

'He's classed as a child until he's eighteen,' Fabian went on calmly. 'And the courts might be persuaded by his advocate that he can be remanded into the care of the local authority, usually with strict conditions such as a curfew monitored by an electronic tag.'

'So—' Sorrel grabbed at Fabian's hand '—will you do it? Will you be Joel's solicitor when he has to go to court?'

'Sorrel, no.' I shook my head. 'No, absolutely not. Fabian's a barrister.'

'Well, I can still be employed as someone's defence advocate,' Fabian said. 'I would imagine Joel's case will eventually be listed in Crown court rather than the local magistrates' court in Midhope. Leeds or Bradford Crown Court?'

'Surely, as a barrister, you have to be appointed to represent someone by a defendant's solicitor?' Mum spoke quietly but everyone turned towards her. 'I mean, someone on the street can't just get in touch with you directly, can they, Fabian? Most people don't have a barrister unless they've done something really serious like murder, and their case is ending up in the Crown court.'

'Mum, what do *you* know about it?' Sorrel tutted impatiently in her direction.

'I read a lot,' Mum said, matter-of-factly. 'When you're bedbound, as I often have been, reading is a way of taking yourself to another time and place. I like reading about police procedures.'

Lola eyed up the last of the hors d'oeuvres hopefully while Mum asked, 'Does Joel have a solicitor, Sorrel?'

Sorrel nodded. 'But Joel's not convinced they've had a great deal of experience with cases like his. I suppose you get what you're given when you're on legal aid.'

'I bet you can charge an absolute fortune, Fabian, can't you?' Lola nodded through a mouthful of savoury shortbread. 'Mum says you're really rich. You know, with your fabulous apartment near where the king lives? Mum says the Soho Slasher would have paid you an absolute fortune to get him off... Mum says—'

'Lola!' Jess's voice cracked like a pistol shot, making us all jump. She'd made her way into the sitting room and was standing just inside the doorway, taking in the whole conversation. 'Excuse me, Lola! I thought you were grown up enough for me to discuss some things with—'

'Gossip with, *I'd* say,' I snapped, embarrassed on Fabian's behalf.

'Food's ready.' Jess, obviously equally embarrassed at being called out for dishing the dirt about Fabian, glared at Lola. 'Come on, come and eat. I've made soup to start.'

'Hope it's Heinz tomato?' Lola said, unperturbed by her mother's censure.

'Whenever has your mother given you tinned soup?' Jayden laughed, pulling Lola's dark curls affectionately.

'She does, you know,' Lola confided in Fabian's direction as Jess ushered us to our seats around the tiny table. Tiny it might be, but it was beautifully set with a snow-white cloth and starched linen napkins, cut-glass water tumblers and Jess's best wine glasses.

'Don't blame her.' Fabian grinned. 'I love Heinz tomato soup. I became absolutely addicted to it, always opening tins and heating them up on the one single gas ring we were allowed at school.'

'A gas ring at school?' Lola appeared puzzled. 'Like a Bunsen burner in the chemistry lab they have at the high school? I love science,' she went on. 'I'm going to be a research scientist when I leave school and help find a cure for Granny's porphyria. Especially if *I* end up getting it.'

'Lola, enough.' Jess shook her head. 'Stop wittering or you'll have to leave the table. We've let you join us for dinner, so try and act like a grown-up.'

'I am,' Lola protested, passing round a warm, fragrant focaccia studded with baby tomatoes. 'I'm discussing my future career and accepting that, one day, I could end up with what Granny's got. Illnesses often skip a generation, my teacher said. We're doing all about diseases in science at school,' she added. 'Did you know—?'

'Lola, can someone else get a word in?' Sorrel snapped in some exasperation. She'd not touched the bowl of soup Jess had placed in front of her but, at a look from Mum, she lifted her spoon.

'This is wonderful,' Fabian said after one mouthful. 'There's fennel?'

'Well spotted.'

'And you roasted the tomatoes?'

'Yep. Is there any other way?'

'No.'

Jess grinned across at Fabian, both locked into the secret language of dedicated foodies while the rest of us simply enjoyed the delicious taste of the soup in front of us.

'So, Fabian, what do you think?' Sorrel had put down her spoon, her soup only half eaten.

'I think this is miles better than Heinz.' Fabian smiled across at Sorrel.

'No! About Joel.'

'Sorrel!' I warned. 'Come on, leave it out. Let Fabian enjoy his dinner. He's a barrister, not a solicitor...'

'Actually, there's no reason I couldn't take on a case like this.'

'Really?' Sorrel's pretty face lit up.

'There's something called Direct Access Portal,' Fabian said. 'In simple terms, it allows members of the public – for instance, Joel – to instruct a barrister directly on their behalf. I could represent Joel either in the magistrates' court or, if his case ends up in the Crown court...'

'Fabian,' I tutted. 'Don't get her hopes up. You left London because you'd had enough of it all.'

'No, I left London because of the awful barrage of abuse I went through defending Rupert Henderson-Smith. And...' Fabian smiled, aware that the rest of us were all concentrating on his words but going ahead anyway '...because I fell in love with some woman who fell off the West End stage and returned to Yorkshire with a crook leg.'

'How *is* your knee these days, Robyn?' Jayden placed his soup spoon in his empty bowl but reached for more bread, chewing contemplatively as he waited for an answer. 'You must want to get back to the West End? You're like me. Performing's in your blood.'

'That would be funny, wouldn't it?' Lola put in. 'Aunty Robyn back in London and Fabian up here in Yorkshire. A sort of swap.'

'I miss it terribly,' I admitted. 'My knee is so much better now. But, you know, I'm nearly thirty. I've had almost six months away from the theatre. I can't see any director taking me on when there's young, fit, talented kids like Sorrel here waiting – literally – in the wings.'

'Don't give up on your dreams,' Jayden warned. 'I can't see you permanently back here in the sticks, Robyn. And teaching, for heaven's sake? How *anyone* can spend even one day in school after the age of sixteen is beyond me.' He physically shuddered at the thought. 'I don't think I went in much after fourteen, to be honest. You're made for better things, Robyn. You're talented. Come on, don't give up. Your knee will get better and you'll be back in London and on the stage again.'

'...And right bang in the middle of the most amazing gardens you've ever seen, is this beautiful, classically styled building. I just stood and stared, couldn't do anything else.'

'Sorry, Mum, where's this? This garden?' I realised Mum was holding forth with great enthusiasm about something, everyone else around the table – except Jayden and me – totally engrossed as she waxed lyrical.

'At the back of Hudson House.'

'Oh, the care home?' I frowned. 'There's a garden behind it?'

'More than just a garden, Robyn. I was amazed. It's like a secret garden that goes on for ever.'

'It's not that secret, Mum.' Jess, in the process of serving dishes of steaming green vegetables and tiny garlic-and-rosemary-laden roast potatoes laughed. 'It's horribly overgrown and no one ever goes there. Haven't done for years really. Even the gardeners seem to have given up on it, to be honest.'

'Exactly,' Mum enthused. 'No one goes in there. I bet you've never been right up to the boundary wall, have you, Jess?'

'No, and I've no desire to. It's all overgrown with weeds and broken paths and tumbled-down walls. Spidery things and slugs.' She shuddered. 'Wouldn't be surprised if there are feral cats... foxes...'

'Who does it belong to?' Fabian took a mouthful of the fish in front of him without waiting for an answer, more interested in the food than a rambling, uncared-for bit of garden. 'Jess, you are an absolute genius. Where d'you get sea bass as fresh as this?'

'I go and see a man about a fish.' Jess laughed. 'Well, several fishes. In Midhope. He drives daily across to Grimsby for the catch of the day. He supplies all the local restaurants. Costly, but, you know, if you want fresh...'

'Bacon, samphire and...?' Fabian chewed speculatively before swallowing the fish and accompanying ingredients from inside one of the delicate razor clams.

'Seaweed,' Jess said proudly.

'Of course.' Fabian smiled. 'Fabulous. Jess, you need to cook for other people, not just for your family.' He swallowed, paused and then asked, 'So, Lisa, some sort of building in the middle of this great big garden?'

Mum nodded. 'Really strange. Someone – presumably the original owners of Hudson House – must have thought it de rigueur to build a summer house in their back garden.'

'Oh, it's a summer house?'

'Much more than that. It's huge, built along Greek classical lines. All white marble and Doric pillars. It reminded me of a miniature White House.'

'In the middle of a Yorkshire garden? How did they get planning permission for that?'

'Did you need planning permission back in the day?'

'Which day?'

'Well, I don't know much about architecture,' Mum said, 'but I assume maybe the twenties or thirties? You can see why the original owners of Hudson House wanted this great stonking edifice in their back garden. They'd have a ball showing off to the local industrialists in the garden.'

'Sounds wonderful,' Fabian said. 'And big enough for the family to eat out there and entertain in it?'

'The family? Fabian, it's huge. It's big enough for a whole restaurant-full of people to eat there.'

'Well, not for much longer.' Jess put down her knife and fork. 'The place is about to be sold. I guess the house, together with this summer house, will be razed to the ground so the Sattars can expand their Frozen empire.'

* * *

'I don't ever want to spend another night without you in my bed.' Fabian rolled me onto my back, easing the weight of his body onto his arms above me while gazing down at me with such love in his eyes, I knew I would forever thank whichever God it was that had decided this man should be mine.

His beautiful dark eyes, in the light from the one single lamp on Mum's bedside table, were deep, almost fathomless, and I fancied I could actually drown in their depths. And die happy. I laughed slightly, embarrassed at my thoughts; wanting to tell him how I felt but unable to find the words, never mind the courage, to lay bare my soul to him.

Fabian reached out a hand, touching my lower lip first with his finger and then with the tip of his tongue, lightly, oh, so lightly, until I almost cried out for more. But he held off, teasing until I found myself pulling him to me, wanting to possess every part of him. Wanting nothing more than to be possessed by him.

Afterwards he moved onto his back, pulling me down onto his chest, wrapping his arms tightly around me, kissing my forehead while wrapping my long black curls around his fingers. Who would have known such a small gesture could be so utterly sexy?

'Hell,' I said, glancing at Mum's little bedside clock radio, 'I have to be up in five hours. What are you going to do with yourself in the morning?'

'I'm going out with your mum.'

'Out with Mum?' I twisted round to face Fabian. 'Out where?'

'I'm going to take a look at this garden of hers.'

'Which garden?'

'The one she was talking about.'

'Oh, the Hudson House garden? Not exactly Mum's garden.'

'I've always been interested in architecture.'

'Since when?' I sat up, leaning on one elbow, looking down at Fabian's closed eyes, moving to gently kiss every bit of his face and neck.

'You continue doing that and you'll end up having four hours' sleep,' he murmured sleepily.

'Since when?' I insisted.

'Since when what?'

'Since when have you been interested in architecture?'

'Since your mum started talking about this classical building sitting in the middle of a West Yorkshire garden.' He opened his eyes. 'I've nothing else to do and it would be good to spend some time with her. Get to know her a bit better.' He sighed. 'I need to work, Robyn. I've had three months of doing little but look after Boris and cook for Jemima and her new bloke. Mum keeps asking when I'm returning to the firm.'

'Blimey, you sound like royalty.' I attempted levity to counteract the feelings of dread I always felt when he talked about returning to London. 'So *do* you want to go back?'

'I don't particularly want to go back to London; I don't want to become embroiled once more in the madness that's the Central Criminal Court, with all it involves.' He sighed again. 'But I need to work. I *want* to work.'

'How are you living? I mean, without working?' Was that a

question I should be asking? A bit personal maybe? 'Listen, I haven't much, but what I have is yours.'

He started laughing. 'Thank you. I'll know where to come when I'm totally on my uppers. I've savings, a trust fund from my grandmother, investments.'

Of course he had. He was a posh bloke from Bucks.

'That's not a problem.' He went on, 'At the moment anyway. The problem is not working. Everyone needs to work and earn a living.'

'So, you're going back?' I felt my heart plummet.

'Savings don't last for ever. And yes, Mum, Dad and, of course, Julius are now on my back wanting me to return from my "little holiday", as Julius calls it. Tempting me back with small cases that won't, according to Julius, have me "running for the hills again".'

'So, nothing doing with taking on Joel Sinclair for Sorrel, then?'

'I didn't say I would, Robyn.'

'You didn't say you wouldn't either.'

'Come back down with me.' Fabian appeared to be ignoring the question of Joel Sinclair. 'You can stay at the apartment in St James with me.'

'And what would *I* do?'

'Audition for theatre parts again.'

'I can't do anything until Easter, Fabian. I can't let the kids down when they're all excited about putting on this production of *Grease*.'

'I thought you said earlier they were more interested in getting pizza down their necks.'

'They're teenagers. Always hungry. Once we get back properly into the new term, rehearsals will start again. And I'll make sure they eat first. And the studio is warm.'

'So, no coming back to London with me, then?'

'Don't ask me to make these big decisions when I'm only five hours' sleep from facing 9CL once more.'

'Let's make it four and a half,' Fabian murmured, a warm hand snaking gently into the waistband of my recently retrieved pyjamas.

8

LISA

'Blimey, Mum, you here again? You'll be hiring a charabanc next and start charging for trips round Hudson House. And why on earth have you brought Fabian?' Jess, Lisa could see, was flustered as she attempted to extricate herself from the shaky yet surprisingly tenacious grip of ninety-eight-year-old Clive, who was equally determined she should not.

'Sorry, darling,' Lisa said, glancing up at Fabian, who was standing quietly at her side. 'We're in your way.'

'It's fine, Mum.' Jess managed a smile. 'Really. Would you like coffee, both of you?'

'Drunk a gallon already this morning,' Fabian said cheerfully. 'We've come to see this miniature White House of Lisa's.'

'Oh, right. Through the kitchens and the door down to your right. Try not to let too many of the residents see you leave or they'll be following you out, in various stages of undress, like the Pied Piper.'

'OK. Lisa?'

Lisa led the way, ridiculously excited at sharing her garden find with someone who appeared to be as interested as herself.

She stopped to deadhead a couple of rusting floribunda that should have been done months ago. 'Do you like gardening, Fabian?'

'I like the finished product...' he smiled. '...but haven't a clue how to go about it. Dad's quite into gardening, but there's always been someone brought in to do most of the donkey work. And then, living in London, in an apartment, there's never been any need...' He broke off. 'Goodness, is that it?' Fabian put up a hand against the weak January sun that was reflecting a kaleidoscope of white light on what remained of the previous day's snowfall. 'I never expected...' He moved quickly forwards, Lisa in his wake, until he came to a standstill at the entrance to the white marble building. 'I see what you mean about the White House. I wouldn't be surprised to hear "The Stars and Stripes Forever" being played.'

Catching up with him, Lisa put a hand to her chest, breathing heavily. 'Amazing, isn't it?'

'You OK?' Fabian was concerned. 'I know you've not been well.'

'Fabian, I'm fine. Just a fifty-four-year-old woman who needs to improve her fitness. Which I fully intend doing with everything else I've promised myself I'll change.'

'You sure? Is it open?'

'It was yesterday. Come on.'

Once inside, Fabian moved quickly from room to room. 'There's an upstairs as well,' Fabian called. 'Marble steps – a bit slippy but totally safe. You stay here if it's too much.'

'Fabian, I'm perfectly fine.'

'There's a balcony up here,' he shouted down as Lisa made her way up to him. 'My goodness, what a view. All the way over to those hills...'

'Those are not just any hills.' Lisa laughed, sounding like an M&S advert as she joined him. 'That's the backbone of England.'

'Hell, something like this where I live in London would be worth millions. I mean, absolutely millions. You'd have everybody after it the minute it came up on the market.'

Lisa laughed again. 'You and Jess could open it as a restaurant. Call it The White House.'

Fabian turned and stared. 'Oh, my God, Lisa. Yes. Yes... Fucking hell – sorry, Lisa – yes!' He turned, running down the stairs, taking out his phone, clicking away from every angle.

'Er, I was only kidding, Fabian.' Lisa smiled nervously, pulling her scarf around her neck against the cold as she made her way carefully back down, holding the rail.

'Who does it belong to?' Fabian demanded. 'Who owns it? Does the care home own it?'

'Well, I would imagine so... Where are you going?'

'To get Jess. Wait there,' he commanded, before sprinting back across the adjacent orchard, through the vegetable gardens, the formal lawns and the rose garden, until Lisa, scrunching her fingers in their red woollen gloves against the cold, had to stand on tiptoe to see him disappear through the kitchen door back into Hudson House.

'Bloody hell!' Lisa sat down on one of the broad window seats, tucking her feet beneath her as she surveyed the inside of this fabulous building once more. 'If only,' she muttered out loud, her breath coming out in a mist in front of her as she spoke. 'Mind you, heating bills would be astronomical.' She stood, slapping at her shoulders to beat some warmth into her body, imagining an eating place right here in this fabulous summer house, the bar area over to one end, the kitchens over to the other end. Or what about upstairs? The view down over the gardens if one were seated up there would be phenomenal. Like being in an eagle's eyrie.

'What? Slow down. Is it Eloise? Oh, hell, she's OK, isn't she?' Jess was tutting loudly, swearing under her breath as she attempted to catch up with Fabian. 'This is all I bloody need,' Lisa heard her shout after Fabian as he took her hand, pulling her into the main body of the building. 'You know, her family saying we've not looked after her properly. She's not... she's not...?'

'Jess, what do you think?' Fabian simply stood, his arms folded, his eyes alive with excitement. He moved to take her hand again, leading her into the centre of the main hall.

'What do I think about what? Is Eloise OK?'

'Eloise?' Fabian was momentarily distracted as Jess's eyes swept the room.

'What do you think?' Fabian repeated. 'About this place?'

'I think it's a huge folly built by rich people with more sense than money. And that it'll be one of the first things to go once the Sattar brothers get their hands on the home. Just think how many fish fingers and chicken nuggets they'll be able to churn out once they build a new factory here.'

'Or...' Fabian spoke slowly and deliberately '...just think how many people *we* could seat here and cook for, you and me, if we were to turn it into a restaurant.'

Lisa had heard of, but never before witnessed, someone's jaw dropping, but here now was evidence of such a phenomenon. Jess's mouth opened but didn't close again and Lisa wanted to laugh at her daughter's reaction.

'Oh, don't be so bloody ridiculous,' Jess eventually managed to get out. 'It's freezing in here.' She shivered dramatically as if to emphasise the point. 'And how would you get any customers in?

Through all those rotting vegetables and rhubarb? Women in their best designer gear and high heels tripping up over molehills to get out to this place? Anyway, it's sold; the Sattar brothers are planning to build one of their factories right here.'

'Is it actually sold, Jess? It can't have gone through yet?' Fabian was calm, his legal training taking over.

'Well, I got the impression it was...' Jess trailed off, glancing first at Lisa and then around at the inside of the summer house as if seeing it for the first time.

'Have you ever actually been up here before?' Lisa shook her head at Jess, who'd never shown a huge amount of interest in the great outdoors. Apart from on a hockey pitch when she was a kid where she'd shown an almost psychopathic refusal to allow a ball in her net. Shame she'd not had that same resolve to keep bloody Dean Butterworth out of her bed.

'Yes, of course,' Jess was saying and Lisa suddenly realised she was embarrassed at being called out in front of Fabian.

'I'm amazed the owners haven't looked after this building better.' Fabian was now tapping at walls, feeling for damp, jumping on the wooden parquet floor for signs of rot. 'Having said that, it's amazingly well preserved. I suppose having been built of stone and marble, rather than wood as modern summer houses and orangeries are today, there's no reason why it should be falling down. Jess, come on, come and look upstairs.'

'You're mad,' Jess said, but nevertheless followed Fabian up to the next level. 'Goodness,' she went on, her voice one of surprise as Lisa followed on behind. 'I'd no idea there was all this room! Blimey, you could sit loads of people – or even have the kitchens – on this second floor.'

'Definitely sit diners up here.' Fabian was excited. 'You wouldn't want to waste this view on kitchens, would you?'

Jess had moved over to the window once Lisa mounted the

steps, and was gazing down and across the gardens and to the rolling hills beyond. 'They've still got snow on them,' she was saying almost dreamily. 'And who'd have thought you could see so much of Yorkshire spread out in front of you?'

'I bet you can see four counties from here,' Lisa surmised.

'Four?' Fabian had joined them at the window.

'Yorkshire, Lancashire, Derbyshire... and Cheshire at a push...'

'You could call the place The Four Counties.' Jess continued to scan the vista.

'How about The White House?' Fabian smiled.

'Too American: people would think you'd just be serving burgers and fries.' Lisa grimaced. 'The Eyrie...?' she began.

'Eerie what?' Jess turned, pulling a face. 'You'd soon put punters off if they thought they were coming to a sort of Hallowe'en do with fake cobwebs and ghostly moans accompanying their starter... oh, right, eyrie as in eagle's nest? Right.' Embarrassed once more, she headed back for the stairs. 'Great dream but a) Hudson House is sold and this building will be flattened and b) it's hairdresser day and it'll be curlers at dawn if I don't get down there to sort them out.' She headed for the door.

'Jess, come on, what do you think?' Fabian wasn't letting it go.

'Well, I haven't got a penny.' Jess laughed. 'So, if you're wanting me to go halves with you on this... Oh, I don't know why I'm even thinking about it when the Sattars have already laid claim to it. Sorry, I'll have to go...' And with that she set off without a backward glance.

'Hmm, I don't think she wants us around.' Fabian frowned.

'Jess is just very stressed,' Lisa soothed. 'She'll have to find a new job soon, I guess. I could do with a coffee though. D'you think we can go and help ourselves in the kitchens?'

'Come on, I'll treat you.' Fabian shook his car keys in Lisa's direction. 'I can't stop thinking about crumpets – I've become addicted to them after moving up to Yorkshire.'

'Good reason to stay up here, then. There's a lovely little café down in Beddingfield village where they do crumpets dripping with butter and a pretty mean coffee.'

* * *

'Best coffee I've had since leaving London.' Fabian smiled, wiping butter from his chin with a gaily coloured paper napkin.

'We're not all whippets and *eeh by gum*, you know.' Lisa grinned, savouring her own coffee.

'You've not exactly got "Made in Yorkshire" stamped all the way through you.' His smile was questioning.

'I was born in Surrey.'

'Oh? How've you ended up here, then?'

'The people I lived with moved to Sheffield when I was nine or so.'

'The people you lived with?' Fabian pulled a face. 'That sounds a strange way of talking about your adoptive parents. I mean I know you were adopted, Lisa – Robyn told me when she and I first met.'

'Hmm.' Lisa picked up her cup once more, draining the contents. 'I know the second cup is never as good as the first, but I'm having another. You?'

Fabian nodded, catching the eye of the waitress. 'And Beddingfield?'

'Jayden was based in Leeds. I met him in a club in Bradford when I was seventeen. After several years out on the road with him...'

'Really?' Fabian interrupted. 'You were a sort of roadie?'

'Yep. I did the bookings, made appointments, made sure he

and the band were fed and watered even if some nights we could only afford to sleep in the van.' Lisa laughed. 'I even joined him on stage sometimes; you know, if his backing group had disowned him because they hadn't been paid.'

Fabian stared. 'I feel like I've had a very staid life compared to you.'

'I was rubbish.' Lisa grinned. 'Kept coming in on the wrong note at the wrong time. And then I realised I was pregnant with Jess. I'd had enough of constantly being on the move – almost five years in total – and, to be honest, I think Jayden had had enough of me cramping his style. We were often abroad, particularly in Denmark, Sweden and Copenhagen.' She laughed. 'I remember throwing up over the side of the North Sea ferry and knew I was totally fed up with it all. I wanted a place of our own and not the horrible rented flat in Harehills in Leeds. We were on our way back from somewhere and heading straight for the flat after being away for a month. The van blew a gasket and we ended up looking for a garage, smoke billowing from the exhaust, in the prettiest village I'd ever seen...'

'Beddingfield?'

Lisa nodded. 'I knew straight away I'd found where I wanted to live; a village with a duck pond, a pub and gift shops and a village school where I'd be able to send this baby I was expecting.'

'What, as soon as it was born?' Fabian grinned at her over his coffee cup and, not for the first time, Lisa knew exactly what it was Robyn saw in this man.

'You know what I mean,' she tutted. 'I wanted to put down roots, give the baby a home, give it a stable upbringing where it would be totally loved and wanted.'

'And your upbringing wasn't like that?' Fabian was insistent, obviously wanting to know more.

'I wanted my baby to know who it was, where it came from. Who its parents were.'

'Of course you did.' Fabian stopped speaking as the waitress placed their fresh coffees in front of them.

'Obviously it didn't work out quite the way I wanted. The *last* thing Jayden wanted was to be stuck in a quiet Yorkshire village – however pretty – with a wife and new baby.'

'You got married, then?'

'Nope. Jayden never asked me. I don't suppose he believes in marriage. Oh, I certainly asked him more than once to put a ring on my finger; to give Jess and me some sense of belonging. Some security. To be fair, I wanted a family. Not Jayden's fault if that wasn't what he wanted as well. I should have left him before I tried the old "coming off the pill without telling him" trick.' Lisa air-quoted the words. 'I celebrated my twenty-third birthday in a beat-up old white van on board a ferry somewhere between Portsmouth and Bilbao. The Bay of Biscay, when pregnant, is not an experience I ever want to repeat. So, we rented a cottage in the village and then, when it came up for sale, Jayden bought it.'

'You were left by yourself a lot of the time?'

'Well, with Jess. I adored her and I was actually really happy. Then, when she was only ten months old, I found I was pregnant again. This time with Robyn. I thought two little girls would be more than enough to tie Jayden down. But, I had absolutely no right to tie anyone down. To curb anyone's freedom when they're still only in their late twenties and trying to make a name for themselves. If there's one thing I've learned, Fabian, it's that.'

'And your own parents? They must have been around to help you with two babies?'

'I told you; they're not my parents.'

'I'm sorry. I'm going on a bit, aren't I?' Fabian obviously didn't know how to answer this. 'But are they still alive?'

'I've really no idea. I've had no contact with the Foleys since I walked out the summer I finished A levels.' Lisa gave a short laugh. 'I didn't even know if I'd passed them or not for a year or so.'

'What? Passed your parents in the street?' Fabian looked shocked.

'No.' Lisa laughed again. 'I didn't know if I'd passed my A levels. I'd been offered a place at Warwick to study biology, but I walked away from it all.'

'And had you?'

'Passed?' Lisa nodded. 'Four A's. Adrian Foley made sure of that.'

'Your dad?'

'I told you, he *wasn't* my dad.' Lisa's face began to close down, her eyes refusing to meet Fabian's. 'I once looked up the definition of adopted. Do you know what the dictionary definition is?'

'Er, no, I can't say I do.'

'To legally take another person's child into your own family and take care of her as your own child.'

'Sounds about right.'

'*Take care of her as your own child?*' Lisa gave a short laugh. 'Despite the fact that they were both trained teachers – and Adrian Foley a headteacher whose job it was to care for, as well as educate, children – neither of them had a clue about caring for the little girl – me – they'd adopted at a few weeks old.'

'I've always known you were adopted but Robyn's never told me any of this about your adoptive parents,' Fabian said gently.

'Because I've never spoken about the Foleys. I didn't want my girls tainted by who they were.' Lisa broke off, frowning. 'Look, I'm sorry, Fabian, my childhood and the Foleys are not something I talk about. I really don't know why I'm telling you all this now.

Your professional expertise, I guess, to wheedle things out of people?'

Fabian put up two hands in apology, but Lisa continued regardless.

'I even made up a totally false story about my childhood, telling the girls I'd been at a local comp in Sheffield instead of St Mark's, one of the most prestigious public schools in South Yorkshire, where Adrian Foley was head. And Jayden, for all his faults, did listen. And listen and listen. Which was probably because of the awful childhood he'd suffered himself...'

'Robyn told me about Jayden's father. Actually, in truth, she didn't tell me until my brother, Julius, did the research. Easy enough to google the reggae artist Jayden Allen. Julius thought he'd hit the jackpot when it came up that Winston Allen, Jayden's father, had murdered Jayden's mother and her lover when Jayden was tiny. A black West Indian murdering his white wife and her lover back in the early seventies must have really hit the headlines?'

'It sure did.' Lisa appraised Fabian for a few seconds. 'But your finding out that her grandfather was a double murderer didn't stop you wanting to be with Robyn?'

'Well, I wasn't pleased that Robyn hadn't told me herself. That it was Julius – he's my half-brother, Lisa, and we've never really got on – who spilled the beans. He really thought I'd have nothing more to do with her when all that came out.'

'As did the Foleys when they learned the truth about Jayden's father,' Lisa said. 'When you love someone their family history's irrelevant.'

Fabian gave a wry smile. 'I'm not sure Robyn sees it that way. She finds it difficult to come to terms with the fact that my family were all educated at Eton.' He paused. 'You know, she sees them as white, entitled Tories...'

Lisa laughed. 'Are they? Are *you*? And now she knows *I* was educated at what is probably one of the country's – certainly the north's – most prestigious public schools, surely Robyn can't still be hanging onto these ridiculous prejudices of hers?'

'I'm afraid I'm not a political animal,' Fabian said, neatly side-stepping any criticism of Robyn from her own mother.

Lisa hesitated. 'You've done the right thing leaving London, Fabian. I think it all got too much for you?'

Fabian nodded, seemingly embarrassed. 'My mother and brother think I've let the family down, abandoning the family firm.'

'They blame Robyn? That you've followed her up here?'

He nodded.

'I'm sorry about that. Never good to be at odds with your parents, no matter how old you are. Right, so, now that we know a little more about each other, how serious are you about turning the white house into a restaurant?'

'The Eyrie, please.' Fabian grinned, animated once more. 'Don't you think it would be fabulous, Lisa? I mean, do you realise just how talented Jess is?'

Lisa nodded. 'I do. Trouble is, she doesn't.'

'D'you not think her coming first in the Yorkshire Christmas TopChef competition has given Jess some confidence about how good she is?' Fabian asked.

'I don't know. If you did look into starting up a business with her, I'm not convinced she'd have the nerve to actually go in with you. If things went wrong, she'd never forgive herself.'

'Better to have tried and lost than never to have tried at all...' Fabian broke off as two designer-suited and booted men, probably in their early fifties, made their way to an adjacent table, sitting down and immediately perusing the menu.

'The Sattar brothers.' Lisa nudged Fabian meaningfully, murmuring their name in a low voice.

'How do you know?'

'Fabian,' Lisa whispered, turning away from the men and continuing to talk in hushed tones. 'This is a small village. Everyone knows everyone round here, but particularly those who employ half the people who live in it.'

9

ROBYN

I was determined that Sorrel was going to get through the audition at the Susan Yates Theatre School with ease, and so was intent on putting her through the three set pieces for her audition in London towards the end of January.

'Come on, Sorrel,' I chided, glancing at my watch. I knew I was being irritable, but time was of the essence. 'There's only twenty minutes left of lunchtime, and I'm teaching Year 7 after that. What? What is it? I'm telling you now, you carry on like this, looking like you have no enthusiasm for what you're doing, and there's absolutely no chance of your landing a scholarship. You won't be the only one being auditioned, you know. I mean,' I went on when Sorrel didn't appear to be listening, 'do you realise just how *lucky* you've been to get this chance...?'

'Luck?' Sorrel muttered, her head down as she started to untie her footwear. 'Are you implying it's all down to *luck* rather than any actual ability I may have? In that case, I might as well call in at the corner shop on my way home and buy some scratch cards and win the lottery. You know, if it's all down to just *luck*...' She trailed off, continuing to slowly take off her trainers and socks before reaching for her black leather dance shoes, and I felt my irritation mount.

'Look, have you gone off the whole idea or what? There's still work to do, you know. Your Sandy piece from *Grease* is just about perfect – you've worked on that for the school production for weeks. Mind you, you'll find in this game, you can never sit back and rest on your laurels: there's always a director narkily suggesting you could do better; always someone in the wings snapping at your heels just waiting for the opportunity to take a part from you. Believe me, I've been there...' I stopped talking as Sorrel lifted her face towards me but gave no response. She eventually stood and moved over to the makeshift barre I'd managed to persuade Jobsworth Ken to put up for us, albeit with many accompanying words of doom and gloom about the school not being around much longer, never mind this bloody cold cellar I insisted on calling a drama studio.

Sorrel moved through a series of stretches and exercises, limbering up, pacing herself, but seemingly without a great deal of enthusiasm for the task. The sparkle, the verve, the downright talent and gusto Sorrel was capable of showing when dancing appeared strangely lacking this lunchtime.

Swallowing the unspoken words of censure on my lips, I crossed the studio floor for my phone, finding the music that accompanied the part of Sandy in *Grease*. 'OK, Sorrel, let's take it from the top.'

'From the top?' Sorrel did little to suppress a tired snigger. 'This is St Mede's comp in West Yorkshire, Robyn, not the effing London Palladium.' Throwing a withering look in my direction, she positioned herself and, once the chords started, began her set piece. Just thirty seconds in, she stopped. 'I need the loo,' she muttered, setting off towards the three wooden steps that led to the lavatory set aside for use of staff.

'You won't be able to have a pee in the middle of a piece next week,' I shouted after her but Sorrel was already out of earshot.

'Have you got a rehearsal?' Mason Donoghue had come into the studio, making his way over to where I stood waiting for Sorrel's reappearance. 'The kids not turned up?'

'Just spending fifteen minutes – ten now – trying to get Sorrel up to speed for her audition in London.'

'Right, OK. Couple of things.'

'Oh?' I turned to look directly at Mason. 'You're not about to tell me I can't have the day off to go with Sorrel to London?'

'I was thinking maybe someone else might go with her. Your mum? Or Jess?' Mason looked hopeful.

'I want to go. *I'm* the one who knows about this stuff, Mason. I know London too.'

'We're so short-staffed...'

'Well, get some money spent and get some supply staff in.'

'I'm already over budget.' Mason sighed gloomily. 'And, as you well know, getting supply staff to stay even for the day, never mind return for another, is almost impossible.'

'Not really my problem,' I said irritably. Sometimes I forgot Mason, my ex-lover, was still my boss. 'What else did you want?' I glanced at my watch and then the wooden steps. How long did it take for someone to have a pee, for heaven's sake?

'You all right, Sorrel?' Mason had turned to see Sorrel make her way over towards her bag and trainers rather than back to where she'd been about to perform.

'Don't feel too good,' she muttered, avoiding looking at me. 'I'm going home. It's only general studies and then RE. Seeing I don't believe in any god, I don't reckon Allah or Jesus will give a flying whatsit if I don't turn up for them.'

'Sorrel?' I moved towards her, concerned.

'Sorrel, you need to go down to matron's room,' Mason started. 'If you're not well.'

'Not much point in doing that,' Sorrel retorted over her shoulder. 'We've not had a matron, have we, since Blane Higson nicked all the paracetamol and Night Nurse from her cupboard?'

'I didn't think anyone knew about that,' Mason whispered in my direction as I began to follow Sorrel's determined exit from the studio.

'Mason, *everyone* knows.'

'Actually, it was about Blane I was coming to see you.'

'What's he done now? Apart from getting high on matron's drugs?'

'He appears to have gone missing. He's in 9CL – *your* tutor group.' Mason's tone was accusatory, as if it were my fault the kid wasn't in school.

'I am aware of that, Mason. He wasn't in registration this morning. But that's nothing new; he rarely gets to school on time, if he comes in at all. He's always bunking off, you know that. How many times have you had to ring his mum and then the local authority's attendance team to go and search for him?'

'The thing is, Robyn, we need to have a point of contact for perennially absent children. With Blane, it's always been his form tutor or head of year.'

'Mason, Celia Logan is not only 9CL's form tutor, but also the Year 9 head of year. As she's now strapped up in a French Alps hospital muttering "*Sacré bleu*", but otherwise enjoying the unexpected extension to her holiday instead of chasing after Blane Higson, I would imagine the point of contact you're looking for will have to be yourself? Hmm?'

'The thing is, Robyn,' Mason repeated, his voice persuasive, 'the concept of a "constant person" to work with a family, once attendance issues become serious, is always seen as the best possible practice...'

'Seen by whom?'

'Sorry?'

'*Who* sees this as best practice?'

'Well, you know... erm... educationalists.'

'Mason, you're beginning to sound like a politician.' I went towards the door, Mason following on, obviously determined to have his say. 'Stop quoting the educational dogma you learned off by heart in order to secure your headship here.'

'Excuse me, will you please remember I'm your boss?' Mason was beginning to sound as irritable as I was feeling. 'You see, Robyn, this person, this one point of contact when a child is constantly absent from school, may not necessarily be a teaching member of staff...'

'Great, that lets me off the hook, then.' I opened the door, Mason still in my wake.

'Indeed, leaders talk about the valuable skills and knowledge brought to this role by staff who have come from social work, police, mentoring or other backgrounds...'

'Other backgrounds? Oh, such as a supply teacher with a knackered ACL, previously dancing in the West End?'

'Perfect.' Mason nodded with some degree of relief. 'You know I hate to ask, Robyn, but with Petra pregnant, I don't want her wandering round the streets of Blane's estate looking for him. I'm so up to my ears with the day-to-day stuff, plus the press constantly wanting to talk to me about the alleged closing down of the school. As well as the attack on Joel Sinclair. And then there's all the meetings I'm having to have with the local authority. I really don't have the time to be Blane Higson's minder as well. It was his mum who got in touch this time; she got a neighbour to ring school. Apparently, he didn't actually go home last night...'

'Well, he's stayed out before. Remember I found him hiding in the girls' toilets overnight because he'd lost his key and couldn't get in his house when his mum had overdosed again...?'

Mason tutted. 'Of course I remember, Robyn. And I know you have a special relationship with Blane.'

'A special relationship?' I turned back in Mason's direction.

'You're good with these kids, Robyn. You *care*.'

'Oh, don't try and get to me through sycophancy...'

'And every time his social worker is back on his case, he's taken into care again. But he just runs back home. I thought...'

'Look, if he's not been home, then it's a matter for the police. Surely you can see that? A missing fourteen-year-old? Social workers and the police need to be involved, Mason.' I did sometimes wonder how on earth Mason Donoghue had been tasked with heading up St Mede's. Exceptionally good-looking, charismatic and persuasive he might be, but after almost five months under his direction, I really was no longer convinced of his leadership. Oh, he was jolly good at talking the talk, walking the walk and, brilliant though he was with these St Mede's kids, knowing just how to handle them, he appeared to have little knowledge of the actual administrative requirements for the day-to-day running of a school.

'Look, I've missed Sorrel now.' I tutted crossly as the bell for afternoon school sounded, shattering the corridor's silence with its raucous clanging. 'Jeez, why does that bell sound so loud down here in the basement?' I headed for the stairs and the Year 7 class I was taking.

'Acoustics,' Mason was saying as he followed me up the two flights of stone steps and into the main body of the school. 'And, *of course*, it's a matter for the police and Blane's social worker and they've been informed. Particularly after the attack on Joel. If the press gets to hear we've a missing child just a couple of days after what happened to Joel, they'll be all over us like a bad rash...'

'Hi, miss. I love your English lessons. You're my best teacher.' Billy Caldwell, his face pale beneath a mass of freckles, tapped my arm affectionately as if I were his mate and, despite the worry about Sorrel's sudden departure and now the missing Blane Higson, I wanted to laugh.

'You see—' Mason continued to follow me even as I brought the class into the room '—you've a special relationship with the children.'

'Are you stalking me, Mason?' I finally asked as he walked in my wake right down to the desk at the front of the room.

'No, no, I just...' he started.

'OK, Mr Donoghue, you let me out of school for the last period. It does mean you'll have to get someone to take 9CL—' anything to get out of teaching that shower '—and I'll drive down to Blane's house to see his mum and find out what's going on. I'm not going after school, Mason – it's getting dark by four and I need to get home to see what's up with Sorrel.'

'OK, OK. Good. We'll do that, then. Good. Good. Very good. Excellent.' Obvious relief that he'd managed to offload one of his many problems made Mason garrulous in his response. Then, apparently deeming even his effusive words of thanks insufficient, he bent to kiss my cheek before quickly leaving.

'Blimey, did you see that?' Lewis Bedford sat open-mouthed, staring after Mason's departing back.

'Cor, sir fancies miss...' Kye Vant chortled.

'My dad fancies her too. Says she's right hot...'

'*I* do as well.' Harrison Wade, staring somewhat dreamily in my direction, suddenly realised he'd spoken out loud and flushed scarlet as his mates started to make what could only be construed as sexually suggestive hand gestures while the low-level giggles started at the back of the room escalated into full-scale ribald laughter.

In no mood for these Year 7 kids getting uppity so soon into their time at St Mede's, I silenced them immediately with a long, low: 'Ex-cuse-me!'

Total silence ensued, apart from a couple of quickly smothered hiccups of laughter towards which I focused my favourite narrow-eyed glare. I stood facing the class of eleven and twelve-year-olds, starting the ten-second silence I reckoned would bring the class completely to heel.

'OK, this afternoon we're going to look at anagrams...'

'Anna Gram's what, Miss Allen?'

'Sorry?'

'You said we're going to be looking at Anna Gram's *something*. You got my last name wrong.' Anna Graham, the brightest kid in the class, interrupted almost kindly. 'You said you loved the poem I wrote last term. Do you want me to read it out again?' Anna started reaching for her bag.

'She's *so* full of herself,' Harper Cooke muttered to her mate. 'You're always showing off, Anna.'

'*Anagrams.*' I laughed in spite of myself. 'OK, any idea what an anagram is?'

'My nan sometimes swears when she's doing the crossword, miss,' Evie Blackburn said seriously. '"Another of them bloody anagrams," she shouts out to my grandad and then *he* says, "Leave it, love, them things is too hard for us. Do the sudoku instead." So, whatever it is, it's hard.'

'I can't do hard stuff,' Billy muttered. 'Can't we read some more of *War Horse* instead? We'd got to a right good bit.'

'OK,' I went on, 'so an anagram is a word or words with their letters mixed up to spell a different word. Or words.'

Silence.

'I can't spell words when the letters *aren't* mixed up.' Billy slumped back in his chair, obviously fed up that, after his bigging me up as his favourite teacher, I wasn't turning out to be quite so accommodating after all.

'So, for example, the word lump – a fruit is the clue...'

'A lump of fruit?' Billy was now almost horizontal across his desk.

'Plum!' Anna Graham shouted.

'Yes, well done, Anna. A cheap fruit.'

'Banana?' Billy offered. 'Me mam says I can have them 'cos they're cheaper than pineapples. An' I really *love* pineapples an' all...'

'If you go to Aldi, they're all quite cheap,' Aria Spencer, already middle-aged as the sole carer for her mum with MS, piped up sagely. 'And you'd be gobsmacked at their carrots and turnips. Right good value...'

'Peach!' Anna shouted, excitedly.

'Yep.'

'There's no rage with this fruit,' I quickly wrote on the smartboard.

'Orange!' Anna was on a roll, pushing back her hair and preening.

'Aw, don't let her get any more, miss.'

'OK, a bit harder now.' I smiled. 'A dirty room – where you might sleep. Work together in pairs, use your jotters. Don't call out, hands up when you've worked it out. Come on.'

There were times when I totally forgot I wasn't into teaching, that I was in a classroom only by default. Lessons like this, with Year 7, were fabulous. Finishing with best in prayers – a female pop singer – and cheering along with the class when Billy Caldwell came up with the solution first, I was as surprised as the kids when the bell went for the end of the session.

Before my final lesson of the day, now that I'd permission to leave school early, I checked my phone hoping for a message of explanation from Sorrel but, instead, found a text from Fabian.

> **FABIAN**
> Can you meet me down in Beddingfield village straight after school?
>
> **ROBYN**
> I can, but it won't be straight after school. I've to go look for a kid down on the estate in Little Micklethwaite first.
>
> **FABIAN**
> OK. Shall I come with you?
>
> **ROBYN**
> See how the other half live, you mean? What's up? Why d'you want to meet me?
>
> **FABIAN**
> Tell you when you get here.
>
> **ROBYN**
> Best if you drive over to school and follow me down. Am free in 45 minutes.

* * *

Exactly fifty minutes later, having left teaching notes for Petra Waters, who had been roped in to take my last class of the day, as well as remembering to send round a note to cancel my weekly extra-curricular dance class for the Year 7s and 8s, I gathered my bags and made for the main door.

'S'OK, Robyn.' Sally, one of the school secretaries, knocked on the glass window of the office before sliding it back.

'What's OK?'

'Blane's back at home. He's turned up there. You don't need to go after all, Mason says.'

'Oh, I'm on my way now, Sally,' I tutted. 'I've sorted my last class and cancelled my after-school session.'

'Well, Mason says—'

'Tell Mason you missed me, that I'd already left.' And, with a cheery wave over my shoulder, I made good my escape, heading into the chilly damp January afternoon. Very tempted to go straight home to see Sorrel, or at least take Fabian down to The Green Dragon for a quick one before he headed back to Harrogate, I decided I was a professional. I'd have to report back to Mason as well. He wouldn't be too impressed if he knew I'd left school early in order to find Blane, only to spend what was left of the afternoon down in the boozer with my lover. Besides, I genuinely wanted to find out what Blane had been up to; where he'd been all night. And, nosy old so-and-so that I was, I wanted to see for myself this mother of his who didn't appear to be doing the best job of looking after her recalcitrant son. Seeing Fabian's silver 911 parked behind my own little red Honda, I waved, jangled my keys in his direction and intimated that he should follow me to the address I'd taken from the class register.

10

The area of Little Micklethwaite around St Mede's High School reminded me of a decaying tooth no one appeared to know how to pull. With the exceptionally pretty villages of Beddingfield and Upper Merton to its left and right, the streets I now drove through held an air of almost embarrassed shame, the area's rich history and tradition, built on the woollen textile industry of the previous centuries, long gone. Any attempt to convert and utilise the solid Yorkshire stone-built mills, turning their vast internal space into single units advertising their new usage as body repair shops, pine stripping, welding services and the like, had in turn given up the ghost, surrendering makeshift shutters to the elements and an excess of graffiti. A long row of nineteen-seventies-built concrete shops, which had replaced the original pretty cottages, the greengrocer and bakers, which today would surely have been listed and preserved, was now made over to the ubiquitous takeaway, betting shops, a laundrette, the heavily protected post office and community centre – which didn't appear to be used by anyone in this broken community. Even the charity shop seemed to have given up in despair. I drove on towards the vast 1950s council estate.

I'd lived in some dives in London – Hammersmith and Soho – but Soho particularly, while often dirty and unkempt, was at the same time colourful and vibrant with a rich tapestry of thriving businesses and life. These streets, which the majority of St Mede's kids walked through to get to school, were soulless, colourless. Lacking hope. Lacking a future.

Waze on my phone directed me along a road of bungalows for the elderly where there were dire warnings of Keep off the Grass (what grass?), Keep Dogs on a Lead (apparently the pit-bull-type animal that was now peeing up against another broken-down sign hadn't yet learned to read) and other signs with their commands long-obliterated by new commands of Fuck Off Filth. With no police presence that I could see, they appeared to have done just that. Something that looked suspiciously like the logo for the EDL was the only colour in an endless sea of brown and grey concrete amidst a profusion of stuffed-to-the-brim black binbags.

Checking in my rear-view mirror that Fabian was still behind me, I pulled up outside Blane's block and cut the engine, locking the Honda's door and walking back to where Fabian had now parked between a large white Transit and a rusting, abandoned caravan.

'Stay here,' I said.

'I'm not letting you go in there by yourself,' Fabian said through the open window of the Porsche.

'Why did you want to meet me anyway?' I asked. 'Are you wanting to go out to eat? You're a bit early. Mind you, I'm starving; I ended up with half a Mars bar at lunchtime.' My stomach growled a reminder.

'You really should start eating properly,' Fabian began. 'Make sure you eat the whole thing next time.'

'Yeah, yeah. Look, I won't be long.'

Fabian was already out of the car. 'But what is it you're here for? You shouldn't have to be doing this. You're a teacher, not a social worker. Or the police.' He tutted. 'I'm coming with you.'

'Oh, don't be daft,' I tutted in return. 'His mother will think you've come to arrest her.' I laughed. 'Look, if you're coming to protect me, just pretend you're a teacher like me.'

'In my jeans and trainers?'

'Oh, I don't know, Fabian. Come on, make your mind up. Pretend you're a social worker, then.'

Together we walked across a muddy piece of sad-looking grass littered with a couple of empty Red Bull cans, a black bin bag, its noxious contents spewing onto the adjacent broken concrete path, and what looked suspiciously like a used condom. Who on earth was having sex out here on this tiny patch of grass? I averted my eyes.

'23B.' I indicated a marked stairwell to the right and together we walked up the concrete steps – a fetid smell of stale urine meeting our nostrils – to the floor above, in silence. I really wished Fabian had stayed in the car; actually, wished he'd stayed back in my own pretty village of Beddingfield. I realised I was now acutely embarrassed that he was seeing me on what amounted to my home turf, vastly different from his beautiful London apartment overlooking Green Park and a different planet entirely from his parents' pile standing proud in the rich, leafy suburbs of Marlow.

'Right, this is it.' I knocked on the door, tentatively at first and then, when there was no response, with a heavier hand.

'Who is it?' A softly spoken voice could just be heard behind the door.

'Mrs Higson? It's Robyn Allen from St Mede's. I'm Blane's form tutor. Mr Donoghue asked me to call round to see what's happening with Blane.'

'It's OK. Thank you, he's back. Don't worry. The police know he's back.'

'Could I come in? Just for five minutes?'

Silence.

'Just for a couple of minutes, Mrs Higson? Just to check Blane's OK? And you are as well?'

'You're not a social worker,' Fabian mouthed crossly, frowning down at me.

Ignoring him, I went on, 'Could I just have a couple of words with Blane? A quick chat with him?'

'He won't want to see you. He'll think you're taking him off again. You know, with the police or into... you know... into care...'

'I promise you, Mrs Higson, I'm his teacher. Two minutes, so's I can have a word with him?'

After a long silence, the door to the flat opened a couple of centimetres and then, when the woman behind the door, after viewing my school identity lanyard, appeared satisfied that I was who I said I was, she opened the door wider, allowing us entry.

I wasn't sure what I'd been expecting of Blane Higson's mother – possibly a caricature of every female heroin addict I'd ever read about – but, although the woman was tiny, pale and obviously anxious, she was well dressed in clean jeans and sweater, a pair of white and gold designer trainers on her feet, her long dark hair tied back in a neat high ponytail.

'Hi, Mrs Higson, I'm Robyn Allen, Blane's form tutor.'

'Actually, its Ms Scaccetti,' the woman replied. 'And I thought Blane's form teacher was Ms Logan?' She turned her head to Fabian, taking in his height, his broad shoulders in the navy jacket, his dark good looks. 'So, who's this with you?' she asked, continuing to stare at Fabian.

'Just a friend of Robyn's,' Fabian said cheerfully. 'No one in authority—'

'I used to go to school with someone called Scaccetti,' I interrupted, silencing Fabian with a look. 'She was several years above me at Beddingfield High.'

'Beddingfield Comp?' Ms Scaccetti held my eye. 'Loretta Scaccetti?'

'Yes, that's it. Do you know her?'

'You could say that. It's me.'

'What is?'

'*I'm* Loretta Scaccetti.'

'Oh, goodness, right.' Well, that was a shock. I remembered Loretta as a slim pretty thing who all the first formers constantly looked over at in assembly. Something of a mean girl. How on earth had the charismatic Loretta ended up here in this awful tower block, a heroin addict and Blane Higson's mother to boot? Mind you, hadn't there been some scandal about her at school?

"Fraid you're not ringing any bells with me,' she said, peering at my face through narrowed eyes.

'Well, I was only an insignificant Year 7 when you were in Year 11. You might remember Jessica Allen, my sister?'

'Sorry, no.' She shook her head, seemingly uninterested in what I was saying.

'But you've older children as well as Blane…?' I started. Blane had talked about his two big brothers who'd recently upped and left home, one, apparently, into the army, both unable to cope with their mother's addiction, according to Blane. By my calculations, this woman in front of me could only be thirty-four at the most.

'Pregnant at fifteen,' (of course, that was the scandal!) 'with

Catholic parents who didn't want to know unless I stopped seeing the boy I was with,' Loretta said, defiantly. 'Anyhow, you've not come about me.' She stepped back into the hallway and we followed her in and then on into the sitting room. The gas fire was on full and a clothes horse of damp washing was splayed out in front of it. The steamy, humid atmosphere made me draw in a sharp intake of breath, after leaving the cold outside.

'Blane,' Loretta shouted. 'Someone to see you.'

'Tell 'em to piss off,' a voice came loudly from the other side of a bedroom door. 'I've had enough of 'em all. Tell 'em *no comment*.'

'Hang on.' I raised a questioning eye at Loretta and the woman nodded. I moved to the door. 'Blane? Blane, it's Ms Allen. Just come to see you're OK, sweetheart?'

Sweetheart? Where'd that come from? Flushing slightly, I tried again. 'Come on out, Blane, or let me come in there.'

'You're not coming in my bedroom,' Blane shouted back. 'I don't know what your intentions might be.'

Fabian stifled a laugh, which he hurriedly turned into a cough. Intentions? Blimey, big words from the kid I'd always called Whippety Snicket on account of his stature and awful behaviour.

'Come on, Blane, Mr Donoghue asked me to call in.'

'Where's Ms Logan?'

'Not in school at the moment. D'you remember? I told you that the other day. If you'd been in school more regularly, you'd have known that she wasn't back yet. Will I do instead?'

'S'pose.'

The bedroom door opened a crack and half of Blane's face – one eye with its accompanying brow, one nostril – could be seen. 'Hang on, who's that bloke? He's not come for me, has he? Is this all a set-up?'

'You've been watching too much bloody TV, Blane,' his mother shouted. 'Get out here and talk to this teacher of yours who's come all the way out from school to see you.'

'But who's the geezer?'

'He's a friend of mine, Blane.'

'Why've you brought him? Is he going to take me off to the police station again? Or into another effing kids' home?'

'No, no, not at all,' I soothed. 'We're on our way out for tea and, as we were passing, I said we'd just call in to see you. Mr Donoghue – and me – well, we've been worried about you.'

'McDonald's?'

'Sorry? Oh, yes, probably,' I lied. I bet Fabian had never set foot in a burger place.

The door opened wider and I found myself in a tiny bedroom smaller even than Mum's box room.

'Where'd you go, Blane? When you didn't come home?'

'I had business.'

'Oh?'

'You know.'

'No, I don't.' I smiled encouragingly. 'Tell me.'

'Can't.'

'Why not?'

'They'd be after me.'

'Who?'

'I'm not telling you that. Look, miss, there's nowt you can do. You saw what they did to Joel Sinclair.'

'Oh, Blane, you've not got yourself mixed up with that lot?'

'I'm working for them,' he said proudly. 'I'm a Sitter now, but soon I'll be a Top Boy, ordering the little kids around.'

'But the other day in school, I got the impression you were frightened, Blane.'

'Me? Frightened? Nah, not me, miss.'

'So where were you last night?' When Blane said nothing, I probed further but speaking gently. 'You didn't come home. Your mum was worried...'

'Only because she might not get her stuff. Only reason *she* was worried.'

'I don't think that's true, Blane. Mr Donoghue was worried. *I* was worried.'

'Well, don't be. It's all under control.'

'Had you kept some of the drug money? Is that why they were after you?'

Blane's eyes narrowed. 'Who's been talking?'

'Just a guess, Blane.'

'Yeah, well, all sorted now. I'd bought myself a scooter off another kid with the money.' Blane pointed towards the electric scooter that had pride of place against the closed curtains. 'But they said it's all right. I'd been using me inish... me inishi...'

'Your initiative?' I finished.

'Summat like that. I can do me work that bit faster now I've got me own set of wheels...'

'And the money?'

'Said I can add it to me debt bondage.'

'Your *debt bondage*?' I stared. 'What the hell's that?'

'Oy, don't swear in my bedroom, miss.' Blane actually grinned at me. 'You know, they give you a load of dosh up front and then you pay it off every time you do a job. They let me off the scooter money because I'd used my inishi... that word you just said.'

'And you told the police all this when they came looking for you?'

'No, course not. I'm not a grass and they 'aven't got nowt on me. I told 'em nothing: "No comment".'

'So, are you coming into school tomorrow? You've got to go to school, Blane.'

'Yeah, suppose. Get off to your Big Mac now, miss.'

Realising there was little more I could report back to Mason in the morning, I said, 'Look, Blane, I'm here if you need to talk.'

'Nah, I'm good. 'S all good.'

* * *

'Come on, let's get out of here. I wouldn't be surprised if the wheels have gone off the car. Or the car itself gone.' Fabian almost ran out of the door of the tower block.

'Well, if you will drive such a posh motor. Actually, Fabian, thank you.' I reached for his arm, pulling it round my waist, loving the warmth and sense of security it offered. 'I'm glad you were there with me. I *was* nervous, to be honest. Kept expecting one of these gang members to pop up. Four wheels all intact? Tyres still inflated? Green Dragon, is it?'

Fabian nodded. 'See you in the car park.'

* * *

'Where are you going? Entrance is this way!' I turned in surprise as Fabian caught up with me in the car park, taking my hand and veering off to the left. 'Oh, you fancy a swim, do you?' He was heading across the road towards the village duck pond where rustling, a series of secretive scurrying and flitting noises made us slow down on the path surrounding the water.

'How do the ducks escape the fox?' Fabian was asking as he continued to lead me around the long edge of the pond.

'Used to outwitting it, I guess – they're more than happy roosting on the water at night. Look, there's a couple over there.' I pointed to a symmetrical pair of dark shapes on the small island in the middle of the pond.

'Aren't they waste bins? They must get off to bed early.' He smiled.

'It's actually beginning to freeze at the edge of the pond,' I said, dipping my toe and immediately breaking the thin ice as I'd so often done as a child. 'Fabian, where are we going?' I demanded once more, following Fabian, who appeared determined to get where he was going. 'Careful, there's always goose poo on these paths. Slippy.'

'There can't be many villages left with an actual duck pond,' Fabian called over his shoulder. 'That's why I fell in love with it.'

'With what?' Panting slightly behind him, I knew I needed to get my fitness back after doing little exercise over the Christmas period.

'*Now* where are we going?' I complained as Fabian took a turning through the churchyard and out towards the cricket pitch on the other side. 'I really could do with getting home to see what's up with Sorrel.'

'There,' he said, five minutes later. 'There!'

'What? What am I looking at?' Sweating now in my big coat after the walk, I stood, turning a complete three hundred and sixty degrees as I tried to work out just what was exciting Fabian so much. He'd brought me halfway across the village, rather than settling down in The Green Dragon with the warming hot toddy for which the village pub had become famous. And which, after the day I'd had, I was desperate for.

'Oh, for heaven's sake, woman.' Fabian took my hand once more, pulling me towards the row of exquisite early-nineteenth-century cottages overlooking both the village green on one side and the cricket pitch on the other. 'To let.'

'To let what?'

'Jesus, you're thick when you want to be, Robyn. The fourth cottage from the left? It has a To Let sign outside.'

'Right?'

'And, I would very much like to extend my time away from London by renting said cottage.'

'Oh?' I felt my pulse quicken.

'And, I would very much like it if you'd rent it with me.'

'Gosh. Are you asking me to live with you?'

'Yes, that's the general idea.' He laughed, but I knew he was nervous waiting for me to say something.

'And you don't want to go back to London?' I asked.

'No. Not at the moment anyway. Not without you, Robyn. I don't want to spend another day without you in my bed.'

'But have you seen it inside? It might be dark and poky. It might be noisy, cold and damp. It might be old-fashioned with no shower and nowhere for you to cook properly…'

'I went round it this afternoon. It's light, airy and, best of all, has a fabulous modern kitchen just waiting for me to get stuck in. It's been totally renovated since the old woman who lived here died and the cottage sold on.'

'So who owns it now? Where are they?'

'Some young bloke who has suddenly upped and gone abroad apparently. The estate agent was happy to show me round, but said I'd need to make a decision pdq as there were a load of other people interested.'

'So, you said you'd have it?' I stared. 'Really? Goodness. But what will you do all day? You know, stuck in the middle of a village where you don't know anyone? While I'm at school? And your family won't be pleased. They'll blame me for keeping you up here.'

'Well, yes, very likely, but, to be honest, I don't really care. We can take each day as it comes. I can be a house husband and have "your tea" ready for you every day. And Boris can come over from

Harrogate with me. You'd be OK with that? Mind you, I never mentioned the dog to the agent.' Fabian pulled a face.

'I love Boris... but, Fabian, what *will* you do all day?' I realised I was sticking my fingernails into the palms of my hands, praying this was real. That Fabian wasn't having me on.

'Take on some legal work, probably. I can work as an agent for the CPS: they're always looking for people.'

'But you're a defence barrister, not a prosecuting solicitor.' I wasn't sure that that was the best way forward for him.

'Or...' And here Fabian took my hand, pulling me inside his unbuttoned warm coat. 'Or Jess and I can look into doing what we really want.' Fabian was animated.

'Your restaurant?'

'*Our* restaurant.' He smiled, kissing the top of my head.

11

LISA

The following morning, Lisa found herself grinning at her reflection in the hall mirror. She hadn't felt this positive about herself for a long time. For years she'd woken each morning with a sense of dread that she might be about to have another seizure, that she was going to end up in hospital again, unable to care for her girls. That any anxiety, any pain and nausea she might be feeling, could be the start of another remission into porphyria. Not forgetting she'd had a good nine months or so of Sorrel being bloody hard work, of being constantly called into Beddingfield High before Sorrel's eventual expulsion. Thank goodness for Mason Donoghue, who'd been prepared to take her youngest daughter on at St Mede's, despite her awful record of attendance and bad behaviour. She'd miss Sorrel so much if she was accepted at the Susan Yates Theatre School but just a bit of her was looking forward to the prospect of having the house to herself; at having a new independence after years of being at the helm of single motherhood.

She hadn't even seen Jayden off on his way up to Newcastle after he'd repacked his overnight case and left Jess's spare room the other day. Had even forgotten he was round there, so excited was she about getting on with her life and all the things she wanted to do with it. She actually laughed out loud at the realisation that finally, finally she appeared to be totally out of love with the man who'd been at the very core of her life from the age of seventeen. She continued to smile to herself as she made her way upstairs to the shower after spending a good hour cleaning and tidying both rooms downstairs and the little box room she'd slept in for the past couple of days after giving up her bed to Robyn and Fabian.

She'd been down to the new gym in the town centre and seen the fabulous 25 m pool, the huge studios where she was going to have a go at Pilates and t'ai chi and something called Sh'bam, which, when she'd watched through the window, had appeared a bit energetic. Nevertheless, she'd told herself, she was up for it.

Lisa smiled at her reflection again, piling her long dark hair up on her head and pouting somewhat coquettishly before moving to turn on the shower. Hearing a sudden bang in Sorrel's bedroom, she stopped dead, straining to hear the sound once more. She'd packed Sorrel off to school with a plate of scrambled eggs inside her, seen her get into Robyn's little Honda for a lift to St Mede's, heard the pair of them say their goodbyes to Fabian, who'd been determined to be first on the doorstep of the estate agent when it opened at eight thirty. If it wasn't Sorrel, who the hell was it? Not burglars? Lisa hesitated, her pulse racing at the thought. Well, let them have what they wanted: the keys to her battered old Fiesta were on the kitchen worktop where they lived in a basket, and they could have the TV if that was what they were after. As long as they didn't run off with Roger Rabbit.

She stood at the door dithering, uncertain what to do. Whether it wouldn't be a good idea to actually lock herself in the bathroom. Then Sorrel's bedroom door flew open and her daughter pushed past her into the bathroom.

'Sorrel?' Lisa turned as her daughter stood heaving, making little mewling noises at the lavatory before vomiting into the bowl.

Relieved that she wasn't about to face an axe murderer, Lisa hurried over to Sorrel, pushing back her hair and holding her head as she had all three of her girls when they'd been ill. 'What is it? Something you've eaten? I do hope there wasn't salmonella in those eggs. I did get them direct from Joe at the farm down the road.'

'I'm OK.' Sorrel stood, turning to the sink to rinse her mouth before wiping her face on a towel. 'I got an Uber back from school.'

'But, Sorrel, Robyn said you weren't well yesterday. That you came home early from school yesterday too?'

When Sorrel didn't answer, but simply gazed at her own reflection in the mirror, Lisa went on: 'Is it nerves at the thought of the audition next week? You'll be fine; Robyn's going with you. Or are you still worried about Joel? I can understand both...'

'I feel anxious all the time. And, Mum, I've got a pain here...' Sorrel indicated and rubbed at her abdomen through her school sweater. 'And now I've actually been sick. Mum, I googled it...'

'What? What did you google, darling?'

'The AP thing.'

'But why? My porphyria is something *I've* been landed with. There's no evidence it's hereditary.'

'You don't know that. You were adopted. You've no idea if your real parents or grandparents could have had it. And, anyway, it is!' Sorrel hissed the final word. 'Look it up. The first thing it says is acute porphyria is passed down through families.' Sorrel scrabbled for the phone in her blazer pocket, hitting the keyboard with the speedy deftness of all teens. 'Look!' She passed her phone over to Lisa.

> Porphyria is usually inherited. One or both parents pass along a changed gene to their child. Although porphyria can't be cured, medicines and certain lifestyle changes may help you manage it...

Lisa didn't have to read the words: she'd researched the condition herself many times over the years, always worried for Jess, Robyn and Sorrel.

'See.' Sorrel put her hands in her head. 'Mum, I feel awful.'

'Right, OK, let's get some tests done to put your mind at rest. We'll get Dr Matt onto it...'

'I don't want to know. I *don't*, Mum.' Sorrel glared at Lisa. 'I'm just going to pretend it's not happening. And it's all your fault if you've given it to me.'

Lisa felt the balloon of happiness she'd been floating on for weeks begin to deflate. Sorrel was right – it *was* her fault if she'd passed on the awful condition to her youngest daughter. Just when everything seemed to be going so well, when she herself was feeling almost reborn, surely this couldn't be happening now to her little girl?

* * *

Robyn

'OK, Mr Carrington, Ms Allen, that appears to be that, then. Nine months, initially, and then you can make any further decisions about extending the rental on the property after that.' Geoffrey Brampton of Brampton and Hornville, the oldest, and generally thought to be the most prestigious, of the two main estate agencies in Beddingfield, proffered a hand. 'The owner, I'm sure you understand, would have much preferred a longer let – twelve months minimum, really – but your reputation goes before you, Mr Carrington. Good to have someone famous in the village at last.' He smirked knowingly.

'My reputation? Famous?' Fabian frowned and, seeing his discomfort, I quickly jumped in.

'Sorry, I'm going to have to get back to school. Bell for afternoon school will be going in…'

'Oh yes, it's not every day we get a world-famous legal eagle in one of our properties. I followed the case of the Soho Slasher from the start. Such a shame you gave up on it, Fabian.' Geoffrey patted Fabian's arm chummily, but his tone was ingratiating and I saw irritation cross Fabian's face. 'Tell me,' Geoffrey went on, lowering his voice, 'are you moving into the village – and just for nine months – because there's some big local case you're taking on? Hmm? Leeds? Bradford? York, maybe? *Local* interest?'

'*Local* interest?' Fabian repeated the words. He eyeballed the estate agent, taking in the greying comb-over doing little to disguise the man's shiny pate, and his inquisitive, pale, porcine eyes. 'You could say that, Mr Brampton.' Fabian lowered his own voice conspiratorially. 'It's because I'm shagging the most beautiful *local* woman in your village.'

'Was that really necessary?' I snapped crossly once we'd walked down the cottage path. Glancing at my watch, I saw I'd exactly ten minutes before I was in front of 8TR taking them for PSHE.

'Probably not.' Fabian sniffed irritably. 'But for heaven's sake…'

'What are you going to do now?' I asked, still feeling embarrassed.

'I'm going to check out what basics we need in the cottage, then I'm going to try and get in touch with the Richardsons. And then I'm going to have to get back to Harrogate for clean pants and the like. There's stuff I need to do over there.'

'We need furniture! A bed. Sheets. Pots and pans.' Hell, where to begin? 'And the Richardsons?' I was already unlocking my car door.

'Who own Hudson House. I want to see if it's a done deal with these Sattar people.'

I smiled. 'You do that.'

'Now you're being condescending, Robyn.'

'Sorry, I didn't mean to be. I need to go.' I moved to kiss him. 'And, Fabian, I'm so glad we're doing this. Even if it's just for a few months until we both know where we really want to be. Give us a bit of breathing space?'

'I can't think of anything I'd rather be doing.' Fabian gathered me up in his arms, bending to kiss every bit of me until I was helpless with giggles and heads were turning in our direction. 'I really don't see why we can't move in straight away.'

* * *

Lisa

'Mum?' Jess, showing round a couple intent on finding the best possible care for an elderly relative, excused herself as Bex opened the front door and she caught sight of Lisa's anguished face on the doorstep. 'What's the matter?'

'I'm fine.' Lisa attempted a smile. 'I'm going to tidy up that garden of yours if that's OK?'

'Why?' Jess frowned, obviously unsure whether to hand over the visitors to one of the carers so she could see to Lisa. She looked at her watch, making a quick decision. 'I'm just going to show Mr and Mrs Connor round. Why don't I make you a coffee, Mum, and I'll be with you in fifteen minutes? Something's happened, hasn't it?'

'There's no need, Jess,' Lisa said irritably. She needed to tell Jess and Robyn about Sorrel's – and now her own – fear that history might be repeating itself with the porphyria. But now, when Jess was so busy, wasn't the right moment. 'I *will* get a coffee, if that's OK,' she said, 'but I'm perfectly capable of getting it myself, darling. And then I'm going to take it out to the garden. I've got my gloves and I've brought my tools.' She held up a sturdy pair of gardening gloves and indicated the heavy bag at her feet. 'Your roses need deadheading.'

'They're not *my* roses...' Jess broke off seeing Lisa's determination to do the job she'd come for. She knew if there was one thing that would help her mother when she was anxious or upset – which she appeared to be right now – it was gardening. 'OK, you do that and I'll come and join you as soon as I can. Mind you,' she added in an undertone, 'not sure why I'm still bothering to show people round when the place is probably going under.' She turned encouragingly towards the couple. 'D'you want to follow me?' Jess looked back at Lisa. 'And for God's sake, Mum, don't overdo it. Just remember how ill you were back in September.'

Lisa beamed at a couple of residents who were holding hands as they made their way to the lounge area. She must ask Jess whether Neil and Pat had come into Hudson House together. Were they married? And, if so, how lovely to be still wanting to hold hands after years of marriage. Or had they lost original partners and had now found new love here? Never too late to find love, Lisa smiled to herself, even though, after Sorrel's little bombshell, smiling was the last thing her face felt able to do.

Lisa made herself a coffee and went straight out into the cold early afternoon air carrying her mug in one hand and her bulging bag of gardening tools in the other.

Oh, these fabulous roses. Someone in the past had adored this rose garden; had known exactly what they were doing. She supposed, in the heyday of Hudson House, there'd have been a whole gang of full-time gardeners on the payroll. Maybe even a head gardener who ruled the roost, terrifying the local boy who came in after school and in the holidays to help for a few pence? Before, Lisa assumed, his going into Hudson's Textile Mill like the rest of his family once he left school at fourteen.

How could anyone who knew the first thing about floribundas and these fabulous climbing roses have allowed this decline? There, against the far wall, soaking up as much of the weak winter sunshine as was possible, were a Danse du Feu and an Alchymist if she wasn't mistaken. But, like prisoners in an exercise yard, they were intent on fighting off their restraint, bidding for freedom by going over the top. The prisoner analogy brought a smile at last and, aware that worrying about Sorrel wasn't going to help her own health, she determined she'd speak to Matt as soon as she could, leaving her to concentrate on what she was doing here. Maybe Sorrel just had a bug? She'd been lucky, bringing up the girls – they'd rarely been ill, rarely having time off school like some other kids.

'Lucky?' Lisa realised she was actually saying the words out loud. 'Having Jayden who was there, but never *really* there? Why the hell was that *lucky*? And why the fuck...' Lisa, unused to using such language, actually whispered the expletive '...didn't I ditch him years and years ago?'

She threw the remains of her coffee onto the grass but, try as she might to stop worrying, continued to carry the thoughts in her head as she surveyed the rose garden in front of her.

She pulled on her thick gardening gloves and set to with her pruning tool, clipping carefully at first and then, realising much of the woody stems and overgrown roots needed to be cut back, bent to her bag for the cordless pruning shears, going for it big time.

Oh, but this was so cathartic: snipping, slashing, stabbing, cleaving, dissecting. She was sweating now and, despite it being a particularly cold January, she took off first her gilet and then her jacket, continuing to slash and prune, getting rid of all the anger she should have directed at Jayden himself. Or was it the bloody Foleys? Mother and Father. Ha! Slash, stab, slash!

'And, for heaven's sake,' Lisa continued the one-way argument with herself, 'Sorrel isn't sixteen yet. Far too young to be starting with porphyria.' And, she reassured herself, once she'd thrown up, Sorrel had appeared much better and, rather than staying at home, which Lisa had said she should, she'd insisted on Lisa dropping her back at school. Said she just *had* to get back to school as she was sitting mock GCSEs in the next couple of days.

'Oh, my little girl.' Lisa put her hand to her face and realised she was crying. Bad enough talking to the roses, but now actually crying was not a good sign. And hell, she didn't appear to be able to stop. She fished for a non-existent tissue, wiping her eyes and nose on her shirt sleeve.

'Are you all right?'

'I'm fine, thank you.' Lisa sniffed and turned, trying to smile at the newcomer who'd appeared almost silently at her side. 'Oh, Eloise. Hello.'

'Have we been introduced?' Eloise looked puzzled. 'And Granny won't be pleased that you've been at her roses, you know.' She handed over an embroidered handkerchief. 'Here you are. Nothing's ever as bad as you think it is.'

12

'There's mildew and leaf spot on the winter pansies,' Eloise said, bending down to remove a couple of the affected leaves.

'You'll get your hands dirty,' Lisa replied, giving a few final sniffs and putting Eloise's hanky up the sleeve of her shirt. 'I'll wash this and get it back to you. Thank you,' she added.

Eloise waved a hand dismissively. 'I've a drawerful in my bedroom at home. Do keep it...' She broke off as Bex appeared at their side, a rather lovely camel cashmere coat over her arm.

'Ah, Eloise, there you are. Come on, we've got all the board games out. Clarissa needs a partner for Snakes and Ladders.' Bex held out her hand.

'Just like at prep school on wet playtimes.' Eloise gave Bex such a look, Lisa wanted to laugh.

'She's OK here with me, Bex.'

'Oh, it's far too cold to be out here.'

'I'm not a child,' Eloise said indignantly. 'Although if I stay in this place much longer, I'll have reverted to being one. Pass me my coat, would you? I'll stay and help the gardener. I think the state of Granny's roses have upset her.'

Bex glanced across at Lisa, taking in her tear-strewn face. 'You OK, Lisa? Jess said you hadn't been well.'

'I'm absolutely fine and more than happy to have Eloise out here with me. Mind you, I think she could do with an old coat and some gloves if she's going to get stuck in.' Lisa took Bex to one side as Eloise continued to examine the pansies. 'She seems absolutely... *with it*, Bex. And she's only what? Early seventies? Why on earth is she in a care home for the elderly, for heaven's sake?'

'Dementia. I gather Eloise set the kitchen on fire when she left a pan on the stove and forgot about it. She's been wandering the streets; the police have had to find her and bring her back on a couple of occasions. I think the idea is that she's here to give the husband a bit of a break. He's almost eighty and not in good health himself. According to him she'd become too much for him. Aggressive even.'

'And her children?'

'Not sure. One lives in Australia, I believe. There's a daughter, although I think there's a problem *there* as well.'

'A problem?'

Bex gave a subtle indication with her hand that the problem was alcohol.

'Oh, right. It all seems a bit strange to me. Anyway, leave her out here with me. She seems to know what she's doing and I'll bring her back in when she's fed up or if she gets too cold.'

'You sure? I'll get Bianca to bring out an old coat. There'll be one somewhere.' Bex patted Eloise's arm and headed back down the garden to the house.

'So, do you have children, Eloise?'

'I have four.'

'Four? I've three myself.' Lisa turned back to the roses.

'Don't think Granny won't be after you.' Eloise raised an eye. 'She hated cutting anything back too much.'

'Granny?'

'Yes, of course. She lived here until Daddy took over the mill and we moved here when Grandpa Frank died. Mummy refused to have Granny living with us – they never got on – so Granny agreed to move to a much smaller house in the village. A lovely cottage down by the duck pond. But, only on the condition that she be allowed back to do the garden.'

'Oh?' Lisa didn't turn, realising that Eloise was much more likely to talk if she wasn't being barraged with questions.

'I never liked this house. And I don't know why on earth I'm back here now. With all these *old* people in every room and not one of them Granny. Mind you, I'm glad Mummy's not here. Now *she* really was a bitch. The biggest bitch of all. And Granny…' Eloise stood, rubbing her back, but giggling slightly '…Granny used to say she was…' she lowered her voice '…common. That Daddy, who'd gone after her because she looked like some Hollywood actress called Lana Turner, had had to reap what he sowed.'

'So, you actually lived here at Hudson House?' Lisa did now turn to stare.

'I still do.' Eloise seemed confused. 'Well, I think I do. I'm Eloise Hudson, you know.'

'Yes, of course.' Lisa knew enough about people presenting with dementia not to argue with them. Certainly not to be confrontational. 'And were you happy here…?' She broke off as Jess appeared at their side with an old Barbour jacket over one arm and a mug in each hand.

'Eloise's just telling me she used to live here, Jess.'

'I think you'll find I still do.' Eloise's tone was imperious once more. 'Ah, coffee. Lovely.'

'You're Eloise Hudson.' Jess smiled. 'Of course you lived here at Hudson House. I think your great-grandfather built the house?'

Eloise nodded.

'So, who built the white house, Eloise?' Lisa indicated with a movement of her head to where the top of the summer house could just be seen poking through the bare branches of a row of oak and beech trees.

'The white house?' Eloise frowned. 'What white house?'

'The summer house? Where I was talking to you earlier.'

'When? I've never spoken to you before!'

'But...'

'Don't confuse her, Mum,' Jess interrupted. 'Have you had enough out here now, Eloise?'

'Hand me that coat and I'll be fine.' Eloise took the coffee but sniffed at the mug with some disdain before placing it, untouched, at her feet. 'There's always been a summer house up across from the top lawn, but Mummy insisted on making it so much bigger. *That's* when Granny said she was common and that she must be trying to compete with someone... The prime minister, was it?' Eloise frowned, obviously trying to remember.

'The president of America?' Lisa ventured.

'That's the one, yes.' She looked surprised. 'Oh, did you know Granny?'

Lisa smiled at that, but to change the subject said, 'Eloise has four children, Jess.' She glanced encouragingly towards the older woman.

'Oh, I thought it was only three.' Jess looked surprised.

'I think I should know how many children I've given birth to,' Eloise said irritably.

'Of course.' Jess nodded in agreement. 'We women don't go through all that and forget anyone, do we?'

'So, you must have been part of the swinging sixties, then, Eloise?' Lisa asked as she secured a trailing rose more securely to its trellis before standing back to see the effect.

Eloise stopped deadheading the floribunda and said, almost dreamily, '1968.'

Lisa and Jess leaned forward slightly to catch what the older woman was saying.

'It was 1968, you know, girls.'

'What was?' Jess asked. 'Was it a good year for you, Eloise?'

'Oh, the *best*.' She gave a little laugh. 'The absolute best year of my life...'

13

SUMMER 1968

Eloise

'Eloise, will you please get out from under my feet and *do* something?' Muriel Hudson was irritable and Eloise knew it was because she, Eloise, was back at home. And this time for good. Thank God, she didn't have to get through even one more day at that bloody awful school in Whitby. She'd never either managed to be invited, or been able to ingratiate herself, into the hierarchical tribes of girls who flocked together dependent on new or old money, academic ability or those, like her, who got through each day, each term, each year, always on the periphery. She had almost made it into Suzy Warrington's little clique in the final term but had totally let herself down by throwing up over Annabel Bellingham's burgundy velvet bell bottoms after downing too much of the vodka being passed round the dorm. The trousers were, as Annabel constantly reminded them all, a gift from some obscure cousin of Prince Charles. Apparently for services rendered. The trousers were ruined, as was her final attempt, after five years at St Bernadette's, to infiltrate the inner circle.

Then, after school, the almost as bad nine months in Lausanne at Château Mont-Choisi where Muriel had insisted she go to be *finished*. 'Actually,' she'd heard her mother laugh in that put-on tinkly voice of hers over the table of one of her lunch parties with *the girls* – spiteful old hags as far as Eloise could see – 'Eloise needs a bomb under her to actually get her *started*.'

Oh, ha ha, Mummy, such a bloody wit.

'But I'm not sure *what* I should be doing,' Eloise now said, trying to be logical as well as polite so as not to irritate her mother further. 'I could walk around with several books on my head to show the world what superb posture I now have? I could lay the dining room table for you...'

'Well, yes, that would be helpful,' Muriel conceded. 'Except we've no one round to dine until the Fairleys on the...' She broke off as a movement in the garden made her stand and peer round the heavy damask curtains. 'What *is* that woman doing now?'

Eloise moved across the room to join her mother at the window. 'Oh, good, Granny's here.'

'Granny? Goodness me, the woman could be taken for the village idiot in that get-up. What is she wearing and what's she *doing*?'

'She's got Mr Bower's old gardening coat on.' Eloise giggled. 'And his hat as well. He'd put them on one side to donate to Fred Hargreaves.'

'Fred Hargreaves?'

'You know, the farmer down Blackley Lane? He's always on the lookout for old clothes, especially hats, to make new scarecrows, but Granny said she'd have them instead.'

'Your grandmother is wearing our gardener's cast-off clothes?

Intended for a scarecrow?' Muriel pulled a face of pure distaste. 'How do you know all this?'

'I took the dog down there for a walk and ended up talking to Mr Hargreaves. He offered to show me his scarecrows.'

'I'll bet he did,' Muriel retorted indignantly. 'You keep away, Eloise. Daddy and I haven't spent an absolute fortune on your education just so you can hang around with… with… *farmhands*. I thought there was a bit of a whiff around you yesterday, but I didn't like to say.'

'It's never stopped you before…' Eloise knew she was pushing boundaries with Muriel and stopped as her mother glared in her direction.

'That farmer has a *reputation*.'

'What sort of reputation?' Eloise was most interested.

'Never you mind. What he gets up to down in The Green Dragon is no concern of ours.'

'Well, it's obviously a concern of *yours*, Mummy.'

'Enough, Eloise, go and tidy your room. And then, perhaps you could help Mrs Baxter in the kitchen. A cake maybe? Don't forget Michael is back home from school the day after tomorrow. You know what boys are like. They spend any time not kicking a ball stuffing themselves with cake.'

'I'm a hopeless cook.'

'But we sent you to Switzerland to learn to cook. All that money and you still can't whip up a Victoria sponge or a batch of scones?'

'They taught us the basics of shorthand and typing as well. Very much the basics, Mummy. They were more interested in the correct way to address the Ambassador to Nigeria if we should ever meet him…'

'Nigeria? Goodness, I hope not. Bad enough with all these…

these *coloured* people from India working in Daddy's mill. The place is getting quite overrun with them.'

'We had two really lovely girls from India at St Bernadette's,' Eloise pointed out.

'Goodness,' Muriel repeated, 'Bombay to Whitby? I assume they were the daughters of someone high up in India? They must have got the money from somewhere?'

God, did her mother never shut up about money?

'I'm going out to help Granny with the roses,' Eloise said, turning to watch as her grandmother made her way across the lawn and orchards towards the beautiful walled rose garden.

'I think *not*, Eloise. She's more than happy out there by herself. There are broad beans to pod in the kitchen – Mrs Baxter never does it properly and…' Muriel broke off as the telephone rang and, hearing her mother safely ensconced with her friend and the town's latest gossip, Eloise slipped out into the drizzle and grey skies of a West Yorkshire July morning.

* * *

'Hello, my darling.' Maude Hudson grinned a welcome across the rose beds whose extravagant blooms, now harbouring droplets of moisture, were worthy of any professional rose grower. 'How's it going? Glad to be home?' Maude held out her arms and Eloise went into them, the earthy, wet-dog smell of the gardener's cast-off coat strangely comforting.

'Well, glad to be back from Switzerland.' Eloise nodded from the depths of the hug.

'But finding it difficult to settle into being back at Hudson House? Back in this backwater of Yorkshire?'

Eloise nodded again.

'Your mother being a pain in the arse?'

Eloise giggled at her grandmother's language. Despite being brought up in the higher echelons of North Yorkshire society and, like Eloise, sent away to school and then to finishing school, Maude Hudson wasn't averse to using the language of the lower orders. 'Granny, what am I going to do with my life? Mummy's insisting that I do the season.'

Maude cackled throatily, reaching into the pocket of the voluminous old tweed coat for her tin of roll-ups. 'What season, for heaven's sake? It's 1968 and we've long moved on from all that nonsense, surely?'

'No, it's still being held,' Eloise said gloomily. 'And Mummy is determined I should be part of it, just like she was back in her day.'

'Darling, your mother was never presented, was never a deb, though she likes to tell everyone she was. She married up when she married your father. Now, *I* had to go through the whole bloody circus when I was a girl.' Maude inhaled deeply, blowing smoke rings up into the leaden sky. 'Load of stuff and nonsense and, after all that rigmarole, I ended up marrying into West Yorkshire trade. My parents were not happy I was marrying and, not only moving to West Yorkshire from Harrogate, but marrying into a woollen textile family. Mind you, the Hudsons had the money. We Berkeleys had spent all our dosh on carousing, inheritance tax and trying to keep up appearances.' She cackled again. 'My mother might have looked down on the Hudsons, but she was jolly glad I was marrying into money and would eventually move into Hudson House.'

'You didn't marry Grandpa just for his money?' Eloise was shocked. She was going to marry for love. When it happened. If it ever did.

'Well, the Hudson trade money helped. Of course, it did. But no, luckily your Grandpa Frank was really rather delicious in his twenties. Thighs that could crack a nut with all that riding he did...'

'Granny!' Eloise giggled nervously.

'Bloody good in the sack was your grandpa.'

Eloise put two hands to her ears, her face flaming with embarrassment.

'Oh, deary me, what has that prudish mother of yours taught you? Nothing, I suppose? Listen, my darling, if I were you, I'd get out of here while you can. There's London just two hundred miles down the A1.'

'Mummy would never let me go.'

'No.' Maude shook her head almost sadly. 'No, I don't suppose she would. And, my sweet, if you were to head off by yourself, you'd be eaten alive.' She was silent for a good few seconds. 'Au pair, that's it. You could be an au pair in London. I'll bring you my copy of *The Lady*. France even... A year in Paris. That should toughen you up a bit...'

'Granny, I'm no further on speaking French after a year in Lausanne than when I left school. "*Je voudrais un gâteau, s'il-vous-plâit*" is about all I managed. Mainly because I was always hungry. No one seemed to eat much at school. Probably because even an orange had to be eaten with a knife and fork.'

Maude laughed. 'I remember it well. So, Eloise, what are you going to do with yourself, then? Because if you stand still, that mother of yours will have you married off to the highest bidder before you know it.'

'I suppose that's what she's aiming for with the season. Mummy is chair of the Yorkshire Young Debutantes Association and is, "determined to uphold tradition".' Eloise air-quoted the words.

'I bet your mother doesn't know that Prince Philip considered the Queen Charlotte's Ball "bloody daft" and...' Maude broke off, laughing, '...Princess Margaret apparently said: "We had to put a stop to it... every tart in London was getting in".'

'I think Mummy is intent on it being local rather than in London. She's planning a big ball at The Queen's hotel in Leeds.'

'Goodness, how utterly common.' Maude turned back to the climbing rose she was determinedly tying to a trellis. 'Mind you, I'm surprised she hasn't considered having the whole of Yorkshire society in that great white monstrosity Frank's father had built up beyond the orchard – it's certainly big enough to fit them all in now she's extended it.'

'Actually, I think Mummy *is* planning something in there. My coming-out drinks do at some point before the big bash in Leeds.'

'So you can be picked over by every beady-eyed, fortune-hunting mama in Yorkshire?'

'Suppose.' Eloise sighed gloomily.

'Come on, darling. Get stuck into a bit of deadheading and then I'll drive you back down to my house for lunch. Cheese on toast with Branston and a little glass of sherry? And I can show you what I've bought you.'

* * *

'It's a late birthday present,' Maude said handing over a rather untidily wrapped box. 'I didn't want to send it over to you in Switzerland – thought it might get smashed. And, it's always nice to have an un-birthday present, isn't it?'

'Gosh, what on earth is it?' Eloise glanced across at her grandmother.

'Open it and see.'

'Oh, Granny. How did you know this is just what I wanted?'

Eloise stroked the box even before opening it to take out the contents inside. 'A Praktica Super TL!'

'I did my research,' Maude said proudly. 'Went into Schofields in Leeds and spent a very entertaining hour with a young man there. Now he *was* gorgeous.' She laughed, delighted with Eloise's response to the present. 'It's a 35 mm, I believe? And SLR. Whatever that means.'

'Single-lens Reflex.' Eloise continued to stroke the box until Maude laughed again.

'Get it open; start using it.'

'There were a couple of 35 mm cameras in Lausanne that we were allowed to borrow, but nothing as up to date as this.' Eloise opened the box carefully, taking the camera out with reverence.

'And here are a few bits and pieces to go with it.' Maude passed over another, larger box.

'More?' Eloise's eyes were saucers.

'Darling, you are my very favourite granddaughter.'

'I'm your only granddaughter,' Eloise tutted.

'Just a couple of accessories to go with it.' Maude smiled.

'Granny!' Eloise took out the wide-angle and long-focus lenses, the teleconverter and leather case, ten rolls of boxed 35 mm film and an instruction book, placing each one on the kitchen table as she did so. 'I can't believe this.'

'Just don't tell your mother. I keep telling her I'm broke,' Maude added.

'You're not, are you?' Eloise pulled a worried face.

'No, darling, I most certainly am not. But I enjoy having your mother think there'll be nothing coming her way once I go. Another little sherry?'

* * *

The grey overcast sky had eventually cleared and, while Maude went to sit in her favourite armchair by the window, immediately closing her eyes, Eloise made her way down the garden path of the cottage, which was situated in the centre of Beddingfield village. Near enough to the village duck pond for Maude to wander round a couple of times each day with Samson, her ancient Jack Russell, as well as just across from the cricket pitch where she wasn't averse to whiling away her Saturday and Sunday afternoons eyeing up the local talent in their cricket whites.

Nervously, Eloise practised taking snaps without film in the Praktica before manoeuvring the film into the back of the camera to take close-ups of Maude's rain- and windblown peonies, convex raindrops shimmering and winking amongst the scarlet petals and stigma, like smooth uncut diamonds.

This, then, was what she was going to do with her summer.

* * *

'Eloise, you really can't spend all summer mooching around taking photographs like some female David Bailey.' Ralph Hudson had arrived home late from the mill where there'd been tension brewing amongst the directors and the union rep over an area of the mill being given over for prayer to the mainly Muslim workers newly arrived from the Mirpur district of Pakistan.

'I should think not.' Muriel, feeling somewhat guilty that she'd spent a too long, but rather lovely lunch with her current squeeze – the town's local Tory MP, Sir Keith Wadsworth – patted her husband's arm in agreement. 'Who is this David Bailey anyway?' she added, affecting the little-girl pout she often put on to portray herself, for some reason, as her husband's inferior.

Eloise knew it thoroughly irritated her father, rather than pleased him.

'Oh, Ma,' Brian Hudson tutted, pouring himself a whisky before lying flat out on the gold-tasselled Knowle sofa, legs splayed, tie loosened. 'The great David Bailey? Where've you been all this time? What a job *he's* got, photographing all those dolly birds, legs right up to their backsides. Beats arguing with Don Whitwam and his cronies round the boardroom table all bloody afternoon. Don's on our side anyway, but has to show he's not. Religion should be kept out of the workplace; we don't let the Baptists or the Catholics go off to pray every two minutes.'

'And surely, Eloise,' Muriel interrupted, obviously refusing to relinquish the issue of her daughter spending her summer taking photographs in return for a deeper debate about religious and cultural differences and inclusion, 'women wouldn't want another *woman* taking their photograph? Surely, they want to pose for men? I mean, I certainly wouldn't want another woman looking at *me* in my brassiere.' Muriel patted coyly at her kitten-bowed blouse with long red manicured nails.

'So, Eloise, what *are* you going to do?' Ralph wasn't letting it drop. 'Your mother was insistent you do this year in Lausanne rather than A levels, which would have got you into university.'

'Oh, we didn't want a blue stocking in the family, Ralphie, darling,' Muriel trilled. 'What would Eloise have studied anyway?'

'I rather liked maths,' Eloise said. 'And I quite fancied doing engineering.'

'Oh pish,' Muriel retorted, irritated now. 'A man doesn't want a wife who is cleverer than him. Look at Pamela Hughes.' She lowered her voice. 'Her husband was soon off with another woman once Pamela started doing that part-time degree of hers in Bradford instead of taking her turn to host Ladies' Lunch.'

'Right, Eloise,' Ralph said matter-of-factly. 'We're desperately short of staff in the offices. You can type? A bit of shorthand? Answering the phone and some filing? Or on Reception?'

'Oh, no, I don't think so, Ralph! The boss's daughter in the offices, with all the town's office girls?' Muriel appeared utterly affronted.

'Dad, she'd be hopeless.' Brian frowned. 'She's so bloody clumsy, she'd file important stuff away and not pass on phone calls…'

'Oy, d'you mind?' Eloise stood, knocking over Muriel's martini from the Hepplewhite side table and, desperately trying to retrieve it, tripped over her mother's Chanel handbag.

'Well, it's either that or actually in the weaving shed? Or with the menders? You need to earn a living, Eloise. You can start in the morning.'

14

Eloise had often accompanied her father down to Samuel Hudson and Sons' Textile Mills between their own pretty village of Beddingfield and the smaller neighbouring village of Little Micklethwaite, just a couple of miles further down the road. She'd always found the crashing looms, the constant noise of machinery and voices shouting to be heard, the smell of grease, somewhat fascinating if not a little scary. She'd been particularly captivated by the towering machines: row upon row of clattering weaving looms in one shed and the long, newly installed carding machine in another. It was the engineering expertise behind these great monsters that had both enthralled and terrified, when she was a little girl, hiding behind and clutching onto Ralph's pinstriped trouser leg, and he'd stopped to speak to the foreman or one of the workers on the shop floor.

The miserable, unusually overcast skies of the previous day had shifted overnight westwards across the Pennines and out towards the Irish Sea, leaving a glorious summer's morning, the sun already warm in a cerulean-blue sky. Part of Eloise – actually most of her – wished she could spend the day wandering the gardens at Hudson House, discovering new plants, breathing in the scents of rosemary, oregano and mint in the herb garden as well as watching how others had grown and changed during her time away in Lausanne. And all the time she could have been taking photographs of the ones she found the most beautiful and interesting with her brand-new camera.

Instead, she was joining the world of grown-ups, becoming part of the day-to-day grind of making a living producing the fabulous worsted cloth for which Hudson and Sons had become internationally famous.

'Right, Eloise, I'm going to leave you with Miss Baker.' Eloise could tell Ralph was eager to be off.

'Your secretary?'

'Yes. She'll take you across to the main suite of offices where Miss Gray, the office manager, will show you the ropes, show you where to leave your coat...'

'I don't have a coat, Daddy.' Eloise held up empty hands.

'I was being metaphorical, Eloise. All right, the Ladies, where you can powder your nose; coffee et cetera...' Ralph was already losing interest, needing to get to his office and sort the problems he'd left behind the previous evening.

'Dad...?' Her brother Brian was at the door to his own office, waving the phone in Ralph's direction.

'Right, Eloise, I'll leave you,' Ralph said vaguely, giving her a little push towards the neatly dressed, but quite tiny woman in her mid-forties standing waiting for her. 'Enjoy yourself.'

'Right, OK.' Eloise, her leather tote bag and precious camera over one shoulder, walked in the direction he'd indicated.

'Hello, dear, your father wants to keep you occupied, I believe? Get you out from under your mother's feet.'

'Well, I don't know about that...' Eloise started, slightly indignant. Why was everyone – apart from Granny Maude – intent on treating her like a naughty child no one knew what to do with or how to keep entertained? 'Actually, Miss Baker, I'm very pleased to be here. I'm interested to learn more about how the place is run: what the sales figures are like – profits and margins et cetera.' Eloise was proud of that last sentence – she'd learned a little in the business studies module at Château Mont-Choisi that only herself and Ting Lo from Hong Kong had signed up for in preference to 'Pick up that champagne glass correctly!' (From the bottom of the stem, she'd learned afterwards from the other girls intent on practising this difficult feat of engineering and good manners.)

'Well, dear, I'd leave the task of actually running Hudson's to your father and brother – men's work, don't you think? – and we'll find you a bit of filing to keep you occupied.'

'I can type,' Eloise demurred as she followed the diminutive woman along a corridor lined with framed proof of the superiority of Samuel Hudson Textiles' worsteds. These were interspersed with myriad photographs of her ancestors and relatives – all men – both past and present, who had directed the company to the dizzying heights of world dominance in the textiles trade. Eloise glanced down at her size seven feet in their flat beige leather sandals, comparing them somewhat unfavourably with the size three (at a guess) navy leather stilettoed feet leading the way along the long, monogrammed-(SHT)-carpeted corridor. A good job, whoever had ordered the carpet, hadn't decided to boast of the mill being *international* textiles, Eloise thought to herself, stifling a nervous giggle when, despite the size of her feet and long legs, she had to break into a run to keep up.

'Ah, Miss Munro.' (Was everyone so polite round here?) Miss Baker came to a sudden standstill as an extremely pretty girl in, Eloise assessed, her late twenties, exited a door on their right, a pile of files in her arms. 'This is Eloise, Mr Hudson's daughter.

We've been looking for Miss Gray, but would you take her to the filing office and show her the ropes?'

'Oh, thank goodness, I thought I was going to have to get someone from the pool again. And Marjorie is never impressed when I pinch one of her girls. I've been on to the temping agency already trying to get an office girl, but it's July and every temp on their books appears to be off to Majorca or Benidorm.' The girl spoke quickly and seemed flustered, appearing unwilling to acknowledge Eloise, who was now patiently awaiting her orders.

'I'll leave her with you, then.' The older woman almost smirked her response and Eloise felt a tension between them, taut as a stretched rubber band. 'I'm sure you've both… plenty in common.' She raised both eyebrows in the younger woman's direction before turning on her heel and heading back to Ralph Hudson's private office.

'So, what do *you* do here?' Eloise asked, putting into practice one of the many ways she'd been instructed during the finishing school sessions of: "Introducing another into polite conversation."

'I'm Mr Brian's secretary,' Miss Munro replied, scurrying along the seemingly never-ending monogrammed carpet towards a door at the end of the corridor.

'Brian's secretary?' Eloise guffawed. 'You poor thing. I hope he doesn't trump in your office like he does in the sitting room at home. And then try to blame the dog.' Then as Eloise realised this mode of conversation most certainly was not, and never had been, on Château Mont-Choisi's curriculum, she blushed scarlet to the roots of her long blonde hair.

Paying scant attention to any attempt on Eloise's part to be friendly, Miss Munro led her past a huge typing pool where, through a glass door, she glimpsed rows of girls, their heads down, clattering away under the watchful eye of a severe-looking supervisor. It reminded her of the rows of chained slaves aboard the Roman galley in *Ben-Hur* – one of her absolutely favourite films – the centurion in charge beating out a rhythm with his two mallets. Were those poor typists actually chained to their station? Eloise mused. She had little time to speculate further as Miss Munro ushered her into the spacious General Office where several women were at work. Eloise thought it a grim, dusty room that wouldn't have been out of place in a Dickens's novel. Several large mahogany desks each held a phone, an in-and-out tray, an impressive array of rubber stamps and seemingly endless towering piles of pink, yellow and blue paper. Four grey metal filing cabinets stood at the far end of the office, presiding over the room like beings from another world.

'Miss Gray? I'm delivering Mr Hudson's daughter to you. She's going to do some filing.' And with that, Miss Munro immediately turned on her kitten heels, her short blonde Twiggy hairdo, her red miniskirt and endless long legs in their pale tights soon to be just a fleeting memory.

'Oh, *hello*, my dear.' Miss Gray at least was friendly. 'My, you've grown since I last saw you. Quite the beanpole, aren't you?' She laughed delightedly, patting Eloise's arm to show affection rather than offence. 'Now, have you done any filing before? It's not difficult. Let me take you through it...' She took a pile of the coloured invoices from one desk, immediately demonstrating how they were to be filed in alphabetical order in one or other of the drawers of the metal filing cabinets.

By lunchtime, Eloise's stomach was growling reproachfully. They'd stopped for ten minutes at ten thirty for a cup of weak Nescafé and a KitKat but now, two hours later, as soon as the buzzer sounded its raucous klaxon warning, the four women in the office immediately downed tools, reached for bags, greaseproof-papered packs of sandwiches and Tupperware boxes and were off.

'Now, what did your father suggest you do for lunch?' Miss Gray asked kindly, but glancing longingly at the pack of ham and mustard she'd brought out of her shopping bag.

'He didn't,' Eloise replied, embarrassed that the other woman had seen her look just as longingly at the sandwiches in her hand.

'Well, there's the canteen across the yard,' Miss Gray suggested. 'You can get a nice plate of pie and chips there as well as the day's specials; they seem to be doing a lot of that awful curry stuff these days. The chippy down George Street will be open, but there's generally a queue... Or, if you head into Beddingfield village – just a five-minute walk – there's a very nice sandwich shop. A bit pricey, but...' Again she trailed off, obviously considering the boss's daughter, straight from finishing school in Switzerland, would not be unduly concerned with spending a few shillings on her lunch.

'Oh, look, please don't worry about me.' Eloise smiled. 'Honestly, I really could do with some fresh air. I'll explore the place; see how much it's changed since I used to come down with Daddy... with my father... with Mr Hudson...' For heaven's sake, what was wrong with her, reminding this woman who'd been in charge of the General Office since Methuselah was in nappies who her father was?

'If you're sure?' Miss Gray looked anxiously at the clock and then towards the door.

'Oh, please, please don't let me spoil your lunch hour.'

'Forty-five minutes,' the other woman warned. 'Back here sharp at one fifteen.'

Miss Gray finally hurried out, a white M&S cardigan round her shoulders, and Eloise blew out a sigh of relief. That didn't stop her being starving though. The thought of a plate of pie and chips (Muriel always held forth that the two together on a plate were for the working class and refused to entertain them in her dining room) had Eloise salivating, and she headed to where she thought the canteen was. She crossed a cobbled yard encumbered with huge containers of greasy-looking raw wool where the mill workers were sitting in the midday sunshine eating sandwiches, fish and chips from a newspaper and drinking from Thermos-flask beakers, while smoking, stuck into a tabloid or simply chatting.

'Excuse me.' Eloise hovered uncertainly where a group of men, all in dark blue overalls, were playing cards. 'I'm so sorry to disturb your game, but could you point me in the general direction of the dining room?'

'Yer what, love? What y'after?' A balding, elderly man looked up at her, his voice kind.

'The dining room?'

"Ey up, Lofty. Canteen, you're after?' A younger man grinned at his mates. 'Aye, love, it's up them steps over there.'

'Thank you so much.' Eloise smiled gratefully. 'I'm actually really rather hungry.'

'Aye, well, you'll get sorted up there.'

She turned to where he'd pointed and started walking, a chorus of laughter following in her wake. Unperturbed, she took the metal steps indicated, her nose following a delicious smell of fried food, her growling stomach once again reminding her how hungry she was. On into a small canteen where she was met by a sea of navy blue interspersed with several tables of women wearing pink, lime-green and yellow nylon overalls. There must have been fifty of the mill workers sitting at tables of four or six, all tucking into plates of what appeared to be chips with everything: sausage and chips, egg and chips, beans and chips as well as the – much lauded by Miss Gray – pie and chips.

Embarrassed as heads turned, Eloise made her way to a serving hatch where four white-aproned women were on duty. Oh, she thought with some relief, not a great deal different from the school refectory at St Bernadette's.

'Could you tell me what's in the pie of the day?' she asked politely with a smile.

'Sweeney's best,' a voice behind her guffawed loudly.

'Lovely, I'll have a portion of Mrs Sweeney's best, if I may?' Eloise continued to smile at the first serving woman.

'Eh, love, he's having you on.' The woman tutted, shaking her head but laughing at the man behind Eloise. 'And whoever's sent you up here's having you on an' all. Office staff are next door,' she added. 'You can get through that door over there.' She indicated with a nod of her head a door in the far corner. 'You'll get something in there.'

'Right, thank you so much.' Her face flaming with embarrassment, Eloise made her way through the tables, cannoning off a couple in her need to be out of where she appeared to have been made a laughing stock. She opened the door and was thankful to see two of the women from the General Office sitting round a big table of other females. Most were eating from their Tupperware containers while talking and laughing; some knitting in between bites of sandwich, a feat which Eloise, staring, found dextrously resourceful as well as riveting.

'Miss Hudson, are you all right?' Shirley from the General Office was on her feet.

'Oh, Eloise, please…'

'Have you not had lunch? I think they've just about finished serving now.' As she spoke, the metal shutters came down on the hatch in the corner of the canteen.

'Oh, not to worry, I really wasn't very hungry anyway,' Eloise lied. 'I'll get a cup of tea back in the office...' And with that, she hurriedly left the room, taking the outer door and the steps on her right, bringing her out onto a patch of grass where ten or more girls from the weaving shed were laid out, stockings and tights off in an attempt to tan their pale legs in the hot sunshine. Trying to avoid their curious stares, while acting as if she always took this route through a sea of sunbathing girls and knew exactly where she was going, Eloise purposefully looked at her wristwatch as though she had an important appointment to keep.

'Did you get your pie?' one of the girls called.

Eloise turned to find half the girls now sitting up, staring after her.

"Fraid not.' Eloise pulled a face.

'You hungry?' The girl, her hair in curlers and nylon headscarf, began to pull on a pair of stockings, fumbling under her lime-green overall for the suspenders to hold them in place. They were an old-fashioned shade of Calvados, Eloise noted, and there was a long ladder in one.

'Starving,' Eloise called back, fed up of answering to the contrary.

The girl stood. 'D'you want a sandwich? I've a couple left. My mum always makes too many for me. Potted meat?'

Eloise's stomach gave another rumble and her mouth watered. She hesitated and then walked over to the group of girls, who were now all sitting up, looking blatantly her way, an obvious object of curiosity.

'That's terribly kind of you,' Eloise said. 'I can't tell you how jolly hungry I am.'

'You look like you could do with some grub down you,' another said. 'Blimey, how d'you keep so thin? You could be a model.'

'Twiggy.' Another nodded in agreement.

'She's taller than Twiggy,' a girl in a pink-checked overall said, eyeing Eloise from head to toe. 'Twiggy's only five foot six. It was in *Jackie* last week.'

'More like Veruschka,' another said sagely.

'Who?' The girls all turned.

'Veruschka. German model. She's six foot. Mind you, she's old. She's nearly thirty.'

'D'you want this sandwich or not?' The first girl proffered the sandwich, its flabby white slices oozing a thick brown paste.

'Thank you so much.' Eloise went to sit on the grass beside the girl and bit, cautiously at first, into the bread. The sandwich was absolutely delicious and she demolished it – paying absolutely no heed to how a lady should eat as taught at Château Mont-Choisi – devouring the lot in three greedy mouthfuls.

'Goodness,' Eloise said, embarrassed as the ten girls watched in awe as she wolfed down the sandwich. 'I ate like a gannet there! Sorry!'

'I wouldn't say that, love,' one of the girls said, her face straight. 'But there was a load of gannets over there tekking notes.' She started laughing and the others joined in.

'So, are you new to the office? Are you with Dorothy in the General Office?'

'Dorothy?'

'Miss Gray. They're all so bloody formal up there. Up their own backsides an' all. They all look down on us weavers.'

'And menders,' another girl sniffed. 'Don't forget us menders.'

'Yes, I'm helping out with the filing.' Eloise smiled.

'Helping out?' The girls were curious. 'Temping, you mean?'

'Something like that, yes.'

'Well, if you want to have your dinner with us, we're always sat here. In the summer, anyhow. Unless it's cold and raining.'

'Listen, would you mind awfully if I take your photograph before you go back in? I've a new camera and I'm still trying it out.'

'Ooh, not with me rollers in, love.'

'You've always got your rollers in, Janice.'

'Yeah, you're right. Come on, then.'

The ten girls ran hands through their hair, backcombed the sides with their fingers, straightened fringes and reached in bags for lipstick and eyeliner. Two minutes later they were ready and Eloise took the first of several photos before the klaxon heralded the end of the dinner break.

With much swearing and tutting, the girls gathered their bags and headed back to the various sheds.

'What's your name?' Janice turned and called.

'Eloise,' she called back, ridiculously happy to have made new friends. And then without thinking added, 'Hudson. It's Eloise Hudson.'

15

LISA

'Mum, she's getting cold.' Jess glanced across at Eloise who, having talked non-stop for the last twenty minutes, was looking slightly pale. 'We need to get her back inside; it's lunchtime.' Jess rubbed at her own hands. 'I need to get back down as well.' She glanced at her phone where a message had just pinged through. 'Kamran Sattar's just arrived and is waiting outside my office.'

'Come on, Eloise.' Lisa smiled, offering a hand. 'Are you hungry?'

The older woman pulled a face. 'Not overly. Goodness, as a girl I was always hungry. Those potted-meat sandwiches! Potted dog, the girls used to call it...'

'Your girls?'

'*My* girls? No, no.' Eloise was irritable now. 'Janice and Kath and Gail... The girls... What was she called, the little dark-haired one? Her fringe was right over her eyes...' She laughed girlishly herself. 'I did buy some potted meat once, you know. Beef spread, they call it now. In Waitrose. Of course, that man turned his nose up, actually sneered when he saw it in the fridge.'

'That man?' Lisa and Jess took an arm each, taking Eloise down the less muddy route back to the house.

'I'm more than capable making my own way home,' Eloise said crossly, pulling her arms from where Lisa and Jess were attempting to steady her. 'Goodness me, anyone would think I'd been drinking. Or you were arresting me.' Eloise suddenly stopped walking. 'What do you mean, that man?'

'You said that man turned his nose up when he saw the potted meat. Even though it was from Waitrose?' Lisa attempted an explanation.

'Mum, don't confuse her,' Jess warned.

'You know, that man I lived with? Have to say I wasn't keen on him. Never was. Friend of my brother Brian. Can't say I was keen on him much either. But Mummy said I had to marry him. Not my brother, of course. I certainly would have put my foot down if I'd had to marry Brian.' Eloise laughed and then tutted. 'Should have put my damned foot down when they said I had to marry the other one... You know, that man...' Eloise stopped, frowning, obviously trying to recall her husband's name. 'D'you think I could have a potted-meat sandwich for my lunch?'

'Ooh, there's lovely roast pork for lunch,' Jess said, slipping slightly on a patch of mud.

'Tell you what, Eloise,' Lisa said, 'I'll bring you some, next time I'm here. The butcher in the village does a lovely home-made beef spread.'

'Mum.' Jess lowered her voice, nudging at Lisa's arm that was round Eloise's back helping to steady her. 'You were upset when you arrived. Do *not* head off home without telling me what's happened. Look, can I leave you to get Eloise back to the day room? Lunch in ten minutes if you'd like to help there as well? We're really late with serving. Goodness, it's almost afternoon tea time. So, can you give us a hand? But only if you're up to it. I still think you're doing too much. Mind you, it's so helpful having you here. I need to speak to Mr Sattar, although I really don't know what it's got to do with *me*. I only work here.'

'It's Sorrel.' Lisa lowered her own voice as they arrived back at the kitchen door.

'Sorrel? What now?' Jess sighed deeply. 'She's not refusing to go to school again? I thought we'd sorted her out – you know, with this audition in London? We can really do without going through all that again.'

'No, no, it's not that...' Lisa broke off as a dark-haired man stood and stepped forward from where he'd been sitting outside Jess's office. She recognised him instantly as one of the two men who'd come into the coffee shop when she'd been in there with Fabian.

'Hello, Mr Sattar, I'm so sorry to keep you waiting. Do come through.' Jess was immediately back in professional mode, politely welcoming the visitor. 'Mum—' she turned back to Lisa as the man went through the open door and Jess made to follow him '—don't go anywhere, will you? I need to know what's going on at home.'

* * *

Lisa spent the next hour helping to serve a very late lunch of roast pork and apple pie to the residents – she really did enjoy being needed, and it stopped her brooding over Sorrel's problems. What did they say? You were only as happy as your unhappiest child? But it was almost impossible to fill your head with whatever might be wrong with your youngest daughter when there was a shaking hand to direct to a plate; when there was a resident who was telling her a funny story about her husband,

Cyril, getting an electric shock from the Christmas tree lights thirty years earlier.

'Goodness, was he all right, Sylvia?' Lisa laughed along with the woman, who was chortling now. 'More custard on that pie?'

'All right?' Sylvia put down her spoon, smiling impishly in Lisa's direction. 'He was *dead*. Very dead. Which was all right with me. Meant I could marry his brother, Rodney, who I'd always fancied.'

'Right?' Lisa glanced across at Bex who, obviously a party to Sylvia's history, grinned, nodding her confirmation of the story.

'Now then, guurl.' Lisa's wide-eyed appreciation of Sylvia's story was interrupted by a slow, lilting Caribbean accent, smooth as milk chocolate, from Denise Donoghue sitting across the table from Sylvia. 'Talking about fancying people, what happened between that daughter of yours and my grandson?' Denise's eyes twinkled. 'Mason cut up that she's back with that barrister boyfriend of her. That southern man come between what was hotting up into nice little romance...'

'Hang on, Denise,' Lisa protested. 'Mason went back to his wife. Nothing to do with Fabian – that's Robyn's boyfriend from London—'

'I know who is Fabian Carrington,' Denise interrupted. 'I read the paper. Big-shot barrister from London defending the Soho Slasher. How do he do that? Hmm? Defending that bastard. She better off with Mason...'

'I'll stop you there, Denise.' Lisa frowned, but she could see the old woman's eyes were mischievous. 'Mason's back with his wife – Angel, isn't it? – and Robyn and Fabian are very much together. So,' she added, laughing now, 'don't *you* start meddling and matchmaking, Denise.'

Eloise, sitting at the far end of the dining room, aloof and refusing pudding, closed her eyes on the noise and people around her, distancing herself, it seemed to Lisa, from her situation and all that it entailed.

* * *

Lunch over, Lisa texted Robyn to make sure Sorrel had stayed in school once she had dropped her back off there after the bout of vomiting. She was relieved when Robyn immediately texted back to say that when she'd spoken to her at the start of the lunch break, before going off to meet Fabian and the estate agent, Sorrel had appeared well and much more like her old self.

Lisa made her way to Jess's office, but the door was still closed. She was about to turn back to the day room where the residents were being organised for the afternoon's activities, as well as a visit from the chiropodist, when the door opened and Kamran Sattar came through, followed by Jess.

'My mother, Lisa.' Jess made introductions.

'Hi, Lisa. Goodness, your *mother*, Jess?' He turned back to Jess but then immediately turned back to concentrate on Lisa, taking in every aspect of her while holding out his hand. 'Weren't you in the café in the village yesterday?'

'Oh, yes, yes, I was.' For some inexplicable reason, Lisa found her heart beginning to race; her pulse speed up. Hell, was she on the verge of one of her seizures? No, this was a quite different sensation. She'd experienced this before – when she'd first set eyes on Jayden Allen performing in that nightclub in Bradford. Oh God, was she regressing to being a teenager?

'You all right, Mum?' Both Jess and Kamran Sattar were staring at her and she flushed, probably most unbecomingly, she'd think afterwards when she recalled the moment.

'D'you work here, Lisa?' Kamran's hand was outstretched and she put her own into it, feeling it warm and dry, looking up into the most beautiful pair of brown eyes she'd ever seen, taking in a subtle scent of some expensive aftershave.

'Just helping out,' she found herself breathlessly twittering, while Jess continued to stare at her pink face. 'You know how it is.'

'Er, not really.' Kamran smiled. 'I'm afraid I know nothing about care homes.'

Despite this man's presence totally flooding her senses; even while there was a strange but vaguely familiar feeling in her nether regions she'd thought she'd locked away for ever, Lisa suddenly remembered who this man was and why he was here. Yes, he certainly did know nothing about care homes! Not concerned how Sylvia and Denise and Ted – constantly wandering the place in his rolled-down undercrackers – would have to be looking for a new home if Kamran Sattar got his way. How Jess was going to be thrown onto the dole; not have the job she loved, despite her often moaning about it. How that beautiful neglected garden, the orchard, the herb and vegetable plots would be bulldozed just for the sake of a few more bloody Turkey Twizzlers and frozen fucking fish fingers.

'I believe you're about to destroy the lives of the residents here, Mr Sattar?' Blimey, it was very difficult not to melt in the face of such a gorgeous man looking down at her with some humour, but she'd got her lippy on and she was going for it. 'Do you not realise the lives you're ruining? Who's going to take Ted, with his bum on show to the world most of the time...?'

'Sorry? Ted—?'

'Mum—!'

Kamran Sattar and Jess spoke as one, but Lisa ploughed on.

'And there's Eloise. She'll have to go back to a husband who won't let her have potted dog when she wants it...'

'Potted dog?' Kamran's face was a picture.

'And there's Denise – St Mede's headteacher's grandmother...'

'Right?' Lisa could see Kamran was trying unsuccessfully to follow Denise's lineage and the woman's relationship to the school, Lisa suddenly remembered, he was *also* intent on razing to the ground.

'...And she won't be able to go back to Grenada, because she left when she was eight – even though she still has that lovely Caribbean accent. Actually, I do think she puts it on a bit for effect... Or she'll have to go and live with Mason and that dreadful wife of his, Angel, who always has her enormous chest out on display...'

'Mum, enough already.' Jess took Lisa's arm, pushing her into her office. 'Mr Sattar, I have work to do. If there's anything else I can do for you?' She closed the door on Lisa, who, suddenly realising the little contretemps she'd created out there, started giggling nervously.

Thirty seconds later, Jess let herself back into the office, closing the door once more. 'Bloody hell, Mum, what was all that about?' Then, seeing Lisa rolling around in hysterics on the small sofa to which Jess always directed the families of prospective residents, joined in herself.

'God, that was priceless,' Jess finally hiccupped. 'You know, Mum, you were always feisty when Robyn and I were kids. Even with Jayden, when he was off again. I think that's what he loved about you.'

'Until I became a doormat, you mean?' Lisa wiped unsuccessfully at the tears of laughter and smudged mascara.

'Until you became ill.' Jess smiled.

'Yes, I suppose I did have a bit more about me when I was in my teens and my twenties.'

'Ted and his bum hanging out, for heaven's sake! Accusing Denise Donoghue of a fake West Indian accent. Telling him Angel Donoghue got her tits out...' Jess started laughing again.

'I didn't say "tits", did I?' Lisa was horrified.

'As good as.' Jess nodded.

'So, why was he here? To gloat? To claim ownership? To put his stamp on the place?'

'To get you into a bit of a tizz, Mum.' Jess chortled. 'I've never seen you behave like that.'

'I was just cross,' Lisa said, not looking at Jess.

'You fancied him.'

'Did not.'

'Yes, you did.'

'Didn't.'

'Well, *I* did.'

'Really?' Lisa's head shot up.

'Well, if he was twenty years younger. Or I was twenty years older. I wonder if he's got any sons?'

'So, why was he here?'

'To ask if I knew what was going on.'

'Going on?'

'John Richardson phoned him this morning to tell him there was someone else after the place.'

'Oh?'

'He wanted to know if I knew anything, wanted to know if it was just a ploy on the Richardsons' behalf to get more money.'

'Have any estate agents actually been round?'

Jess shook her head. 'I think the sale was going to go through privately. I don't think the Richardsons were even really considering selling up until the Sattars approached them face to face. Same golf club apparently – you know how it works. Right, OK, Mum, what had upset you when you got here today?'

'I told you: Sorrel.'

'She's at school, Mum,' Jess said. 'Well, she was. I rang her at 9 a.m.'

'She came home around ten. In an Uber.'

'An Uber? How much is that costing her? And why did she come home?'

'She says she's not well. And Robyn said she'd not been well at school yesterday – she even left the lunchtime practice session Robyn's been putting her through. She paid for an Uber to get herself home then too. The audition's next week, you know.'

'I do know.'

'And then, as I say, she came home from school again this morning. That's twice now she's come back home feeling ill. She threw up.'

'Actually vomited? Or just told you she had so she wouldn't have to go to school?'

'Jess, I held her head. She was sick.'

'A bug?'

'Dunno.' Lisa sighed. 'She's got herself into a bit of a state, Jess. She's been googling porphyria and now realises it can be a hereditary condition, although we've always denied it. She's terrified she's starting with it.'

'Oh no, poor kid. It's something Robyn and I have known for years. Something we've had to live with.'

'So, let's get Matt to talk to her. Reassure her. Maybe even do some tests?'

'That might be a bit difficult.' Jess pulled a face.

'Oh?'

'I'm not seeing him any more, Mum.'

'Oh, Jess.' Lisa tutted. 'But he's perfect: he's kind, he's clever, he really liked you.'

'I'm sorry, I know all that. But it just wasn't right. And there's absolutely no reason why *you* can't approach him directly – he is your consultant, after all.'

'I wondered why we hadn't seen him for a while. Is he upset?'

Jess nodded. 'The thing is, Mum, I see how Robyn is with Fabian, how you used to be with Jayden, how *I* used to be with Dean...'

'Oh, please don't tell me you're having Dean back? I just wouldn't be able to be civil to him over the dinner table.' Lisa felt her heart plummet.

'Now you know why my relationship with Jayden is shot. I've hated seeing the way he messed you around all these years. Why I find it difficult to be friendly, and, yes, civil, to my own father.'

'I know, I know.' Lisa suddenly felt thoroughly depressed at the wasted years.

'But I can see you've got the hots for Kamran Sattar.' Jess was laughing at her.

Lisa perked up. 'Is he married, do you know?'

'I've really no idea. Talking to him face to face, he's totally different from what I expected. And, he couldn't stop looking at you, Mum.'

'Don't be daft... really?' Lisa felt a flicker of excitement and then, remembering Sorrel, said, 'OK, I'll speak to Matt. Ask his advice on how we can reassure Sorrel. I think it's just stress. She's worried about whether Joel is to be remanded as well as stressed at her mock GCSEs when she's got herself so behind not going to school. And, of course, the audition next week. Right, I'm going home and I'll ring Matt.'

Lisa turned at the door. 'Oh, did Mr Sattar let on who was after Hudson House?'

Jess shook her head. 'He wouldn't say and, to be honest, I don't think he knew. I had to say I'd absolutely no idea. But I'll tell you what, I'll give you three guesses, Mum.'

'Fabian? With this mad idea of a restaurant in the white house?'

Jess nodded. 'Must be him. Fabian seems absolutely obsessed with the idea.'

16

ROBYN

The next day I spent my lunch break with the Pink Ladies. I'd persuaded Maggie, the formidable cook, to prepare and have ready in the drama studio a picnic lunch the girls could tuck into after being put through their paces. A sort of carrot on a stick to keep them going when they were 'absolutely starving, miss'.

'Only 'cos it's you, Robyn,' Maggie, who regularly donned her Lycra and joined in with my after-school Zumba class, had said tartly. 'Pushing me over my budget, you know, doing this sort of thing. The PE staff'll all be after the same for footie practice, if they get wind of it. And, mind, I want the best seats in the house.' Maggie's usually strident voice had turned dreamy. 'God, I loved John Travolta when I was younger.'

The girls were shaping up nicely. Isla Boothroyd was absolutely superb as Betty Rizzo, the tough, sarcastic and outspoken leader of the Pink Ladies. Great casting, I smiled to myself, shouting praise in the girl's direction.

'Got to go, miss,' Isla shouted back at me, reaching for her bag before stuffing a tuna sandwich into her mouth and a Scotch egg into her one free hand. 'Got my mock physics exam in fifteen minutes. Miss Hussain'll have a fit if I'm late.'

'Still determined to be a vet, Isla?' I called to the girl's retreating back.

Isla turned, flushed with the success of a good rehearsal. 'Yep. Or on the stage in London like you were,' she managed to get out through a mouth full of sandwich. 'Haven't quite decided yet.'

'You go for it, Isla,' I called. 'You're quite capable of doing either. You follow your dreams...' But Isla had gone, banging the door of the drama studio behind her.

I then spent the next half an hour with Frenchy, Marty and Jan, the other main female character leads who made up the Pink Ladies, putting them through their paces. They might lack the natural talent of both Sorrel, and Isla Boothroyd, but they were shaping up nicely and once they'd done what I wanted, I let them have free rein on Maggie's picnic lunch. Glancing at my phone, I realised that, with ten minutes to go before drama with 8TR, I'd better avail myself of a somewhat flabby-looking Scotch egg if I was to survive the afternoon sessions.

'Any left for me?' Sorrel had let herself into the drama studio, apparently changed and ready for some action.

'Help yourself.' I indicated the remains of the picnic. 'You feeling better? I can't believe you got an Uber home yesterday and the day before. Why didn't you just go and sit it out in the sick bay?' When Sorrel didn't reply, her mouth too full of the remaining piece of quiche, I laughed. 'You're obviously feeling better today.'

Sorrel nodded. 'Right,' she said, once the Pink Ladies had left for their afternoon classes, 'have you got five minutes to help me with that tour jeté you're so good at?'

'You sure?' I frowned. 'If you were actually sick yesterday, I don't think flying through the air is the best thing to be doing.

Why didn't you just stay at home for a couple of days until you felt better?'

'Need to revise for my maths mock exam. Mrs Gledhill's giving a few of us some extra tuition on quadratic equations... they're still beyond me.' Sorrel looked at her watch and then at the studio wall clock. 'Come on, Robyn, I've only got ten minutes.'

Goodness, Sorrel was so accomplished: an absolute natural; a latent talent that would, I was sure, take her to huge success in the West End. The world was her oyster and, for a fleeting moment, I felt nothing but a bolt of pure envy. At almost sixteen, Sorrel had all her musical career in front of her while here was I, pushing thirty and stuck in this backwater.

Oh, but I had Fabian and the excitement of the new cottage in the village. Suddenly much happier, and mentally kicking myself for feeling jealous of my little sister, I launched myself forwards, shadowing Sorrel's movements across the wooden floor until we were both dancing in perfect harmony.

'Ooff! Hell!' I exhaled, coming to a standstill while watching Sorrel's final steps of the dance I'd choreographed for her audition. 'We've just got time to go through your main Sandy pieces; my class will be in soon.' Then, seeing Sorrel's pale face, despite the exertions she'd just put herself through, I frowned. 'You OK, Sorrel?'

'You see,' Sorrel said, tutting and holding onto the barre. 'I feel woozy again. Robyn, what's the matter with me? I've got what Mum's got, haven't I? *I'm* the one that's inherited it.'

'Can you *inherit* a condition? Isn't it just money or a house from a rich uncle?' I tried to make light of Sorrel's worries, which, I could see, were threatening to overwhelm her. I walked over to her. She was breathing heavily, beads of sweat on her pale face. 'You're far too young, Sorrel. Mum was in her thirties when she was diagnosed. You're just doing too much: your mocks, this audition in London, the lead part in *Grease*, trying to sort Joel...'

'He's been bailed,' Sorrel said, some colour returning to her pretty face.

'Well, that's good, then, isn't it...?' I turned as my first class of the afternoon started gathering at the door, noses and big bags pressed against the glass to see what was going on with their teacher and her sister.

Sorrel shook her head. 'Bailed to the local authority.'

'What does that mean? Oy...' I turned crossly to the kids now pushing at the slightly open door '...you lot know the rules. One line. Outside. And I'll be with you.' I turned back to Sorrel. 'What does bail mean?'

'He says he's being taken to Castleford.'

'Castleford?' I stared.

'Out of the area. It's not safe for him here. He's got to stay with his mum's sister. It was what his solicitor and the YJS officer came up with. The alternative, which Joel said the CPS were pushing for, was Wetherby and youth detention.'

'OK,' I soothed. 'Get him away from what he's got himself involved in round here.'

'What about his mocks? He's clever. *You* know that...' Sorrel trailed off as a collective 8TR finally fell through the door.

'I'll have a word with Mr Donoghue. Are you OK now?' Sorrel's colour was back and she was breathing normally once more. 'You've just overdone it.'

'You know as well as I do, Robyn, I'm going to have to do a lot more than the ten minutes I've just done when I'm in London. It's no good. I'm not up to it.'

Upset at knowing Sorrel spoke the truth, I rounded irritably on the Year 8 kids who were now swinging bags at each other.

'What do you lot think you're doing?' I glared, torn between sorting out the class and listening to what Sorrel was telling me.

'Just establishing the rivalry between the Montagues and the Capulets, miss,' Tyler Jacobs shouted back. 'You know, like you said last lesson.'

'Right, OK, then.' Slightly mollified, I turned back to Sorrel. 'Well, at least they've remembered.'

Sorrel tutted but smiled.

'Look, meet me after rehearsal this afternoon. I've got the T Birds until five fifteen. Come and see the cottage we're going to rent.'

'Is Fabian going to be there?'

'Yes. He's got the key. He's been here, there and everywhere yesterday and all day today doing a ton of stuff. I'm going to meet him there about 6 p.m. when he's back.' I thrust a paper plate of remaining picnic items towards Sorrel, covering them with a white paper napkin. 'Make sure you're eating enough and spend the time in the library revising, Sorrel. I'll come and get you when I've finished and drive us down there.'

'Jobsworth Ken will throw me out. He'll want to lock up.'

'I'll have a word. Right, you look much better,' I soothed. 'Off you go. And don't worry. Panic and worry are making you ill – I think you've been having slight panic attacks. There's nothing physically wrong with you!'

I turned to the class. 'OK, you Montagues and Capulets – "Draw if you be men. Remember thy swashing blow."'

* * *

'Oh, it's lovely.' Sorrel, for once, was speechless. 'Really lovely. How on earth have you managed to rent this place? Mum and I always thought it was the most beautiful cottage in the village.

Right next to the duck pond and the cricket pitch. Isn't it called the Dower House or something like that?'

Fabian's Porsche was already parked up outside the cottage, the light from the one central naked bulb inside projecting ghostly rays onto the frosty garden path as Sorrel and I walked towards the front door.

'We'll need some lamps,' I said, feeling excited at the prospect of furnishing the place. 'Lots of lovely lamps.'

'Oh, wow, it's so much bigger than it looks from the outside.' Sorrel stood in the hallway staring.

'The new owner has recently put on an extension.' Fabian was animated, smiling in anticipation, and drawing not just me, but Sorrel as well, into a bear hug of a welcome.

'Er, ger off,' Sorrel gasped. 'I can't breathe.' But nonetheless she stayed in Fabian's embrace. 'If the owner's done the place up, why isn't he living here?' Sorrel asked, gazing round at the beautiful newly renovated open-plan kitchen whose bank of glass windows and doors led out to the patio and onto a lawn, illuminated with strategically placed garden lights.

'Unexpectedly sent abroad.' Fabian smiled. 'How lucky are we?'

'You're going to need some furniture.' Sorrel pulled a face.

'Go upstairs.' Fabian smiled, his excitement palpable.

Sorrel and I galloped upstairs, both determined to arrive first, laughing as we opened the door onto the spacious main bedroom and en suite.

'They've left their bed.' Sorrel frowned.

'No, they haven't.' Fabian was behind us. 'I spent all morning looking for one almost exactly like the one in my apartment in London that Robyn loved so much.'

'Do I really need to know about Robyn's preferences in the bed department?' Sorrel pulled a face and I suddenly saw my little sister was feeling left out. A virtually absent father, and a mother who'd suffered badly from post-natal depression and seizures as Sorrel had grown up, hadn't left her with a great sense of familial security.

I squeezed her hand, wanting to include her in my and Fabian's excitement. 'And it was delivered? This afternoon? Even Amazon can't do that.'

'Told him it was essential it was in place for this evening. Gave him a backhander.'

'Money talks, doesn't it?' I tutted. 'Mind you, I'm glad it does. And you've got duvets and pillows and everything.'

'Of course. I brought up a whole load of my stuff when I moved to Harrogate to live with Jemima. These, Robyn, are the actual London bedsheets...'

'All right, all right.' Sorrel pulled a face as only a fifteen-nearly-sixteen-year-old could pull. 'Get a room, the pair of you!'

'Hey.' Fabian smiled, taking Sorrel's arm and heading for the second bedroom. 'This can be *your* room. Whenever you deign to grace us with your presence from London.'

'Really?' Sorrel's eyes lit up and then her face closed down once more. '*If* I get there. *If* I'm not already dying from some terrible condition.'

'Bloody hell, Sorrel, you're more of a hypochondriac than Boris.' Fabian folded his arms.

'Boris?'

'My dog. He'll be moving in as well.'

'And he's a bit of a hypo?'

'Always checking himself over for ticks, kennel cough, distemper and hair loss and other worrying signs he might peg out at any moment.'

'Now you're laughing at me.'

Fabian patted Sorrel's arm. 'I'm really not. I was the same

when I was your age. Convinced I had bone cancer in my leg, MS, bird flu, kidney failure... The list is endless.'

I stared. I'd never known this about Fabian, although his giving up the case of the Soho Slasher after the trolling he'd suffered at the hands of mainly women's groups was surely indicative of a sensitive nature?

'And,' Fabian went on, glancing back at Sorrel as we returned downstairs, 'most of it a reaction to stress and worry: *I* hated being away at boarding school. *You've* a lot going on in your life at the moment. Right, I'm starving – I've a picnic here.'

'We've had one picnic already, today,' I said, immediately wishing I hadn't.

'Oh?' Fabian looked crestfallen.

'But nothing like this one.' Sorrel was already at the huge kitchen island, rifling through boxes and bags. 'Oh, yum.'

'Nothing much wrong with you.' Fabian smiled as we all tucked into the Waitrose goodies he'd bought from the Harrogate store. A beautifully soft sourdough with the crispest of crusts was, in turn, slathered with butter, hummus and whipped Feta with beets. Tiny sweet tomatoes, black olives and coleslaw accompanied the feast together with a small glass of pink fizz to toast the new cottage.

'Woah, that was heaven,' Sorrel said, lying back on the new cream carpet. 'This carpet isn't going to last long with a dog,' she added. 'I'm surprised the landlord's allowing a dog here. Didn't the estate agent say anything?'

'He never asked.' Fabian gave a little laugh. 'And I certainly didn't offer any information regarding the third tenant. As I always advise my clients: do not offer any information other than that asked for.'

'Which reminds me, have you thought any more about it, Fabian?' Sorrel sat up.

'About having Boris here?'

'No.' Sorrel was suddenly serious. 'About representing Joel in court. His case is actually being sent to Leeds Crown Court.'

'Serious, then, if that's what's happening, Sorrel.' Fabian sat up himself, his long jeaned legs out in front of him at right angles.

'So, will you?'

'Sorrel...' I interrupted, putting a hand on Sorrel's arm.

'Look, find out what's happening,' Fabian said. 'Who Joel is being represented by. I'd need to speak to his mother and to Joel, but primarily to his solicitor.'

Sorrel stood, scrabbling in her bag for her phone, scrolling through until she got what she wanted. 'OK... it's a firm called Braithwaite Anderson... and... hang on... the solicitor is... someone called... hang on... I've got it... Alex Brookfield...'

'Alex Brookfield?' Fabian spoke the name calmly but I thought I saw a flicker of something – of recognition? – on his beautiful face. Since leaving London, he'd taken to sporting a dark beard and, gazing over at him now, wearing the navy cashmere sweater I loved, I didn't think I'd ever seen him looking more utterly gorgeous.

'D'you know the firm?' I asked when, slightly pink at Fabian catching me staring at him, longing for his touch, I looked away and began clearing the remains of the picnic.

'A bit. Leave it with me, Sorrel.'

'Fabian, don't get her hopes up.' I frowned across at him.

'Just leave it with me,' he insisted. 'Right, changing the subject, there's something for you in the fridge, Robyn.'

'The fridge? Is there one?' I looked round. 'Is it switched on and working?'

'Yes, on both scores.' Fabian gave me what could only be described as a particularly lascivious grin and I knew instantly what was in there. I only had to think about ice cream and my knickers were on fire. It had really been quite difficult at times, when the ice-cream van had been parked outside St Mede's during the still warm days of the previous September and October, when I'd first fled London.

I looked at Fabian and we continued to share the secret. Until Sorrel tutted. 'Oh, for heaven's sake, give me a quick lift home, Robyn, or I'll get Mum to pick me up. I'll leave you to your ice-cream kisses.' She turned to Fabian. 'I know all about how you seduced Robyn with ice cream on the riverbank on your first date.'

'How d'you know that?' Fabian and I spoke in unison, laughing.

'Jess told me.'

'Typical. Don't tell my big sister *anything* if you want it kept quiet. Mum said she was going out when I rang her to say you were coming down here with me,' I went on, standing and clearing away food, paper plates and the bamboo cutlery and napkins that had accompanied the feast. 'But you don't need to go, Sorrel.'

'Oh, I think I do.' She sniffed and then sighed. 'Anyway, maths mock tomorrow.' She turned. 'Keep yourself and that pud on ice, Fabian. She'll only be twenty minutes.'

* * *

All the way from the centre of Beddingfield out to the rural open countryside where Mum and Jess's row of ten cottages were snuggled together down a lane in the lea of a particularly pretty wood, Sorrel talked constantly about Joel and how wonderful it would be if, with all his expertise, Fabian could be, was prepared to be, his defence barrister.

'Don't get your hopes up, Sorrel,' I warned once more. And then, when no reply seemed imminent, I turned from the wheel. 'You OK?'

'Stop the car, Robyn.' Sorrel was already scrabbling with her seat belt. 'I feel sick.'

'Again?'

I pulled up at the side of a quiet country lane, five minutes from home, where a white-faced Sorrel dry-heaved for several minutes.

'Water.' I was by her side, offering the bottle I always carried with me.

'You see, Robyn, there *is* something wrong with me.' Sorrel turned her beautiful brown almond eyes towards me, her face pitiful.

'Maybe something going round? Maybe you ate too much back there? We're nearly home. Can you make it back?'

Sorrel nodded, wiping her mouth on her navy coat sleeve before levering herself back into the passenger seat and closing her eyes. I put the car into gear again and set off home.

Once the kitchen door was unlocked and lights and gas fires switched on, I went to fill the kettle for a hot-water bottle for Sorrel. 'Bed.'

'Got maths to do.'

'No, come on, bed. It's only a mock, not the actual GCSE.'

'I'm OK now...' She broke off as Jess came in through the door.

'I thought I heard the car. You'll never guess – Mum's really going for it. She's taken herself off to some new choir she's joined.' She paused when she saw Sorrel's still pale face. 'What's the matter?'

'She's thrown up again.'

'You're not throwing up on purpose?' Jess asked, her arms folded.

'On purpose?' Sorrel glared. 'D'you not know how horrible it is to vomit? Especially at the side of the road? Are you trying to make out I'm bulimic?'

'Sorry! To be fair, I can't remember the last time I threw up.' Jess paused to think. 'Must have been when I was first pregnant with Lola. D'you remember, Robyn? I couldn't keep anything down and...' She trailed off and stared at Sorrel.

'Oh, so now you're accusing me of being *pregnant*, are you?' Sorrel stared furiously at Jess. 'For heaven's sake! What's the matter with you?'

17

LISA

'Matt, thank you so much for seeing me.' Lisa had made her way along the unusually empty – almost serene – corridors of Green Lea wing at Midhope General, stopping to greet those she knew and who had helped her so much over recent years. Old friends they were really, although, as the wing had expanded over the past year under Matt Spencer's professional lead, there were a lot of faces she didn't recognise.

'Lisa, why wouldn't I see you?' Matt, looking tired and rather washed out, rose and came forward from his desk, giving her a kiss on each cheek before offering a comfortable chair.

'What on earth are you still doing here at...' Lisa glanced at the clock on the wall '...goodness, it's after 9 p.m.? You're a consultant, for heaven's sake. I thought you did nine to five?'

'Oh, come on, Lisa. You should know better than most, the hours we put in.'

'D'you not have a home to go to?' Lisa teased, immediately regretting her words when she saw Matt's face.

'Not much there for me except an unlit fire and an empty fridge. And Tinder,' he added meaningfully as an afterthought.

'I'm sorry, Matt.'

'So am I.'

They both knew without further words what they were referring to.

'Look...' Lisa hesitated and then her words came out in a rush '...if it makes you feel any better, I thought you and Jess were really well suited. I don't understand her.'

'One of those things. I really fell in love with her, you know.'

'I know.'

'Is that why you're here?' Matt smiled, running a hand through his thinning sandy hair. 'When Jill told me you'd asked to come and see me...'

'Jill?'

'My new secretary.'

'Gosh, more new people. The wing really is extending.'

'And expanding all the time. Exciting research being done here, Lisa.' For a moment, Matt's face and voice were animated. 'Anyway, when Jill told me you'd asked to come and see me, I hoped you might be coming as a sort of go-between. You know, with an olive branch from Jess...?' Matt trailed off when he saw Lisa's face. 'No?'

'I'm so sorry, Matt.'

'She back with Dean?'

'No, no. NO! Well, I hope not anyway. If she was, she'd be too embarrassed to tell me. Having said that, I was no positive role model in the way I behaved with Jayden over the years. Genes will out: learned behaviour, isn't that what they say?'

'OK, so if you're not here to matchmake, why are you here? You're not feeling ill, are you? Medication all right? Not having any problems with that? I have to say, Lisa, you're looking fabulous.'

'Matt, I've not felt as well as this since I was in my early thirties. In fact, I've just been singing!'

'Singing?'

'Joined a choir. Obviously, it's Jayden who has the fabulous voice but, I was only telling someone the other day, I used to work with him on stage if one of the backing singers had upped and left. Which they often did. Anyway, I've walked into the village hall by myself, and had a wonderful time singing. Musical theatre stuff. Loved it.' Lisa was animated, proud that she'd found the confidence to make the initial move and gone for a taster session. 'So, yes, I'm feeling great.'

'Well, that's a relief.' Matt smiled. 'OK? What, then?'

'You know we've discussed in the past about this bloody awful condition being hereditary?'

'Hmm?' Matt leaned forward at his desk.

'You've always said it can be.'

'Yep.' Matt stared. 'Jess isn't ill, is she?'

'No. It's Sorrel.'

'Sorrel?'

'She's been feeling terribly anxious, had stomach pains, nausea and vomiting. Some tingling, she says.'

'Remind me again, how old is she?'

'Fifteen. Well, sixteen next month. And she was so excited about getting the audition for the Susan Yates Theatre School. You know?'

'I do.' Matt smiled. 'Fifteen is very, very young to start with porphyria.'

'Suddenly, instead of being excited and spending time with Robyn being put through her paces, she's throwing up, tired and tearful. Very tearful. Very anxious.'

'OK, let's hope it's not porphyria. I doubt it is. Sounds more like nerves and panic at what's in store for her in London. You know, she's probably desperate to be accepted at the school, but she *is* only fifteen. Leaving home and everything.' Matt sat back, reaching for a notepad. 'We need to run some tests. Can you get her in?'

'She says she doesn't want to know if she's carrying the gene.'

'Well, if she is starting with it, the sooner we begin tests and treatment, the better.' He stopped writing. 'Lisa, we need to know if *you* inherited the condition.'

'But, you're aware, Matt, I've no idea who my birth parents were.'

'Of course. It was one of the first things I asked you, if you remember?'

'Vaguely. When I was brought in, back in September, the last thing I was capable of doing was discussing my family tree.'

'I think we need to find out. For Sorrel's, Robyn's and Jess's sake. And Lola's, of course.'

'The girls have always turned a blind eye. Frightened, I suppose. You know, Jess only told me the other day that Dean had always said if *she* ended up with it, he'd be off.'

Matt raised an eye at that, but said nothing.

'I don't know how I'm going to persuade the girls...'

'You need to get Sorrel to come and see me. Not only for her sake, but here at the hospital we're starting databanks, amassing what little we know about the condition.'

'OK. You're right.' Lisa smiled uncertainly.

'What *do* you know of your birth parents, Lisa?'

'Very little. The people who brought me up wouldn't tell me anything.'

'Your parents, you mean?'

'The Foleys.' Lisa relented. 'My adoptive parents.'

'Any idea why they weren't cooperative?'

'They were terribly racist. Actually embarrassed that I had "a touch of the tar brush".'

'What? No! Surely not? Your own parents? Against their child?'

Lisa looked at Matt but said nothing.

'And you've never wanted to find your birth parents?'

'No. They gave me up to be brought up by a quite dreadful couple. Incapable of love, racist, misogynistic. Is it any wonder I turned constantly to Jayden?' Lisa's eyes filled with tears. 'I'm sorry, Matt, I thought I'd got over it all.'

Matt pushed the box of tissues across the desk. 'Lisa,' he asked gently, 'have you never thought about having some counselling?'

'I'm fine.'

'*I* don't think you are.' He paused, holding her eyes until she looked away. 'OK, but for all the girls' sake, and any children they might go on to have, you could do with investigating your birth mother and father.'

'I wouldn't know where to begin.' Lisa started to stand. 'All I know, according to my mother – and I never knew if she was giving me the wrong information – is that my birth mother was from India and my birth father obviously white. British presumably. Karen Foley used to hint at *honour killings*. You know, a girl from an Indian family becoming pregnant by a white boy? If that's the case, I really don't want to know. It's enough that Jayden's mother and lover were killed by Jayden's father. It would be just too much for my girls to take in if both sides of their family are murderers.'

'Goodness, I can see why you've not gone into it.' Matt paused, obviously debating whether to probe further. Eventually he said, 'You were born in Surrey? I remember you telling me. But came up to Sheffield when you were nine?'

Lisa nodded, making her way to the door. 'There's always something, Matt. Isn't there? Always something that won't go away, no matter how hard you try to make it.'

* * *

Lisa was surprised to see all the lights on when she pulled up on the drive of her cottage. Jess's cottage too. It was gone 10 p.m. Robyn had said she was staying with Fabian and yet her car was in the drive. She did hope Sorrel wasn't still up, cramming those equations. Or worse still, feeling ill again.

She certainly wasn't expecting, when she let herself through the kitchen door, all three of her daughters sitting round the kitchen table, a plethora of cups and mugs in front of them.

'Oh?' Lisa stared. 'What's the matter? Is it Lola?'

'Lola's fast asleep next door with the door locked. She knows I'm here and she's got my phone.' Jess was tense.

Lisa turned to Sorrel. 'Are you not well again? What?'

'Sit down, Mum.' Jess appeared to take charge. 'There's tea in the pot.'

18

ROBYN

'I thought you were staying with Fabian tonight? Or has he driven back to Harrogate?' Mum looked from Sorrel back to me.

I shook my head. 'This is more important.'

'OK, go on.' Mum sat down without taking off her coat.

'Where've you been, anyway?' Jess asked almost accusingly. 'What choir goes on until after ten at night? We were getting worried.'

'What, you've all gathered here to wait up for me? Just so you'd know I was home safely?'

'Mum,' Sorrel suddenly blurted out. 'I'm pregnant.'

There was silence in the room as the three of us kept our eyes on Mum, waiting for her response.

'But you're fifteen, Sorrel. What do you mean, you're pregnant?' Mum appeared dazed.

Jess held up the evidence of the pregnancy test, hiding behind the teapot, waving it crossly in Mum's direction. 'I drove down to the all-night pharmacy in the village.'

'Oh? So everyone in the village now knows, do they?'

'Does it matter? Anyway, it's not me, is it?' Jess tutted crossly.

'Right? Joel, I suppose? The father of your child is a sixteen-year-old drug pusher in prison?' Mum was close to tears. 'What is the matter with this family that we all make such totally awful decisions about the men we choose?'

'You're as bad, Mum.' Jess, knowing Dean was being dissed, was immediately on the defence.

'I never said I wasn't including myself,' Mum snapped.

'Hey, and what's wrong with Fabian?' The bloody awful mess Sorrel had got herself into was making me more than irritable. 'I thought you liked him?'

Ignoring both Jess and me, Mum turned back to Sorrel. 'Well, what do you want to do about it?'

Sorrel shrugged.

'If you're old enough to be having sex with this boy, then you're old enough to make some decisions about what to do with the consequences.' Mum was almost beside herself.

'Mum, you can't call a baby a consequence.' I shook my head.

'Well, what would *you* call it?' She turned on me now, glaring in my direction.

'I thought... you know... I thought...' Sorrel started '...thought I could have it and then Jess – or even Robyn – could look after it. You know, until I was old enough to have it back.'

'What?' Jess, Mum and I spoke as one.

'Lending it to me?' Jess's face flushed with anger. 'Like a sodding library book that I have to return, once you decide you're ready to send me a reminder? That you actually have a child?'

Mum and I tutted in unison.

'I don't *want* another baby,' Jess went on crossly. 'If I'd *wanted* another baby, I'd have *had* another baby.'

'But, Jess, you like children; you've fostered children.' Sorrel started to weep.

'Short term, Sorrel. The last thing I want is another eighteen years of bringing up your child.'

'And count *me* out, Sorrel.' I put up two hands against the very idea. 'Can you imagine, going down to the cottage and telling Fabian, now that I've got him back, that actually there'll be two of us moving in with him?'

'This just goes to show how immature you are, Sorrel.' Jess was on a roll.

'OK, I'll have an abortion, then.'

'I *hate* that word.' Jess closed her eyes. 'Can you not say...' she lowered her voice, visibly upset '...termination?'

'A rose by any other name,' I murmured.

'Oh, don't you start quoting your precious Shakespeare at us,' Jess countered, glaring in turn at me.

'Isn't it against the law for a boy to have sex with someone under the age of legal consent?' Mum folded her arms, sitting back in her chair.

'If that was the case,' I snorted, 'half the kids at St Mede's would be being arrested.' I turned to Sorrel. 'Does Joel know?'

'*I* only found out myself an hour ago,' Sorrel protested. She put her head down on the table and wept. 'I don't know what to do.'

'Oh, sweetheart.' Mum was immediately up on her feet, cradling Sorrel, who clung to her. 'This is all Jayden's fault.'

'What's *he* got to do with it?' I pulled a face.

'If he'd been a proper father to you girls, this wouldn't have happened. It happened to you too, Jess, don't forget. About to go to uni and, instead, you make the decision to stay here with that pillock next door.'

'Dean's not next door, is he?' I asked, tutting in Jess's direction.
'No!'

'But, Mum.' Sorrel lifted her head. 'At least my being... you know... pregnant... means I've not got porphyria.'

'I never for one moment thought you had,' Mum said, obviously feeling some relief at what Sorrel had just said. 'Actually, that's where I've just been,' she went on. 'To see Matt.'

'At this time of night?' Jess stared. 'You said you'd been singing. Was he, you know, was he... *all right?*'

'Not great, no, Jess. How you can let go a wonderful man like *Dr* Matt Spencer...' Mum emphasised his profession as proof of his brilliance and suitability for her eldest daughter '...is utterly beyond me. And, I have been singing. And it was fantastic. And I'm going again. As long as I can continue to get my life on track and not now be stuck at home changing sodding nappies!'

'Matt was singing?' Jess pulled a Jess face. 'Matt can't sing. He can't rub two notes together.'

'Mixing your metaphors,' I muttered.

'Will you please stop doing your teacher act on me?'

'Matt said I should do what I always said I never would do.' Mum looked up from stroking Sorrel's hair.

'What, finally boot Jayden out?' Jess sniffed.

'Will you leave your father out of this?'

'You keep bringing Dean into it!'

'Matt says I should try to find my birth parents. Look into whether the porphyria is in my family. If there is a gene that is being passed down the generations.'

'If that's the case, does that mean you're more likely to pass it on to us in turn?' I exhaled. 'I really don't think I want to know.'

'Me neither,' Sorrel sobbed. 'Let sleeping dogs lie and all that. Don't go opening cans of worms.'

'Good use of imagery.' I was impressed.

Mum looked at the clock. 'It's well after eleven,' she said

calmly. 'I think we've all said things this evening that should never have been said...'

'*I* haven't,' Jess protested. 'Jayden *is* a pillock and...' she raised an eye in Sorrel's direction '...I am *not* prepared to bring up another baby that's not mine.'

'That sounds like Lola wasn't yours either,' Sorrel said mulishly.

'Sorrel, I sacrificed my career and my body: my bosom, my pelvic floor, my mental ability – and stability – to bring Lola into the world. I can assure you I was there at her conception and her birth and, while I adore my daughter, I do *not* want another.' She stood up, crossly. '*I* want what Fabian wants,' she added, giving me a somewhat challenging look while pushing back her chair.

'He wants *me*.' I tutted, looking at my watch. 'Right now, and wearing very little apart from the black basque he bought me for Christmas. *And* with a spoonful of ice cream in my...'

'Enough!' Mum held up both hands, silencing all three of us as she'd so often done in the past.

'I was going to say in my mouth.' I started to laugh and then, realising that wouldn't now be happening, as well as remembering the reason behind its non-occurrence, moved over to Sorrel. 'Oh, you silly girl. We'll sleep on it and sort it out tomorrow.' I turned back to Jess, who was at the door. 'And what the hell do you mean, you want what Fabian wants? You used to call him that "Bastard Barrister from Bucks". So don't you come all matey, best friends forever with him now.'

'I want,' Jess repeated grandly, 'what Fabian wants. He and I are going to open a restaurant.' And, with that, she slammed the door behind her, loftily striding past the kitchen window as she made her way back to her daughter asleep in her own cottage.

19

JULY 1968

Eloise

'Eloise? Eloise, come on, come and have your dinner with us.' Janice was beckoning a hand and shouting as Eloise somewhat hesitantly began making her way towards the patch of grass in the hope that one of the girls would invite her to join them again. Her second day helping out in Samuel Hudson and Sons Textile Mills' General Office, and this time she'd come prepared, having got up early to make sandwiches to eat once the klaxon sounded to down tools.

'Eloise, what are you *doing*?' Muriel, nursing one of her heads and looking for aspirin, had come into the kitchen in her housecoat, her feet, despite the warm July morning, ensconced in fluffy pink mules.

'I'm making a pack-up,' Eloise had said, standing at Muriel's newly acquired LEC fridge and gazing into its chilly depths. 'Only there doesn't seem much to put into it.'

'A pack-up? What on earth is a pack-up?' Muriel closed her eyes, drawing long red talons across her forehead. 'Surely you're having lunch in the directors' dining room with Daddy and Brian and... and... the others?' She waved a pale hand in Eloise's direction, indicating her daughter must know who the others were even if Muriel herself, having nothing whatsoever to do with the mill – other than spending its profits – did not.

'Brown Windsor soup and the roast of the day?' What had sounded an absolute feast yesterday, had she been invited to join the directors, now sounded utterly stuffy and banal compared to a picnic shared – hopefully – with the girls from the weaving and mending sheds. 'Mummy, what can I put in my sandwich?'

'Well, you're looking in the wrong place for the bread, to start with. The bread bin's over there.'

'Yes, I know that, but what can I put in it? We must have some cheese and... and tomatoes or something.'

'Of course there is. You're just not looking in the right place.'

'Is there no white sliced bread?'

'Mother's Pride? Oh, for heaven's sake, Eloise.' Muriel tutted her distaste, but finally relented. 'There's a large sliced loaf somewhere. It's the only thing that'll keep Michael from starving to death once he's home, this afternoon. You know what thirteen-year-old boys are like.' Muriel's sour face softened at the thought of her favourite child. 'Just don't take it all or he'll soon be complaining when he needs feeding. And don't let anyone in the office see you with the stuff, Eloise. They'll think it's what we eat here.'

'Nothing wrong with Mother's Pride,' Brian said, coming into the kitchen and shaking his keys in Eloise's direction. 'Lived on the stuff when I was over at Huddersfield Tech. Come on, if you're coming. Dad went an hour ago; he's off to Bradford. Five minutes,' he warned when he saw Eloise collecting bread, butter and a huge hunk of Gorgonzola.

'Is this the only cheese we've got?' Eloise sniffed at the package. 'I can't make a sandwich with this.'

'No, you can't. That's for your father – insists on the stuff after dinner. Oh, I don't know, Eloise, just eat with Daddy in the dining room. You are a Hudson, after all. I'm taking my head back to bed.' Muriel had picked up a copy of *Woman's Own* and her cup of tea and left the kitchen, giving a string of instructions to Mrs Baxter, the daily, on her way out.

'Don't see how she can go back to bed without her bloody head,' Eloise had muttered to herself and, hearing Brian impatiently revving up his little Austin-Healey on the drive, had grabbed the forbidden cheese, placing huge sticky lumps of the stuff between two slices of white bread, before hastily wrapping her lunch in greaseproof paper and heading for the door.

* * *

'Eloise, don't be so stuck up! Come on,' Janice shouted once more in her direction as she made her way across the scrubby patch of grass towards them.

'She's the boss's daughter, Janice,' Eloise heard Gail mutter under her breath as the rest of the girls, bright as a flock of tropical birds in their different-coloured nylon overalls, turned as one in her direction. 'She'll be off to the directors' dining room for her dinner. Or at least to the office canteen.'

'Thank you.' Eloise, finding herself tongue-tied under the girls' continued scrutiny, went to sit beside Janice, folding her long legs underneath herself like a newborn colt.

'Blimey, what's that's smell?' Susan, to Eloise's right, swallowed her mouthful of currant teacake, sniffing the air like a Bisto Kid. 'It's your bloody feet again, Andrea.'

'No, it bloody well isn't,' Andrea said indignantly. 'Stop

having a go at my feet.' She bent over, grabbing hold of her stockinged foot and sniffing it before thrusting it towards Susan. 'See!'

'Ugh, summat smells,' Rita agreed. 'What is it?'

'Are we sitting in dog shit?' The girls all turned to inspect their own patch of grass, while Eloise unwrapped her cheese sandwich.

Following their noses, the girls turned again, this time to Eloise.

'What you got in that sandwich, love?' Janice spoke first.

'Cheese,' Eloise said.

'Not Kraft slices!' Janice exhaled, waving the evidence of her own orange, but odourless, cheese sandwich in the other's direction.

'Oh, sorry!' Eloise was scarlet. 'It's Daddy's Gorgonzola. He does like a bit every evening after dinner. Mummy's not keen on it, but...' Eloise broke off when she saw that, for some reason, her words appeared to amuse the others. 'I'm so sorry, but I'm starving.' Eloise bit into the pungent sandwich, her expression immediately acknowledging she'd been overzealous with the amount of cheese. 'Golly, that *is* strong,' she eventually stuttered. 'Shall I go and sit somewhere else?'

Janice patted her leg as Eloise began to rise. 'No, don't be daft...' She broke off as four navy-overalled men in their early twenties walked past, the girls' attention now thankfully off Eloise and her smelly sandwich.

'Ooh, Janice, you've gone all red.' Jean elbowed the girl.

'No, I haven't.'

'Haven't you got anywhere with him yet?' Susan spoke through her too-ambitious mouthful of Wagon Wheel biscuit.

'She'd have told us if she had,' Jean said. 'Y'aven't, 'ave you?'

'I'm doing my best,' Janice said, pulling at her long dark fringe to hide her red face. 'He's off to the Regent Rooms on Saturday night. I asked him.'

'I wouldn't bother with him, Janice,' Gail said. 'Now that Paul McCartney's free again.'

The others turned. 'What? He's finished with Jane Asher?'

'She finished with him. On the telly. On Saturday night. On the Simon Dee show.'

'No!'

'Yes, didn't you know?' Gail nodded. 'Don't suppose *you* know Jane Asher?' She turned to Eloise who, having demolished the overloaded sandwich, was now wishing she'd brought a drink with her. 'I mean, you're a posh lass like her.'

"Fraid not,' Eloise said.

Attention away from herself and back on Eloise, Janice said, 'So, are you just here for the summer? Helping out? Are you going back to school in September?'

'Golly, no, I've left school now. I came back from Switzerland last week.' Eloise shook crumbs of Gorgonzola onto the grass.

'Switzerland? Were you on holiday?'

'No, I was at school there. Just for a year.'

'One of them finishing schools?' Janice asked. 'See, I said you could be a model. Did you walk around all day with a pile of books on your head?'

'Well, not *all day*.' Eloise smiled. 'I hated it, to be honest. I was really homesick. I missed my granny.' Eloise reached for her camera. 'It was Granny who bought me the camera.'

'Blimey, a bit different from St Mede's Sec Mod, I bet?' Susan stared. 'What did you learn? What were you finishing?'

'Herself, you moron.' Janice laughed. And then, turning back to Eloise, 'What did you learn there, love?'

'Oh, you know…'

'No, tell us.' All the girls leaned in.

'Well, primarily the school taught etiquette, manners, how to manage a household. Some cooking – which I wasn't wonderful at – a lot of French, which, again, I'm probably no better at speaking than when I went there. Deportment and how to dress.'

'Department? Like Lewis's department store in Leeds? I'm after a job there actually. Must be better than this place.' Then, remembering it was Eloise's dad who owned this place and handed over the brown paper packet with her wages every Thursday afternoon, Gail shut up.

'Deportment.' Eloise smiled.

'What's that, then?'

'Oh, you know, how to carry yourself, alight from cars without showing your pants and the like. How to cut a pineapple and eat an avocado...'

'Avocado...?' Gail pulled a face.

'How to find a rich, suitable husband. And what to do with him once you've found one – which I most certainly haven't. You know, the best way to be a good wife and look after and support your husband.'

'Hmm, not doing much to help the fight for gender equality and education there, then.' Kath, one of the older girls, pulled a face.

'Oh, Kath, just because you're doing your sociology O level at night school, you think you know it all.'

'You ought to get together with that lad in the carding shed,' Janice advised once she saw Kath was about to retaliate.

'Who, me?' Kath snorted.

'No, Eloise.'

'Mr Hudson's daughter with a lad from the carding shed?' Gail sniggered and the others joined in.

'That Asian lad. The good-looking one.'

'Half of 'em are Asian in there. Are any of 'em good-looking?'

'The one who's always got his camera out?'

'Better than having something else always out.' Susan smirked. 'My mum says I've to keep away from that lot. They're not like us.'

'He's a really good photographer. I've seen some of his stuff...' Janice started.

'You need to be careful, Janice.'

'You're being racist, Susan,' Kath said. 'Stereotyping and being prejudiced.'

'Oh, stop throwing words around you've just learnt from night class, Kath. I've no idea what they mean. And I bet you don't either.' Gail was irritable, turning her back on Kath. 'So, Eloise, did you meet some right nice lads in Switzerland? Speaking French and smoking them right nice French cigarettes?'

Eloise smiled. 'Not really...'

'And have you got a boyfriend here, Eloise? What's he like? Posh, like you? A bit stuck up...?'

'Gail, shut up,' Janice interjected before turning back to Eloise. 'So *have* you got a boyfriend?'

Eloise shook her head. "Fraid not.'

'Well, I'm not surprised with your hair tied back like that. And no make-up on. Your eyebrows could do with...'

'Shut up, Gail!' Janice said crossly, seeing Eloise's face fall. 'Listen, Eloise, what are you doing on Saturday night?'

'Saturday night?' Eloise looked blank. 'Staying in and watching TV, I suppose. I might be at Granny's house.'

'It was my birthday last week,' Janice said. 'I'm eighteen, so I can have a drink...'

'Never stopped you before, Janice,' Gail said, still smarting at being told to shut up.

Ignoring Gail, Janice went on, 'We're all going to the Rooms.'

'The rooms?' Eloise pulled a face. 'What rooms?'

'The Regent Rooms down Bradford Road, just out of Midhope town centre. We go most Saturdays, unless we're off to the pictures.'

'*Up the Junction*'s on at The Essoldo,' Susan said.

'Ooh, it's a bit mucky, isn't it?' Gail's eyebrows shot up.

'I went last week with Billy. It's a look at society today,' Kath started. 'It's about some rich posh girl played by that Suzy Kendall – she's a really good actress, isn't she? Anyway, she takes a job in a sweet factory to get away from her rich... her privileged upbringing because she wants to make her own living...'

'She must be mad. Why would you work in a sweet factory, work anywhere, if you didn't have to? If you had rich parents...?' Gail trailed off as all seven girls turned to look at Eloise, who was saved from speaking, literally, by the bell.

Eloise gathered her things. 'Thank you for having me,' she said, as she did when leaving any social occasion. She stood, starting to walk back in the opposite direction from the girls heading to the weaving and mending sheds.

'So.' Janice caught up with her, taking her arm. 'Are you going to come out with us on Saturday? I live in Little Micklethwaite, so you could come down to my house first if you wanted and we could get the bus together.'

'The bus?'

'Yes, you know, a big red thing that picks people up and takes them places?'

'I'll have to ask Mummy.'

'Why? You're seventeen, Eloise. Why can't you just say you're off out? Or wouldn't your mum and dad want you going out with us?'

Eloise felt her face redden, knowing Janice had insight into the truth. 'No, no, no, it's not that at all...' she stuttered.

'Great, then come down to our house – it's a fifteen-minute

walk into Little Micklethwaite from the centre of Beddingfield where you said your granny lives. We can get the bus down to the Rooms together.'

Eloise left the girls and made her way back to the office, reluctant to be swapping the warm July sunshine for the overpowering fug of Lenthéric Tweed – Sandra's – and BO – Carole's – that permeated the air each afternoon as the warm summer days progressed.

She stopped suddenly, coming to a standstill as a figure in front of her stood as if playing a child's game of statues, his arms raised slightly as he dropped slowly and noiselessly to a crouched position. The man in the blue mill overall, obviously sensing Eloise's presence, turned slightly, immediately tutting and swearing under his breath at the flurry of activity from the adjacent privet.

'Oh, for heaven's sake,' he snapped. 'You've disturbed it now.'

'I'm so sorry, what was it?'

'The most beautiful song thrush. I've been trying to get a decent picture of it for days.' The man – boy really, probably only a couple of years older than herself, Eloise thought – turned back to his camera, ignoring Eloise, who didn't know if she should carry on speaking or simply walk away.

'How d'you know it was a song thrush?' she finally asked. 'And not a mistle thrush?'

'Brown above, with a white belly covered in black, drop-shaped spots. It's smaller and a warmer brown than the mistle thrush.' His voice, testy, was accented and when he turned once more, Eloise stared, feeling the air almost sucked from her lungs as she came face to face with what she knew to be the most beautiful face she'd ever seen. Coffee-coloured skin, the beginnings of a dark beard and huge brown eyes, which were now fixed crossly on her own.

'Are you all right?' The boy stared, almost impatiently, in her direction. 'You've gone very white. You're not going to faint, are you?'

Eloise immediately felt herself flush the unbecoming beetroot that appeared par for the course whenever she came face to face with an attractive male. Would it ever stop?

'Sorry, so sorry...'

'Oh, wow. Fab!'

Eloise turned to see who was behind her. What had suddenly delighted him? He relaxed his cross face into a smile showing the most amazingly white straight teeth.

'What?' Eloise, realising he was staring at her, put up a hand to her face, to her hair. Had she got the remains of the cheese sandwich round her mouth?

'A Praktica Super TL.' He breathed the words reverentially, and was reaching a hand towards where the camera was strapped over her shoulder when the klaxon warning rent the air again and a shout of, 'Oy, Sattar, stop pissing about with that bird and get back on the shop floor.'

'Does he mean me?' Eloise was most indignant.

'No.' The boy smiled, heading off in the direction of the carding shed. 'He means the song thrush.'

* * *

'Eloise, dear, can I have a word?' Dorothy Gray was waiting at the door of the General Office as soon as Eloise returned from lunch.

'Yes, of course.' Her head full of the beautiful boy with the camera, she couldn't think straight or even speak properly. She took a deep breath, trying to concentrate on what the older woman was saying. Oh God, had she filed Wm Armstrong and Sons under Wm Armitage and Sons again like yesterday?

'I don't think sitting on the grass with the mill girls is quite the thing, dear. You get my meaning? You must come and eat your lunch with us in the office canteen. I should have taken you there from the start, but I got the impression you wanted to walk into the village to buy your lunch? Have a bit of a look round? Mrs Wilson has some very nice Sirdar patterns and wool to knit yourself a nice cardi...'

'Mrs Wilson?' Eloise shook her head slightly, not wanting to disperse the fading image of the boy from her mind.

'Haberdashery, dear. She'll put the wool away for you if you want to pay weekly...'

'Right.' Eloise frowned. 'I can't knit to save my life. And I really enjoy sitting with the girls. They're so interesting. They've invited me...' Eloise broke off, sensing danger.

'Invited you...?' Miss Gray leaned in until Eloise could smell the fish paste from the woman's lunchtime sandwich on her breath.

'Oh, just to sit with them every day at lunchtime.' Eloise gave a little forced laugh. 'It's so wonderful to be out in the sunshine and fresh air, don't you think? Now, you said you might let me try my hand with a few invoices this afternoon.' Eloise was feeling brave. After all, her family did own the place.

'As you wish.' Miss Gray sniffed, reached for a monogrammed handkerchief up her sleeve and led Eloise to a somewhat battered Imperial on a desk at the back of the office. 'But really, dear, I know for a fact Mr Hudson wouldn't want you... *fraternising* with the men from the shop floor. But particularly with... you know... our Indian brethren...? Really not the ticket. Not the thing at all.'

20

ROBYN

What should have been a lovely Saturday was marred by Sorrel's predicament. Was being pregnant a predicament? Hell, yes, if you were fifteen and about to be auditioned for a place at the most prestigious theatre school in the country. An opportunity given to so few, and one that would change a life for ever.

As would being pregnant.

'Oh, you silly girl, you silly, ridiculous girl.' I spoke the words out loud as I filled kitchen cupboards and the fridge with my haul from Sainsbury's, unaware that Fabian had returned from the car with yet another load of stuff both from Jemima's place in Harrogate and more of my clothes from Mum's cottage.

'These things happen, Robyn,' Fabian said. 'You, above all others, should know that, dealing with teens as you do.'

'But the audition, Fabian? All she's worked for. All she's ever wanted.'

'Can she not still go? She's only a few weeks pregnant, isn't she?'

'Probably more, the way she was throwing up.'

'Not necessarily. I remember one of the young barristers in

the London chambers throwing up from day one.' Fabian placed a paper bag on the kitchen counter. He patted my bum affectionately. 'Crumpet?'

'Again?' I looked up. 'D'you not think we christened that new bed enough last night? And again, this morning...?' I trailed off as I saw Fabian reaching for the toaster and butter. 'Oh? Yum! *Actual* crumpet. Ooh and coffee? Please.' I stood from where I was crouching down to fill a low cupboard, rubbing at my knee where the ACL injury still gave me pain. 'I suppose she can still go to London. Our trains are booked. But I can't imagine she'll be on top form. She's already sleeping for England and says she feels heavy and clumsy. Not the best way to be feeling when you've to give the performance of your life.'

'And she doesn't want to... you know... not have it?'

'Oh Fabian, when I left her after school yesterday, she looked absolutely drained. She just doesn't know what to do.'

'Well, she *had* done her maths mock exam in the morning. And history in the afternoon. A couple of two-hour exams are enough to finish anyone off. Never mind doing them in the early weeks of pregnancy.'

'You seem to know a lot about it?' I pulled the two plates and mugs I'd filched from Mum's from the cupboard. 'D'you want to go shopping this afternoon? We could drive over to John Lewis in Leeds for crockery and the like.'

'Later on, maybe? They're open until seven tonight. Then we could go and eat at The Ivy Asia? I'd much rather go and explore those moors above Marsden while the sun's out.'

'Really?' I frowned. 'I find them a bit desolate.'

'You're such a towny,' Fabian scoffed. 'It's after living in Soho – you've forgotten to appreciate the beauty of your natural surroundings. And remember, I'm now officially in charge of

Boris. I need to walk him. I've been desperate to get out on those moors since I viewed them from "The Eyrie".'

'That poor dog, he's been passed from pillar to post. First with your parents, then Jemima and now with you and me. Where is he?'

'He's out exploring the garden. Right.' Fabian expertly caught the two crumpets as they popped up from the toaster. 'Breakfast, a long walk on the moors and then Leeds.'

* * *

'So, there's something I need to tell you.' Fabian took hold of my hand as we crossed the road leading from Holmfirth, which, as I informed him, stretched out in front of us towards the Isle of Skye. He paused, frowning. 'The Isle of Skye? We're not walking all the way to Scotland, are we?'

I laughed at that. 'We're heading out to Dovestones. Apparently, so the story goes, an Irish navvy, with a very strong accent, was building this road through the moor. He looked up through the grey mist to see a bit of blue sky and said, "Look, there's an 'ole in the sky."'

'That's a great Irish accent.' Fabian grinned down at me. 'Have you ever thought of going on the stage? Isle of Skye,' he went on, mulling over the words. 'That's what we could call the restaurant.'

'Not sure about that.' I pulled at the sleeve of his jacket. 'So, what did you want to tell me?'

'My parents are here.'

'Here?' I stopped short, turning as if the Lord Chief Justice of England and Wales and his wife were following on behind.

'Well, not here, obviously. They're in Harrogate. With Jemima.'

'Where are they staying?' Anywhere, I thought, through a rictus of a smile, as long as it's not with us.

'Mum and Dad with Jemima. And Julius...'

'Julius is here as well?' I hadn't crossed paths – or swords – with Fabian's brother since he'd gone through my past life like someone at a jumble sale, rummaging through it until, with a cry of triumph, he'd uncovered, amongst all the detritus of my family history, the juicy little titbit he'd been convinced would end my and Fabian's relationship.

'And Claudia, his wife. They're staying at The Old Swan in Harrogate.'

'Well, that's lovely for you. Lovely that they're coming up north and accepting that both you and Jemima have a life here.'

'Hmm.' Fabian's sigh left me in no doubt there wasn't any actual acceptance of Fabian leaving Carrington's, the family's prestigious law firm that was started eons ago. More felons had been saved from the noose and from incarceration by now long-dead Carringtons at the Central Criminal Courts than I'd eaten bowls of porridge.

'When are you going over to meet them?'

'I said we'd drive over to Harrogate for lunch tomorrow.'

'We? Oh, I don't think so, Fabian. Sorry, no, really. It's you they want to see, not me.' I turned from him, setting off down the moorland road, heading for a footpath I knew, which overlooked Wessenden reservoir.

Fabian, dragging Boris from where he was happily sniffing the grass verge, caught up with me, grabbing at my hand. 'Hang on. Slow down. Don't go off on one.'

'Fabian, really. They don't want to see me.' I smiled, trying to show I wasn't sulking, hadn't, as they said in these parts, *got t'monk on*.

'Dad's booked a table for us all at The Beech Tree.'

'Upmarket.'

'Always wanted to go there.'

'Of course you have. And you must go.'

'I'm not going without you. Come on, Robyn, I've integrated myself into your family...'

'Integrated?' I laughed. 'Sounds like a new fridge fitted into a kitchen unit. Anyway, *my* family aren't scary...'

'What? Jess and Sorrel not scary? Between them they're enough to scare the pants off any poor soft southerner with a posh accent.'

I laughed again but accepted that, yes, Fabian had done everything to become a part of my family while I, on the other hand, having had my fingers burnt on both occasions I'd met Julius Carrington on his home territory, wasn't ready for another round with the racist misogynist. I sighed, calling for Boris, who'd wandered off. Maybe on neutral ground I'd fare better? Actually get on with him this time?

'Fabian, I want your family to accept me.'

'Jemima already does. You know that. She loved you from the minute she met you. And Dad thought you were pretty amazing too...'

'Your dad was able to come to that conclusion after just five minutes with me at a charity barbecue?' I gave Fabian a look before turning back to the path through the peat bog of the Pennine moorland, slipping slightly on the tussocky mounds of winter grassland.

'It's not just you that'll be under scrutiny,' Fabian argued, taking my gloved hand once more as I stumbled, placing it with his own in the deep pockets of his navy woollen jacket. 'They're going to be meeting Jemima's Bruce for the first time as well, remember. That'll take the pressure off you and me.'

'OK, OK, I'll come with you, and I promise I'll be on my very best behaviour.'

'No parroting the West Indian patois like you did last time you met them?' Fabian laughed at the memory but then stopped suddenly, taking my hand from his pocket before wrapping both arms around me. 'Robyn, it will be all right, believe me. I'm not going anywhere for the moment – we've rented the cottage for nine months – let's just take it a day at a time.' He lowered his head, kissing my eyes, my cheeks, my very cold nose and I knew I didn't want to be anywhere else on this freezing January afternoon but out on these glorious moors with this heavenly man who seemed only to want to be with me too.

'You know,' Fabian said an hour later as we headed back to the car, 'I think you should persuade your mum to find out more about her birth parents. It might help the three of you girls – especially Sorrel – to come to terms with her condition.'

'How would it do that?' I frowned. 'Mum does some searching and ends up finding out all her blood relatives have suffered from porphyria?' I shivered slightly. 'Better not to know what might be in store for us, I reckon.'

'Knowledge is ammunition.' Fabian smiled as he unlocked the car door, towelled Boris's large feet and encouraged him into the small space in the well of the passenger seat.

'To blow off our heads with?'

'Knowledge is power,' Fabian amended. 'It might be that no one else in your mum's family has suffered from the condition.'

'That doesn't mean to say Jess, Sorrel and I aren't going to have the gene. I suppose it has to start somewhere and, like Sorrel said the other night, why go round opening a particularly wormy can of worms?'

'If *I* knew there was a possible defective gene in my family—'

'I've already seen that your brother Julius is pretty defective in pleasantness.' I thought that was rather clever and chortled at my own witticism, startling Boris, who looked up as I continued to giggle.

'Will you let me finish?' Fabian tutted. 'All I'm saying is, I'd go for genetic counselling: be prepared; know thine enemy.'

'Sounds a bit biblical that.' I smiled and then frowned. 'Look, I wouldn't know where to start looking for Mum's birth family. As far as she knows, her mother was from India and she was born in Surrey. How on earth do you start looking? And how can we do that if Mum doesn't want to know?'

'Pretty obvious, I reckon.'

'Oh?'

'Get Lisa to tell you more about these Foleys who adopted her and then go and see them. They'll have answers.'

'Mum's kept the Foleys from us all these years, Fabian. I don't see why she'd start divulging information now.'

'She started opening up to me, Robyn, in the café the other day. Someone not in the family, I suppose. She's seen how anxious Sorrel has become about the thought of carrying the gene...'

'Fabian, Sorrel's carrying *a baby*.' Oh, God, out on these glorious ancient moors, Fabian by my side, I'd managed to push the huge worry about Sorrel to the back of my mind. Now it all came rising to the surface once more.

'Genetic counselling, Robyn. Goes on all the time.'

'OK, OK.' I looked at my watch, not wanting to face these problems any longer. 'Hot chocolate and a big fat bun down in Holmfirth before heading off to Leeds and John Lewis? I've made a list.'

* * *

The following morning, despite it being a Sunday, I was out of bed by 8 a.m.

'Now where are you going?' Fabian, eyes closed, snaked a hand in my direction. 'Our first Sunday morning in our new bed in our new cottage. Get yourself back in.' He opened one eye and yawned.

'If I'm to impress your family, I need to look good.'

'You don't have to impress them, Robyn.' Fabian opened the other eye and, sighing, hauled himself up onto the pillows. 'And you'd look good in a sack.'

'Course I need to,' I said, already feeling extremely nervous at the thought of running the gauntlet of the Carrington family in a posh restaurant. I'd been awake since 6 a.m., trying to work out what to wear for lunch, and knew the only dress I wanted – a soft pink woollen L K Bennett – was still hanging up in the wardrobe in the box room back at Mum's.

'I want my dress and Mum's lovely new suede boots. And I want to see what Sorrel's decided. If she's not going to London, we need to cancel the appointment.' I sighed heavily. 'She'll never get another opportunity like this one. I won't be long. What time do we need to set off?'

I drove the two miles from the centre of Beddingfield – St Bede's church bells already ringing out a welcome from the overenthusiastic parish campanologists – back to Mum's cottage, making a mental list of any other things I needed to pick up as I went. The kitchen door was locked when I got there, but I had my key and let myself in, shouting 'Hellooo?' so as not to alarm Mum and – particularly – Sorrel, who I assumed, like any fifteen-year-old on a Sunday morning, would still be fast asleep in bed.

I called again. 'Hello? Only me! Just come to collect a few things as I'm off to some posh...' but didn't finish my sentence as

Mum appeared in front of me at the top of the stairs, holding a finger to her lips.

'It's OK,' Mum whispered, but her face was pale.

'What is?' I whispered back, climbing the stairs.

'Shh, she's asleep.'

'Sorrel?'

Mum nodded. 'She's lost the... you know... the pregnancy.'

'Oh goodness! She's had a miscarriage?'

Mum nodded again.

'Should we get her to hospital?' I asked.

'I don't think it's necessary. She woke me up about 1 a.m. Said she had tummy ache. I saw she was bleeding. Obviously need to keep an eye on her, but I think it's like a very heavy period. She wasn't very far gone.'

'Mum, how do you know that? Don't you have to have a D and C or something after you've lost a baby?' I seemed to remember reading something of the sort in a magazine.

'I rang 111. They said if it's an early miscarriage, to let nature take its course. If she seems to be bleeding a lot or if she's in a lot of pain, then I'll take her up to A & E. But, to be honest, Robyn, sitting for hours with the last of the Saturday-night drunks while we wait to be seen... you know, she's better here where Jess and I can take care of her.' Mum held my eye. 'It's for the best, Robyn. She's far too young to be putting her life on hold at fifteen. She's young and healthy. She can stay in bed all day and we'll see how she is.'

'Do you want me to stay?'

'No, there's no need. She'll be feeling very tired and emotional but, as I say, it's for the best. Don't cancel those train tickets just yet.'

'Mum, come on, she can't be facing the audition of her life if she's just lost a baby.'

'It's a pregnancy at this early stage,' Mum said.

'You try telling that to women who find themselves unexpectedly not pregnant any longer. There's *been* a baby.'

'I know, I know. I'm sorry. That was callous of me.'

'I don't think I should go out for lunch. Better to stay here with you and be here for her instead.'

'Will you two stop discussing me?' Sorrel appeared at her bedroom door, her face white. 'It just feels like a very heavy period. I've a bit of cramping but yes, Robyn, it was early. I know exactly when it happened. It was just the once.' Sorrel rubbed at her eyes. 'And yes, it is for the best.'

'Do you want me to stay?' I went to hug her. 'Go back to bed and stay there today.'

'No, I'll be fine. But, Robyn, the thought of dancing in London this week when I feel so tired, so heavy…' Tears welled and rolled down Sorrel's cheeks.

'Come on, back to bed,' I said once more. 'Take some paracetamol and sleep.' I turned Sorrel round, leading her back to her single bed while Mum set off downstairs to make tea. I arranged pillows, tucking the duvet around Sorrel's beautiful elfin face. She looked so much like Mum, and I remembered with a start how Jess and I had often done the same for Mum when she'd had to take to her bed when we were in our early teens. Before Sorrel was even born. 'You OK? It's a truly awful and terribly sad thing you're going through, Sorrel.'

A large tear slid down Sorrel's face. 'It really is. And I would have had the baby. I couldn't have done anything else.' She sniffed before turning back to me. 'You know Fabian's been in touch with Alex Brookfield?'

'Who?'

'Alex Brookfield, Joel's solicitor.'

'No, I didn't know. He never said.' I pulled a face.

'Probably client confidentiality or something.'

'Suppose. Right, listen, Sorrel, I'm going out for lunch with Fabian's family...'

'With the horrible Julius? And the horrible mother?'

'They're up in Harrogate to see Jemima. I'm only going to go out for lunch if you promise me if the bleeding becomes heavy, or if you feel feverish or you have a lot of pain, you let Jess and Mum know. Deal?'

'OK.' For once, Sorrel was not in combative mood.

'Did Joel say what was happening with Fabian? You know, with his court case?'

'Not really.'

'And you told him about... you know...'

'Being pregnant?'

'Hmm.'

'No. I didn't want to add to his worries. His bail conditions have him on an electronic tag and a curfew. I didn't want him breaking them by coming over to Beddingfield.'

'That's very mature of you.'

'I thought so.' Sorrel gave a little smile. 'Now, go, will you? I need to sleep and get better.'

21

'There's nowhere to actually park at the restaurant, Fabian.' I looked over at the stunning eighteenth-century former farmhouse that was The Beech Tree restaurant in Ilkley. 'Gosh, that is so pretty.'

'Nearly as gorgeous as our cottage.' Fabian smiled.

'Actually, you're right. They must have been built around the same time.' I attempted a smile myself, but was feeling sick with nerves at the thought of meeting the arrogant Gillian Carrington for only the second time. Virtually ignored by Fabian's mother on the one occasion I'd been presented on a plate for the woman's approval chez Carrington, I really wasn't ready for another dose of the same.

'Hang on, I can park here.' Fabian pulled the Porsche onto a side street. 'Oh, and there's Jemima with Bruce.' I looked across the street to where Fabian's sister and her lovely new man were alighting their own vehicle.

'Hi, you two.' Jemima sprinted across the street, narrowly avoiding the wheels of a Sunday cyclist who swore something unpleasant, before hugging me and then Fabian. 'Are you ready for this?' She grinned. 'Lunch *en famille*. The four of us under inspection from Ma?'

'Fabian says your parents haven't met Bruce yet,' I said, linking with Jemima's arm.

Jemima shook her head. 'No, we've both been so busy we've not really had a chance to go down south. Bruce went back to his dad's in Newcastle when Fabes and I went back home for Christmas.'

It was a great comfort to have another outsider in Bruce, whose Geordie accent was even more pronounced than my Yorkshire one, up for inspection at this lunch.

'Hi, Robyn. How you doin'?' He grinned in my direction, squeezing my hand slightly, and I knew, despite his being one of the north's top oncologists, he was as nervous as I was. 'Come on, let's do this.'

Roland, Gillian and Julius Carrington were already seated at a round table near the stained-glass window and, as the men stood in greeting, Gillian remaining regally enthroned, Claudia, Julius's wife, appeared at my side from somewhere. A mirror, probably, I surmised, marvelling at the large, immaculately outlined and lipsticked mouth that surely she couldn't have actually been born with? Her very black eyebrows formed two perfect arches, her long straight hair was pulled back tightly from high contoured cheekbones and, as she turned to greet Jemima and Fabian, Claudia's profile now towards me, I could only think of a cartoon cod. Goodness, where on earth did she put those lips when she went to bed at night? Glancing now at her husband, I realised that was probably a superfluous question.

'Robyn. You are looking more than fabulous.' Julius pushed back his chair and came forward to meet me, his hand immediately on my pink wool backside, remaining there despite my attempting to edge away. 'Do come and sit next to me so that we can catch up.'

'Catch up?' I wanted to knock his hand from my bum but, trapped between the standing and kissing Carringtons and the edge of the beautifully dressed table, found I was unable.

'Ah, Robyn, my dear. Do come and join us. How lovely to see you again.' Sir Roland Carrington was at my side, kissing my cheek and seemingly genuinely happy to see me. 'How's life with you? Hmm?'

'Good, good, thank you.' I felt myself begin to relax. Maybe the Carringtons were not the enemy I'd conjured them up to be after that one awful meeting with Fabian's family in the summer? A glass of Sauvignon Blanc down me and I might actually be purring contentedly in the bosom of my in-laws. The thought made me smile and, as I took the proffered chair from Julius – unable to come up with a polite reason not to – Sir Roland patted my arm.

'Now,' he said, 'just let me go meet this young man of Jemima's she's kept from us all these months.'

'A glass of champagne?' Julius was already pouring me a glass as I sat down beside him, searching across the table for Gillian Carrington, the woman who had made so patently obvious her disapproval of, not only my heritage, but also my West Yorkshire working-class background and my career on the stage. Would she approve any more of my working as a teacher in a northern sink school?

Gillian, tall, raw-boned and red-haired, offered an on-off smile across the white starched tablecloth and cut glass. 'Hello, dear. How are you?'

'I'm very well, Gillian, thank you. And you?' Oh hell, should I have addressed her as Mrs Carrington rather than Gillian? Lady Carrington? Your Honour, Judge Lady Carrington even? Which came first? Lady or Judge? I knocked back the champagne, immediately refilled by Julius, who appeared entertained by my obvious nervousness.

'So, dear, we meet again on your home territory.' Gillian lifted a glass of Evian to thin pale lips, eyeing my second glass of alcohol with patent disapproval.

'Home territory?' I wanted to laugh at that. Was the woman throwing down a gauntlet? The bell sounding and gloves on in readiness for a second round of confrontation?

'Oh no, of course.' Gillian offered a little smirk. 'You're in *West* Yorkshire, I believe? Huddersfield, Bradford, Midhope...?'

'As well as Ilkley and Wetherby.' I smiled. 'Everyone appears to think because Ilkley is so pretty it must be in North Yorkshire along with Harrogate and Richmond.'

At my correction of her geographical knowledge, two tiny spots of colour appeared in Gillian's already red-veined cheek and I wondered idly if, drinking water instead of the quite delicious champagne that was sliding down very nicely indeed, the woman wasn't perhaps a recovering alcoholic. Gillian, obviously put out, not just at my presence at the table, but now at my cheek at correcting her in front of her whole family, turned instead to Bruce, who was being introduced to Claudia.

'You're a consultant ornithologist, I believe?' Claudia tinkled merrily, flashing Bruce, not only large doe eyes, but a quite magnificent view of her sumptuous chest, which was totally at odds with the rest of her stick-thin figure.

'Ornithologist?' Bruce appeared somewhat nonplussed and then laughed raucously, the sound booming across the table and into the restaurant until Gillian offered up a pained expression in his direction. It gave much comfort to know I wasn't the only one not to meet with Lady Gillian's approval.

'Oncologist, darling,' Julius drawled. 'Shame, he's not – he'd have been well suited to working out what goes on in that bird brain of yours.'

Flushing, Claudia glared at her husband and I felt sorry for the girl. What must it be like to be married to such a horrible man? I thought, not for the first time, how glad I was that he and Fabian were only half-brothers, Gillian having married Sir Roland after seeing her first husband off to an early grave.

A waiter was hovering, obviously desperate to get everyone seated and orders taken. The restaurant was busy and, having worked at Graphite, I offered a smile of sympathy in his direction.

'Right, right, come along, let's order.' Sir Roland was in an effusive mood. 'Jemima, my darling, come and sit next to your old dad and tell me where you've been working and which part of the world you're heading off to next.'

'If she'd stayed at Carrington's, she wouldn't be heading off anywhere but back to London.' Gillian sniffed. 'Mind you, if that were the case, we wouldn't have needed to be dragged halfway up the country to have lunch.'

'You wouldn't have come up to see me, Mum?' Fabian smiled, but I knew he was put out.

'Oh, you'll be back in London very soon, Fabian.' Gillian arched an eyebrow in his direction. 'Once you've got over this ridiculous idea of finding yourself. Of leaving your vocation.'

'I'm not convinced law was ever my vo—'

'But of course it was. You were a superb defence barrister. You're a Carrington. All Carringtons go into the business of issuing justice.'

'Er, and I'm not a Carrington, then, Ma?' Jemima arched her own eyebrow, but didn't appear overly upset.

'Oh, you, Jemima!' Gillian tutted. 'You always were contrary. Always determined to do your own thing with no thought for the firm. But Fabian...' Gillian flashed me a look of dislike '...was well on his way, after being one of the youngest barristers in London, to be made KC. And now, to give it all up, to—'

'OK, I'm going to have the crispy Arlington egg,' Roland interrupted loudly. 'There's a new head chef here, I believe?'

Fabian nodded gratefully in his father's direction, obviously glad to get Gillian off his back. 'A new culinary lead I believe is the term these days, Dad.' He scanned the menu and I knew he was taking it all in, excited by the innovative dishes. 'Celeriac, I think,' he went on.

'Celeriac?' Claudia looked mystified. 'I thought the new culinary lead was someone called Celino?'

'Celeriac, my darling, is a knob celery...' Julius tutted.

Only one knob at this table, I thought, grinning to myself.

'...and on the starter menu.' Julius gave Claudia a look. 'With pickled mushrooms and coriander yoghurt. I'll join you, Fabian.'

'Pressing of rabbit, I think,' Gillian barked, not looking up from the menu.

'Ooh, no, not rabbit!' I spoke before I could stop myself.

'You have something against rabbits, Robyn?' Gillian stared in my direction.

'Well, not per se: I actually love rabbits; I just don't want to eat one.' I found myself going red as everyone, including the waiter, turned in my direction. 'We have Roger at home, you see. You know, it would be a bit like eating Boris.'

'The ex-prime minister?' The young waiter, unable not to, joined in the conversation. 'Blimey. You'd have a mouthful there!'

'The dog.' Fabian laughed. 'And Roger is the house rabbit.'

'You have a house rabbit?' Gillian stared at me. 'Hopping around the kitchen?'

'And the sitting room. If he's feeling particularly put out with Mum or my sister, Sorrel, he's not averse to hopping up the stairs to mark his territory on our beds.'

'Goodness. How... how *northern*.'

'Whippets and coal in t'bath, Robyn?' Bruce grinned in my direction.

'Aye, lad,' I said, straight-faced, enjoying the banter. 'The bath...' I emphasised the flattened vowel '...in front o' t'fire every Friday night. Whether we need it or not.'

The waiter – Marcus, according to his name tag – finally managed to take everyone's order for starters and mains before moving to clear the one remaining place setting of its cutlery and glasses.

'Please, would you leave it?' Gillian instructed, laying a hand on Marcus's arm.

'Oh, there's someone still to come?' Marcus appeared worried, glancing up at the large antique clock on the far wall.

'If they can make it.' She smiled. 'They might just join us for dessert.'

'Who else is coming, Ma?' Jemima pulled a face. 'It's supposed to be a *family* lunch. Bruce and I want to tell you something...' She turned to Bruce, reaching across the table for his hand.

'Sorry, Mr and Mrs Carrington.' Bruce smiled. 'I should have asked your permission...'

'Permission?' Roland turned to Gillian and then back to Bruce.

'I'd like permission to marry your daughter.'

'And, just to be clear, if you don't give permission, tough.' Jemima laughed. 'We're getting married next month.' She turned to Fabian. 'Sorry, Fabes, should have told you really.'

'Next *month*?' Gillian stared. 'But that won't give us time to send out invitations, choose the cake, actually find a venue...'

'Don't want any of that,' Jemima said cheerily. 'We're off to Mauritius. Just the two of us.'

'Oh, not one of these beach jobbies? Please, don't say that, Jemima.' Gillian looked so taken aback, I almost felt sorry for her.

'But what about your family, Bruce?' Roland, I could see, was visibly upset at not being allowed to accompany his only daughter down the aisle.

'Just my dad at home now,' Bruce said. 'I've no siblings and I don't think my dad will be too upset at missing out on a big do.'

'Right. Well, congratulations, then.' Roland turned to kiss Jemima and then shake Bruce's hand. 'Welcome to the family, Bruce.'

'Glad to be here.' Bruce grinned.

'Great, I can put my ring back on now, then.' Jemima reached for her clutch, taking out the small solitaire band and slotting it onto her finger. 'Oh, yes, and there's one more thing.' She smiled. 'You're going to be a granny, Mum.'

There was a split-second stunned silence around the table before there were more congratulations from Fabian and Roland, both men standing to hug Jemima and shake Bruce's hand. Gillian's face held a rictus of a smile, but Claudia's large eyes filled with what I could only read as pure envy. Interesting: a baby was obviously on Claudia's Christmas list but not, I surmised, glancing across at Julius, whose hand was now being taken by his wife, on her husband's.

And, for some unknown reason I couldn't quite grasp, I suddenly felt left out. Fabian and I had been together longer than Jemima and Bruce. Had Sorrel's pregnancy unsettled me? Was it, now I was almost thirty and no longer bound for West End stardom, my baby body clock telling me something? Fabian wasn't meeting my eye as if to say 'how about us?', as happens in all good romance novels. Oh, I was being ridiculous. We had only been together nine months and for three of those we'd not been speaking. The last thing either of us wanted was a baby when we didn't know where we were going to finally end up living; when Fabian was out of work; when all he wanted was to fulfil his dream of owning a restaurant. And a baby had never been on my agenda.

I reached for my glass of champagne, which, I saw, had been filled once more. I sipped at it, reminding myself I'd never been much of a drinker, especially on an empty stomach. Two glasses were my limit before I either fell asleep, talked too much, holding forth in a silly accent – I was particularly good at Scouse – or became downright combative. I glanced towards Julius on my left and, instead of concentrating on Claudia, who was still holding on tightly to his hand, he was staring at me. When I raised an eyebrow in his direction – what was he playing at when his wife so obviously needed his attention? – he smirked and turned back to his own drink.

I needed Fabian, needed to know he was there for me – there was so much undercurrent around the table I was afraid of being pulled under – but he was sitting between Bruce and Jemima, happily talking Mauritius, babies and the role of, not only uncle but, apparently, godfather as well. I was just about to start on the warm bread roll that Marcus had popped onto my side plate, for something to do with my hands, when my attention was caught by an exceptionally beautiful girl, probably around my own age, who had just come through the main door. Dressed in a fitted cream wool midi skirt, which showed off her amazing figure, as well as brown suede boots, which did the same for her long legs, and with beautiful swishy caramel hair to her shoulders, she was a vision of utter loveliness and I found I could only stare. As did the majority of diners at the other tables, turning heads; one woman even nudging her neighbour, indicating the girl.

Maybe she was famous? A local celebrity? Did Ilkley have

celebrities along with its Cow and Calf stones on the moor and its song about being without a hat?

'Darling girl.' Gillian was instantly on her feet, giving all the attention and welcome she'd denied Bruce and me to the newcomer. 'Do come and sit down – so glad you were able to join us. We've saved you a place.' The girl's invitation and subsequent appearance at the restaurant had obviously not been shared with *all* the Carringtons. There was a slight pause in the proceedings as everyone else – apart from Bruce, me and Julius – appeared slightly stunned and then there was more standing up, more kissing, and another bottle opened as Marcus and a second waiter hovered with our starters, unable to actually get through to place them on the table.

I glanced across at Bruce, who grinned, shrugged his shoulders and waited to be introduced.

'Oh, sorry, how rude of me.' Gillian Carrington paused, looking towards Julius for several seconds before addressing the girl. 'Let me introduce you, darling, to our guests today.' She turned to Bruce. 'This is Bruce, who is apparently about not only to join the Carrington family but also to present us with our first grandchild.' She then turned to me and, with what could only be described as a malicious smile, said, 'And the girl next to Julius is Robyn, a friend of Fabian's from West Yorkshire. And *this*, Bruce and Robyn, is the very lovely Alex Brookfield, my best friend's daughter and particularly *special friend* to Fabian.'

22

JULY 1968

Eloise

'Eloise!' Muriel Hudson's strident voice flew up the stairs at Hudson House like a pistol shot. 'Come down from that bedroom. I need some help.'

Eloise, sitting cross-legged on the bed while poring over the photography books she'd borrowed from Beddingfield library that morning, tutted, hoping that if she ignored her mother she might go away. No such luck. There was a rattle of the door handle and then, when Muriel realised it was locked, she rapped smartly.

'Why are you locking the bedroom door?' she called impatiently. 'What are you doing in there?'

Eloise sighed, but went to the door, turning down Emperor Rosko, who was holding forth on Radio 1 on her transistor.

'What are you doing?' Muriel repeated once she was in the room, and, seeing the dishevelled bedspread, added, 'I'm sure they don't allow sitting on one's bed in Switzerland. And turn off that infernal noise, do, Eloise. Now, I need some help with these guest lists.'

'Guest lists?'

'Eloise, it's your coming-out ball...'

'No, it's not, Mummy. It's *yours*. It's *you* who wants me out in society.'

'Out of my hair, to be honest, Eloise. Sitting up here on your bed, listening to this racket. It isn't good for your posture, your ears or... or your standing in society.'

Eloise actually laughed at that. 'I don't think there's much society here in Beddingfield.'

'Exactly.' Muriel smelt victory. 'And *that's* why we're having the ball in Leeds. At The Queen's hotel. Now, Mrs Livesey is coming round later for both of our dress fittings.'

'But the party's absolutely ages off. Next year! I'm going down to Granny's. She says I can stay the night.'

'Why on earth do you want to spend the night with Granny?' Muriel, at loggerheads with her mother-in-law since the day they'd first been introduced, was genuinely perplexed.

So I can go out with Janice and the others to the Regent Rooms. If I can pluck up the courage. The words, in Eloise's head, remained unspoken. Instead, she said, 'Granny actually knows quite a bit about cameras. She doesn't let on that she does, but—'

'Oh, cameras, art, photography. Fiddle. Maude Hudson has always considered herself an artist. Bohemian, I'd say. Anyway, Eloise, I need you here this evening. Daddy and I are off to some do in Bradford.' Muriel sighed. 'It will be an absolute bore, the usual bankers and accountants and the like fawning over your father trying to get him to do business with them.'

'Don't go, then.'

'One has to show willing.' Muriel gave a little on-off smile to convey the graciousness that went hand in hand with being the wife of a wealthy mill owner. 'So, I need you to look after Michael.'

'Babysit Michael? You're not serious, Mummy.' Eloise felt her pulse race at the unfairness of it all.

'Totally serious. He's thirteen. He can't stay here by himself – he'd eat everything in the larder and the fridge.'

Probably down the contents of her father's drinks cabinet as well, Eloise mused. She'd mopped up three inebriated adolescents and helped dispose of the evidence back in the Easter vac when Michael's two friends from St Cuthbert's had come to stay. So, that was her evening out with Janice and the girls up the swanny, then. To be honest, she knew in her heart, even if she'd gone down to stay with Maude, she wouldn't have dared take the next step, turning up at the address Janice had written down for her, before telling her to be there at 7 p.m. on Saturday. Well, Saturday was here and it didn't look as if she was going anywhere except watching *Opportunity Knocks* with Michael. She adored her little brother: there was something very endearing about his naughtiness, about his arrogance. He was a gorgeous-looking, floppy-haired thirteen-year-old, the world his oyster, and one day he'd be out there, ruling it. But until then, he commanded his big sister to bowl endless balls to him down the lawn and to feed him ham and beetroot sandwiches and tell him what she knew about sex. Which wasn't a great deal. Michael himself had opened her eyes to what went on in the big bad world when he'd surreptitiously passed her a tattered paperback copy of *The Perfumed Garden* he'd brought back from school. Goodness, there were things in there...

'Oh,' Muriel tutted, hearing a door bang and Michael's voice calling up the stairs. 'There's Mrs Livesey now. Why can't these people keep to their appointed time? I do hope you've clean underwear and your roll-on on?'

Eloise sighed but reached into her underwear drawer for her M&S rubberised roll-on, drawing it upwards over her long legs and, without admiring the effect in the long mirror, pulled down her skirt and followed Muriel along the landing to her mother's bedroom where Mrs Livesey was already unpacking pins.

* * *

'Oh, Eloise, darling? I thought you said you had to babysit Michael?'

'Reprieve at the last minute.' Eloise swung her camera towards Maude, catching her profile as she sat in the deckchair in the warm late-July evening sun, gin in one hand and the racing page in the other. 'One of his school friends from Mirfield invited him over to stay. His father arrived to pick him up for the weekend. I think they're going over to Filey to do some sailing.'

'So, you and me, then? Lovely! There's that funny little chap on *Opportunity Knocks*...'

'Funny little chap?' Eloise took another snap of her grandmother, wanting to take even more but conscious, as always, of the film's capacity.

'Les Dawson, darling. Pulls the most incredible faces. So, that's on at seven and then there's a film...' Maude took the spectacles from around her neck, turning the pages of her newspaper to the TV listings '...*Carry on Cruising*.'

'Granny.' Eloise suddenly felt brave. 'Would you give me a lift?'
'A lift? To where?'
'Over to Little Micklethwaite?'
'Oh?'

'I've been invited to a friend's house.'

'In Little Micklethwaite?'

'Hmm.'

Maude peered over her glasses, examining Eloise's pink face. 'A boy, is it?'

'A boy? No, Granny, it's *not*. It's a girl.'

'You're not one of those lesbians, are you?' Maude continued to stare and then cackled. 'Mind you, doesn't matter if you are. I always quite liked girls myself. Beatrice Harding and I got up to all sorts in the dorm. I think I could have been... what's it called these days?' She paused to think. 'Bisexual... you know?'

'Granny!' Eloise's face was puce.

'So, a friend?'

'I'm going out with some of the girls from the mill.'

'The office girls?' Maude pulled a face. 'What does your mother think to that?'

Even less if she knew she was off out with the weavers and menders, Eloise thought, without correcting her grandmother. 'Would you drop me down there?'

'And your parents don't know?'

When Eloise deigned not to answer, Maude sniffed, put down her drink and reached for the keys to her old Morris Minor. 'Not sure I totally approve but come on, then, lead the way.'

* * *

'Janice!' The acne-faced teen who answered the door at 26 Petunia Way on the large Micklethwaite council estate managed to call behind him without turning his head, a feat Eloise found mightily impressive. 'There's some posh bird here says she knows you.'

'Get out the way, Stuart,' Janice said, pushing him back into the kitchen once she saw Eloise on the doorstep. 'Oh, good, you came, Eloise. I never thought you would. Just getting ready. Come upstairs.'

Eloise followed Janice, in her full regalia of curlers and face pack and stripped down to bra and pants, up the stairs.

'Watch the step at the top,' she warned. 'There's a hole in the carpet – nearly went arse over tit a few days ago.' She led Eloise into a tiny but immaculately neat bedroom, the outfit Janice had put out for the evening hanging over the door. 'Right,' she said, 'let me get myself sorted and we'll work out what you're going to wear.'

'What *I'm* going to wear? I've not brought anything else with me.'

'Well, thank God for that if the rest of your stuff's like what you've got on now. I thought with all your money you'd have had some fabulous clothes?'

When Eloise felt herself redden and started to say that, really, she'd just popped in to say hello, but she'd be off now, Janice took pity on her. 'Sit down there. We're about the same size although you're much taller than me. God, I wish I was willowy like you.' She moved to a single wardrobe, rifling through its rail of clothes until she found what she'd obviously had in mind for Eloise. 'Right, see how that looks. Let me just finish my make-up and then I'll help you with yours.'

'Oh, I couldn't. I'll never fit into that.'

'Just try it,' Janice said patiently.

Scarlet-faced once more as she removed her blouse and skirt, Eloise had the A-line pink and contrasting single white flower dress over her head when she heard another, much older voice.

'Who've you got in there with you, Janice?'

'It's Eloise, Mum. From work.'

The door opened. 'Oh, hello, love. Ooh, that dress doesn't half look good on you.'

'Mum made it,' Janice said proudly, turning to Eloise, a mascara wand in hand. 'I just showed her a picture of the Mary Quant dress in *Jackie* and she was off to get the material from the Monday market. She got her Singer out and there you go.'

'Oh!' Eloise had caught sight of herself in the mirror. 'Oh, it's so pretty.' She tried to pull it down over her knees. 'But it's way too short for me.' She reached for the zip at the back once more but Norma Atkinson stayed her hand. 'No, it's not; shows off those fabulous pins of yours. It's beautiful, love. You're beautiful. Just let our Janice put you a bit of make-up on.'

'Right.' Janice turned from taking out the curlers and brushing her now bouncy hair down to her shoulders. 'Which dress, Mum? This one I've already got out?'

'How about the little yellow-and-white one I copied from *Vogue*? The daisy dress.'

'Ooh, yes, I've not worn it since we went to Blackpool last summer.'

Eloise stared, taken aback at the girly banter between Janice and her mother. Never in a million years could she imagine Muriel chatting to her like her best friend while she stood there in her undergarments. She felt a flash of envy. What must it be like to have a mother like this one?

'Oh goodness, you look wonderful,' Eloise breathed once Janice was fully made up and had the yellow dress on.

Obviously not fully. 'Not got me lashes on yet.' Janice laughed. 'Bald as a wotsit without them.'

'Right, come on, over here, Eloise,' she ordered two minutes later. 'Sit down.'

'Put a towel round her, Janice,' Norma advised. 'Your mum

does know you're here, doesn't she, love? She knows you're off out with our Janice and her mates?'

'Granny does.' Eloise breathed, swivelling round on the little stool to face Janice as a crepe bandage was placed around her hairline and a tan pan stick applied to her cheeks and forehead. 'I'm staying with her tonight. She's just dropped me off.'

Five minutes later, once a final coat of Rimmel had been applied to her eyelashes, she was allowed to swivel back to the mirror to view the results. Staring back at her was a face she didn't recognise, and she almost turned round to view the beautiful girl who must have taken her place on the stool.

'What shall we do with her hair, Mum? Mum,' she told Eloise, 'used to be a hairdresser when she left school. But she gets paid so much more as a mender at Hudson's.'

'Better on me legs, but terrible on the eyes.' Norma smiled. 'You've beautiful thick hair, Eloise. Why don't we just take it out of the rubber band – never use rubber bands in your hair, worst thing for it – then, let's see, pull it up off your face, twist this round a bit.' She secured it with a couple of clips, threaded some ribbon the same colour as the dress into its height before twisting the blonde locks dangling down around her fingers and fixing her handiwork with a blast of Elnett.

'You, Eloise, could be a model. Have you never thought about it?'

'I think my mother would see modelling as akin to selling myself on the street.' Eloise blushed at the near mention of prostitution. 'How *do* I stop blushing?' she entreated.

'Green powder, love. Here you go.' Norma reached for the powder and brushed a tiny amount onto Eloise's cheeks, standing back to see the result.

'Right, we need to go, or we'll miss the bus.' Janice stood, and then frowned as she saw Eloise's footwear. 'Scholl sandals? She can't dance in those.'

'Well, she'll have to. You've got big feet, love, or we'd lend you a pair.'

'I know, I know,' Eloise said, embarrassed as the three of them stared down at her feet. 'I've always been a clodhopper.'

'Don't you believe it,' Norma said as they left the bedroom and headed for the stairs. 'Now, Janice, you're to look after Eloise. She's not used to being out with you lot. And no alcohol. She's not eighteen yet.' She turned back to Eloise. 'I don't think you're eighteen yet, are you...?' Norma broke off, the question left unanswered, as the door on their right opened.

'Woah, who's your mate?' A tall, good-looking boy of around twenty was coming out of the bathroom, booted and suited and ready for Saturday-night revels.

'Never you mind, Gary. She's far too posh for you. You stick to your usual scrubbers.'

* * *

'Your mum's lovely,' Eloise said, once they were upstairs on the red double-decker taking them into Midhope town centre. 'But she seemed to know who I was.'

'Everyone knows who you are, Eloise. You've been the talk of the mill ever since you started there.'

'Really?' Eloise digested this little nugget of information in silence.

'Really. Right. Gail, Jean and Eileen get on here.' Janice stood, opening the vehicle's narrow top window before yelling down: 'Oy, we're up here, you lot.'

The three of them clattered up the bus's steps, wobbling slightly on too-high heels, laughing raucously as they did so.

'Blimey, nearly on me arse there.'

'You lot had a drink already?' Janice asked.

'Yep, we called in for a Babycham at The Albion. Jacko and Ernie from work were in and bought us one each. Heck, you scrub up well,' Jean went on as if suddenly realising, not only who Eloise was, but that she was with the group. 'You look great.'

'Janice's mum was so utterly kind,' Eloise explained, her cut-glass vowels, she was painfully aware, terribly out of place on the smoky top deck of the Number 32.

'Right, I need a fag.' Gail took out a pack of menthol Consulate, lighting up and immediately blowing smoke rings to the ceiling of the bus.

'They're like smoking bloody Polo mints,' Eileen said. 'But I've run out of me No.6. Come on, give us one. I'll pay you back.'

Fifteen minutes later the bus, having stopped every two minutes to pick up more and more Saturday-evening revellers, came into the town's bus station, spewing out its occupants into the warm July evening.

'Hey, girls!' A couple of lads in Levi's and checked Ben Sherman shirts were standing on the pavement outside The Boot and Shoe, drinking pints. 'Come and have a drink.'

'They won't let you into the Rooms in jeans,' Janice advised. 'It's Saturday night. Suits only.'

'Well, come and have a drink with us first, then, if you won't be enjoying our company down there. Who's your mate?'

'Shall we?' Eileen asked. 'Come on, we're too early to be going down to the Rooms. We don't want to be the saddos in there first.'

'You all right with that, Eloise?' Janice asked.

'Oh, don't worry about *her*,' Gail said slightly cattily. 'She's fine. If she's out with us, she needs to join in with us.'

'Really, yes, lovely,' Eloise stuttered. Maude had pressed a couple of pound notes into her hand – 'For a taxi back if you need one,' she'd said. 'And no walking home in the dark.' How did she pay her way? Did she pay for a round? But the other four girls appeared happy to have their drinks bought for them and Eloise ordered a vodka and tonic – Muriel's drink of choice – while, to her embarrassment, the other girls asked for halves of lager and cider.

'So, are you from round here, then?' Bob, who was apparently a neighbour of Eileen's, asked, placing an arm around Eloise's waist and drawing her in to him. His breath smelt strongly of beer, but there was another overpowering scent she couldn't identify.

'Erm, Beddingfield,' she finally said, not sure what to do with the sweaty hand that was moving down to her buttocks, pulling up the fabric slightly. In the short Mary Quant dress, she felt if it moved any lower it would be on her pants' elastic. Nervously, she downed the vodka quickly, the tonic refreshing her mouth, which seemed to have dried up of any conversation. Château Mont-Choisi had never offered instruction as to what one should do when an unwanted stray hand was inching up towards one's knickers.

'Get your hand off Eloise's backside,' Janice warned. 'Buying us a drink doesn't mean you get to handle our bums. And, you've totally gone overboard on the Brut.' Janice waved a hand in his direction. 'Never heard of subtlety?'

Bob laughed, obviously finding Eloise's lack of response an utter turn-off. He moved instead to Gail, who didn't seem to mind him peering down her low-cut dress.

The alcohol swirling in her veins was making Eloise feel unsteady and she wished she were back home in the garden at Hudson House, the heady scent of night-scented stocks pervading her senses as she bowled endless cricket balls to

Michael. Wished, even, she were back with Maude and Les Dawson.

'Come on, it's nearly nine,' Janice ordered the girls. 'Let's get off. I'm dying for a dance.'

'You're dying to see if Paul Dyson's there,' Gail chortled, poking Janice in the ribs.

Janice linked one arm firmly with Eloise, while Jean took the other and, laughing, they swept her off the pavement and across the road to the Regent Rooms.

Escape, it appeared, was no longer an option.

23

ROBYN

The day after the extremely stressful Sunday lunch with the Carringtons, I drove over to Mum's place once school was over. I'd enough worries what with my lesson planning, which, Mason had informed me, was not up to scratch, as well as with Sorrel's problems. The biggest elephant in the room – that which had come to light over lunch in Ilkley – I was refusing to even think about at the moment. Time for all that when I was back home with Fabian.

We'd left the restaurant as soon as we could, me driving the Porsche – very badly, convinced the one glass and a bit of champagne would have me over the limit – once I saw Fabian was pale and incapable of being at the wheel after developing one of his debilitating migraines. Concentrating on the early Sunday evening traffic, I'd allowed Fabian to drift off and, once home, he went straight to bed. For the first time ever, we slept turned away from each other, going to sleep without making love and without loving words.

I'd had a 7.30 a.m. start at school that Monday morning – Mason demanding an early staff meeting, where I knew he was going to be on the rampage about both planning and marking – and I'd left Fabian to sleep.

Mum, Jess and I had all insisted that Sorrel stay in bed instead of going to school, despite her insistence that she needed to be up and going through her routine for the audition that week.

'You're looking much better,' I now said, pleased to see that Sorrel was dressed and sitting on the sofa with Roger Rabbit, revising for her final mock exam the following day. 'D'you feel all right? Should we still have a word with the GP?'

'Since when can you actually get to see a GP these days?' Jess had immediately come round to Mum's. 'Look, I had a word with the doctor who was up at Hudson House this morning to see one of the old ladies. He was happy to give me some general advice about Sorrel. Good nutrition, plenty of sleep and, when she feels like it, go out for a walk. An iron tablet, just in case, and if she has a fever or heavy bleeding, that's when we get her to A & E.'

'She has youth on her side,' Mum said, 'but I'm not convinced she should be heading for London. I really don't think it's a good idea. What if something happens? What if she starts bleeding heavily? She shouldn't be dancing.'

'Will you stop talking over me as if I wasn't here?' Sorrel snapped. 'I'm fine.'

'You've been through an awful experience, darling,' Mum soothed. 'You shouldn't be going to this audition in London.'

'Good job I've cancelled it, then.' I folded my arms, looking directly at Sorrel.

'You've done *what*?' Sorrel's eyes immediately filled with tears. 'You'd no *right*. How could you, Robyn?' Tears streamed down her cheeks and Mum was immediately at her side. 'You're just jealous,' Sorrel sobbed. 'Of my chance of being in the West End... Just because you've had it... you'll never dance again...'

'You're not ready, Sorrel,' I said gently, taking her hand, which she immediately shrugged off. 'You won't do your best if you insist on going on Wednesday. So, you've got Covid...'

'I haven't got bloody Covid.' Sorrel stared at me through her tears. 'What are you talking about?'

'I rang the Susan Yates at lunchtime, told them you'd had Covid and needed to rest. So, the audition is postponed...'

'Why the hell didn't you say postponed instead of cancelled, Robyn?' Jess was cross. 'For heaven's sake.'

'Oh, really?' Sorrel took my hand again while wiping her tears with the other. 'Honestly?'

'It's on the Monday after now.' I smiled. 'The last audition of this round, apparently. You get yourself up and about, have a chance to get your hormones calmed down, and then we've a few days when we'll really go for it, putting you through your paces.'

'Thank you, thank you.' Sorrel grabbed hold of Roger Rabbit, burying her face in his fur.

'Right, I'm off,' I said, bending to kiss my little sister. 'I'll see you back at school later on in the week, Sorrel. Make sure you have your dance stuff with you all the time and we'll take it from there.'

Jess followed me out to the car. 'You OK?'

'OK?'

'Something's up. I know it is. I know you, Robyn.'

'A couple of things.' I sighed. 'This whole thing with Sorrel and Joel is getting to me, but with Sorrel convinced she was following Mum down the porphyria road, that's got me worried as well. Am I going to end up with the condition? Are you?'

'Pointless us worrying about it.' Jess was matter-of-fact. 'You'll worry your life away.'

'So, I want to know more about Mum's past.'

'Good luck with that.'

'She's agreed, for our sakes, that we can find out what we can.'

'Our sakes?'

'Try to find out if there's a history of the porphyria in her birth parents' families.'

'And how are you going to do that?' Jess shook her head.

'I always fancied being a detective.' I gave a little smile. 'Anyway, when I should have been at an English and drama planning meeting at lunchtime, I was ringing the Susan Yates school to plead on Sorrel's behalf.'

'What's that got to do with Mum's birth parents?'

'Absolutely nothing. Once I'd done that, I thought, sod it, I'm in enough trouble with Mason, might as well be hung for the proverbial—'

'Will you get on with it?' Jess looked at her watch. 'Is it because you're an actor, Robyn, you like to spin a tale out? Hold an audience?'

'Very likely.' I grinned. 'So, I spent the rest of lunchtime chatting with Jo Cooper, who's Head of History.'

'Right?'

'She has a little sideline business.'

'Oh?' Jess threw up her hands in frustration. 'What? Street walker? Another village drug dealer?'

'She traces people's family history.'

'Really?' That was enough to spark Jess's interest.

'Hmm, I told Jo what we already know, that Mum was born in Surrey. Gave her the birth date, adopted family name, that Mum's been told her mum was Indian – that should be a good clue.'

'Why don't we see if we can find the Foleys?' Jess's interest was really revving up now. 'I've always wanted to, but Mum was adamant we shouldn't.'

'Yes, let's.' Jess's excitement was contagious. 'You know, it's not just Mum's history – it's *ours* as well.'

'It shouldn't be difficult seeing as Adrian Foley was headteacher of St Mark's school in Sheffield. I'm going to start googling this evening.'

'Me too.'

'You? Thought you'd be feathering your new luuuurrrve nest with Fabian?' Jess laughed but stopped when she saw my face. 'What is it?'

'I met Alex Brookfield yesterday.'

'Who's he?'

'She.'

'OK, who's she/they/her?'

'A Leeds-based lawyer who's Joel's brief.'

'Oh, well, that's nice.' Jess paused. 'Isn't it?'

'Not only is she Joel's solicitor, she happens to be Gillian Carrington's best friend's daughter.'

'Cosy.'

'Oh, and yes, I forgot to mention, she's also Fabian's ex-girlfriend.'

* * *

Fabian's car wasn't parked up outside the cottage and, for once, I felt relief. Although only 6 p.m., it was pitch-black and spring seemed a long way off. I shivered, rubbing at my hands in their woollen mittens, and let myself in. With neither of us at home all day, there was an air of sadness to the place, which, only a couple of days previously, I couldn't have imagined. I filled the kettle and then thought, sod it, and instead took a bottle of white wine from the fridge, pouring myself a large glass. I lay on the cream carpet, propped myself up on cushions and wondered whether the sofa and chairs we'd chosen in John Lewis only two days earlier would still be needed. And why on earth the sudden – and obviously well-orchestrated (what an entrance!) – appearance of the very beautiful Alexandra Brookfield at The Beech Tree restaurant had been enough to make me doubt my relationship with Fabian.

'Hi.' Fabian, in dark suit, white shirt and carrying his briefcase, crossed the floor, not stopping to drop a kiss on my head as he normally would, but immediately making for the kitchen and the open bottle of wine.

'You feeling better? That's the second time now I've seen you almost out of it with a migraine. Good job I'd not drunk much more than one glass of champagne or we'd have been stuck in Ilkley.'

'I suffered a lot from them when I came back from Dijon after my year out from university.'

'Because you didn't want to come back?'

'Something like that.'

There was a lot about Fabian I still didn't know. When he didn't expand further, I said, 'So, why didn't you tell me?' I pushed myself up from the floor, pulled a hand through my mass of curls, which needed a good brush – probably a good cut too – remembered the huge hole I'd arrested with red nail varnish in my black woolly tights, and immediately crossed my legs to hide it. Next to Fabian's gleaming – if still a little pale – beauty, I felt dowdy, provincial, *teacherish*. I'd bet anything Alexandra Brookfield dressed for work in expensive little black suits and smart, crisp shirts, her caramel blonde hair shiny and fragrant, her legs clad in unladdered tights. Stockings, even?

'Tell you what, Robyn?' Fabian stood in front of me, looking down with raised eyebrows. 'What is it you want to know?'

'OK.' I took a deep breath, numbering off the points on my fingers. 'One: why didn't you let on that Alex was actually Alexandra? Two: why didn't you tell me you knew who Alex Brookfield was when Sorrel first told you she was Joel's brief?

And three: how special – and I quote your dear mother here – how special was your friendship with the woman?'

'Alex and I were together for two years.'

'Two years?' I stared, feeling my heart lurch.

'Yes.' Fabian was straightforward, stating the facts very much as I'd seen him do when he was in court. When I couldn't quite get out the words I wanted to say, he continued. 'Robyn, I am entitled to a life before I met you.'

'Of course you are. I would find it very strange if I was your first relationship...'

'So what's the problem?'

'You've never told me about Alexandra.'

'Because I knew what your reaction would be.' Fabian spoke calmly. 'You carry an aura of self-possession, of tenacity and independence but deep down, for whatever reason, you lack confidence. The minute an old girlfriend of mine turns up, you're running for the hills.'

'Rubbish!' I felt my pulse race, knowing there was more than a glimmer of truth in what Fabian was saying. 'And your mother and Julius cooked it all up between them that she'd swan in and make an appearance. It was all planned. A way to make me feel embarrassed, left out... Silly!'

'Yes.' Fabian nodded. 'But that's my problem. They're my family and their behaviour yesterday was unforgivable. I've already had words. As has Dad on your behalf.'

'Your mother wants you and Alexandra together again.' It was a statement rather than a question and I scowled across at Fabian.

Fabian nodded again. 'Yes. With Alexandra being the daughter of my mother's best friend, both families were delighted when Alex and I got together.'

'I bet they were.' Pictures of Fabian and Alexandra at family

Christmases; Fabian and Alexandra on family holidays; Fabian and Alexandra planning their future together crowded and fought for space in my head, and I shook it to dispel the images.

'And distraught when you were no longer a couple?'

'Yes.' Fabian drained his glass before reaching for the bottle to pour more wine.

'Should you be drinking after such a bad migraine?'

'What are you now? My doctor?' Fabian scowled back in return, but replaced the bottle on the floor without refilling his glass.

'So, were you childhood sweethearts or something?' I was determined not to let it go.

'Alex and I broke up last March.'

'*March?*' I stared. 'But that was just two months before we met.'

'It was.'

'No wonder your mother was so upset when I turned up at her charity do on your arm: Alexandra gone and me in her place.'

'Alex and I were on a break,' Fabian said. 'Trying to work out what we wanted. Where the relationship was going. If anywhere.'

'A break? How much of a break? A total rupture or just a fracture that needed a bit of a sticking plaster to make it mend and whole again? Could you be a little more specific, Fabian, please? And you didn't think to tell me this when you were intent on tracking me down at Graphite? When you were feeding me ice-cream kisses on the riverbank on our first date?'

'I didn't want to scare you off. Alex and I were on a break because I was unable to get my head around where Alex and I were going. What I wanted.'

'What do you mean where you were going? What you wanted?' The sick feeling I'd had all day didn't appear to be shifting at Fabian's explanation.

Fabian shrugged. 'I was already beginning to realise that continuing to defend murderers and violent rapists wasn't what I wanted. It was making me ill. Alex couldn't understand what I was feeling. I wasn't much fun to live with... She had a fling with one of her colleagues... I don't blame her... I wasn't in a good place...'

'Well, *I* blame her.' I was furious, hating the thought of Fabian being cheated on. Hated the beautiful blonde who'd done this to him. 'Were you terribly hurt?'

Fabian nodded. 'But I can only blame myself. I wasn't giving her any attention. I guess I was very depressed at where my work was taking me.' He smiled, reaching for my hand. 'But then I met you. You were utterly different from anyone I'd known before.'

'Well, yes, I've nail-varnished holes in my tights and a dysfunctional family.'

'Robyn, I fell in love with you. You *must* know that. You *do* know that.'

'But, Fabian, what the hell is she doing in Yorkshire? Joel's brief, for heaven's sake? Did she follow you up here?'

'Alex was at university in Leeds. She says – although I'm not convinced – she always loved this part of the country and, as her twin sister now lives in Ilkley—'

'Jesus, there's two of them?' Despite my anguish, I felt a little nervous chortle start and quickly swallowed it down. This was no time for laughter. 'Bloody hell, that's all I need – another one just like her.'

Ignoring me, Fabian continued. 'When we decided to call it a day, she took the opportunity to move up to be near her sister, taking a promotion with the large firm of solicitors that's dealing with Joel's case.'

'Bit of a coincidence, isn't it? And you didn't know?'

'I'd no idea who Joel's solicitors were. Why would I? I'd never even met Joel. Until today.'

'You've met Joel now? You've actually agreed to taking his case?' I stared, taking in the dark suit and briefcase at Fabian's feet.

'Not if you don't want me to.'

'Does it mean working alongside your ex?'

'Of course. That's what happens when solicitors appoint a barrister.'

I was silent for a while, mulling over the information Fabian had laid out in front of me. Then I said, 'When you came up to live with Jemima in Harrogate?'

'Yes?'

'And I didn't know you were living in Yorkshire?'

'Yes?'

'Did you start seeing Alex again then?'

Fabian sighed. 'Robyn, when you ran away back north, running back up here...'

'I wasn't exactly running – I'd badly injured my ACL, for heaven's sake.' I glared at him.

'...ran away back up here...' Fabian repeated calmly.

'Stop speaking to me like I'm in the dock,' I interrupted, knowing exactly where Fabian was heading.

'...blocking my calls, refusing to have anything to do with me? How long, Robyn? How long before you were in your headteacher's bed? Hmm? Hmm?'

When I didn't answer, Fabian smiled sadly. 'I rest my case, Robyn.'

24

LISA

It was a mistake coming down to the gym in the town centre thinking she'd be able to do what all these Lycra-clad bodies in front of her were putting themselves through. As a little girl she'd been pretty good at gymnastics, cartwheeling around the garden of the schoolhouse and doing handstands up against the wall, school uniform tucked into her knickers. Until Mother had told her to stop creating such an exhibition of herself; she was the headmaster's daughter, for heaven's sake, and she was to remember that. Did she really want the school porters to be viewing her underwear? It was pretty obvious, Mother said on more than one occasion, just from where she'd inherited this lewd behaviour. Her *real* mother – the dirty tramp – had obviously passed on her predilection for showing her knickers to all and sundry.

Lisa had gone into Father's study, from which she was barred, on pain of a slap, to look up both *lewd* and *predilection*, in the huge dictionary Adrian Foley kept in there. She had learned from the dictionary that her real mother was crude and offensive in a sexual way but then had to also look up both 'crude' and 'sexual'.

Not very nice words to describe her real mother. But then, as the seven-year-old Lisa conceded, she must have been a pretty awful woman not only to have given birth to her when she didn't have a husband, but to throw her away as well. Unwanted, *a half-caste* as Karen Foley so often reminded her (usually when she'd done something to disappoint – and that list was endless), she had been thrown out by the real mother. For years, Lisa thought she must have been thrown into a dustbin by the real mother, mingling amongst potato peelings, apple cores, scrapings from Sunday lunch plates, until she was rescued by Mother and Father and given the comfortable and Christian home and excellent education other unwanted little bastards could only dream of…

'Lisa?' A powerfully built young man stood in front of her, smiling. 'Shall we have a chat about what you want from the gym?'

'Oh, I'm not convinced I can do any of this.' Lisa looked longingly towards the main entrance, but the man – Ari, from his lanyard – just laughed.

'You look to be in pretty good shape already.'

'I do a lot of gardening,' Lisa said, following him into an office where he took an iPad and began punching in some details. 'I want to swim again, maybe do some classes?'

Ari nodded. 'Absolutely. If you've not done any gym work for a while…'

'Never, actually,' Lisa broke in. 'And, you need to know, I do have a medical condition.'

* * *

An hour later, not only had she been given a tour of the gym, she'd also tried out some of the machines, had a swim and a sauna and was now about to shower in really quite upmarket surroundings. Jayden had said, months ago, he'd pay for Lisa to join the gym, but she wanted some independence, wanted not to be beholden to Jayden Allen any longer, and had raided her savings to pay for the membership.

Gosh, this was fabulous, Lisa thought as she peeled off her wet swimsuit. She was actually here, had done a bit of a workout and was feeling good. More than good. Shy at first of stripping off in front of the other women in the communal changing room, she took a surreptitious look around. OK, there were the ubiquitous beautiful yummy mummies, highlighted hair swishing as they hoisted designer bags over shoulders, shouting loudly to Camilla, to Tia and to Darcy that they'd see them at school pick-up, and whose turn was it to book tennis? To host Supper Club next? But over in the corner were some of her own tribe: women in their late forties and fifties hiding middle-aged spread and stretch marks behind large fluffy white towels. Lisa rubbed at her long dark hair before moving over to the mirror to finish the job with a fancy blow-drier, which left her locks in soft tendrils round her elfin face. She gazed at her reflection before reaching for blusher and lipstick and the new mascara she'd read a review on in *The Sunday Times* and which, for once, totally lived up to the hype.

'Wow, you've long eyelashes.' One of the women from the oldies corner of the changing room was at her side, reaching for the styling wand Lisa had just replaced in its holder on the mirror.

'Thank you.' Lisa smiled. 'It's been a long time since I've treated myself to a new mascara.'

'Well, you look fabulous!' The woman smiled back.

'That's so kind, thank you. I've suddenly realised I'm over fifty and need to sort myself.' Why on earth was she telling a stranger this?

The woman stared. 'Over fifty? Goodness, I thought you were one of the school Right-on Rangers that take over the place every morning. Terrifying lot, they are. Mind you, I suppose you could still be one? Apologies – women do have their kids in their forties now, don't they?'

'Apparently.' Lisa pulled a face. 'I had my first two in my early twenties.'

'Well, you look bloody good on it. I'd have put you in your early forties; you've got some great genes there.'

'Wish I knew where these genes came from,' Lisa murmured, staring at her face in the mirror, suddenly feeling strange, confused.

'Sorry?' The woman looked confused herself, glancing at Lisa's Levi-clad bottom. 'Where they've come from? No,' she laughed, 'I meant genes not, you know... not your jeans.'

'I know. I know exactly what you meant. Gosh, I'm sorry. Offloading to a total stranger.' Lisa attempted a smile but still felt adrift. Here she was, at fifty-four, just beginning to emerge from years of not being able to do the things she wanted. But emerging from what? Who was she? Where had she come from? 'I don't know who I am,' she blurted out. 'I don't know any of my history. I don't know who I am,' she repeated.

'Oh, I'm so sorry, I've upset you.' The woman put out a hand.

'No, really, you haven't. I'm just so cross with myself for leaving it until now to try and find out who I actually am.' Lisa picked up her bag, slung it over her shoulder and smiled at the woman. 'Thank you,' she said. 'Really lovely to talk to you. Thank you.'

* * *

'Ms Allen? Lisa?' Lisa looked across at the 'in' turnstile as she was making her way towards the 'out'. For a split second, she couldn't work out why this incredibly good-looking man would know who she was.

'Oh, Mr Sattar.' She flushed, remembering the tirade she'd directed at him just a few days earlier at Hudson House. 'Hello, how are you?'

'Good, good, but all the better for seeing you.' He smiled, and for some strange reason Lisa felt her pulse race. 'Listen.' He made his way through the turnstile until he was standing at her side. 'Have you a minute?'

'Well, I was just on my way up to Hudson House. There's such a lot of work to be done in the garden...' Lisa trailed off. 'Mind you, not much point, I guess, seeing you're going to be in there with your bulldozers.'

Ignoring the rebuke, Kamran Sattar said, 'Do you fancy a coffee?' He indicated a hand towards the gym's coffee bar. 'I've a PT session, but it's not for half an hour.'

'PT?' Lisa pulled a face. Hadn't they done PT at infant school in yellow Aertex and big brown knickers?

'Personal Trainer.' Kamran smiled. 'I've been working so hard lately I've been neglecting the gym. New year, new resolutions...'

'New projects for the village?' Lisa realised that if she could think of Kamran Sattar as the enemy, as the man behind the redevelopment of St Mede's school and Hudson House and not as this gorgeous man who was making her pulse race, then she could converse with him on his level, find out more about what the Sattar brothers were up to. Arm both Robyn and Jess with information about what was going on in their respective places of work.

'Thanks, coffee would be great.' Lisa followed Sattar as he went to the bar. 'Flat white, please.'

'So.' Lisa went straight for the jugular once he sat down, placing a cup in front of her. 'What are your plans for Hudson House, Mr Sattar?'

'It's Kamran.'

'OK. Kamran. Your plans for Hudson House?'

'I honestly don't know yet.'

'Oh, come on, you don't honestly expect me to believe that?'

He smiled. 'OK, OK, I've a pretty good idea. I mean, we'd like to buy the place wholesale and then decide.'

'You're not prepared to tell me, are you?'

'No.' Kamran grinned across at her. 'I'm curious, Lisa. Why do you have such an interest in the place?'

'Apart from my daughter losing her job? Apart from the house being lovely and my not wanting to see an aspect of Beddingfield's industrial history go to the wall in the name of modernisation?'

'Of jobs for the locals?' Kamran raised an eye in her direction. When she didn't reply, he asked, 'What's your history, Lisa? I know Jess is your daughter yet you don't have the Yorkshire accent she has.'

'Eeh, lad, ah can put one on if yer want.' Lisa smiled. 'I was brought up in Surrey but moved to Sheffield when I was nine.'

'And your background?'

'My background?'

'How've you ended up here in Beddingfield.'

'I sometimes wonder.' Lisa smiled. 'No, it's wrong of me to say that. My husband and I came across the village by chance. I loved it...' She shrugged. 'Had my girls here and been here ever since.'

'You have a husband?' Kamran Sattar's eyes held her own. 'Still?'

'Actually, that's a moot point. I've *never* had a husband...' Lisa broke off as a tall, toned blonde in shocking pink appeared beside them.

'Ah, caught you! Coffee, Kamran! I thought we'd decided to cut it out?' The girl, arms folded, glanced from Kamran before focusing on Lisa.

'We all fall off the wagon sometimes, Tamsin.' He smiled, standing and stretching. 'Lisa, thanks for the company. I enjoyed our chat.' He held Lisa's eye for longer than was probably necessary, and she felt her heart skip a beat. This man was so gorgeous. Her pleasure in his company was dented only when she heard Tamsin laugh affectedly. 'Kamran, I never had you down as fancying older women!' And with a hand on his backside, she laid claim to him by kissing his cheek proprietorially.

25

ROBYN

'I'm not convinced we should just be turning up like this,' Jess said for at least the tenth time since we'd set off. 'I mean, what's the likelihood that the Foleys are still going to be here anyway? Still actually alive? They must be knocking on now, the pair of them. And it's eight o'clock already. Old people go to bed early. We should have left it until the weekend.'

'Mum has suddenly got a bee in her bonnet about this; wants to uncover her past, to find out more about the porphyria. And so do I,' I added. 'Jo at school got so excited about doing Mum's history,' I said. 'She's spent the past few evenings at her computer until two in the morning apparently, searching and researching.'

'She must be mad.' Jess pulled a face. 'And then up and teaching history to your horrible St Mede's kids after just four or five hours' sleep? What's she charging you for all this?'

'Mates' rates. She says it's totally addictive: you get taken down one route and then another opens.'

'Right.' Jess didn't appear overly interested in the intricacies of family history, parish records, electoral rolls and Ancestry.co.uk. Instead, she said, 'So, Robyn, you've kept pretty quiet about you and Fabian after this Alex Brookfield woman appeared out of the woodwork?'

'Fabian and I are being polite and skirting round each other. I do blame him, Jess, for not telling me about Alexandra. That he was practically engaged to her until two months before we met. If you must know, I'm furious that he kept her from me. I feel there's a side to him I just don't know.'

'And you told him all about Mason? That you'd had a couple of months' fling with him?'

'Yes, he knew about Mason.'

'You actually told him?'

I hesitated. 'Sort of.'

'Sort of?' Jess turned from concentrating on the road ahead through the now foggy darkness. 'What's that supposed to mean?'

'Can you watch the road?' I tutted. 'I just said Mason and I had become good friends during what had been an extremely difficult time in my life.'

'You didn't mention the sex, then?'

'Why would I?'

'Maybe the same reason Fabian didn't tell you about this Alexandra woman?' Jess gave me one of her speciality looks.

'Bit different.'

'Oh?'

'He was with her two years, Jess. Mason and I were friends for two months.'

'Enough already with the "friends".' Jess, stopped at a red light, air-quoted the words. 'You were in a sexual relationship with Mason. With your headteacher. So don't go all Julie Andrews on me now.'

'It's Fabian's bloody family again...' I started.

'You're not with his family, Robyn. You're with Fabian, And Fabian's fabulous.'

'Apart from him not thinking it appropriate to mention the ex.'

'Robyn, he's up here in Yorkshire with you; his family are in London. He's got his suit out – and on – and is taking Joel's case. Give the man a break.'

That shut me up and, unable to come back at Jess, I stared out of the window at the tall stone terraced houses in the residential area the satnav had now brought us to.

'You do know they're probably dead,' Jess said, breaking the silence. 'Or in a home?'

'The Foleys are on the electoral register from a few years back. They're obviously not at the same address as when Mum upped and left thirty-seven or so years ago with Jayden – that was the St Mark's school house address – but they've only moved a mile or so down the road...' I broke off as a somewhat austere school building set behind gates, but with acres of fields sporting both rugby and football posts, was suddenly in front of us. 'Hang on, slow down,' I instructed. 'Look, that's the school. St Mark's! That's it. How weird to think Mum was brought up here. And she never let on. Never told us she was educated at a public school. D'you realise, she's actually still Lisa Foley? I know she goes by the name of Allen, but in reality she's Foley.'

'No, that hadn't occurred to me.' Jess peered through the dark at the poorly lit road ahead. 'Just let me concentrate on this satnav.' Following instructions, she took a left, carried on a main road for a good five minutes and then turned onto a road of large gloomy Victorian villas.

'Over there,' I almost shouted. 'There, Jess, the green painted door. Pull up, there's a space.'

Jess drew up outside the house, but didn't switch off the

engine. 'Just remind me what we're saying if they answer the door? Hello, Grandma? Grandad?' Jess gave a nervous titter.

'We just tell them the truth. That we're Lisa's daughters and we need to know more about her condition.'

'Yes, but they won't know anything about her porphyria. She didn't have any symptoms of it until she was into her thirties.'

'Well, we'll explain all that,' I said. 'It's her birth family we want to know about. Let's just get inside. Play it by ear. Come on.'

'You sure about this?' Jess said as we walked to the door. 'I feel nervous now.'

'Me too. Mum said they were always pretty religious. Maybe we should say we're Jehovahs? The Sally Army? That we want to pray with them? Over them?' I started giggling.

'Don't be ridiculous.' Jess shot me a look. 'Act your age, Robyn.' Which made me titter more. She reached for the metal door knocker in the shape of a hand. Green with age, it resembled a grisly specimen at a murder enquiry and, once she'd given the door a good bang, Jess let go of it, repelled. 'They're coming. Look serious, kindly, interested...'

'Which one?' I panicked, trying each one on for size.

'All of them,' Jess whispered as the door slowly opened on us.

'Yes?' The stoop of the woman behind the slightly ajar front door belied her actual height. I could see she was, in fact, exceptionally tall for a woman in her eighties and of her generation. She narrowed her eyes suspiciously. 'What is it? I'm not buying anything. I'm not interested in your politics, if that's what you're about.'

'Is it Mrs Foley?'

'Who's asking?'

Jess glanced across at me and tried again. 'Mrs Foley? My name's Jessica Butterworth. This is my sister Robyn...' Jess swallowed and smiled. 'The thing is...'

'Mrs Foley?' I took over, trying the kind, social-worker-type smile Jess had suggested. 'Do you think we could possibly come in and have a chat?'

'Are you from the papers again? Because, if you are, I've nothing to say. I've said it all.'

'The papers?'

I hesitated and Jess, finding her second wind, announced in a too loud voice, 'Karen? May I call you Karen? We're Lisa's daughters. Lisa Foley's daughters.'

The woman stared and her hand on the door edge trembled slightly. 'She's dead.'

'No, really, Karen, she's not. She's alive and kicking and—'

'Dead to *me*,' the woman spat, attempting to close the door on us.

'Please, Karen, could we come in? We really need some information.'

'What sort of information?'

'What you might know about Lisa's birth mother and father?'

Karen Foley stared hard at us for a good few seconds before lifting a trembling hand to her head. 'I need to sit down...' She crumpled slightly, hanging onto the door for support.

'I'm so sorry, we've upset you,' Jess said, immediately taking charge again as though she were at work with the residents at Hudson House. 'Let me help you.' Jess gently pushed back the door, taking one of the woman's arms and indicating to me that I should take the other. 'Feeling a bit dizzy? Come on, Karen, we're here to help. Will you let us help you?'

'I'm fine.'

'I don't think you are,' Jess soothed. 'Is Mr Foley at home? A cup of tea? In here?' Jess guided the older woman into a room on the left where a TV was on, helping her into a chair, placing a cushion behind her back. 'Is the kitchen through here? Tea? Always helps, don't you think, Karen?'

'Don't leave me,' I mouthed at Jess. 'You sit and talk to her, and I'll make us some tea.'

'Is that all right, Karen?' Jess said, reaching for the woman's hand. 'Is it OK if my sister goes into the kitchen and makes us all some tea? You've gone very pale.'

Karen Foley nodded, her eyes closed, and I set off down the gloomy corridor in search of the kitchen. The house, despite the January cold outside, was stuffily warm. I opened a door on my right and tried the light switch on the wall, but to no effect, my heart immediately racing in fear as a pair of malevolent eyes met my own. The huge ginger tomcat glared in my direction before racing for the open door, brushing past me into the hallway and up the carpeted stairs beyond.

'Shit,' I said out loud. 'Biggest bloody cat I've ever seen.' I tittered nervously and was about to close the door on what I assumed to have been the dining room when a disturbance from the far corner of the room had me straining my eyes. Another cat? The room certainly smelt as if there was more livestock in there and, repulsed, I breathed shallowly against the rank odour as two more pairs of green eyes met my own. Hell, Karen Foley must be a cat lady. But cats didn't normally mutter, I conceded, as a stream of incomprehensible words followed by a couple of thuds reached my ears.

'Hello? I'm Robyn. I'm looking for the kitchen to make Karen some tea.'

More muttering and strange little grunts. Was there a lamp I could turn on? My vision becoming accustomed to the soupy, fetid gloom of the room, I saw a lamp on a table in front of me and switched it on, my eyes immediately drawn to a sort of chair bed and what, at first, I assumed to be a pile of blankets and clothes and on which were parked three more cats. I moved further into the room, realising that the pile was actually a person whose eyes were staring at me with as much hostility as the ginger tom a minute earlier.

'Hello, I'm Robyn. Er, we've just come to have a word with Mrs Foley about Lisa. Lisa? Lisa Foley's our mum, you see...'

I trailed off as the man's eyes bulged – actually bulged – and I could see he was paralysed down one side, his mouth twisted into a horrible grimace. 'Right, well, I'll be off then... to make this tea... I don't want to disturb you if you were sleeping...' I made my exit, pulling the door quietly to. Jesus, that was like something out of the film *Psycho*.

I found the kitchen through an adjacent door, hurriedly filled the kettle, took three of the upturned cups drying on the sink and found a tin marked TEA on the counter. I made tea in the cups, dropping a bag into each, found milk and hoped Karen Foley took milk but not sugar. Carrying the three cups of hot tea in my two hands, I sidled past the room with the cats and grimacing man – presumably Adrian Foley – and went back into the sitting room.

Karen Foley was sitting back against a couple of cushions, eyes closed, but she opened them as I stood in front of her, reaching for the proffered cup and gulping at the scalding liquid as if her life depended on it.

'I've just been telling Karen here what a good life Lisa has had, settling in Beddingfield and mum to us three girls,' Jess said, indicating with a nod of her head that I should sit on the other side of Karen. 'Apart from the horrible porphyria, of course.'

'Karen, are you able to tell us anything about Lisa's birth family?' I asked. 'The thing is, this porphyria is possibly genetic – you know, could be passed on down to me or my sisters. We'd really like to know if you had any idea whether Mum's birth mother or father could have been a carrier.'

'I really don't know what you're talking about. I've never heard of this porphyria. Lisa probably made it all up to get attention; she was always attention seeking.'

'OK.' Jess smiled, encouragingly. 'Can you tell us anything about who Lisa's birth mother was, then, Karen?'

There was a good thirty seconds' silence while Karen appeared to make some decisions. Eventually, she said, 'I can tell you as much as you want to know about that mother of yours.'

'OK?' Jess's voice was gentle. 'We'd love to know more.'

Karen went to speak, but then suddenly swung round to look at me. 'You look like her,' she said, staring and pointing a finger. 'Apart from the hair. Lisa had long straight hair. I cut it off because it did nothing but make her think she was better than everyone else; everyone telling her how beautiful it was. How beautiful and talented she was. Vanity is such a sin; the good Lord teaches us that.' Before I could reply, Karen turned back to Jess. 'But you don't look like her. Take after that scruffy black man she ran off with, I suppose? And there's another one of you at home? Three girls? I wanted boys... she should have been a boy...' She broke off, her eyes wide and quite scary. Mad. 'Boys are so much easier than vain, affected little girls who think they know it all. And who men drool over. Well, they don't. And, I'm telling you now, they're not.'

'Not what, Karen?' Jess's voice was gentle.

'Not what everyone thinks they are,' Karen cackled. 'Lisa, the little tramp, was a thief.'

'No! I don't think so!' Jess's face was scarlet. 'No! Mum is one of the most honest people I know.'

'Just proves how much you don't know, then,' Karen sneered. 'You ask her. Ask her about the thieving from shops. How we had to go down to Sheffield city police station when she'd been caught with all that make-up.'

Stunned, Jess and I took refuge in our tea. When Karen said nothing further, the gloating smile still on her face, I asked, 'Is that Lisa's father in the other room?' Jess, unaware of his presence, looked up in surprise.

'Mr Foley, yes.'

'He doesn't appear too well.'

Karen snorted. 'Of course he's not well. Would you be well if you'd had such a miscarriage of justice hanging over you all these years?'

'A miscarriage of justice?' We both leant in.

'Are you sure you're not from *The Courier*?' Karen's eyes narrowed. 'Four years, he was given.'

'A prison sentence?' I breathed. 'For what?'

'I told you,' Karen said crossly. 'Adrian was innocent. He did nothing. He's a headmaster, for heaven's sake. Of one of the most prestigious schools in the country.'

'Well, not any more, Karen,' Jess said gently, not sure what to say next. 'I'm sure he must have retired years ago.'

There was another good minute's silence and I wondered if we should be going. 'Do you have any photos of Mum?' I eventually asked. 'You know, as a little girl? We've never seen any.'

'I do not,' Karen snapped crossly. 'I burnt any we did have – school photos and the like – once she turned out to be a trollop. Just like that mother of hers.'

'Oh, so you did know Lisa's birth mother?' I said quickly, seizing the opportunity.

'Of course, I did. I wasn't likely to take on the bastard child of just anyone.'

'She was of Indian descent, I believe? Mum's birth mother?'

For a few seconds Karen looked puzzled and then offered up

another little smile. 'I told her that because I didn't want her finding out who her mother really was. I didn't want her snooping, going off to find her like they all do, these adopted children. They're given a good home, a good Christian upbringing and then what do they do once they turn eighteen? Go searching and upsetting people. After all we'd done for the ungrateful little bitch. The top education she received. The good, God-fearing home we gave her.'

'So, Karen, would you tell us what you do know about Lisa's birth mother, then?' I asked, smiling encouragingly, despite the old woman's vitriol.

'She was always asking the same.'

'Who was?'

Karen Foley waved her empty cup angrily at us. 'Lisa, of course – that so-called mother of yours. Can't imagine she was any good at it, being a mother.' She cackled again. 'Oh, she might have had a beautiful face, might have been clever academically – and she *was*, Mr Foley made sure of that – but she was sly, that one, sly and manipulative, always wanting to *know*. To know... to find out...' The woman leaned back, clutching at the arms of the chair.

'What was it she wanted to know, Karen?' I asked.

Karen glared at me. 'She wanted to know where she'd come from. Who her real mother was. But there was no way I was letting on how we ended up with her.' She cackled almost maniacally. 'D'you think we were mad?'

* * *

'Yes, I do think you're mad, Karen Foley!' I fastened my seat belt, speaking for the first time after leaving the house. 'Mad as a bloody hatter. Poor Mum, being brought up by those two.'

'Oh, Robyn, she was horrible.' Jess sat back in the driver's seat, not attempting to start the engine.

'You didn't see the old man in the dining room. He was like something out of a horror film. All twisted and... and bulging eyes. He's obviously had some sort of stroke. I wonder if they get any help. Are social services involved?'

'Not your problem. Don't go there,' Jess said angrily. 'Poor Mum.'

'So, her mum wasn't from India? Which means her dad must have been, then?'

Jess shrugged. 'I don't think I'd believe *anything* Karen Foley says. She probably changes her story all the time. And what on earth was that about Mum being a thief?'

'Well, I certainly don't believe that! Interesting though, about Adrian Foley. Headteacher of one of the most prestigious public schools in the country and yet he ended up doing four years in prison.'

Jess turned on the ignition, resetting her satnav back to Beddingfield. 'You don't think he was some sort of... you know...?' Jess trailed off. 'You don't think he was *inappropriate* with the kids in his care?'

'Well, it won't be difficult to find out more. Hang on...' I reached for my bag, taking out the phone. 'I'll google him.'

'Can you do that without being car sick?' Jess glanced across. 'I couldn't.'

'Out of battery,' I said crossly, tossing it back into my open bag. 'We're not getting very far, are we?'

26

JULY 1968

Eloise

The large, red-faced bouncer on the door of the Regent Rooms nodded at Janice, Gail, Eileen and Jean, glancing briefly at their membership cards before allowing them in.

'Hang on, are you a member, love?' He stepped in front of Eloise, barring access as she attempted to follow the others.

'Er...' Eloise glanced towards Janice for help. If she wasn't a member, she wouldn't be able to go in, she thought. Then she could get a taxi back to the safe haven of Maude's cottage.

'She's with us,' Janice called over her shoulder. 'Give her a guest pass, Roy, and if she likes it, she'll get a member's card next time. She's posh, is Eloise. You should be bloody grateful to have her in this crummy place. Don't you dare turn her away. If she doesn't get in, none of us are coming in. We'll be off to Moonlight instead.'

'She is that.' Roy grinned admiringly, his small eyes moving over every part of Eloise's body until she felt herself grow hot with embarrassment. 'Don't know where you've come across this one, Janice,' he added, the sweaty hand tapping at Eloise's backside apparently giving the consent needed to follow the others. 'Right, you're in, love, and I'm out here all night if you get lonely.' He leered in Eloise's face and she hastily followed Janice into a darkened, smoke-filled room, a DJ at one end, stairs, apparently leading down to a bar, at the other.

Janice and the others immediately made their way to an adjacent flight of red swirly-patterned-carpeted stairs, Eloise following in their wake, her shoes lifting stickily with each step. The door at the top opened to reveal a bank of washbasins and mirrors, each surrounded by a posse of girls backcombing hair, spraying Elnett, adding more black to already darkened eyes and pale colour to pouting lips.

'Bloody hell, watch what you're doing,' a fiery redhead was saying to another girl. 'The bloody stick's gone in me eye now.'

'Well, get out the way, then, stop hogging the mirror – let someone else in.'

The mixed pungent smells of Youth Dew – Eloise recognised her mother's choice of perfume – Coty's Masumi and the smell of urine from a broken-down toilet on her left were making Eloise feel sick. She stood on the periphery of the restroom, not sure what to do, but eventually reached into her bag for the one piece of make-up – a pink lipstick – she had with her, taking her time to outline and fill her lips, copying how the other girls completed the task.

'Hey—' one of the girls she didn't recognise broke off from applying yet another layer of pan stick to her face '—that lad from the carding shed – you know, that right good-looking Asian lad – is here.'

'*Here?*' Several of the girls turned in surprise. 'Why? What's *he* doing here? I've never seen any of his lot in here before.'

'Well, he won't be here to dance, will he? Or drink. I don't think they're allowed, are they? Isn't it against their religion?'

'Yes, I've seen him too. He's wandering round with that camera of his,' another girl said.

'His camera? There aren't any birds in here, are there?' Eileen started laughing. 'Not the feathered type anyhow.'

'Ugh, that's weird. He's not taking *my* photo.' The redhead pulled a face. 'My Ronnie would soon be after him if he caught one of that lot looking at me; taking photos of me.' She fluffed up her hair in the mirror, admiring her reflection.

'He's a superb photographer. I've seen some of his stuff. Why wouldn't you want him photographing you?' Janice frowned.

'Well, you know.'

'No. What?' Janice wasn't letting the girl's racist remarks go.

'Well, it's not right, is it? One of them taking pictures of us.'

'Would you let David Bailey take photos of you?' Janice asked.

'Yeah, course, don't be daft.' The redhead was indignant. 'I'd strip off to me knicks if he could get me to be a model.'

'So, Junayd, like David Bailey, is a man. Yes?' Janice was warming to her theme.

'Yes?'

'And Junayd is as good looking as, if not better looking than, David Bailey?'

'Suppose.'

'I think he looks like Omar Sharif,' Eileen started. 'You know, in *Doctor Zhivago*...?'

'He doesn't look anything like Omar Sharif, Eileen,' Janice snapped. 'Omar Sharif is Egyptian for a start, and much older: he must be pushing forty. Junayd Sattar is only our age.'

'I wouldn't know.' The redhead turned to her mates, tutting and pulling a face towards Janice in the mirror.

'Well, I'm telling you, he is.' Janice was cross. 'And you're being downright prejudiced.'

'Oh? And what's that supposed to mean?' The redhead turned, squaring up to Janice, who stood her ground.

'It means judging someone on their skin colour, not on what's inside them.' Janice's face was almost the colour of the other girl's hair. 'It means you're uneducated...'

'Oh yeah? You're just as uneducated as me, Janice Atkinson, leaving school at fifteen, so don't get all high and mighty, full of yourself, with me.'

'Yes, well... well... I'm doing O levels at night school...' Janice trailed off as Jean, Gail and Eileen all turned in surprise.

'Are you?' Gail said, giving Janice such a look, Eloise almost wanted to laugh. 'What for?'

'Because I want to travel. I want to be a travel agent. I don't want to work at Hudson's all my life, get married and have a load of kids while my husband's down the pub. Or...' Janice paused '... I might even try to be a teacher.'

'A teacher?' Eileen laughed out loud. 'You're mad. What do you want to be a bloody teacher for? We hated school.'

'*I* didn't. I liked it.'

There was silence for a split second before the girls who'd obviously been at St Mede's Sec Modern with Janice started to laugh. 'Oh, you daft bugger, Janice.' Eileen took her arm. 'Cut it out. Come on, "Jumpin' Jack Flash" is on. I need to dance.'

* * *

Eloise spent the next hour trying to work out how she should be dancing. She followed the moves of the other girls as they bopped and gyrated in a big circle, handbags in the middle of the dance floor. Lads gathered at its edge, watching, laughing and occasionally breaking free from their group – usually in a pair – to herd a couple of girls they obviously fancied out of the circle. Goodness, Eloise thought, it was all a bit different from marking your dance card at the start of the evening. She watched as, one by one, Eileen, then Jean and then Gail were separated from the group, had a couple of token dances with their captors before following them down to the bar where they remained.

She and Janice were left on the dance floor with several other girls Eloise didn't know and, after Janice had rebuffed the attention of several potential suitors, Eloise realised the other girl was not prepared to leave her. When Eloise recognised, at the edge of the dance floor, smoking and laughing with his mates, the boy from Hudson's, the one who Janice obviously had a thing for, Eloise made a decision.

'Look, go and say hello to him,' she instructed Janice. 'I can look after myself. I'm desperate for the lavatory, to be honest.' With an encouraging smile in the boy's direction, she picked up her handbag and moved through the crowd back to the stairs and the ladies' restroom. Once in there, she leaned her head against the cool mirror and then, as the door opened and a gaggle of girls came in, fled into one of the cubicles.

'Did you see that beautiful blonde girl on the dance floor?' one was saying. 'Hair up in a ribbon to match the fabulous pink flowered Mary Quant dress? It must have cost a fortune.'

'Do you think she was a model? Up from London or Manchester?'

'All the lads were looking at her.' The girl laughed. 'Not one of them dared to make a move on her. Oh, to be as gorgeous and upmarket as that...'

'In your dreams, Barbs. Come on, I'm going to get more lagers down me and then I'm going to ask Kevin Conlon to dance...'

The restroom door banged shut and Eloise, who'd been holding her breath, slowly exhaled then left the cubicle while wondering how to make an exit from the club. She stole a look in the long mirror, smeared now with make-up. Had those girls been talking about her? She looked at the blonde hair, the pink ribbon, at the pink-and-white Mary Quant dress. Her face, alive and pretty, seemed to belong to someone else.

'Hello, Eloise Hudson,' she murmured at her reflection and then, feeling foolish, looked at her watch – 10.30 p.m. Granny Maude would be getting worried. She left the restroom, standing at the top of the stairs to watch the people down below. The crowd was thinning out, probably heading to the bar for last orders. She scanned the room looking for Janice and was delighted to see she was now chatting to the boy she'd had her eye on. Good, she could make her goodbyes and get herself a taxi from the rank outside the nightclub. Or would one of the doormen do that for her? Or was that just at Claridge's in London? She smiled, remembering a trip to the capital city with Maude a couple of years back when they'd stayed at the hotel. They'd been to the theatre and had dinner at the revolving Post Office Tower restaurant where Mick Jagger and Chrissie Shrimpton were also dining. Gosh, that had been exciting. Maude had become quite animated, and Eloise had had to restrain her from going over for a chat with the pair.

Eloise headed for the door, wanting to catch Janice's attention, worried suddenly about how she was going to return the dress. What if Janice wanted to wear it the following day?

'Oh, are you going?' Janice was immediately by her side, concern etched on her face. 'Are you all right? I thought you must be with the others.'

'No, no, honestly, please, don't worry about me. I'm going to get a taxi.' Eloise could see the other girl was torn between going with her to the taxi rank and accompanying the boy as he began to turn away. 'I'm fine, really.'

'You've got money for a taxi?'

'Yes. I'm just worried about your dress.'

'Why?' Janice laughed and the boy caught hold of her hand, smiling down at her. Eloise felt a flash of something. Envy? Lust? Sadness? The recurring dream that so often was there, the images always tantalisingly disappearing before she could form them into a tangible memory on waking? 'Just bring it with you to work on Monday. You sure you're OK?'

'Oh, absolutely! Utterly fine.' While she did her best to smile and reassure Janice, Eloise herself wasn't convinced. How ridiculous, here she was at seventeen and had never taken a taxi by herself. Did she have to jump out into the road and shout 'Taxi' as Maude had done so efficiently and imperiously on Bond Street?

Eloise made her way past a couple locked around each other on the stairs, the boy's hand burrowing under the girl's skimpy shirt in the manner of an enthusiastic mole; on past a pair arguing, the girl sobbing as she pulled at the boy's reluctant hand. She skirted round Roy the doorman, who suddenly jumped out at her, leering, his own red sweating face just inches from her own.

'Where's your mates, love? If you hang around for another half an hour, I'll give you a lift home.' Eloise smiled politely, declining the man's offer as she left through the main exit. Avoiding a pool of vomit and three football-chanting men, she set off towards where she thought the taxi rank was.

She walked through the Saturday-night revellers, the bus queues full of hot-dog-eating men and women, and Eloise, who'd always been censured that to eat in the street was appallingly bad manners, was quite taken aback. She really had no idea where she was going and eventually braved a posse of girls, asking if they could point her in the direction of a taxi rank.

'What's wrong wi't'bus?' one of them jeered through a mouthful of fried onion and tomato ketchup, a couple of specs of masticated hot-dog landing on Eloise's neck and dress.

'Are you all right?' The boy with the camera from the mill was suddenly at her side, taking her arm gently and leading her away from the bus-stop horde.

'Oh, hello!' Eloise said brightly. Too brightly. 'I don't really know the geography of the town centre. I'm trying to find a taxi. I believe I should be looking for a rank?'

'You're going in totally the wrong direction,' the boy said. 'You need to be up at the railway station. Come on, I'll walk you there; you look as if you're about to be eaten alive by this lot.'

'Oh, that is so kind,' Eloise said gratefully, doing an about-turn as she followed him. 'I'm Eloise,' she added.

'I know exactly who you are,' he said without smiling.

'It's Junayd, isn't it? I believe you've been at the Regent Rooms this evening?'

He nodded. 'I saw you there.'

'Oh? Really?'

'You looked out of your depth.'

'I think I was really. I'm not convinced I'll repeat the experience.' And then, worried that the boy might think her snobbish, above herself, added, 'I rather enjoyed myself though.'

He laughed out loud at that. 'You looked as if you were about to be executed, to be honest.'

'Really? Oh dear. I'll try harder next time. If there *is* a next time.'

'You look very different tonight from when you scared my thrush away.'

'Oh, I'm so sorry about that. Yes, I've been with Janice from the mill – this is her dress.'

'She's OK, is Janice. She'll speak to me when others won't.'

'Who won't speak to you?'

'Oh, Eloise, come on, you must know your dad's workers from Pakistan are looked down upon by the rest of the shop floor.'

'I can't imagine why,' Eloise said hotly.

'You can't?' The boy gave a bark of laughter. 'Come on, Eloise. "Ovver 'ere, tekking what's ours! Tekking our jobs? Foreigners? Eating all that curry muck?"' The boy adopted a broad Yorkshire accent totally at odds with his appearance. He might be wearing Levi's and a shirt, but his dark good looks were very different from the pale-skinned, fair-haired Yorkshire-born youths they were now walking round and through. 'So, tell me about your camera. Your photography.'

'I'm just starting, really. Granny bought me the camera as a late birthday present.'

'It's a good one. You must know that.' Junayd smiled down at her.

'Oh, I do, but I'm going to need some lessons on its finer points. So, what were you doing at the Regent Rooms this evening?'

'I've become pretty good friends with the editor of the *Midhope Examiner*'s son.'

'Oh?'

'We met doing A levels at night school. David had been at the boys' grammar school, messed about, failed all his exams and his dad said he'd have to retake them at night school, which he did. He's at Bradford University now, training to be an optician. Anyway, when David's dad is short of a photographer – and so many from the *Examiner* are off on holiday at the moment – I get a note through the door asking me to step in.

There was some celebration going on at the Regent Rooms this evening, so I went along with the features writer and took a load of pictures.'

'Oh? And did you pass your exams too?'

'I've another couple of years to do. Starting from scratch and doing them part-time takes a lot longer than simply doing resits.'

'That must be dreadfully hard, working in the carding shed all day and then off to do A levels at night?'

'My dad's convinced I'm going to be an engineer or even a doctor.'

'And you're not?'

'We're here,' Junayd said, ignoring her question, but taking her hand and running across the road towards the town's railway station where a line of white taxis was waiting for customers. 'There you go, you're safe now.'

'How are you getting home?' She turned to look into Junayd's face, struck once again by his beautifully chiselled features, his dark brown eyes, his dark hair.

'I live just at the other side of the bus station. Where all the newcomers live. The Irish and Poles have moved on and upwards. It's the turn of the West Indians and us now.'

'You sound slightly cynical.' Eloise was proud of that word.

'I suppose I am. Workers are invited here from the old British Empire to fuel the local industries – to keep Britain going – but we're not appreciated. And downright frowned upon if we try to get the education we have to have in order to move up in life.'

'I'm sorry.'

'Sorry? Why on earth should you be sorry? Oh, because of who your dad is?'

'I suppose so.' Eloise paused and then, knowing her face was aflame, suddenly asked: 'I say, I know this is awfully cheeky of me, but would you perhaps give me some lessons?'

'Lessons? Oh, with the camera?' Junayd frowned. 'What would your dad and your brother say if they knew about that?'

'I think they'd be delighted,' Eloise lied.

'I think they'd be horrified, Eloise.' Junayd stared at her, taking in the earnest face, the full mouth with its long upper lip, the naturally streaked blonde hair that was beginning to escape from its pink ribbon. 'Encouraging me to teach you to use your camera would never be on their agenda. And you know it.' He turned and, before Eloise could thank him properly, he was gone.

27

ROBYN

'So?' Mum, looking after Lola in Jess's absence, had been standing watching at Jess's sitting-room window for us to return from Sheffield. Once she saw Jess's car pull up in the drive, she was at the open front door waiting for us.

'Let us get in, Mum,' I called up the drive. 'Is the kettle on?'

'So?' Mum asked again once we were inside.

'Oh, Mum.' I went straight in for a hug. 'You poor thing, having her for a mother.'

She didn't say anything but sat down heavily on the sofa and then jumped up again, going to the kitchen and filling the kettle noisily as if, by this action, she could rid herself of unpleasant memories. I checked my phone once again. There was nothing from Fabian. But then, why should there be? He'd gone back over to Harrogate to help Bruce put together a particularly puzzling flatpack wardrobe that Jemima had earlier given up on. Said he would stay and eat with them. I just hoped Alexandra Brookfield wasn't helping as well.

'So?' Mum demanded a third time and I could see her hands, tucked around the mug for warmth, were trembling.

'Yes, they're both in Sheffield, and at the address Jo gave us from the electoral roll,' I said.

'I thought they might have gone back to Surrey.'

'Mum, where's your birth certificate?' I turned to Jess. 'Oh, for God's sake, why didn't we ask Karen Foley for the birth certificate?'

'Because she'd never have given it to you.' Mum pulled a face. 'Don't you think *I* asked? And searched for it? She said it was lost in the move from Surrey. The Foleys didn't tell me for years that I was adopted and then, I can't remember how, it somehow came out. Mother just said I was lucky, that I'd been chosen and given a good Christian home and the best education ever that no other *little bastard* like me could ever dream of.'

'She didn't call you that?' Jess was horrified.

'And the rest.'

I shook my head. 'Mum, she's horrible.'

Lisa gave a mirthless laugh. 'Is it any wonder I tried to forget about her? Got out as soon as I could? And him? Adrian Foley? He was just as bad.'

'In what way?'

'Unpleasant, spiteful, cruel.'

'Cruel? Did he… you know… did he hurt you?'

'He hurt me with words.' To my horror, big fat tears rolled down Mum's cheeks unchecked. 'What did he say to you? I can't imagine he welcomed you in, once he knew who you were.'

'Mum, he's in a bad way,' I said, taking her hand. 'He must have had a stroke, I think. Paralysed down one side and couldn't speak. Surrounded by his cats.'

'Cats?' Mum pulled a face of disbelief. 'Cats! He hated dogs and cats. But particularly cats.' She frowned, obviously remembering. 'I always wanted a cat but he said they were filthy creatures…' She broke off and gave a slightly maniacal giggle. 'This'll be Mother getting her revenge; she never let anything go without getting her own back. He's paralysed? Can't move? So, she brings a load of cats into his room, probably onto his bed? On his pillow...?' Mum brought a shaking hand to her open mouth, her eyes wide.

'Revenge for what?' Jess leaned forward, taking Mum's other hand.

'Adrian Foley embezzled funds from St Mark's, from day one, apparently. He was sentenced to four years for fraud, theft.'

'Oh, that's why he'd been in prison?' I stared. 'He'd been fiddling the school finances; hiving off money? And you knew this, Mum?'

'It was in all the papers. About fifteen years ago. The Sunday tabloids went to town on him.'

'Did Jayden know?'

'Yes, of course. I made him promise not to tell you girls.'

'But why not?'

'It was nothing to do with you and I didn't want reminding of him. He was in my past. I began to realise – probably didn't realise until after I'd left – that she hated me. Not because of anything I'd done, I don't think. It was because she was jealous of me; didn't want Adrian Foley to have any sort of relationship with me. She is exceptionally warped, is Karen Foley. Father would take me off to his office to drum Latin and maths into me and, in revenge for him daring to spend so much of his time on me, she'd sit me down and make me read and learn great tranches of the Bible "for my own good" or, later, as punishment.'

'Punishment for what?'

'I wasn't the easiest child to bring up.' Mum gave a little smile. 'When you're denied love and affection, you'll do anything to get attention. The thing was, I was pretty bright: I loved school, loved the teachers who were particularly kind to me, especially as I was the head's daughter. There were some perks to being Adrian Foley's daughter.' Mum gave another little laugh, but devoid of all humour. 'I became his protégée, I suppose – he was determined I'd go to Oxbridge like he had.'

'Bloody hell, Mum,' Jess breathed. 'It's like something out of a Victorian novel. You sure you weren't locked up in the red room like Jane Eyre?'

'Oh, the pair of them would certainly send me to my room to "contemplate my misdemeanours" if I didn't eat everything on my plate; didn't get full marks in a spelling test; forgot to do—'

'Mum,' I said gently, 'Karen said you'd been shoplifting.'

'Yes.' Mum's voice was calm, but her face flushed scarlet. 'Another reason I didn't want you girls to go hunting to find out things about my background. It's not something I'm proud of. When Sorrel started misbehaving, I sort of assumed genes would out.'

'Did you get into trouble with the police then?'

'No, it was only once.'

'Mum, loads of kids do a bit of shoplifting,' I said.

'*I* never did,' Jess countered.

'Well, me neither,' I mused. 'So just once? Karen Foley made out you were a total tealeaf.'

Mum tutted, shaking her head. 'She would. I got friendly with a girl down the road when I was fifteen... now, she *was* light-fingered. We were in Boots in Sheffield city centre and they knew her. Security came and sent for the police because they were fed up of her nicking all the Rimmel make-up. I'd taken a lipstick too. They called the Foleys.'

'Not the most heinous of crimes, Mum,' Jess said.

'No, but I was made to feel like a mass murderer. They reminded me of it at every turn. Which, when you think how much Adrian Foley stole...' She gave another mirthless laugh.

'So, more importantly, are we any further forward finding out who my birth mother might be?'

'Oh, gosh, yes.' I suddenly remembered. 'Your birth mum was white. Presumably from Surrey. It was your dad who must have been originally of Indian heritage.'

'Oh, really?' Mum's eyes widened. 'Mother liked me to believe my birth mother was Indian and had been done away with in an honour killing. It was a horrible thing to think about. So, I didn't. Goodness.' She was silent for a long time. 'I really want to find out more now.'

'Are you OK, Mum?' I asked. 'Do you want me to stay with you tonight?'

'No, no, of course not. Sorrel's here, and why on earth would you want to be back in the box room when you've Fabian waiting for you?' Mum laughed.

'Is Sorrel OK?' I asked, ignoring Mum's question.

'She is.' Mum smiled. 'I'm keeping an eye on her. Miscarriage is a horrid experience for any woman to go through, but particularly a young girl. Don't forget it's her birthday next month. Sweet sixteen. Right, I'm away.' Mum stood and then turned to back to Jess and me. 'I want to find out more now, girls. I want to know everything. Everything!'

28

LISA

The following morning Lisa didn't know what to do with herself. Sorrel had insisted she was fine and able to be back at school so, after dropping her off at the school gates, she decided she'd head to Hudson House. She knew there were jobs to do in both her own and Jess's garden, but she wanted the company that Radio 4 wasn't able to give her. She hoped getting stuck into little tasks at the care home might be an antidote to the myriad flashbacks Robyn and Jess's visit to Sheffield had reignited.

The home was a carer down. Jess, unsure whether, in the light of the Sattars' move on the place, she should be employing a permanent member of staff, had turned to an agency, who weren't overly helpful. There'd be plenty of little jobs Lisa could assist with and, while she also packed the new gym kit she'd treated herself to, she was happy to be with people who needed her company and her help.

It was lovely when the staff – Bex, Stephie and Azir – greeted her, obviously pleased to see her and have her there. Lovelier still, when the residents made their way over to pat at her arm, hold her hand, call her over to their chair or even salute her, as Geoffrey always did.

'Where's Eloise?' Lisa asked when Jess asked if she'd assist in the kitchen with morning coffee.

'I don't know.' Jess turned to Stephie, who was emptying biscuits from a packet onto plates. 'Stephie? Have you seen her?'

'Couldn't get her out of bed this morning,' she replied. 'She said she was tired and wanted a lie-in.'

'We could do with getting her up and dressed,' Jess said. 'Her daughter's just phoned to say she and Eloise's husband are coming over shortly. Any chance they get to be critical of her care and they'll be in there.'

'Do you want me to go up to Eloise?' Lisa asked. 'See if I can persuade her to get herself dressed and her make-up on?'

'Would you, Mum?' Jess was harassed. 'I've so much to do. That all right with you, Stephie?'

'Sure.' She grinned, stuffing another Garibaldi into her mouth. 'I'm better down here.'

'Yes,' Jess sniffed. 'But just leave something for the paying guests, if you don't mind.'

* * *

Lisa made her way up to Daffodil floor where those with some dementia had their rooms, walking along the carpeted corridor until she came to Eloise's room and knocked.

'Can I come in, Eloise? It's Lisa.'

'Lisa? Oh, Lisa, yes, yes...'

'You know who I am?'

'Yes, of course, you're Granny Maude's gardener.'

'That's right.' Lisa smiled, remembering Jess's instructions to go along with what people with dementia believed to be the case.

'Are you feeling tired this morning, Eloise?' Lisa looked at her watch. 'It's nearly eleven. Did you have a bad night?'

'I don't want to go to Canada, Lisa,' Eloise said, struggling to sit up.

'Have to say, Eloise, it's never really been on my wish list either.' Lisa smiled, lying through her teeth – it was the one country she'd always aspired to visit. 'I'm not keen on the cold and snow, although I believe it's a very beautiful country.'

'It's a despicable place.'

'Oh?' Lisa moved to help Eloise as she swung her legs from the bed and headed to the shower.

'Despicable. And, I really don't need the gardener helping me to dress. I'm not going, you know.'

'You don't have to, if you don't want to,' Lisa called from the other side of the room's en suite door. 'Can I help you in there?'

'Absolutely not.' There was a minute's silence and then: 'Are you saying I can stay with you?' Eloise's hand and then her blonde head appeared back round the bathroom door.

'Of course you can, if you want.' Lisa hoped she was saying the right thing.

'Well, don't tell Granny. She's booked the tickets.'

'Oh? To see what? A film? The opera?'

'You know perfectly well what. She'll have told you; she tells you everything.' Eloise stared, obviously confused. 'You're not Granny.' She continued to stare. 'Your skin is the same colour as Junayd's.'

'Junayd?' Lisa encouraged.

'Shhhh. Don't let Mummy know...'

'It's all right, Eloise. I won't tell her.'

'Well, somebody did.' Eloise, still in her nightdress, suddenly crumpled and made her way back to the bed, sitting down beside Lisa, who took her hand. 'She knew about the baby.'

'The baby?'

'My little boy. Mummy told Granny to take me to Canada. They came up with the idea between them. And nobody knew, not even Daddy.'

'You had a baby boy?' Lisa asked, staring at the other woman. 'In Canada?'

'Yes.' Eloise glared in Lisa's direction.

'And where is he now, Eloise?'

Eloise shook her head. 'In Canada, I suppose. He must be quite a big boy now. I've never stopped thinking of him, you know.'

'I bet you haven't. When was he born?' Lisa moved nearer to hear Eloise's response, but Eloise was struggling with her gold bracelet and didn't reply.

'Do you want that off before you shower?'

'There,' Eloise said in some triumph, turning the flat face of the identity bracelet over and pushing it towards Lisa for inspection.

'What? What am I looking at?' Lisa bent closer trying to work out what was very faintly engraved there. 'Adam? Is that what it says? And a date – 5 May 1969?'

'Yes.' Eloise turned, picking up her pillow and cradling it as one might a child.

'But that's *my* birthdate,' Lisa said, staring. 'Exactly! To the very day! How strange. What a coincidence...' She broke off as a knock came at the door and Jess popped her head round.

'Mum, Eloise's husband is here. He's pretty unsteady on his feet so I've kept him downstairs. Let me help you get dressed, Eloise.' Jess turned to Lisa. 'Wouldn't she listen to you, Mum?'

'Sorry, Jess, we just got chatting.'

Jess, all efficiency now, fetched a facecloth, encouraging Eloise to wash her hands and face. 'Right, Eloise, how about your lovely red shift dress? With the red cashmere cardigan? You always look like a model in that. I'm not sure what we can do with your hair except give it a good brush. It looks lovely to your shoulders. Makes you look so much younger.'

Five minutes later and Lisa and Jess were accompanying Eloise down the stairs.

'Really, you know,' Eloise tutted, 'I may be forgetting things and, for some ungodly reason, known only to yourselves, I've ended up back here at Hudson House, but I'm more than capable of descending a flight of stairs without help.' And with that she was off, heading for the lounge, where Christopher Howard and his daughter were waiting impatiently in the doorway.

Lisa turned at the bottom of the stairs, debating whether to tackle some of Hudson House's garden, go to the gym or simply go home and rest. She hadn't slept wonderfully well the previous evening after Robyn and Jess had returned from their visit to the Foleys and she was beginning to feel tired. She mustn't overdo it – too much too soon now that she was feeling so well could put her back in bed. She looked at her watch and made the decision to go home and prepare Sorrel's favourite spaghetti carbonara before driving to St Mede's to pick her up. She'd insist Sorrel eat a good tea and have another early night.

'Lisa?'

Lisa turned back towards the front door where Kamran Sattar was standing looking towards her. 'Hi, how are you?' What was it about this man that made her mouth go dry whenever she bumped into him?

'I'm good. Listen, Lisa, er, do you fancy coming to the opening of a new restaurant I've been invited to?'

'A new restaurant?'

'Yes.'

'With you?'

'Yes, that's the general idea.'

'Oh, er, well, yes, thank you. That would be lovely. When were you thinking?'

'It's tomorrow evening.'

Lisa wished her phone weren't in her bag in the staffroom. Wished that she could be seen to be perusing a diary before accepting. She didn't want to appear too keen. Wasn't that part of dating rules these days? Oh, you ridiculous woman, Lisa Allen, she scolded herself. Who said this was a date? He was probably just trying to find out what she knew about Fabian's interest in the house.

'So, is that a yes, then?' Kamran was smiling at her, his arms folded as she continued to dither.

'I don't *think* I've anything on tomorrow,' she lied, knowing all that would be on was the new drama on the box that Jess had recommended.

'Well, shall I give you my number and then you can confirm when you've had a good look at your diary?'

'Lovely.' Lisa swallowed back her nerves. 'Why don't we do that?'

'And, if that fits with you, I'll pick you up about three. It's quite a drive.'

'Three? You mean 3 p.m.? Goodness, it must be if we need to set off at three. Where is this restaurant?'

'Montmartre.'

'No, I mean where is it? Not what it's called.' She smiled across at him.

'Montmartre.' He laughed at her confusion, obviously enjoying the game.

'The one in Paris?'

'The very one.'

'Right, OK. Er, so how do we get there?'

'To be honest, Lisa, if the weather isn't wonderful, we won't get permission to take off. It is January, after all. But the forecast is for a cold and clear day. Hopefully we should be OK.'

'You have your own plane?'

'I share it with my brothers. We're all qualified to fly.'

'Well, I'd hope so,' Lisa said faintly. 'I can't imagine going up in a tin can over the English Channel if you weren't.'

'Not had to bail out yet,' Kamran said cheerfully. 'It's been great for the three of us getting about when we've business in Europe. I want to look round this place a bit more now, so if you'll excuse me? I'll leave my number with Jess… Oh, and don't forget your passport.'

And with that he headed towards the front door and the gardens leaving Lisa feeling utterly winded.

* * *

'You're doing *what*?' Jess was immediately round on her return from Hudson House, handing Lisa the piece of paper with Kamran Sattar's number written on it.

'Am flying off t'Montmartre for me tea,' Lisa repeated in her best Yorkshire accent. Which was never very convincing.

'In his plane? In January? Over the sea?' Jess stared and Lola, knowing something was afoot, and following in her mother's wake, shook her head.

'You can't do that, Granny.'

Lisa, who had been thinking exactly the same all afternoon, replied, 'Absolutely I can.'

'Won't you need one of those Biggles' helmets and goggles, Granny?' Lola stared.

'Mum, he's the enemy.' Jess tutted, ignoring Lola's concern re Lisa's sartorial headgear. 'You can't fraternise with the enemy.

He's about to turn out all the residents into the cold just so he can extend his fish-finger empire.'

'I like fish fingers...' Lola started.

'Well, maybe I can find out more about what he's up to,' Lisa said. 'And then report back.'

'What? Thirty-five thousand feet up above the North Sea?'

'Isn't it the English Channel?' Lisa said, feeling cross. She'd made new year resolutions to take every opportunity going and now she was being thwarted at every step. 'And isn't it only jumbo jets that fly so high?'

'I wouldn't know, I've never actually been up in a jumbo,' Jess snapped, concern for Lisa making her irritable. 'The furthest we ever got with Dean was Malaga and Benidorm with Ryanair.'

'Well, then, time to expand your horizons and live a little now that you're single,' Lisa said, eyebrows raised.

'Single? Mum, you're not divorcing Dad, are you? I thought he was coming back.' Lola pulled a face.

'We'll talk about Dad later,' Jess said, shaking her head in Lola's direction. 'I'm more concerned about your granny taking herself off with Kamran Sattar. You do know you'll need a passport?'

Lisa glared across at her eldest daughter. Surely, she wasn't taking that waste of space Dean back? Again? 'I have a passport, thank you very much. If you remember, Jayden and I travelled extensively in Europe before you girls were born. You may also remember, he took me to Amsterdam for my fiftieth.'

'I'd forgotten that.' Jess frowned. 'The one time he came up trumps.'

'I think it's brilliant,' Sorrel said, coming into the kitchen and joining the conversation. She helped herself to a spear of the raw broccoli Lisa had just prepared. 'So, what are you going to wear, Mum?'

'I shall go shopping in the morning,' Lisa said, glancing at Jess, daring her to contradict her. 'There's that fabulous dress shop in the village. I've already got my eye on a dress I was going to treat myself to.'

'It's not your birthday, Granny, is it?' Lola frowned.

'Not yet, darling.' Lisa laughed. 'The dress and the whole restaurant experience will be early birthday treats to myself.'

'But *we* always treat you, Mum,' Jess said, visibly upset.

'And you still can, Jess,' Lisa soothed. 'In May, when it's actually my birthday.' And then, remembering, went on, 'It was so strange today, talking to Eloise...'

'Who's Eloise?' Sorrel and Lola spoke as one.

'A very lovely lady who is up at Hudson House. Her family actually lived there when she was a girl.'

'They were all residents at the care home? Weird!' Sorrel broke off from the broccoli to pull a face.

'No! Her family owned Hudson's mills and actually built Hudson House and lived there before it became a care home. Eloise was *Eloise Hudson*. Anyway, what is weird is that she showed me the bracelet she always wears, and engraved on it was my birth date.'

'So she'd remember your birthday and buy you a card?' Lola laughed. 'That's really kind.'

'Now, that is weird.' Sorrel grinned, finishing the last of the broccoli and pulling a daft face at Lola.

'No, of course not.' Lisa shook her head. 'She had a baby, born on exactly the same day as me.'

'Hey,' Sorrel laughed, her eyes wide, 'now you know your mum was English and not Indian as you've always thought, maybe this Eloise woman is your mum?'

'Good try, sweetheart.' Lisa smiled. 'But the baby was a boy. Called Adam. And, he was born in Canada.'

'Right, Mum,' Sorrel said, obviously bored with the conversation about old ladies and babies she didn't know, 'pick me up from school at lunchtime tomorrow and I'll do your make-up and your hair.'

'Absolutely not,' Lisa said. 'You've missed enough school. And, besides, I've an appointment at Luigi's in the village in the morning. You may think I'm past it, but I'm more than capable of doing my own make-up. Right, anything else or can I get on with this carbonara?'

29

LISA

'Oh, how did you know I was coming?' Jayden had let himself in and was sitting in the kitchen, eating the last of the pack of Sorrel's strawberry yoghurts. 'Wow, you look absolutely fabulous, Lisa.' He whistled appreciatively, his eyes taking in the beautiful aubergine midi-dress and the brown suede boots Lisa'd managed to filch back from Robyn.

'I didn't,' Lisa said. 'Did you tell me? Message me? I don't recall any such notifications, Jayden.'

'Ooooh? What's up with *you*?'

'I thought we'd agreed, last time you were here, that you weren't just to turn up expecting me to drop everything. Expecting me to welcome you into my house and my bed.'

'I think you'll find it's my house, Lisa.' Jayden laughed without rancour. 'Me who has paid the mortgage all these years.'

'And me who's brought up your three daughters. Alone. Brought them up by hand.' Lisa felt no anger, just slight irritation that the man had turned up once again just as she was going out on her first date for over thirty years.

'Of course. And a fabulous job you've done too. You know you and the girls are my life. Even Sorrel appears to have turned a corner. Come on, Lisa...' Jayden flashed the seductive smile she'd always fallen for, the one she could never resist. Until now. 'I'm here to take you all out for Sorrel's birthday.'

'That's next week.'

'I know that. Thought we could have an early birthday celebration.'

'Well, you'll have to celebrate without me. And, if you want a bed for the night, I suggest you try Robyn down in the village, as I can't see Jess putting you up again.'

'Robyn's in the village? With Wotsisname? The lawyer?'

'He's called Fabian, and he's a barrister. And yes, they're renting a place together.'

'Serious, then.'

'Of course it's serious.' Lisa tutted, irritation mounting.

'Where's Sorrel?'

'At school, where do you think? And, as far as I know, she's practising for the Susan Yates audition before going round to Jess's for tea.'

'I thought the audition was this week. I sent her a good luck message.'

'Good, that's what dads do.'

'Why hasn't she had the audition?' Jayden finished the yoghurt, flinging the carton expertly into the open bin.

'She's been a bit off,' Lisa lied. 'Covid. The theatre school's been very good at rearranging the audition.' She didn't want Jayden suddenly becoming the righteous, heavy-handed father, blaming Lisa for the mess Sorrel had got herself into. She, Jess and Robyn had dealt with the situation. Well, one particular aspect of it. She knew Sorrel was still in contact with that Joel Sinclair.

When she heard a car on the drive, Lisa's heart skipped a beat and she felt her face grow pink. The last thing she wanted was Kamran Sattar coming face to face with Jayden.

'That's my lift,' she said, heading for the door. 'If you want to see Jess, Sorrel and Lola, I suggest you wait here until they're back from work and school. Then, maybe, as long as it's OK with Robyn, you pop down there to be with your other girl?'

'But, Lisa, *you're* my girl.' Jayden tried once again with the seductive smile.

'Oh, grow up, Jayden,' she eventually snapped, worried that Kamran would be out of the car and on her doorstep. 'I'm a grown woman. Make sure you turn the lights out and lock up once you go.'

'But where are you going?' Jayden's voice was plaintive.

'Paris,' Lisa said with some degree of triumph. 'Paris, Jayden.'

* * *

'You know, I've only flown a couple of times before,' Lisa said as Kamran put the car into gear and headed for the small private airfield just five miles out of the village.

'Oh?' Kamran smiled across at her.

'Any travelling I used to do with my ex-partner was on the road in a huge Transit van. Or on the ferry from Hull to Zeebrugge or from Dover across to Calais. The thing is, I'm a bit nervous of this plane of yours.' Lisa was beginning to feel totally sick with nerves.

'Don't be, really. I'm honestly not a bad pilot.' He grinned. 'And, before I joined the family firm, I was a pilot with BA.'

'Oh, really? Oh, well, if you were able to take a great big jumbo across to Australia...' Lisa glanced across at Kamran for confirmation '...then a little two-seater across to Paris must be chicken feed for you?'

'Well, they are very different.' Kamran's hands, on the steering wheel of the Evoque, were strong, dependable, in control and Lisa began to relax. 'And actually, the plane we have at the moment is a four-seater.'

'So, I'm assuming we'll be strapped into some sort of parachute? You know, just in case?'

'Er, 'fraid not.' Kamran smiled.

'No?' Lisa exhaled. 'Lola said there would be.'

'Lola?'

'My ten-year-old granddaughter.'

'If it makes you feel any better, the plane itself does have a sort of parachute.'

'Really? Goodness.' That did make her feel – marginally – better. 'How long's the flight?'

'If we can get a good take-off slot, we should be able to land at Orly airport before 6 p.m. and then it's just 25 K or so in *le taxi* to Montmartre. A lovely meal at the restaurant and then I'll have you safely back on English soil in the early hours. We're lucky, it's perfect flying weather – it's not often we can get up in January.'

'So, what happens if the weather suddenly changes and we're buffeted about on clouds?' Lisa hugged the car's seat belt. 'Or it starts snowing...'

'It's cold and clear – but not so cold that the wings will ice up and drop off.'

'Oh, thanks for that.' Lisa wished she were back on the sofa with Roger Rabbit, watching a catch-up of *Coronation Street*.

'I'm sorry, that was just me teasing.' Kamran smiled across at her. 'I promise you, Lisa, I wouldn't be setting off myself if I thought there was any danger. Really. Just relax.'

Twenty minutes later they'd parked the car, walked over to a rather snazzy little plane ('*a Cirrus SR 22T*', Lisa would later report back to the girls) and Kamran was doing the checks in preparation for take-off.

* * *

'You OK?' Kamran executed what, even with her eyes closed in terror, Lisa could tell was a perfectly smooth take-off from the tiny airfield. Nothing like the smaller version of the tarmac runway at Manchester airport she'd been expecting. The order from the disembodied woman instructing: *'Pull up, pull up, terrain, terrain'* had her actually clutching onto Kamran's arm, but he simply smiled, saying, 'Sorry, should have warned you she always says that,' before patting her arm in response. She opened one eye. 'I need to concentrate,' he said, 'so just plug yourself into some music—' he handed over headphones '—and enjoy the flight. Once we get to the restaurant, I want to find out everything about you, Lisa.'

He smiled again and Lisa had a sudden need to lean over and touch his face; trace the contour of his cheek, his mouth. She sat on her hands and as he turned back to the wheel – joystick thingy? – Lisa turned slightly in his direction. From under not fully closed eyes, she took in the rest of the man: tall, but not excessively so, slim, toned (from exercise in whatever form with the pink-leotarded beauty at the gym?) and really quite stunning.

Did finding out about her mean he was interested in her? Or was this a ruse to find out what Fabian's plans were for the white house?

'When does the duty free come round?' Lisa smiled weakly. 'I'm out of gin at home.'

* * *

Two hours later, and after an experience she'd now decided she'd be happy to repeat on the return journey, Lisa felt her ears pop as Kamran made his descent onto the private tarmac at Orly airport. Fifteen minutes later, they'd made their way through Customs and were in *le taxi*.

Heading into Montmartre, it soon became obvious to Lisa that Kamran knew the area well and loved the place, waxing lyrical about the buildings and restaurants but particularly its artists. 'It became a place of refuge for artists such as Van Gogh, Picasso and Dali,' he explained. 'And nowadays, the Bohemian neighbourhood is one of the most-visited areas in Paris and home to some of the best restaurants in the capital.'

'You're obviously knowledgeable about both art and food.' Lisa smiled, staring out at the early evening night life.

'I love both. And Montmartre is one of my favourite places in the whole world.' He pointed a finger. 'The Chevalier de la Barre, and the Sacré-Coeur. The Square Nadar offers a great resting place after climbing up those hundreds of steps... and a great view of the Eiffel Tower. There you go, just visible now, see? We couldn't have picked a better evening.'

'So, whose restaurant is it we're going to? In Montmartre?' Lisa turned back from the window where she'd been taking in the famous landmarks.

'My cousin Khadija's. She's married to a Parisian; lived here for years. It's their second place: this one is French Asian fusion, reflecting both their heritages... Hang on, we're here, I think. Yes, this is it.'

There were a good twenty minutes of welcome: introductions all round and handshaking as well as Gallic kissing on both cheeks followed by a tour of the restaurant and the kitchens. Here, many chefs, all dressed in black, heads down and working shoulder to shoulder, were fully occupied with food preparation.

'I've seated you here, Kamran.' Khadija smiled, leading them back into the restaurant itself. 'Best table in the house. We need to show you what we can do if Zain is going to have any chance with you back in Yorkshire.'

'Who's Zain?' Lisa asked, once Khadija had moved off to welcome more guests.

'Khadija's son,' Kamran said, but didn't expand further. 'Right, glass of champagne?' he asked. 'I'm afraid I can't join you.'

'Religious reasons?' Lisa murmured, immediately wondering if it was a polite question to ask someone she'd only just met.

He smiled. 'No, not at all. I've a big bird to get back over the Channel in a few hours. You?'

'Me what?' Lisa wasn't quite sure what he was asking. 'Would I like champagne?'

'Well, yes, but I didn't know if your religion might frown on alcohol. I think maybe you and I have a similar heritage?'

'I've no religious beliefs,' Lisa said. 'I had the Bible thrust down my throat at every opportunity when I was a child. It kind of puts you off any religion.' She hesitated and then bowled straight in, unable not to. 'The thing is, I've just found out my mum – my birth mother – was English. I don't know any more than that. My father, I believe, was from India.'

'Similar, then. My mum's born and bred Yorkshire; her family go back generations in the north, but my father's family originated from the Mirpur area of Pakistan.' Kamran paused. 'What do you mean you've only just found out about your mum? And you seem uncertain about your father?'

'Long story and tonight, I don't think, is the time for discussion.' Lisa found tears welling.

'I'm sorry, I've upset you.' Kamran paused, indicating to the hovering waiter the glass of bubbly was for Lisa, which she sipped at gratefully, concentrating on the menu that had been placed in front of her. She hadn't realised all this churning up of her history, of her background, was making her feel so emotionally drained.

'The thing is, Kamran, I don't know who I am. It's probably why I insisted on staying with my ex for so long. At least with him, I had an identity – I was Jayden's partner.'

'Jayden Allen, the reggae artist?'

'You know?'

'Yes, someone told me.'

'Right.'

'Sorry, I just wanted to find out more about you.'

'And you?' Lisa asked, finding herself grow pink at the compliment. 'Are you married?'

'Not any more. Clare and I split up a few years ago. We have a very amicable relationship now.'

'Children?'

'Georgia has just finished at Newcastle; Sophie is in her first year at uni in Warwick and Sammy – Samar – is still away at school.'

'And the pink leotard?'

'Sorry?'

'The personal trainer at the gym.'

'Just that – a personal trainer.' Kamran smiled. 'I'm old enough to be her father.'

Lisa grinned at that. 'And?'

'And what?' Kamran laughed, hesitated and then said, 'Lisa, I'm not in the market for running after young women in pink leotards. I've been single now for several years and, although I found it very difficult at first to admit that I'd messed up my own marriage...'

'You had an affair?'

'No, not at all.' Kamran frowned. 'You seem determined to portray me as some sort of womanising Lothario, Lisa.'

'I'm sorry.' Maybe, Lisa thought, she assumed all men were tarred with the same brush as Jayden? 'But you just said you messed up your marriage?'

'I was too much in love with my work, constantly missing social occasions my wife had arranged, often working until the early hours; flying back early from family holidays. Determined that Frozen should be up there with Iceland and the other competitors.'

'In love with your fish fingers?' Lisa smiled.

'And our Black Forest gateau and lemon meringue. If you've not tried them, you should. Even though I say it myself, they wouldn't be out of place in a restaurant like this...' He trailed off as the young waiter arrived back at their table.

'Bonsoir, monsieur, madame, que souhaitez-vous en entrée?'

The next few minutes were spent in discussion over the menu, Kamran conversing in perfect French. While Lisa herself hadn't used the language much since schooldays – apart from in Calais many years ago when the exhaust had fallen off the Transit van – she was pleased that she was able to follow what was being said.

'Asian traditional dishes but adapted with French gastronomy focusing on refining classic flavours,' Kamran explained. 'Really exciting stuff.'

Whether it was thanks to the champagne combined with the delicious food – *raviolis croustillant crevettes* with a sweet and spicy sauce that was placed theatrically in front of them – or Kamran's apparent genuine interest in her, Lisa began to relax, talk, telling this man just about everything in her life.

'Gosh,' she eventually apologised. 'I'm so sorry, talking so much about myself. That was a bit like *This Is Your Life*. It was one programme Karen allowed herself to watch. I think she had a thing about Michael Aspel.'

'Didn't all mothers?' Kamran laughed and then took hold of her hand, stroking the wonderfully sensitive spot between finger and thumb until Lisa found herself leaning in to him. 'Lisa, you *must* find out about your birth parents. You might have a whole family in India you've not met. Mumbai? Delhi? Jaipur?'

'I've really no idea. It's only this week I've found out that it wasn't my mum who was Indian; that she wasn't taken out in an honour killing as Karen always used to tell me.'

'Why on earth did she tell you that if it wasn't true?' He frowned. 'Lisa, you need counselling: I'm a big believer in it.'

'No, I don't.' She laughed. 'I just need lovely evenings like this and champagne to loosen my tongue and make me talk. This is as good as counselling.'

'You know, we have met before.' Kamran drained his glass of water.

'Oh? I'm sorry, I don't...'

'Clare, my wife, came into the little gift shop where you were working a few years ago. I was waiting outside, impatient as always to be off, and eventually I came in to find her and hurry her along. The shop was busy but you were calm, smiling. I know this is utterly stupid, but I felt a connection with you...' He trailed off, obviously embarrassed.

'Really? I'm sorry, I don't remember.'

'You wouldn't. You were being so lovely, laughing along with a customer about something. I stood by the door and watched, just taking in everything about you. You were utterly beautiful and I couldn't get the picture of you out of my head. I actually came back into the shop a few weeks later. I couldn't not. You weren't there.'

'I was probably ill.' Lisa felt her happiness at being with

Kamran begin to evaporate. What right did she have to be flirting and smiling with this gorgeous man when the reality was that she could have another attack of the bloody awful porphyria at any time? That would soon put him off this *connection* he was apparently feeling. Needing – wanting – only to have a wonderful evening with this heavenly man without the spectre of her condition coming between them, she attempted to change the subject.

'So, Kamran, are you still going ahead with the plan to knock down Hudson House?'

'Knock it down?' Kamran frowned. 'There was never any intention to knock it down.'

'Oh!' For a few seconds, Lisa couldn't think what to say. 'Why did you go along with it, then, when I was ranting on at you about turning the oldies out?'

'We – I – do want to find new homes for the residents. I don't think that will be too difficult, and we certainly wouldn't do anything until new homes had been found for them all.'

'Not difficult?' Lisa finished her glass of champagne. 'Not difficult? *Of course*, it's difficult to move on, to move into new care facilities, to even *find* care homes with space.'

'I accept that, but you know, Lisa, care homes close all the time, some go under…'

'So, if you're not going to knock it down, what are you going to do with it? You're not moving your factory into it, are you?'

'No, of course not.' Kamran laughed at the very idea. 'Hudson House is far too beautiful a house, and in far too beautiful a position, to even think about knocking it down. It's listed anyway – grade two, I believe.'

'So what? You're going to renovate it and live there yourself?'

'Well, I did think about that. Although, as a single bloke, living by myself, it would be far too big. I'd rattle around playing Lord of the Manor like some saddo.' He laughed again. 'I've talked to my three kids about living there, but they were all dead set against it. And, by the time I'd taken it back to being a family home, the kids would have fully flown the nest.' He paused. 'It's so interesting, Lisa, I've been doing a lot of research about my family – the Sattars – and the Hudson family, who originally built the house. There's a connection, Lisa.' Kamran's face was animated.

'A connection?' Lisa frowned. 'What sort of connection? Oh, you mean your family was employed at Hudson's Textile Mill?'

'Well, yes.' Kamran stared. 'How did you know that?'

'I didn't.' Lisa smiled. 'I just remember Jess saying something about the large number of workers who came from the Mirpur area of Pakistan to West Yorkshire after partition. You know, invited here to work in all the mills? I assumed Hudson's was no different. You do know one of the Hudson family is a resident at the home at the moment?'

'No! No, I didn't know.' Kamran put down his glass of water and stared.

'Mrs Howard.'

Kamran shook his head. 'Means nothing.'

'Why would it? I wouldn't have thought she'd ever have had anything to do with her family's mill workers.' Lisa laughed. 'She's very upmarket.'

'And you're saying I'm not?' Kamran grinned, shooting the cuff of his expensive shirt as if to prove a point.

'You know exactly what I'm saying.' Lisa smiled. 'Eloise Howard looks like Grace Kelly. Tall, beautiful and very posh.'

'Eloise?' Kamran stared.

'Yes. Eloise. Eloise Howard. She *was* Eloise Hudson. Lived at Hudson House as a child, apparently.'

'Well, well, well.' Kamran sat back in his chair. 'Well—' he gave a bark of laughter '—who'd have guessed?'

'Guessed?'

'Nothing, nothing.' He shook his head, obviously lost in thought.

'It's clearly something,' Lisa said encouragingly, but Kamran shook his head.

'Just some family business that wouldn't interest you.' He smiled then, taking her hand, before saying, 'Listen, I thought you and Jess realised.'

'Realised? Realised what?'

Kamran smiled again, obviously willing Lisa to understand his intentions for the care home. 'I'm planning on turning Hudson House into a fabulous restaurant.'

30

AUGUST 1968

Eloise

'Unlike formal coming-out balls, Eloise,' Muriel said crossly, 'which are always held during the social season in spring or summer, one's individual coming-out party may, according to social convention, be held at any time of the year. So please do not contradict me when I tell you yours is at the end of August.'

'Coming-out balls?' Michael, drowning a bowl of cornflakes in a pint of milk, sniggered. 'I don't have to get my knackers out at this do, do I?'

Muriel, reaching for a copy of the *Midhope Examiner*, slapped Michael around the head with the Classifieds section while Maude Hudson, who'd arrived uninvited in the kitchen, made her way past Eloise to the kettle, patting her granddaughter's arm as she did so.

'What's wrong with the kettle in the gardener's hut?' Muriel snapped, eyeing Maude's muddy boots with distaste. 'And d'you think you could leave the mud where it belongs, in the vegetable patch?'

'Blown a fuse,' Maude said unapologetically. 'Can't prune the lavender or sow the annuals without tea and a smoke.' She went to sit by Eloise, reaching for her tobacco tin.

'Do *not* light up in here, Maude,' Muriel instructed, glaring in her mother-in-law's direction. 'And, Michael, stop stuffing food down your throat at a rate of knots. And elbows off the table...'

'I hear the Yorkshire Debs' Ball at The Queen's in Leeds is off?' Maude winked conspiratorially across the table at Eloise.

'Not definitely,' Muriel said huffily. 'We've time yet to up the numbers. And, if it doesn't go ahead, all the more reason for Eloise's coming-out party here at the end of the month. Invitations have gone out and there's a wonderful take up for *that*.'

'People round here won't turn down a pint and a pie and mushy pea supper.' Maude winked again at Eloise and this time, despite feeling utterly miserable at the thought of being flaunted in front of the cream of Yorkshire's society, Eloise laughed out loud.

'Pie and peas, for heaven's sake.' Muriel's neck turned an unflattering shade of turkey red and she dabbed at her face with the tea towel she was holding.

'Menopause, Muriel?' Maude's tone was nothing but sympathetic.

'Are you in that already, Ma?' Michael looked up with interest from his cereal.

'Excuse me!' Muriel snapped. 'Would you mind your language, Maude, in front of Michael? And, I'll have you know, the Veuve Clicquot is already ordered while a very expensive and tasteful supper will be prepared and presented by the chefs from The George hotel.'

Maude nodded her approval but then shook her head. 'And you're seriously expecting everyone to troop up through my gardens, trampling over my flowerbeds in order to get up to that great monolith on the lawn?'

'Absolutely. Mr Bower and his underlings are laying down... laying down... something for people to walk on. Can I remind you, Maude, they're no longer your gardens...? Where d'you think *you're* going, Eloise? I need you to sort out what you'll be wearing and—'

'Sorry, Mummy, must dash.' Eloise made for the door. 'I promised Sarah I'd help her with arrangements for her engagement party. May I take the Mini?'

'Oh, absolutely, yes. And make sure you give her your party invitation.' Muriel turned to Maude. 'Do you know this Sarah, Maude? One of the Harrogate Huntington-Greens apparently; an old school pal of Eloise's living just twenty minutes away? Eloise and Sarah are great chums – she's spent every minute of the past few weeks with the family. This is the sort of friendship we need to be encouraging; I'm led to believe Sarah has several older – single – brothers and then there's a whole pool of Huntington-Green cousins—'

'Can't say I have,' Maude said, cutting Muriel off mid-sentence. Tired of listening to the litany of Muriel's hopes and expectations regarding a suitable match for Eloise, she quickly made her tea and headed once more for her roses.

* * *

'Where does your mum think you are?' Janice asked, opening her front door to Eloise.

'At Sarah Huntington-Green's near Mirfield.'

'And why aren't you?'

'Because she's a total figment of my imagination.' Eloise,

feeling braver with each passing day she spent as Janice's mate, laughed, nervously at first and then with more confidence.

'You be careful, love.' Norma Atkinson, at the sink, turned. 'I'm not sure your dad and your brother would approve of you hanging about down here.'

'Oh, I'm so sorry if I'm in your way.' Eloise's confidence shrivelled to embarrassment.

'Don't be so daft, Eloise. You know you're more than welcome here any time. Are you staying for a bit of dinner? Our Gary's just off to the chippy.'

'That's awfully kind, Mrs Atkinson, but I'm meeting a friend and heading out to take some photographs.' Eloise indicated the camera over her shoulder. 'I don't seem to be able to stop snapping these days.' She knew she was talking too fast, knew also that Norma probably had a jolly good idea who the friend was.

'Be careful, love, that's all I'm saying. They're not like us. Different, you know?'

'I'll be off, then,' Eloise said, her face flaming, Janice following her down the path to the Mini.

'Look, Eloise,' Janice said. 'This is all my fault. If you hadn't come to the Rooms with us the other week, you'd never have started all this.'

'Janice,' Eloise said, smiling, 'I fell in love with him the minute I saw him taking the photo of the thrush…'

'But Eloise, he's… look, I know he's absolutely gorgeous; I've always fancied him myself, to be honest, but, you know, that's as far as it went…' Janice was genuinely anxious.

'Janice, I feel alive for the first time in my life.'

'Oh, now you're being dramatic.' Janice tutted. 'How about a date with our Gary? He fancies you like mad.'

'Stop worrying. All will be well.' Eloise opened the Mini and slid into the driver's seat.

That, she realised, was the second lie of the morning.

* * *

As soon as she saw him, standing waiting for her by his rusting old Triumph Herald out on the moor above Wessenden reservoir, Eloise marvelled again just how utterly gorgeous he was. She pulled up behind the Triumph, crashing the gears as she did so.

'You sure you've passed your test?' Junayd smiled through the open window.

'Well, only a month ago and, to be honest, only because it was absolutely pouring down and the examiner couldn't open the door to see how far I was from the pavement when reversing.'

'Right, well, hopefully we'll see a curlew or a dipper if we're lucky. Got plenty of film?'

Eloise nodded, hoping Junayd would take her hand but, instead, he set off at pace, heading down a tussocky path looking over Wessenden reservoir.

'You know, I'd never been up here until you suggested it.'

'I can't believe that,' Junayd said. 'It's absolutely glorious. Look at that heather. Shh...' He suddenly bobbed down behind a huge boulder, taking Eloise's hand and pulling her down with him.

'What?'

'A skylark.'

'Well, you won't be able to take a photo of that,' Eloise whispered. 'It'll turn out just a black dot.'

'But, oh, *the beauty* of that black dot.' Junayd continued to gaze into the cerulean-blue sky. 'Have you never read Meredith's poem "The Lark Ascending"?'

'Er, no, can't say I have. I was more into maths and sciences, I suppose, than, you know, literature.' Eloise felt embarrassed at her lack of poetic knowledge. She leaned forwards to take her camera, wanting to preserve Junayd's image for posterity. Well, at least so she could gaze at his picture in the secrecy of her bedroom. 'How do you know about English poetry?'

'Why wouldn't I? As soon as I knew A levels were the only way out of the mill, I made sure I enrolled at night school. Mind you, the sciences I needed to study medicine – my parents' dream for me – are pretty much beyond me. I've swapped over to English, art and photography. I want to go to university.' Junayd's eyes were wide with anticipation at the prospect.

'Do you miss home?'

'I *am* home,' Junayd said almost crossly. 'Where I am now is home.' He threw Eloise a look, staring down at the reservoir instead of up at the black dot that was beginning its rapid descent. 'Do you have any idea, Eloise, why my family and I were, not only invited to this country by your government, but actually driven out of our homes?'

'Driven out? By whom?' Eloise was indignant.

'After partition – you do know about partition? – the Mangla dam was commissioned by a consortium of eight US companies. The Jhelum River, in the Pir Panjal mountains, was diverted, sending billions of gallons of water into the dam.'

'Surely that's a good thing?' Eloise frowned. 'You know, clean water for drinking, hygiene, industry?' She glanced down at Wessenden reservoir below them.

'Hydroelectrics? The whole lot?'

'Well, yes.' She paused. 'No?'

'Not wonderful for the people like us who were living there. When my family has known nothing but farming and agriculture. When our village, and hundreds like it, disappeared under the water. When, in order to live, to survive, my family had to move.'

'But you were invited to work here? In Daddy's mill? I thought you *wanted* to come?'

'Oh, a great opportunity? Is that what you're saying? We should be grateful?'

'I wasn't saying that,' Eloise stuttered.

'Do you think you Brits want us here?'

'Well,' Eloise said stoutly, flushing as she spoke, '*I* certainly want you here.'

'You're such an innocent, Eloise.' He leaned forwards to stroke her face gently with his thumb and she found herself moving towards him, unable not to. 'And when I turn up at your coming-out party—' Junayd smiled as he spoke the words '—your father will welcome me, one of his Pakistani workers from the carding shed? Your mother will come forwards, take me by the hand, introduce me to her guests?'

'My party? How do you know about my party?' Eloise felt panic setting in at the thought of Junayd turning up unannounced; Muriel's face as he laid claim to her over The George hotel's devilled eggs and mini prawn cocktails.

He was laughing now. 'Oh, don't worry, just something I overheard at the mill. The problem is, Eloise, we're worlds apart and, before I fall totally in love with you, we have to stop meeting like this, on the pretence of taking photographs. I wait every dinner break for you, desperate to see you, talk with you, pretending it's our cameras that've taken me there, when really...'

'Really?' Eloise held her breath.

'You know what I'm saying. Your family wouldn't approve in a million years. And, I have to tell you, Eloise, neither would mine. My father is already questioning me...' Junayd took her face in both hands, cupping it gently, bending to kiss her eyes, her nose and eventually her open mouth. Never having been kissed before, she wasn't sure what to do, but instinct somehow, magically, took over and she closed her eyes, loving the feel of him, his breath sweet, his heart beating until she wasn't quite sure where he ended and she began.

'This is not good, Eloise,' Junayd finally said, sitting up and gently pushing her away from him. 'This is wrong.'

'This *is* good,' she pleaded. 'It's right.' And, reaching for him, she pulled him down into the heather-strewn grass behind the rocks.

* * *

Muriel had insisted Eloise wasn't to go into the mill – *playing at being secretary* – the week leading up to the party, when, instead, she was to stay at home and help with arrangements, as well as visit the hairdresser and beautician. Eloise, unable to contemplate five days of not seeing Junayd, had been equally insistent she should. She and Muriel had eventually compromised on her being at home on the Thursday and Friday prior to the do. By offering to pick up some dry-cleaning, as well as sneaking off early from Beddingfield Beauty Bar on the Friday, she managed to meet up with Junayd after work, both driving out to the moors for their secret assignation. When, later that evening, Muriel demanded to know why there were bits of heather stuck in Eloise's crocheted sweater, the mythical Sarah Huntington-Green and all three of her tall, handsome and rich brothers were quickly resurrected in explanation.

Saturday dawned with a warm hazy morning, the August sunshine quickly burning off the last of the mist to leave a perfect day for a party in the garden. Eloise had longed to invite Janice, Jean and Eileen, but had the good sense to quit while she was ahead: Muriel, she knew, would have had something to say about Hudson's menders and weavers being on the guest list.

She actually rather liked the dress Mrs Livesey, her mother's tailor, had made for her. While it wasn't as short as she'd have liked (and certainly not the black wide-legged trousers and floppy hat she'd squirrelled away upstairs in her wardrobe after a shopping trip in Leeds the previous Saturday with Junayd, who certainly had an eye for women's fashion) she went along with the cream layered creation Mrs Livesey had come up with. While it did make her look like a royal-iced wedding cake, once on, and her blonde hair in the up style suggested by Angie the hairdresser, Eloise accepted the look, knowing the whole shebang would be over and done within a few hours.

* * *

'Eloise, do come and stand at the door to welcome everyone,' Muriel instructed, a rictus of a smile on her over-made-up face. 'And, Michael, don't you dare help yourself to any more of those vol-au-vents.' She pronounced the final word to rhyme with *rents*. 'Now, d'you think there's enough food...? Eloise, are these Huntington-Green people coming? I didn't have an RSVP – poor form... Michael, no, you're not allowed champagne, there are bottles of Orangillo for the non-drinkers... Eloise, will you please pay special attention to Christopher Howard when the Howards arrive...?'

'Who?' Eloise, wanting only to pay special attention to her dreams of Junayd, shook her head irritably.

'The Howards, Eloise. You know – Christopher is Brian's chum – the pair were at prep school together: caused mayhem when Mrs Dixon had to have a term off for her down-below bits and that dreadful young woman straight from college took the class with her newfangled ideas on education. She had the boys sitting together round tables rather than in rows... Anyway, the

Howards are all en route... Ah, Lady Saville, delighted... And Bunty and Bobo as well! How lovely...'

Eloise was seriously beginning to think Muriel was on something. She'd not stopped talking in this ongoing stream of consciousness for the past thirty minutes.

'Good God, what *is* your mother wearing now, Ralph?' Muriel shot a look of distaste towards Maude in a purple crushed-velvet trouser suit.

'Hello, Granny, you look lovely.' Eloise hurried over to the entrance to the white house, taking Maude Hudson's arm and handing her a glass of bubbly before leading her to a table of septuagenarians, all Maude's mates from when she ruled the roost up here before being tipped out into the dower cottage down by the village duck pond.

'Christopher, do you remember Eloise?' Muriel was at her side once more. 'I'm sure you do! I seem to think I have a snap of the pair of you playing in the paddling pool totally in the ruddie nuddie when you were tiny. *Too sweet.*' Eloise thought Muriel just *too silly* for words, but Christopher, in a sober dark suit and tie, didn't appear to have noticed. He was already on his second glass of fizz and was looking past Eloise, eyeing up the talent who all seemed to belong to her brother Brian. 'I'll leave you with the party girl, Chris,' Muriel said, patting his arm matily, 'and attend to my other guests.' She exited with a warning nod and wink in Eloise's direction.

'Hello, Eloise, you look different with your clothes on.' Christopher Howard, having spent a year in the States desperately trying to drum up business for his family's failing engineering company, finally deigned to look her way. He spoke a strange mixture of educated public school peppered with native Yorkshire, and an undertone of pseudo-American twang every time he remembered he'd been living Stateside. 'Hey, you have grown up since I last saw you. Quite the beanpole, aren't you?'

'Seeing that must have been sixteen years ago, that's no surprise, I suppose.' Eloise took in the round pink face, the fine blond curls hiding an already receding hairline and a gut straining at his trouser belt and shuddered. Give him a trumpet and take his clothes off – Eloise breathed a silent yuck – and he'd be a dead ringer for one of the cherubs in Raphael's *Sistine Madonna*.

In reply, Christopher reached for another glass of champagne from the waitress, gave the girl a friendly squeeze on her backside and knocked back the drink in one.

Eloise suffered almost an hour of Christopher Howard talking about himself, his racing cars, his tennis, his golf, his family's engineering business before returning to yet more birdies and holes-in-one. She was just about to excuse herself and join Granny Maude and her mates, who all seemed to be getting well stuck into the champagne, chortling merrily and thoroughly enjoying themselves, when a man, dressed in full black morning suit and obviously in charge of proceedings, produced a huge gong and announced food was served.

Supper, to Eloise, seemed interminable as the sixty or so guests piled their plates with the delicious delicacies, either standing to eat or making their way back to tables. A tiny woman on a harp, brought in at great expense to *aid the guests' digestion*, seated herself and began the commencement of many pieces neither Eloise, nor, she suspected, anyone else, had ever heard before. She was just about to set off to find Michael, who Muriel said had been looking somewhat green around the gills five minutes earlier, when her mother headed over.

'Eloise, Eloise, *Eloise*, the photographer is here...'

Still in Manic Muriel Mode, Eloise noted.

'I was hoping for at least *Yorkshire Life* or even *The Yorkshire Post*, but we end up with the *Midhope Examiner*... And...' she lowered her voice '...a *coloured man*, for heaven's sake. Don't tell me there wasn't an Englishman available... what will our guests think...? I shall have words. Now, do go and freshen up, Eloise, brush your hair, pull your dress down, don't want the whole of Yorkshire to think you're a tart... don't want the photographer to see your knickers...'

'I beg your pardon...?' Eloise didn't hear her mother's response, wasn't sure if there had actually been one, because all she could hear was a buzzing in her ears and she felt the blood drain from her face before returning in a whoosh of burning red. Slightly hysterical, she only just managed to stop herself from saying: 'Too late, Mummy, he already has!'

'You all right, Lou?' Michael, as pale as she was scarlet, was standing at her side. 'I've just been sick in the rosebushes,' he added cheerfully. 'You don't look too good either.' He laughed. 'Ma's gone off on one too. She can't understand why the *Examiner*'s sent a coloured bloke to take the photos of you.'

31

ROBYN

I longed for January to be over, longed for birdsong and lighter evenings, for summer dresses and sitting in the garden with a glass of Pimm's. And for Fabian and me to be back as we were before Alex Brookfield had reared her ugly head in our lives. Ugly! Ha! Alexandra Brookfield was absolutely ravishing: one of those stunning women who had obviously been blessed by every good fairy invited along to her christening. The little people had probably been bickering to be first in the queue, determined to bestow nothing but fabulousness on the baby Alexandra: perfect in-proportion figure, perfect shiny swishy hair, perfect white teeth; brains, health, wealth and happiness. As well as the knight in shining armour – or was it the handsome prince in the castle? – in the form of Fabian Mansfield Carrington.

And if, by trampling on the fairies' plans for the oh, so beautiful Alexandra, I was about to be carted off to a Fabian-free world as punishment by the little tinselled feckers, then I wasn't sure what I could do about that. I was a big believer in fate, and if my path towards happy-ever-after in a cottage in West Yorkshire was suddenly yawning with a bloody great pothole, then who was I to argue otherwise?

'Oh, don't be so bloody wet,' Petra Waters admonished me when finding me skulking and sulking in the drama department's wardrobe, and I'd finally opened up about Fabian and Alexandra. 'I mean, has he left you? Gone back to her?'

'Well, no...'

'Was he happier with her than he is with you?'

'I don't know...'

'Have you discussed her with him?'

'I refuse to talk about her.'

'Is he seeing her now?'

'Yes, every day. He's been up before I'm awake, off down the M62 to miss the Leeds and Manchester traffic in order to work on Joel's case with her.'

'And she's gorgeous?'

'Yep!'

'His family like her?'

'Adore her.'

'Does Fabian know about Mason?'

My back was to Petra as I sorted what amounted to a pile of fusty-smelling rags in the cupboard, and I swung round to face her.

'What about Mason?' I asked, my cheeks burning.

'That you had a fling with him within a few weeks of starting here.'

'You knew?'

'Of course I knew, Robyn. And, if you say this ex of Fabian's is gorgeous, that he sees her every day *and* that he knows about Mason into the bargain...' she paused somewhat theatrically, a hand to her seven-month-pregnant belly '...then yes, I'd say you were well and truly skating on thin ice. Particularly if you're acting like a spoilt adolescent, sulking when he gets home, determined to punish him for having a life before he met you, giving him the cold shoulder, turning away from him in bed. In that case, you're doing nothing but encouraging him back into *her* bed.'

'Don't see how,' I muttered, knowing she was right. 'Oh, Petra, you just have to look at her to see why she'd win any race with the two of us in it.'

'So, one, why did they split up in the first place? And two, why didn't he go back to this Alexandra goddess when you and he were no longer together in London?' Petra looked at her watch. 'You've exactly one minute before the bell goes for afternoon lessons.'

'OK!' I started. 'One, apparently, she had a fling with a work colleague, and two, I can't get him to admit whether he did start seeing her again when they both ended up here in Yorkshire. Probably because we're not really speaking except for polite conversation. You know: "have you finished in the bathroom? I'm not sure there's any milk for your Shreddies" sort of thing.'

'That gorgeous man of yours eats Shreddies?' Petra pulled a face.

I tutted. 'You know what I'm saying. And he did.'

'Did what? Eat Shreddies? Or go back to her when you were doing what you did with our headmaster?'

'Fabian didn't know that at the time.'

'How d'you know he didn't?'

'I just do. Mason somehow let it slip when the two of them first met that he and I had been... you know...'

'Shagging?'

'For a deputy headteacher you don't half have an arsenal of bad language.' I scowled. '*An item.* That's what I was about to say.

Mason and I had become *friends* and then become what's known in polite society as *an item*!'

Petra was silent for a few seconds, her thought process interrupted by the raucous ringing of St Mede's bell. 'OK,' she said, putting two hands to her swollen abdomen. 'Close your ears, baby.' She nodded in my direction. 'Yep, Robyn, I'd say you were well and truly fucked.'

* * *

I needed to see Fabian, needed to tell him that once again I was acting like an immature moron rather than the grown-up adult I actually was. I needed to tell him that, even though his family might not think I was good enough for him, even though Gillian and Julius Carrington wanted Fabian heading back to London and down the aisle with Alexandra, I was ready to fight for him. For us.

'I'm ready to fight for us, ready to fight for what we've had, what we've got and what we may have in the future.' I practised saying the words out loud in my form room after 9CL had dashed out, desperate to start their weekend, trying out the sentence over and over again, placing emphasis on different words.

'Ready to *fight*... ready to fight for *us*...'

''Ey up, miss, who you getting into a scrap with? D'you need any help?' Whippety Snicket, aka Blane Higson, was behind me as I articulated the words.

'Sorry?' I whirled round. 'Oh, Blane.'

'I'll help you sort 'em, miss.' Blane was in a jaunty mood, brand-new, gleaming white trainers, laced up à la mode of all fourteen-year-olds, on his feet.

'Just practising a few lines from *Grease*,' I lied.

'Don't remember anybody saying them words in the film, miss.' He frowned. 'Which one of 'em said that, then?'

'Mr Donoghue or Ms Waters will be after you for not wearing school uniform black shoes.'

'Don't really care,' he crowed, admiring his footwear. 'I'm going to be leaving this dump pretty soon.'

'Oh, yes? And?'

Blane tapped his nose. 'Big things happening, miss. I'm being promoted...'

'Listen, Blane, this has gone far enough. You're in deep, deep water, laddy.' Oh, hell, now I sounded like Superintendent Hastings in *Line of Duty*. I'd be bringing in Jesus, Mary and Joseph and the wee donkey next. I tried appealing to Blane, softening my words and intonation. 'We need to see Mr Donoghue so he can report this to the authorities.' I knew Mason was already working with the local authority gang team on Blane's behalf, taking a softly, softly approach, coordinating with the police and Youth Justice Service. 'D'you want to end up like Joel Sinclair? On a tag? On bail miles away from your mum in local authority care?'

Blane frowned at that. 'If you remember, miss, I've done me time in local authority care.'

'That was different. That's when your mum couldn't look after you.'

'Joel was stupid.'

'One thing that Joel Sinclair isn't, Blane, is stupid.'

'Stupid for going against 'em. Trying to go straight.'

'Oh, for heaven's sake, Blane,' I said angrily. 'You're fourteen, not some hardened criminal in a police drama. If you're not careful you're going to get hurt. And I mean really hurt.' I couldn't help but wonder if we should be handing Blane over to the police and local authority for his own good. I determined I'd go straight down to Mason's office and suggest it was time to escalate things.

Blane shot out a wrist from his grubby grey school shirt cuff, insistent I should see the upmarket watch he was wearing. 'Joel chose the wrong side. He should have joined our lot when he had the chance. Look, miss, don't you worry about me. If I get done, then their sharks just get the NRM involved. They can't touch us then.'

'Sharks? NRM?'

Blane tutted. 'Solicitors! You know! Bent probably.'

'Have you been watching *The Godfather*?'

'Godfather? I 'aven't got no godfather.'

Ignoring the double negative without pulling him up as I would have done in an English lesson, I said, 'And NRM?'

'You know.'

'No, I don't know.'

'Well, the NRM lot anyway.'

'National Railway Museum? For a quick getaway?' Then censured myself: not the place and time for flippancy.

'Now, you're being daft, miss.' He smirked, but I could see him pondering the possibility of the acronym.

'Look, Blane, I have to get off.'

It was already nearly four and I'd made the decision I was going to drive over to Leeds, to where Sorrel had said the solicitors defending Joel were situated and where Fabian had told me he was going to be working all day. I didn't want to miss him, so I quickly texted him.

> My lovely Fabian, sorry for being my usual pig-headed self.

> Am driving over to Leeds in ten minutes. Meet me in Alchemist at 6pm for a drink? On neutral ground?

> Let me know if you've finished early and are either heading over to Harrogate to see Jemima or back home to Beddingfield. Love you, R xxx

Walking Blane down the corridor, I saw Mason coming back in through the main school entrance from doing his usual afternoon duty overseeing the kids leave the premises.

'Mr Donoghue,' I called. 'I have to dash, but I know Blane here would like a chat with you.'

'No, I bloody wouldn't,' Blane scoffed, scowling in my direction. 'I come to see you, miss, not him.' And with that he sauntered, actually *sauntered*, past Mason, who was smiling and beckoning him into his study.

I dithered, recognising I needed to update Mason about Blane, but also knowing what the motorway to Leeds was like at this time of day. I turned back, spending just five minutes apprising Mason of Blane's current situation, before heading for my car once more.

* * *

The M62 into Leeds was thronged even at 4.30 p.m. and I had to keep glancing at my phone on the passenger seat, worried that Fabian might already have left work and be speeding down the opposite carriageway back towards Beddingfield. If I'd had time I would have gone home first, put on my favourite red sweater and jeans instead of my usual teacher's skirt and shirt, and redone my make-up before setting off again. But the late-January sun was already going down on a clear ice-blue and fiery horizon, heralding another cold and frosty evening ahead, and I didn't want to miss him. I wanted Fabian and me on neutral ground: somewhere one of us couldn't flounce off to another room, where

I couldn't drink too much wine, which could make me garrulous, prone to talking over him, desperate to put my point of view.

I kept an eye on the westbound carriageway for Fabian's silver Porsche, but when I had to brake suddenly, I realised I needed to concentrate on the road ahead. It took me twenty minutes to get to the NCP car park on Albion Street where I always left my car when in Leeds.

Stopping only to reach into the back seat for the lovely camel cashmere trench coat Fabian had bought me for Christmas, I quickly refreshed lipstick, eye liner and perfume and pulled a hand through my unruly mass of curls. I headed to the exit, pulling up the coat's collar and tying its belt securely against the cold, before heading for the Trinity Centre and The Alchemist on the second floor. I decided to ring him as I walked to make sure he actually was in Leeds. Impulsive again, Robyn, I chastised myself. Why the hell hadn't I just gone back to the cottage, made Fabian's favourite fish pie and opened a bottle of wine in readiness for him coming home? We could have talked in the relaxing warmth of the log burner and I could have apologised for my immature reaction to being unexpectedly faced with Fabian's ex in a family reunion. A meeting which, to be fair to me, had been cooked up by Gillian and Julius Carrington with the sole aim of making me look silly and out of place.

Instead, I had stopped, phone clamped to my ear, and was being subjected to impatient tutting as I blocked the way of last-minute shoppers and early-evening restaurant-goers while I endeavoured to work out just where Fabian was.

I'd googled the firm of solicitors Sorrel had told me was dealing with Joel's case and where Alexandra Brookfield and Fabian were presumably now working together. Without an office of his own, he'd taken over the spare bedroom in the cottage and, as the atmosphere of *froideur* had continued between the pair of us, he'd increasingly escaped in there, working until the early hours of the morning, coming to bed only when I was fast asleep.

Boris! He must have Boris with him. How on earth could he meet me in a bar in this busy city centre when he had Boris with him? God, I was even more of a bloody idiot than I thought. The coolly elegant, clever and beautiful Alexandra, who presumably made calm and collected decisions on a daily basis, must be looking a decidedly better alternative to this impulsive teacher in her scruffy, muddy boots – I'd taken a shortcut over what was left of St Mede's playing fields – being buffeted by Leeds shoppers.

No answer from Fabian – the call went to voicemail – so I left a message. Then remembered I'd earlier texted him about meeting in The Alchemist, so had to ring him back, leave another message and tell him I was heading for The Alchemist just in case, despite having Boris with him, he was possibly on his way to meet me.

The Alchemist had huge windows looking out onto a roof terrace lit by pretty fairy lights, but I wanted cosy warmth and was given a table inside where I ordered a single gin and tonic. It was good to sit down – I'd taught several dance and drama sessions that Friday, and had run a *Grease* rehearsal in my double free period as well as getting Sorrel up to speed for her audition. She would be fabulous. She was back to her old self: sparkling, full of zest, putting 100 per cent effort into her pieces and I could think of no reason why she wouldn't make the London school's highly competitive grade.

The gin was soothing and I closed my eyes for a few seconds before turning to retrieve my bag, reaching for my phone once more. I froze, mid turn, my eyes caught by a couple standing from where they'd previously been sitting at a table just the other side of the huge glass door.

There was no mistaking the tall, dark-haired, wonderfully

attractive man who was being embraced by the beautiful blonde, her hand possessively on his arm as she leant in to kiss him before bending to fondle the dog's ears seated at the man's feet.

I turned away, not wanting them to catch me gawping. Pulse racing, I didn't know what to do. Did I skip gaily over, shouting: 'Surprise, surprise! Mine's a double gin?' Walk coolly between them with a 'Well, how lovely! Fancy seeing you two here!' Or did I race round and through the glass door, saying, 'Mine, I think,' before grabbing Fabian by the scruff of the neck, taking hold of Boris and pouring my gin over Alexandra?

Before I could get either my brain or my legs into gear, man, woman and dog were walking to the main exit leading out onto the corridor and lift back down to the shopping area. I jumped up, grabbed my coat and pulled up its collar, determined to follow them. But at the door, the bartender shouted me back.

'Would you like to settle your bill, love?'

By the time I'd scrabbled for my phone, paid for my unfinished gin and left the bar, the lift had already descended, and a posse of fifteen or so pink-and-silver cowboy-hatted women, clamouring loudly – and drunkenly – for its return, was blocking my way.

32

OK, so if Fabian had fallen back in love with the gorgeous Alexandra, then there was little I or anyone else could do about it. How could I blame him? He'd been with her for years; she'd given up on him and now she wanted him back, even following him up to Yorkshire to achieve that. How could I blame *her*? I'd seen enough of the pair of them, back in The Alchemist, Alexandra draped possessively all over Fabian, to know when I was beaten. Between Gillian and Julius Carrington, and now Alexandra Brookfield, I needed to come out waving my white flag.

I surrender.

The Friday shopping crowd had thinned, but the evening revellers were out in force, already seated and drinking underneath the ridiculously large gas patio heaters outside Restaurant Bar and Grill and Banyan in City Square. The huge equestrian statue of Edward, the Black Prince, gazed down stonily as I crossed over the road in front of him, making my way back to the NCP car park.

'You been dumped as well?' I asked, glancing up at Edward.

He didn't reply but a grizzled street sleeper, bedding down for the night in his sleeping bag and cardboard, shouted back at me: 'I 'ave that, love!'

I found a fiver in my pocket and handed it over to him. 'Sorry, I can't do more just at the moment.' I realised I was crying.

'D'you want to join me in 'ere, love?' he asked, revealing brown stumps instead of teeth and opening his sleeping bag in invitation. 'Come on, have a wee drink wi' me and wipe them tears off.' He proffered a can of cider in my direction.

'Come on, Robyn,' I censured myself. 'Get yourself home.'

I realised, in my misery at seeing Fabian with Alexandra, I'd come out of Trinity the wrong exit and now had to walk back up to the car park on Albion Street via Park Row and Bond Street.

Get yourself home? Back home where? To the Dower Cottage? Without Fabian? He'd be off back to Harrogate – or was it Ilkley? – now Alexandra had reclaimed him. Eventually, presumably, back to London with her.

Oh, and poor Jess! She'd been utterly sold on the idea of her and Fabian turning the white house into a top restaurant.

One more dream squashed flat.

I finally made it to the multistorey and, too weary to take the stairs, tried to take the lift to the top floor where I'd managed to park the car. I say, tried: the door closed behind me, and then reopened, closed and reopened and closed once again. I pressed the relevant buttons and the lift trundled up to the first floor, wheezing and groaning as it went until it stopped. And remained stopped! Then, after a good minute, suddenly, without warning, descended back to where we'd started.

Fuck's sake.

I turned back to the buttons, pressing every one in turn until the lift door suddenly opened, someone got in and, just as quickly, despite my yelling: 'Don't, don't! Get out! I think it's broken!' the door clanged shut once more on the pair of us.

The woman's head was down and she was crying, real shoulder-heaving sobs as she stood, not caring, it seemed, where she was, or where she was trying to get to.

She eventually lifted her head, obviously trying to work out what was going on; why we weren't moving.

We stared at each other, realisation at who the other was almost immediate.

My heart appeared to stall.

'You're crying.' She seemed surprised.

'So are you,' I sniffed.

'Look...' we both started.

'I'm sorry...' we tried again.

'The lift's broken,' I said.

'So's my heart,' she said.

'*Your* heart?' I said. Actually, it came out as a sneer. I cleared my throat and tried again. 'Why *your* heart?'

'Why d'you think?'

'I've really no idea. I've just seen you wrapped around Fabian in The Alchemist. Your heart appeared far from broken there!'

'You were there?' She stared. 'Where?'

'In the bar in The Alchemist. I'd sent Fabian a message to meet me there, but he never replied. And then I saw why he hadn't replied... You know...'

'He's been without his phone all day,' she interrupted. 'Left on the kitchen table, he thought.'

'I saw you together and realised he still... you know...' I broke off, unable to speak further. We stared at each other for a good five seconds until eventually I blurted out, 'Fabian never even told me about you. I'd no idea he'd been with you for so long. That, when I met him, you and he were...' I air-quoted the words '..."on a break". Sounds like a weekend in Blackpool.'

'That's strange.' Alexandra gave a little sob. 'He told me everything about you.'

'To make you jealous? To make you come back to him?'

She stared. 'I tried everything to get Fabian back. Even moving up to Yorkshire to be near him when he left London.'

'Not to be near your twin sister, then?'

'No! I followed him up here – can't bear the bloody north to be honest: you all talk funny and say you're having your tea instead of supper.'

'Not all the time,' I objected, put out at her rudeness about my beloved Yorkshire. 'We can be quite posh when we want to be. We do eat "lunch" instead of "us dinner" these days.' More air-quoting of words. I shook my head, to clear it. 'So, just a second, are you saying, you and Fabian are not...?'

'No, you've won, you've got him. He loves you. He said so.'

'I wasn't aware there was any competition going on,' I lied.

'No competition? Oh, don't give me that. Listen, I've known everything about you since you first set your cap at him in the Old Bailey. Inveigled your way into his life, didn't you? What he sees in you, I really can't imagine. But there you go, there's no accounting for taste...' She pushed past me to reach the lift buttons, pressing each one in turn, her voice rising in panic once it appeared we were going nowhere. 'I need to get out... I need to get out of here... I get claustrophobia...'

'I'm not wonderful in enclosed spaces myself,' I said. If what she'd said about Fabian was true, I could afford to be magnanimous. She'd said Fabian loved me. He *loved me*. 'Alexandra, you need to calm down. I'm so sorry, but you need to *calm down*. Or we'll use up all the oxygen.'

That probably wasn't the best thing to say, because she now started hyperventilating.

'Please, Alexandra, just try taking deep breaths... right, alarm, there must be one... here it is. We're still on the ground floor, I think. We've not moved since you got in the lift.'

A disembodied male voice crackled over the intercom. 'Lift engineer. You called? What's up?'

'What's up?' For heaven's sake. 'We're stuck in the lift. We're on the ground floor and it won't move.'

'Ground floor? Well, that makes it a lot easier. Have you tried pressing the open-door button?'

'Oh? Open-door button? Silly me, why didn't I think of that?' I gave it another couple of pushes for good measure. 'No, no go.'

'Hang on, we'll be with you in five minutes.'

It was very strange standing in a tiny enclosed space with your lover's ex-lover (make a great title for that book I always intended writing one day: *My Lover's Ex-Lover*) waiting to be released. Did we conscientiously avoid looking at each other, remaining silent, or should I try striking up a conversation such as, *What's the weather been like with you up in Ilkley? Doing anything interesting this weekend? Been away yet this year?* Which, seeing we were still in January, was a bit pointless. Mind you, girls like Alexandra probably went off *en famille* to the slopes of Gstaad or Cortina d'Ampezzo...

Alexandra had stopped crying and hyperventilating but was simply standing, stony-faced, and I truly didn't know what to say to comfort her. What was there to say?

Voices, some banging, some laughter (this was funny?) and the next moment the lift doors were being forced apart with something metallic and three men in yellow hi-vis jackets were peering in at us.

'You're out now, love,' one man was saying as another attached an 'Out of Order' notice to the door.

Alexandra went to exit and I laid a hand on her arm. 'I'm sorry, Alexandra. I'm *truly* sorry.'

She gave me one final look of distaste, shook her head at me before elbowing the three men out of her way and shooting up the stone steps towards her car. I waited a good five minutes, not wanting to bump into her again (as one inevitably did down every aisle in Sainsbury's after an initial 'hello, how are you?' with someone you'd not seen for years and had to then pretend to be finding something incredibly interesting in ladies' incontinence pads or the tinned pilchards in order to avoid eye contact).

I took out my phone and saw there were three messages:

> Robyn what are you playing at? What the hell are you doing in Leeds? I'm here, with an open bottle of wine and two steaks that are ready to go under the grill! Love you, you know that.
>
> Fabian xxx

And:

> Oh, girls, the flight here was so exciting. I'm in a posh restaurant in Montmartre with the very lovely Kamran. I think he likes me too! See you all tomorrow. Oh, and I need to tell you something.
>
> Mum xx

> PS, Jess, can you make sure Roger has plenty of water in his bowl?

And:

> Robyn, it's me, Jo. Just been doing a lot more research on your mum's birth mother but not getting very far really. But then, my mum's just been round and we got talking!!!! Ring me tomorrow, would you?!!!!!
>
> Jo xxx

Ten minutes later I was heading home. Home to Dower Cottage.

Home to Fabian.

33

On the Saturday morning, I revelled – utterly revelled – in staying in bed with Fabian. No school, no longer any huge concerns about Sorrel, no having to worry about Mum, who appeared to have had a whale of a time with Kamran Sattar the previous evening. She'd texted at two in the morning to say she was safely back at home and we could all stop worrying that Kamran's plane had gone down in the Channel and she was now swimming with the fishes. If my mum appeared to be rubbing noses with the family who was intent on knocking down St Mede's as well as Hudson House, then really who was I to be self-righteous? The St Mede's plan didn't appear to be moving forwards yet but, when it did start, I'd be there with the rest of the protesters with my 'Hands Off St Mede's' banner. I wanted nothing more than to get Sorrel through her audition in London in two days' time, put on a successful production of *Grease* in eight weeks and never ever let go of Fabian Mansfield Carrington.

Ever again.

'How could you doubt me?' he'd asked once I'd got back to

the cottage the previous evening. 'Don't you trust me? You still don't get it that I want nobody but you? How do I get it into your obstinate head, Robyn?' He'd shaken his own head in my direction, still cross and frustrated with me, but then had scooped me up in his arms, taken me upstairs, leaving me in no doubt of his love for me.

'Oy,' I said now as Fabian stood with his binoculars searching for the pair of swans that nested on the village pond, 'you'll be arrested if you keep standing at the window with no clothes on. They'll think some naked pervert has moved in. And, you could try bringing toasted crumpets and a pot of coffee back to bed with you,' I went on. 'I think that might go a long way as compensation for my having to witness another woman wrapped round you in The Alchemist in Leeds.'

'It wasn't easy, Robyn,' Fabian said, turning back to me, and not for the first time I marvelled at his bloody gorgeous body. 'We'd been working all day on Joel's case and I couldn't say anything to Alex in the office – not professional at all for us to be discussing our personal relationship. I suggested a drink so that I could break it to her as gently as I could that any relationship we might be having...'

'Relationship you might be having?' I asked crossly, sitting up in bed.

'...would be purely professional to help Joel. That I'd only taken on this case because of Sorrel. I'd see it through but after that, I don't care what it takes or where it takes us, Jess and I are going into the restaurant business together—'

He broke off as my phone rang.

'Leave it, Robyn,' he said, coming over, raining little kisses down my back, reaching a hand to lift my hair as his mouth moved to that little hollow above my collarbone he'd discovered was my downfall...

'Hang on, it's Mum,' I breathed reluctantly. 'Just let me take it. You do breakfast and I promise, after that I'll give you my undivided attention... sorry, Mum, I was talking to Fabian then... sorry, you want to do *what*...? Today...? Why now...? You and Jess are going over...? And Sorrel as well? Right, OK... yes... yes... I'll come as well... don't think you'll get anywhere though...'

Mum carried on talking for another five minutes, one minute slightly tearful, one minute animated. I put the phone down, lying back on the pillows, but my phone rang immediately once more.

'Hi, Jo... You OK...? Today...? Later this morning...? I don't know where *here* is, Jo...' I laughed. 'Oh, I didn't realise you were in Beddingfield too. For some reason I thought you lived near school... What's up...? OK, tell me when I get there...' I quickly wrote down the address she gave me. 'I promised I'd take Boris for a walk... I'll call in on my way if you're OK with a Goldendoodle...?'

'Who're you talking to?' Fabian, followed by a salivating Boris, was back with a tray piled high with breakfast goodies. 'Hang on, let me get this dog back downstairs.'

'Mum...' I said, biting into a crisp crumpet, butter running down my chin. 'God, I don't know how you manage to get these crumpets just right, Fabian. Mine are always soft and floppy...'

'*Never* have I countenanced *anything* floppy.' He grinned, leering lasciviously like a dirty old man, and I started to laugh through my mouthful of crumpet.

I took another wonderful bite. 'Not even floppy disks, years ago?' I mumbled.

'You had floppy dicks, years ago?' Fabian started laughing. 'No wonder you were hot on my heels in Leeds last night looking for what you knew you'd be missing...'

'And then Jo from school on the phone – you know, who's

trying to work out Mum's family history for us? I said I'd pop in when I'm out walking Boris. I know you've some work to do.'

'Is your mum grounded?' Fabian was slightly indignant. 'I can't believe you allowed her to go off with the enemy.'

'Grounded?' I stared as a picture of Mum, ordered to her room for daring to fly off with Kamran Sattar, flashed before me. 'Oh, you mean, literally!' I laughed. 'We were hoping Mr Sattar might spill the beans about what he's up to with both Hudson House and St Mede's.'

'And did he?'

'That's what we're hoping to find out. But—' I swallowed, reaching for my mug '—Mum says she wants to go over to the Foleys' herself.'

Fabian swallowed his last bit of crumpet, both he and Boris – who'd crept back upstairs – looking longingly at my remaining one, and whistled. 'Why?'

'No idea, unless it's because Jess and I have already tried to get things out of them and failed. She'll feel a lot braver facing them with the three of us behind her.'

'Jesus, I'd like to be a fly on the wall when this Foley woman opens the door on all four of you Allen women.' Fabian pulled a scared face. 'One of you at any one time is more than enough, but the four of you on the doorstep...?' Fabian exhaled. 'Good luck with that one.'

* * *

'Whoa, he's a big boy.' Jo Cooper, Head of History at St Mede's, laughed as Boris, ordered to sit, quivered excitedly, desperate to greet her. 'Bring him in, he's fine.'

'Watch your ornaments,' I cautioned. 'He's a bit like a bull in the proverbial.'

I followed her into a tiny kitchen and then through to a beautiful but untidy sitting room where a woman, probably in her mid-seventies, was attempting to clear the papers and books from every surface. She looked up and smiled, her arms full of back copies of *The Guardian* as well as piles of *Family Tree* and *Find Your Ancestors*. A large Mac computer was drowning under a deluge of school planning, papers and marking. Three piles of St Mede's red history exercise books were open, obviously awaiting Jo's attention.

'Jo, how the hell do you work like this?' The older woman tutted before smiling at me and bending to give Boris the attention he craved.

'God, sorry,' I said as Boris scattered two of the piles in his eagerness to greet the woman.

'Oh, don't worry!' Jo laughed. 'The Year 9 essays on the Treaty of Versailles probably make as much sense with a few paw prints on them… Mum, this is Robyn from school. Robyn, my mum, Janice. Mum used to teach at St Mede's twenty-five years ago.'

'Oh, really?'

'Needlecraft, we called it when I started. The girls made their aprons, covers for their cookery baskets and even summer dresses. Did quite a bit of teaching cooking in domestic science as well. Then it all changed to CDT…'

'CDT?' I grinned. 'Gosh, I remember that – craft, design and technology.'

'…and after that it wasn't my thing.' Janice smiled. 'Ended up teaching infants, for my sins.'

'On the phone you sounded as if you'd discovered something exciting, Jo?' I said, finally managing to rein in Boris, before sitting down on the one chair devoid of papers.

'Well, not me. Mum here…'

'Oh?'

'So,' Janice started, 'before I decided to train as a teacher, I was a mender at Hudson's – the huge textile mill at the far end of the village? All apartments now, of course.'

I nodded and she carried on.

'I did my O levels at night – in those days you could do a Cert Ed at teacher training college with just five O levels, especially if you were classed a mature student.'

'My sister, Jess, is in charge up at Hudson House now it's a care home,' I said. 'You know, the fabulous great house the Hudsons built years ago? Which the Sattar brothers are about to knock down?'

'I'd heard that. Along with St Mede's?' Janice sniffed crossly. 'And yes, I know your sister – I've met her up there a couple of times when I've been visiting.'

'Oh? You know it? My mum's always up there too at the moment,' I said. 'Loves the garden.'

'I know. I've met Lisa there as well.' Janice was obviously trying to get on with her story.

'Really? Gosh, small world.'

Janice was silent for a few seconds. 'The thing is, love,' she began, 'and, you know, Eloise made me promise not to tell anyone...'

'Eloise?'

'Eloise Hudson. Who I go to visit up at Hudson House. She's the daughter of Ralph Hudson who was in charge at Hudson's until Eloise's brothers Brian, and then Michael, took over when he ran off.'

'*Who* ran off?' I shook my head, trying to work out who was who.

'Mr Ralph, Eloise's father. Bit of a scandal. He'd been having an affair with Mr Brian's secretary for a year or so – what was she called?' Janice paused, closing her eyes to think. 'Linda, Linda

Munro, that was it. She was a right dolly bird! We menders and weavers all had a good idea although we never let on to Eloise. Linda was pregnant and they both just upped and left. Went off to South Africa where Ralph had contacts – started another textile business, I believe.'

'Mum, get on to Eloise; tell Robyn what you told me.' Jo, obviously listening from the kitchen, was back with mugs of coffee.

'Once I heard Eloise was back in Beddingfield – she and that husband of hers, Christopher Howard, lived out towards north Leeds, so I'm not sure why he brought her back here – mind you, not easy finding a spot for someone with early-onset dementia... anyway, Bex, who also works up there, lives next door to me and she happened to mention that Eloise was a resident. So, I started to visit her just before Christmas.'

I shrugged, smiling. 'OK?'

'I blame myself, really.' Janice pulled a face.

'For what?'

'For encouraging her to come out on the town with us when we were seventeen and eighteen. She used to come down to my house – we lived near St Mede's when I was a kid – and borrow my clothes...'

'Nana Norma was a whizz with a needle,' Jo put in.

'...and I'd do her hair and her make-up,' Janice continued. 'Hang on, I've been up in the loft this morning when I knew you were coming. I've some photos. And letters she sent me.' Janice reached for a brown envelope, passing over several photographs of a beautiful blonde in a short dress. 'That's Eloise Hudson. So, the thing is, I'm wondering if Eloise could be your grandmother.'

'Sorry?' My head shot up in shock.

'Eloise fell in love with one of the mill workers; his family was from the Mirpur area of Pakistan. Junayd Sattar came to work at Hudson's when he was just fifteen and he'd been there four or five years when Eloise started temping at the mill. Educated himself at night school like me. He was very bright. And exceptionally handsome into the bargain. They were both brilliant photographers... they got together.'

I shook my head, trying to make sense of what Janice was saying. 'Sattar? Any relation of the Sattar brothers?'

Janice shook her head. 'I hadn't thought of that. I've no idea. Anyway, Eloise got pregnant...'

'To one of her father's Pakistani mill workers?' I exhaled. 'Blimey, I bet that went down well?'

'Eloise came straight down to tell me. She was distraught. Mainly because Junayd's family, thinking he was spending too much time with – how shall we say? Not one of *them*? – were intent on sending him back to Mirpur. An arranged marriage to get him out of the way...'

'But, honestly, Janice, I don't see where you're going with all this?'

'Just listen, Robyn,' Jo encouraged, her eyes wide with excitement.

'Eloise didn't know what to do. My mum and I didn't know how to help. Getting pregnant when you weren't married, in the late 1960s, was bad enough, but when the father is a... you know... and one of the mill workers to boot...?' Janice pulled an imaginary knife across her throat. 'Out of the blue, Junayd was sent back to Mirpur to get married; the plan was to bring his new wife back here to Yorkshire, I suppose. That's what happened in those days.'

'Still does, to some extent,' Jo added, sagely.

'Eloise was utterly distraught and ended up telling her granny she was pregnant. What was her granny called...? Maude, I think. Or was that her mother? No, her mother was Muriel. Muriel Hudson, that's it. *She'd* been having an affair with the local MP but that's neither here nor there. Anyway, Eloise thought her granny was the one person she could trust when my mum and me didn't know what to do to help.'

'And?'

'Well,' Janice went on, 'obviously her granny wasn't to be trusted. Together, Muriel and Maude Hudson cooked up some story, saying Eloise was going to work as an au pair in Canada. Maude's sister, apparently the black sheep of the family, had settled in Quebec, falling in love and living in the wilds with some lumberjack just after the First World War. You know what it's like, the one member of the family who's always been persona non grata! No one talks about?'

I nodded.

'Quebec was the least... shall we say socially accepting... of all the Canadian states in the 1960s?' Jo had her history teacher head on. 'You know how awful it was for young, pregnant and unmarried girls in Ireland at the time?'

'Not so good here, either.' Janice frowned.

'Well, just as bad in Canada, if not worse.'

'Maude and Eloise stayed with this sister of Maude's until she had the baby...' Janice interrupted. 'Eloise wrote to tell me what was happening. She was beside herself about Junayd.'

'I was up until late last night, Robyn.' Jo got the conversation back to herself. 'Researching what it was like for an unmarried mother in Canada. They were often bound to a hospital bed, over-medicated and told to forget their "illegitimate" child, or to pretend the baby had never been born at all. I didn't realise, but societal norms and religious organisations played a profoundly controlling role in the lives of Canadians right up to the seventies. I was looking at statistics last night and, apparently, 600,000 babies – over half a million, can you imagine? – were born to unmarried mothers, and most of these girls were coerced into surrendering their babies to married couples wanting to adopt...'

'Right, I'm going to stop you right there.' I actually put up my hand. 'Mum wasn't born in Canada. She was born in Surrey. Her adoptive parents moved up to Yorkshire when Mum was nine, but there's absolutely no connection apart from that. She and my father – Jayden – happened to break down in Beddingfield on their way back to Leeds when Mum was in her early twenties. Mum loved the village and decided it was where she wanted to have her baby – my sister Jess...'

'But your mum's birth date is exactly the same as the one Eloise has engraved on her bracelet. You said so, Robyn.' Both Jo and Janice were looking crestfallen, obviously disappointed that I'd burst their bubble. 'And—' Jo gave it one last shot '—your mum's dual heritage. It would fit perfectly.'

'Well, it would, but there must have been many babies born in Quebec on that particular date.'

'Well, I'm still looking,' Jo said. 'I'm doing it for Eloise now. I want to know what happened to *her* baby.'

'Do you even know if she had a daughter, Janice?'

Janice looked slightly embarrassed. 'When she wrote to me – you know after she came back from Canada – she just said she'd had the baby and it had been immediately taken away for adoption. She married Christopher Howard fairly soon after that and we lost touch. In her last letter to me, she said her husband had no idea why she'd been away in Canada; assumed she'd been visiting her great-aunt as well as working as an au pair in Montreal. When I was up at Hudson House, last week, she told me she'd had a son called Adam, but she was very confused and her being quite deaf doesn't help. I'm not convinced she really knew who I was.' Janice gave a little laugh. 'Aw, I'm sorry, love, I think our Jo and I've got a bit carried away with all this.'

'That's the big problem with ancestry,' Jo said, equally embarrassed. 'You go down one track, convincing yourself it's the right one, because you want it to be—'

She broke off as my phone rang.

'Sorry, Jess... I'll be back at the cottage in fifteen... Just need to bring Boris back and then we can get off.'

I turned to the other two. 'Thank you so much, for all your help. Sorry, it turned out to be a bit of a wild goose trail.'

Jo was cheerful once more. 'Oh, don't worry. I'll keep on, but now I'm going to concentrate on tracking down Eloise's baby in Canada. This ancestry lark is more bloody addictive than heroin...' She laughed. 'See you at school next week.'

34

'Fabian doesn't mind you not spending Saturday with him?' Mum asked once I'd decanted Boris back to the cottage and was strapping myself into the back seat of Jess's van.

'He's got a load of stuff to do.' I turned to Sorrel. 'Joel's stuff.'

'I know, I know. I can't believe he's doing this for him. Honestly, Robyn, we're so grateful.'

'Oh, Sorrel, you're far too young to be worrying about this. Too young to be involved in something as serious as this. Too young to be "we".' I air-quoted the words. 'You should have your head free of it all, looking forward to your audition.'

'Looking forward to it? I'm terrified! I'm only coming with you this morning to take my mind off it.' She laughed. 'And to see if my grandparents are as horrible as you and Jess have made out. I'm dying to see the cat-ridden monster in the dining room for myself.'

'They're NOT your grandparents,' Mum snapped crossly. She was pale, nervous and irritable.

'I don't know why you're putting yourself through this, Mum,' I said, reaching forward to stroke her arm.

'Because I don't know WHO I AM.' She almost shouted the last three words. 'And now... well, now I need to know.'

'OK, OK, we get that.' I sat back, chastised, as Jess set off towards the M1 and Sheffield, but then leaned forwards to Mum once more. 'So, you had a great time last night? Woah, Montmartre, for heaven's sake? Paris? In a private jet, you little gadabout...'

'Patronising!' Mum tutted, and I realised she really was, very unusually for her, in a mood. 'And it wasn't exactly a jet, more a little tin can.'

'Not good enough for you?' The three of us all laughed. 'Aiming for a proper jet next time, are you, Mum?'

'It was lovely. Really lovely.' Mum paused. 'The loveliest evening I've ever had.'

'Ever? Blimey!' I exhaled.

'He was lovely...'

'Even though he's the enemy?' Jess gave Mum a quick glance, before concentrating on the road once more.

'Exactly. That's why I won't be seeing him again.'

'But does he want to, Mum?' Sorrel leaned forwards. 'You know, get it on with you?'

'Get it on with me?' Mum tutted again. 'For heaven's sake.'

'Did you kiss him?' Sorrel grinned.

'For someone who's been up to what you've apparently been up to with Joel Sinclair,' Mum snapped, 'that comes over as being particularly childish, if not downright condescending, Sorrel.'

The three of us sat back at that, well and truly told off.

After five minutes' silence in the car, Mum relented. 'I can't see him again. You're right, all of you, he is "the enemy".' More air-quoting of words from Mum. 'Listen, particularly you, Jess – but, I suppose you as well, Robyn, seeing it concerns Fabian...'

'What?' All three of us spoke as one.

'Kamran's definitely knocking Hudson House down?' I asked.

'The sale can't have gone through so quickly!' Jess put in.

'No.' Mum paused. 'He's...' she exhaled '...he's turning Hudson House into a restaurant.'

'What?' I actually put up my hands.

'Oh, marvellous!' Jess snapped, narrowly missing a pigeon that had dared venture off the pavement into her path. 'Fucking marvellous! Wonderful!' She breathed deeply, hands clutching the steering wheel tightly. 'Did you tell him that was *our* idea? Mine and Fabian's?'

'No, I wasn't going to give any information like that away. I'm not stupid,' Mum said. 'So, another reason not to see him again,' she added crossly.

'Hey,' Sorrel said, 'just keep in with him, Mum, because you can then get him to take on Jess as Chief Chef.'

'Head Chef,' I murmured, ever the pedant.

'I don't want to work for the bloody Sattars,' Jess hissed. 'Especially once they've thrown out all the old dears from Hudson House. I want to work *with* someone – own our own place. I want to be with Fabian!'

'Steady on,' I murmured, half laughing. 'I've only just wrestled him out of the clutches of Alexandra Brookfield.'

'Do you fancy Fabian, Jess?' Sorrel asked, laughing herself.

'Oh, don't be so effing stupid, Sorrel,' Jess snapped crossly but, catching her eye in the rear-view mirror, I realised she was suffused with embarrassment. Well, this was interesting!

'Excuse me, can we have less of the bad language?' Mum said irritably. 'Anyway,' she went on, 'Jess wouldn't get a look-in, even if she *was* prepared to work for the Sattars in their restaurant.'

'Oh?' We all leaned forwards once more.

'His nephew, Zain, presently working in Paris, is champing at the bit to come over and work at what would be the first Pan Asian fusion restaurant in Beddingfield.'

'What's that?' Sorrel asked.

'Fusion cuisine,' Mum replied knowledgably, obviously quoting Kamran, 'is producing inventive and flavourful new fusions of what we tend to eat in the West by using traditional Asian-style ingredients, dishes and cooking methods.'

'Great stuff,' Jess growled.

'Well, maybe you and Fabian could still do what you wanted to do, then?' I said, knowing how disappointed Fabian was going to be when I told him the news. Hell, I hoped this wasn't going to mean him heading back to London, his dreams in tatters. 'You know, the pair of you take on the white house in the garden and—'

'Don't be so bloody ridiculous,' Jess snapped again. 'The white house is part of the Hudson House estate. And you can't open two restaurants within a few hundred yards of each other. Oh, I'm so fed up now!'

'You're speeding, Jess,' Mum censured her. 'I knew I shouldn't have said anything about Kamran's plans. Can you slow down? I feel really, really sick. I'm frightened,' Mum went on. 'Terrified of seeing them again after all these years.'

'Shall we turn round, Mum?' I soothed. 'Go home for a nice cup of tea and one of Jess's scones? Forget all this wondering who you are? We know who you are! You're our lovely mum. And that's all that matters.'

She turned to me in the back seat, her face pale. 'No, it's not, Robyn, it's not all that matters. I need to know.'

* * *

'Goodness me!' The woman on the doorstep peered round the front door but said nothing more.

'Is that her?' Sorrel whispered as the pair of us stood behind Mum and Jess.

'No!' I mouthed back.

'What do you want, Lisa?' the woman asked.

'I want to know,' Mum said, staring in obvious confusion at the woman. 'I want to know who I am. Who my birth mother is... Is it Wendy? Aunty Wendy?'

'Aunty Wendy...?' I whispered, nudging Sorrel, whose eyes were saucers.

'Yes, well, we'd all like to know that, wouldn't we?' The woman opened the door to let us in. 'I don't know what you're going to find out from *her*, Lisa. Goodness,' she said again, 'I'd have known you anywhere, you've not changed a bit. Still as beautiful as when you were a little girl. As beautiful as the day you left... the day you ran away.' Aunty Wendy led the way back down the same hallway Jess and I had been in only days earlier.

'You've visitors, Karen,' Wendy said.

Karen Foley turned from where she was huddled in a chair, a blanket wrapped round her bony shoulders. 'You again?' she snapped as Jess walked in, followed by Sorrel and me. Then, her face white and unmoving, she simply stared as Mum came into the room last, ushered in by Aunty Wendy. I actually thought Mum was going to keel over and, always mindful of the seizures she'd suffered in the past, I held onto her arm.

'You all right, Mum?' I asked gently.

'I'm fine,' she whispered in a strangled voice before walking over to Karen and standing in front of her. 'Hello, Mother. How are you?'

'Well, well, well, look what the cat's dragged in. What are *you* doing here?'

'I thought it was about time we put our differences behind us.' Mum smiled, only the slight tremor in her voice and her pale face belying her obvious anguish at being there. 'Time we were friends, don't you think? I know you met Jess and Robyn the other day, but I'd like you to meet Sorrel as well.' Mum stepped backwards, taking Sorrel's hand before bringing her towards Karen.

'Hmm, another one, no doubt, who thinks a pretty face will take her places. Looks like you, Lisa.'

'Mother – Mum – I've come here today to ask you – *to beg of you* – to tell me who I am. You must know more about who my birth parents are? Please? Let's... you know... let's put the bad times behind us and just tell me. I'll go away then and not bother you again. Was my birth mother English? Or Indian? You never would tell me the truth, always changing your mind from one to the other, and I don't understand why.'

'Go away, Lisa. Go back home. I'm telling you nothing. Nothing. Show them out, Wendy. She's making me feel ill.'

Wendy shrugged, turning to Mum, who was almost in tears. 'I'm sorry, dear. You're going to have to get yourself on that *Who Do You Think You Are?* programme. Come on, into the kitchen: I'll not send you off without showing some manners.'

Jess, Mum and I followed her down the corridor and into the kitchen where I'd made tea just a few days earlier. Four cats sat outside the door to the dining room, behind which, I assumed, was still Adrian Foley.

'Mr Foley in there?' I asked.

'Hmm, I try to come as often as I can – I moved back to Buxton when my husband died a couple of years ago – to check if my brother's OK. He hates those cats and they always manage to get into his room somehow. I have an awful feeling she lets them go in deliberately. I'm at the stage of trying to get Adrian into a home, although Karen won't hear of it. The situation's awful.'

'Oh, you're *his* sister,' I said. 'I thought you were Karen's sister.'

'Goodness me, no.' She gave me a hard stare before going to fill the kettle. 'Sit down, dear,' she instructed Mum, giving her a pat on the shoulder. 'Come on, fill me in on your life now. You've three lovely girls – where's the little one? Oh... lavatory, right... Lisa, dear, it's not your fault. Karen always was a very, very strange woman. Bad enough before the pair of them went off to Canada...'

'I never knew they lived in Canada!' Mum said, staring. 'When?'

'Oh, before you were born, dear. They were teaching out there. Some mission school – Pentecostal, I think it was – in the back of beyond. Your Uncle Philip and I had gone to live in Australia, so we weren't actually around at the time. I always found Karen a strange fish – too religious for my liking – never understood what Adrian saw in her. Although, to be fair, Adrian was always a bit strange as well. Your Uncle Philip couldn't abide the pair of them. We had little contact – I first saw you when you were about ten and had moved up here to Sheffield, when your Uncle Philip and I came back from Oz for several months to see to my parents...'

'Wendy,' I finally managed to get a word in, my pulse racing with excitement, 'could you tell us when Karen and Adrian actually went out to Canada?'

'Well, I don't really know, dear. We'd become estranged – Karen didn't get on with me or my parents. She wanted Adrian to have nothing to do with his family. Very, very, possessive of him, she was. We emigrated to Australia, as I said, and we came back fleetingly just before both my parents died – cancer, the pair of them – young, in their sixties. We'd heard Adrian and Karen had adopted a baby while they were living in Surrey, but we didn't get to meet you, Lisa, until Adrian got the headship of St Mark's and moved back up here to Sheffield while we were in the UK looking after my parents. To be honest, dear, I'm only here now because Adrian's the only family I have left in the UK. More than likely, I'll be heading back to Australia very soon to be with my boys. I just don't like leaving him here, in that dining room, with *her*... and those cats...'

'Where's Sorrel?' Jess suddenly asked. 'Has she gone back to the car?'

Leaving Mum catching up with Wendy, Jess and I headed back down the hall to find her. I hoped she hadn't gone to take a look at Adrian Foley for herself. The sitting-room door was open and we could hear Sorrel talking to Karen. Jess was about to go in, but I put a finger to my lips and my ear to the door. Sorrel was sitting on the arm of the chair, her back towards us, so I couldn't hear everything that was being said.

'...obviously very early on...' Sorrel was saying.

'...and fifteen...?'

'...sixteen next month...'

'...typical of Lisa not to bring up her daughters properly... fifteen... and pregnant... goodness me... that was God punishing you for...'

'...I don't believe in a vengeful God... never had babies of your own? Why adopt...?'

'...my Adam... he died too...'

'...so sorry, Karen... mine was just a few weeks... and that was awful... why...?'

'...I don't know... he came early... God took him back...'

'What are you *doing*?' Mum was behind us and Karen, hearing her voice, immediately clammed up.

Sorrel walked over to the open door where the three of us were standing, trying to listen. 'I was just getting somewhere,' she mouthed, shaking her head. 'I'll tell you in the car.'

I went into the room, knelt down by Karen and took her hand. 'Would you tell me just one thing, Karen?'

Karen Foley looked up and I could see utter desolation in her small blue eyes as she held my own.

'Karen, was Mum – Lisa – actually born in Canada?'

She said nothing, but the look of fear that passed over her face was enough.

'I think she was, wasn't she?' I asked gently.

Still nothing, but no denial.

'And I think you've known all along who her birth mother is.'

'She was a trollop,' Karen eventually said. 'Wealthy, from a good family, but threw it all away, tomcatting around when she got the itch in her pants with one of her father's workers. She'd had a public-school education, *a finishing school in Switzerland*, for heaven's sake.' Spittle formed at the corners of her mouth, tiny flecks landing on my arm as she spat *Switzerland*. 'And then she slept with a man before she was married. A... a foreigner as well. She didn't deserve to have her baby live when *my* little boy died.' Karen's voice broke but she still didn't cry. 'Her grandmother told me everything. Distraught, the poor woman was. Couldn't wait to get the girl's baby adopted with a good, God-fearing family and get the girl back to England and brush it all under the carpet. And we did that, Mr Foley and I. We took that... that *bastard* child on, brought her up, did everything for her. Made sure she kept on the straight and narrow. And look how that turned out.'

'Mum, you mean? Lisa?'

'Of course, Lisa! Who else would I be talking about? I tried to beat the devil out of her... You said she'd got some illness now? Well, that's the devil. You need to watch that little sister of yours;

she needs exorcising too...' Karen broke off as the front door banged, glaring at me. 'You got what you came for,' she growled. 'Leave me alone now and don't *any* of you come back.'

35

'I think we should go straight to Jo's place,' I said, once we were all in the car. 'What Jo and Janice told me this morning must all be true.'

'Jo?' Sorrel demanded. 'Ms Cooper from school? What did she say? Tell us!'

'I think Mum's had enough,' Jess said.

'I'm starving,' Sorrel interrupted. 'Can we go and get something to eat? And, if you hadn't let on you were outside the door, earwigging,' she went on, 'I bet Karen would have told me everything.'

Mum, sitting upright but ashen-faced, didn't say a word.

'Coffee, Mum?' Sorrel asked. 'A coffee and a bun? Would that help?'

'Shhh, Sorrel,' I admonished. 'Just shush two minutes while we work out what to do.' I turned to Mum. 'Mum? What do you want to do?'

She still didn't say a word but stared stonily ahead out of the window.

'I think she's in shock,' Jess whispered, turning to Sorrel and me in the back.

'Hot sweet tea, then?' Sorrel mouthed back. 'And a big doughnut?'

'Sorrel, shut it, will you? Oh, Mum...' I leaned forwards to comfort her but she remained utterly still and I began to seriously worry about her. Should we be getting her to Dr Matt at the hospital? 'D'you think we should ring Matt?' I asked.

'Oh, yes,' Jess said, obviously relieved at the thought of passing Mum on to a professional when we three didn't appear to have a clue what to do. 'I think so...'

'Have I got this right?' Mum spoke slowly, but succinctly. 'I was born in Canada?'

We all nodded.

'So, I'm Canadian?'

'Yes, I reckon you're Canadian,' Sorrel said sagely. 'You know, like Celine Dion and... hey, does that make me half Canadian? Will it help me get a green card to work on Broadway...?'

'Sorrel, shhh.' Jess and I tutted in unison.

'I've always wanted to go to Canada,' Mum said, almost dreamily.

'Look, Mum,' I now blurted out. 'I think Jo from school, who's been looking into your family tree, is on the right track after all...'

'Well, then, take me there, please.'

'Really?' Jess exchanged looks with Sorrel and me before turning back to Mum.

'Absolutely. You don't think I can go home and sit down to listen to *The Archers* with a cup of tea when I've my own personal drama going on, do you?'

'Can we stop on the way there?' Sorrel piped up. 'Because if I don't get something to eat, I'm going to *die*.'

* * *

'Oh, good, Janice, you're still here,' I said as we all trooped through Jo's kitchen and into her sitting room once more.

'I wasn't going anywhere when our Jo told me you'd rung her and were bringing your mum round. I'm on absolute eggs.' Janice turned to Mum, taking her hand. 'Oh, love...' but didn't seem to be able to say anything further.

"Lo, miss,' Sorrel said, slightly embarrassed at being in her favourite teacher's home. Probably, like all kids, Sorrel assumed teachers actually lived in the staffroom at school.

'I was just on the point of ringing you when you called,' Jo said, her face alight with excitement. 'Look at this. Found it on a Canadian website this morning once you'd left. Eloise Hudson had obviously been trying to find her lost child.'

Jo handed me a printout from a website aiming to match children adopted in Canada with their birth mother, and the four of us gathered round to read.

Birth Date: 5-5-1969
Adoptee Gender: Male
Adoptee Birth Race: White & Pakistani
Name Given to Adoptee by Birth Parents: none
Adoptee Birth Mother's Name: Eloise Muriel Howard
Adoptee Birth Mother's Maiden Name: Hudson
Adoptee Birth Mother's Race: British
Adoptee Birth Father's Name: Junayd Sattar
Adoptee Birth Father's Race: Pakistani
Adoptee Birth Hospital: Barrett Tower
Adoption agency: ?
Age of Adoptee When Adopted: at birth
Name Given to Adoptee by Adoptive Parents: Adam

'This doesn't tell us anything we didn't know,' I said, frowning, 'apart from the fact that Eloise herself had been trying to find her child years ago. And, that she was looking for a male child. And look, the father was from Pakistan which fits with what you said about Eloise being pregnant to Junayd Sattar, the worker at her dad's mill. But nothing here links Mum to Eloise and Junayd.'

'She told me she'd had a baby boy in Canada.' Mum nodded, disappointment etched on her face. 'That her granny had taken her there. And she knew he'd been named Adam.'

'But, listen, listen.' Sorrel was finding it hard to get her words out in her excitement. 'Didn't you hear Karen tell me she'd had a baby of her own before she adopted Mum? That *he* was called Adam. You know, when I was telling her about me being...' Sorrel trailed off, face scarlet, obviously not wanting Jo and Janice to know about her own lost pregnancy.

The slightly tense atmosphere was broken by Mum's phone ringing. When she didn't answer, it rang again. And again.

'I bet that's Kamran, Mum,' I said. 'Go on, go and answer it. He's probably up for another round of Dambusters with you.'

Once it started ringing again, Mum took herself off into the kitchen while the three of us told Jo and Janice the full details of the morning's visit to the Foleys. Five minutes later Mum returned, her face ashen, handing the phone silently to Jess.

'What?' Jess said, surprised. 'You want me to talk to Kamran? About Hudson House and this restaurant idea of his?'

'It's not Kamran.'

Jess took the proffered phone. 'Hello? Oh, Wendy...? I didn't realise you had Mum's number... Right... Right... OK... No...! Oh, my goodness... well... of course not... no... thank you... you did right... I can't tell you how grateful... no, of course we won't... Karen will never know... I promise you.'

'Bloody hell!' A full ten minutes later, Jess finally calmed down enough to sit down. 'Bloody hell!' She took hold of Mum's hand.

'What?' We all spoke as one.

'It would appear Eloise Howard – Hudson – is my mother.' Mum spoke calmly.

'So,' Jess interrupted, 'this is the story, according to Wendy. After we left, Wendy went into Adrian's room. Apparently, she in particular, and to some extent the carers who go in daily, are able to communicate with him – although he and Karen haven't spoken for years. After we'd gone, Adrian was in a state, wanting to know who'd been visiting, what was going on. When Wendy told him why Mum had been back after thirty-odd years, he broke down and it all came out.'

'What did? What came out?' We all leaned forwards eagerly.

'He and Karen had been teaching in some Pentecostal church school in Quebec somewhere... Wendy couldn't remember where...'

'Doesn't matter – go on,' I urged.

'Karen was pregnant and they were to return to England to Adrian's new job in Surrey before the baby was born. She gave birth early – too early – to a little boy she named Adam. In those days, stillborn babies were quickly taken away without the mother seeing or bonding with her lost child. She was in a terrible state, apparently, beside herself with grief. She wandered onto the ward where girls like Eloise were hidden away to have their babies. Eloise had just given birth to you, Mum, and you were whisked away before Eloise could see you. She wasn't even told whether she'd had a boy or a girl.'

'That's awful,' Sorrel exclaimed. 'How *awful* is that?'

'Wendy was speaking quickly,' Jess went on, 'obviously not wanting Karen to know she was on the phone to Mum and me so it was all a bit garbled,' she added, 'but as far as I can make out,

Karen saw *you*, Mum, knew you'd be immediately put up for adoption and obviously decided to get in there first.'

'She couldn't just do that,' I said, stroking Mum's arm. 'Lay claim to Mum like that. There'd be papers to sign, hoops to jump through...'

'Apparently not. Wendy said Adrian told her money had passed hands...'

'They bought you?' I stared at Mum.

'That kind of thing did go on,' Jo put in. 'I've just been researching it: some Canadian adoptions from years back have now been denounced as cultural genocide. The Sixties Scoop involved the removal and adoption of lots of Native American babies, for example. Many were adopted into non-Native American homes both in Canada, across the border in the States and maybe even further afield. There was a sort of black market in babies...' Jo shook her head. 'I reckon where money is involved and with churchy, respectable people offering it...' She trailed off, obviously concerned her words were upsetting for Mum.

'Maybe,' Janice put in, 'Eloise's granny had told the hospital that the baby's father was Indian – you know, rather than Pakistani – and the nurses there assumed she meant Native North American Indian...? Just a thought...'

'So,' Jess went on, trying to speak calmly, but the words tumbling out as she continued, 'Wendy said Adrian told her that Karen was so beside herself with grief that she picked you up, Mum, refusing to let you go, convincing herself you were her baby, that you were a boy, that you were Adam. Wendy appeared to think Adrian didn't know about the money until much later – she said her brother was always tight and he told her *he* certainly wouldn't have shelled out—'

'He was!' Lisa interrupted with a humourless laugh. 'He'd

lose his temper if you put too much butter on your toast, if you left the lights on...'

'So,' Jess went on, 'a lot of money passed hands with the proviso that Eloise must be told she'd had a little boy called Adam...'

'But why?' I still didn't get it.

'Why d'you think?' Sorrel tutted. 'So that Eloise wouldn't ever be able to come looking for her baby. And Mum wouldn't be able to ever find her birth mother.'

'Wendy seemed to think Adrian and the pregnant Karen were on the point of returning to England to take up Adrian's new job in Surrey when Karen unfortunately went into labour. They simply came back with a baby.'

'What about the birth certificate? And a passport for Lisa?' Janice asked.

'A birth certificate and adoption certificate would have been ordered showing all the correct details. Not a problem. And babies travelled on the mother's passport,' Jo explained. 'It was all a lot lot simpler fifty years ago and in the wilds of Canada to boot. I assume this Karen Foley made sure you never saw either, Lisa?'

Mum shook her head. 'I gave up trying to find out anything, to be honest. Once I knew they were biologically nothing to do with me, I was just thankful and left it at that. Luckily, before I ran off with Jayden, I did manage to filch the passport the Foleys had got for me. We'd spent one – really miserable – February half-term holiday when I was fourteen on a rainy conducted bus tour of some horribly boring classical Greek sites. Karen did nothing but moan and complain, and what fourteen-year-old enjoys that sort of thing? Anyway, I've never had a problem renewing my passport.'

'I think you'll need some sort of counselling, love,' Janice advised.

'Possibly.' Mum nodded. 'Although all this *still* doesn't tell me if the porphyria is inherited.'

'Well, Eloise doesn't have any condition other than the dementia she's suffering with now,' Janice said. 'And I never heard that Mr Ralph or Mr Brian at the mill were struck down with anything.'

Mum stared at us all. 'So, for some reason, for some chance in a zillion, Jayden and I ended up in the very village where presumably I was conceived?' She turned her beautiful brown eyes on the three of us and then started a little chortle. Which gained momentum until she was giggling, unable to stop.

'Do something, Jess,' I said, frightened, as we all moved towards her.

'I'm fine,' Mum managed to get out between hiccups. 'I'm really fine.' She paused, turning to Janice. 'And my dad, Janice? This Junayd Sattar? Where is he? Is he still around? Does *he* even know about me?'

'Sattar? Hey, Mum, you were out with Kamran Sattar last night.' Sorrel's eyes gleamed mischievously. 'You'll have to ask him if he knows this mysterious Junayd. They've the same surname after all. That would be funny, wouldn't it, if he knows him?'

36

'I've got it, I've got it, I'm in. They *want* me!' Still in her leotard and ballet pumps, Sorrel dashed down the stairs, throwing herself into my arms as I stood, two days later, in the waiting area of the Susan Yates Theatre School in Camden, north London.

'They've told you already?' I managed to get out. 'They said they'd write...'

'She has a place, Ms Allen.' A rather stern-looking elderly woman had followed Sorrel down. 'And on a full scholarship. We're at the end of the interviewing process; we were extremely impressed with Sorrel here and saw no reason to keep her in suspense.'

'So, when...?'

'After Easter. At the start of the summer term. She'll begin training with us straight away.'

'Her GCSEs?' I asked.

'Of course. She'll sit them here. We are an academic as well as a theatre school. Then, if appropriate, she'll continue with A levels.'

'Oh, I don't want to do *those*,' Sorrel said, eyes shining. 'Just let me dance.'

'We'll see.' The woman smiled. 'Let's take it step by step. We'll send consent and admission forms to Sorrel's parents.' She stopped and paused, her own eyes bright. 'I believe Jayden Allen is Sorrel's father...?'

* * *

'I do hope I haven't got a place just because Susan Yates fancies Jayden,' Sorrel said once we were on the train and heading home.

'Was that actually Susan Yates herself?' I asked, slightly taken aback. 'I didn't know there was an actual Susan Yates.'

'Yes, yes.' Sorrel appeared anxious, her initial excitement being replaced, I could see, by the reality of her new life ahead. 'What if I'm no good? What if I'm homesick? I'll miss Roger.'

I laughed at that. 'Not me, Mum and Jess, then?'

Sorrel tutted. 'And I feel I'm abandoning Joel.'

'There's nothing you can do to help Joel at the moment, Sorrel, you know that. Fabian's defence will be that he was coerced into modern slavery and, as such, he *has* to be referred to the National Referral Mechanism to receive the appropriate support. This all takes absolutely ages. He's in the best possible hands with Fabian, and out of the area over in Castleford.'

'I know, I know, and we're both really grateful. But Joel is so talented, Robyn. He's a brilliant dancer. I feel bad that I'm getting this opportunity while he's mouldering away over there, just waiting for his day in court.'

'I get that,' I said. 'And if there's anything I can do to help him, I will.'

'So, you and Fabian are OK, then?' Sorrel looked at me from under her lashes.

'OK?'

'Jess said... you know... Joel's solicitor, this Alex woman, has left and gone back to London because she was in love with Fabian?'

'Jess tittle-tattling again?' I tutted and then relented. 'Really, Sorrel, everything is fine. More than fine... Hang on, it's Mrs Gossip Gusset herself again...' I reached for my phone, which had been a hotline since leaving London, talking for a good five minutes as the train hurtled back north.

'What? What was all that about?' Sorrel's eyes were wide as she caught bits of the conversation. 'What now? What's happened?'

'Kamran Sattar wants to have dinner with us.'

'Us? Who's *us*?'

'Mum and me and Jess and Fabian.'

'Why?'

'Dunno. We're meeting him this evening.'

'It's almost evening now,' Sorrel said, looking at her watch. 'And are there actually any restaurants open on a Monday?'

'Not a restaurant. His house, apparently, on the other side of Beddingfield.'

* * *

'Blimey, what an amazing place.' Jess's face was a picture as we walked up the drive of the beautiful honey-coloured-stone manor house. 'Did you know he lived out here, Mum?'

'No, why would I?'

'He's not been in touch since Friday, then?' Jess asked.

'Jess, you've asked me that same question constantly over the past three days. No, he *hasn't*! Is that good enough for you?' Mum was nervous. She looked absolutely ravishing, even though she was dressed simply in a short black skirt, black polo-necked sweater and cream jacket.

'And you've no idea what this is all about, Lisa?' Fabian now took his turn as Grand Inquisitor, but was silenced as the huge oak front door opened to reveal a man dressed in jeans and black V-necked sweater, his feet bare. I immediately saw what it was that Mum had fallen for.

'Hi, come in, come in, you found us OK?'

We trooped in past him, Kamran Sattar greeting both Mum and Jess with a kiss to the cheek. 'We've not met.' He smiled, offering a hand to me and Fabian.

We followed him down a beautiful hallway into a sitting room on the left, decorated in neutral cream. Colour came from two full walls of books and several large vases of flowers: winter jasmine and Christmas roses, as well as a huge jug of very early daffodils.

'What can I get you to drink?' Kamran indicated bottles of rather upmarket white and red wines, as well as an impressive array of gins.

Once we were settled with drinks, the four of us sitting somewhat expectantly on the edge of two squashy sofas, drinks politely to hand, Kamran immediately started speaking.

'Sorry I didn't give you much notice.' He smiled.

'No problem,' I said, wanting to put him at his ease. 'Gets me out of the usual Monday-night lesson planning I should have done over the weekend—'

'The thing is...' Kamran interrupted, obviously not interested in my schoolwork, '...the thing is, I think we're possibly related.'

Jess, Mum and I exchanged glances and I saw Mum's face begin to close down. Here was the first man I knew she'd fallen for since Jayden, and now she was being told he was actually family rather than a potential lover.

'What evidence do you have for that, Mr Sattar?' Fabian had his barrister head on and I gave him a warning look.

'Kamran, please. The thing is, I'm really fascinated by family history—'

'You should get together with my friend Jo Cooper from school,' I interrupted.

'I've been with Janice, her mum, this afternoon.' Kamran smiled.

'Oh...? Right...! Oh...!' Mum, Jess and I looked at each other again, our eyes wide.

'Janice?' Fabian asked.

'Jo from school's mum,' I reminded him. 'Janice. You know, who we were with all Saturday after going over to see the Foleys?'

'Look.' Kamran shook his head slightly. 'Janice says she hopes you don't think she's been speaking out of turn...'

'But how on earth do *you* know Janice?' I asked, frowning.

'I don't.' Kamran laughed slightly. 'I mean, *I didn't*. Not until today anyway. I'd called in to see *you*, Jess, up at Hudson House... I wanted to talk to you about Eloise Howard...' He spoke the name slowly, watching our faces for any reaction.

'I've been at a funeral all afternoon,' Jess said. 'Maurice, who died last week...'

'Yes, Bex told me. I didn't stay but, as I was leaving, I was jumped on by Janice.'

'Jumped on?' I laughed at that. 'Even though you'd never met her before?'

'She obviously knew who I was.'

'Most people in Beddingfield do.' I sniffed, remembering his plans for the village. 'And the KS 9 car registration is a bit of a giveaway.'

Ignoring me, Kamran continued. 'She was on her way to see

Eloise Howard... Hudson...' Kamran looked at us with raised eyes but said nothing further.

'And? Could you tell us what was said next, Kamran?' Fabian was still in courtroom mode and I nudged him irritably.

'Of course.' Kamran looked at Mum for a long time and I knew immediately anything she might be feeling for this man was totally reciprocated by him. 'The thing is, back in the mid-sixties, quite a lot of my relatives left Pakistan, invited by the government to work here in the UK. Several ended up working at Eloise Hudson's family's mill.'

'You *know*, don't you?' I asked.

'About Junayd and Eloise?' Kamran nodded. 'But not until recently. It's been the big Sattar family secret for years: Junayd packed off back to Lahore to an arranged marriage once his family got to know what he'd been up to.'

Jess took Mum's hand. 'And did Junayd bring his new wife back here? Back to Beddingfield? Is he still here?'

Kamran shook his head. 'No, according to the story, he became very ill...'

'Porphyria!' Mum said softly, her eyes closed.

'Sorry?' Kamran frowned. 'If that's the posh name for a burst appendix with complications, then yes.'

'Oh!' The relief on all three of our faces must have been comical to see.

'Junayd apparently was really poorly,' Kamran went on, 'and was in Lahore General for a long time with probably what we'd called sepsis, today. Anyway, once he was well enough, he was married to Alina...'

'He married her?' Mum interrupted, her eyes huge. 'Even though Eloise – my mum – was pregnant with me?'

'Family, tradition, religion,' Kamran said. 'You have to understand, Lisa, things were so different fifty years ago in a traditional Muslim family in Pakistan. Junayd had brought great shame on his family.'

'And I guess the plan was to bring his new wife back to Yorkshire?' I asked Kamran.

'As far as I know, Alina wasn't allowed to come to the UK immediately after the marriage because of the nikah...'

'The nikah?' Fabian frowned. 'Isn't that a religious marriage contract that can be held separately to buy time, or to circumvent British legal or immigration systems?'

'You know more than me, Fabian.' Kamran smiled. 'Suffice it to say, their return to the UK was delayed again and again. By which time Junayd had found work as a photographer with local, and then with national, newspapers in Pakistan.' Kamran paused. 'Junayd Sattar is today renowned for his beautiful nature photographs – particularly of Pakistan's birdlife.'

'So, he never returned to the UK?' Fabian asked. 'Not to see his family even?'

'No.'

'Is he still alive?' Mum asked, leaning forwards. 'Is my dad still alive, Kamran?'

'Yes, he is.'

'Does he know about me?'

'I wouldn't imagine so, Lisa. I'm sure Eloise would have told him she was pregnant, but he was whisked off back to Pakistan even before Eloise was sent to Canada. With Eloise thinking you were a boy and adopted overseas...' Kamran smiled '...Janice filled me in on the details in the car park... well, presumably Junayd knew he'd never have contact with his child. The Sattars have always known of the scandal of Junayd and the boss's daughter. It's only in the past few weeks, with our intention to buy Hudson House, that I've really looked into all of this in relation to Eloise Hudson.'

'So, on Friday, when you took Mum flying, you'd no idea she was Eloise and Junayd's daughter?' I asked.

'No! Why would I? Why on earth *would I*?' Kamran turned to Mum. 'It's come as much of a shock to me as to you, Lisa.'

'I doubt it!' Jess said tartly.

'And...' Mum started '...do you know... how... *how* related are we...?'

Kamran appeared to forget Jess, Fabian and I were in the room. Or he just didn't care. Walking over to Mum, he took her hand and bent to kiss her cheek, smiling down at her. 'Junayd Sattar is my grandfather's cousin's son. My grandfather and Junayd's father left Mirpur together back in the early sixties and both came to work at Hudson's. I can't quite work it out. Fabian? You're obviously a clever bloke – what does that make us?'

'You and Mum are cousins twice removed, I believe,' Jess said archly, her mathematical brain obviously working overtime. 'All totally above board to—'

'Jess,' Mum and I both hissed together.

'So, Jess – and Robyn – do I have your permission to take Lisa out again?' Kamran was laughing at us both. 'Oh, and one more thing...' he now turned specifically to Fabian and Jess '...how do the pair of you feel about pitching in with me and turning the white house into a fabulous, upmarket restaurant?'

'Oh, I don't think so, Mr Sattar,' Jess said crossly. 'It was our idea first. Mine and Fabian's—'

'Hang on, Jess,' Fabian interrupted, turning to Kamran. 'What makes you think we had any notion of doing that?'

Kamran smiled. 'Beddingfield, like any other village, is a hotbed of gossip. Rumours abound. The Richardsons were quite open about someone else being after the place and their intentions for it. It won't be an easy project and, as my two brothers are not remotely interested in opening a restaurant, I'd very much like someone along with me who is. My cousin's son, Zain, wants to be in on it but he's very young and only a pastry chef.'

'But...' Jess began.

'Hang on, Jess,' Fabian said again. 'The white house rather than Hudson House itself?'

'I think so,' Kamran said.

'An equal partnership?' Fabian demanded.

'I wouldn't want anything less,' Kamran said solemnly.

'Does that mean the residents won't be turfed out?' Mum asked. 'Eloise won't have to find somewhere else to live?'

'Certainly not for the foreseeable future if that's what we decide.'

'And what about St Mede's?' I asked, butting in, desperate to know. 'Are your plans to knock the school down still going ahead?'

'That's something else entirely,' Kamran said gently, but I could tell he wasn't prepared to give anything away regarding his plans for the school.

I glanced across at Jess and Mum and finally towards Fabian. All three were looking animated, excited, but particularly Fabian who, I could see, was more than happy to have Kamran on board. Here was an exceptionally successful businessman, one whose family had a wealth of restaurant experience, wanting to be a part of Fabian's dream.

'How do I tell Eloise?' Mum suddenly blurted out. 'How on earth do I tell Eloise Hudson that she never had a son called Adam? That she had a daughter called Lisa. And it's me! Will she believe me? Will it send her over the edge?'

'We've been discussing this, Mum,' Jess said. 'All weekend. Perhaps best to speak to her brother, Michael, who's been over quite a few times to see her. He seems a nice bloke. His wife's pleasant too. Yes, I'd speak to Michael...'

'Can I propose a toast?' Kamran was saying, popping a bottle of champagne. 'To Lisa and Eloise, may you soon share a relationship that's been a long time coming.'

We raised glasses, murmuring, 'Lisa and Eloise.'

'My turn now,' Mum said, wiping away a tear. 'To the white house – may your plans come to fruition. I really, really hope they do. Goodness,' she went on, smiling across at Kamran before reaching out one hand each to Jess and me, 'this has been one hell of a January.'

* * *

Later, much later, when Fabian and I were back in the Dower Cottage, when, looking at my watch, I knew I had only six hours before I was back with 9CL, I turned to Fabian.

'You sure about this, Fabian?' I asked, raising myself up on my elbow and looking down at the beautiful man at my side. I gave him a gentle nudge. 'How can you sleep when you're about to make such a momentous decision?'

'Already made it, Robyn.' He smiled, his eyes still closed. He opened them then, pulling me into him so I could feel the steady beat of his heart, hear the resolution in his words.

'Robyn, I love you and only you. I don't want to be anywhere else but here in our lovely cottage overlooking the duck pond in this beautiful village with you and your mad family. And I can't wait to get started with Jess and Kamran on the restaurant at the white house. Now, unless you want that horrible lot of kids in 9CL totally out of control in the morning, I suggest you close your eyes, tell me you love me and go to sleep.'

Which, knowing I was exactly where I wanted to be, and with

the man I loved more than anything in the world, was exactly what I did.

* * *

MORE FROM JULIE HOUSTON

Another book from Julie Houston, *A Class Act*, is available to order now here:
https://mybook.to/ClassActBackAd

ACKNOWLEDGEMENTS

Lessons in Life is my fifteenth novel and my second writing for the fabulous publisher Boldwood. A big thank you to all the team at Boldwood, and particularly to editors Sarah Ritherdon – who was my very first editor when I started out on this writing journey – and Emily Yau as well as the eagle-eyed Sue Smith whose copy-editing skills are legendary!

Thanks, as always, to my lovely agent, Anne Williams at KHLA Literary Agency, for her unstinting help, advice, friendship and loyalty.

To all the wonderful readers and reviewers who read my books and write such lovely things about them, a huge, heartfelt thank you.

ABOUT THE AUTHOR

Julie Houston is the author of thirteen bestselling novels set in and around two fictional West Yorkshire villages.

Sign up to Julie Houston's mailing list for news, competitions and updates on future books.

Follow Julie on social media here:

- facebook.com/JulieHoustonauthor
- x.com/@JulieHouston2
- instagram.com/juliehoustonauthor
- bookbub.com/authors/julie-houston

ALSO BY JULIE HOUSTON

Class Act

Lessons in Life

BECOME A MEMBER OF

THE SHELF CARE CLUB

The home of Boldwood's book club reads.

Find uplifting reads, sunny escapes, cosy romances, family dramas and more!

Sign up to the newsletter
https://bit.ly/theshelfcareclub

Boldwood

Boldwood Books is an award-winning fiction publishing company seeking out the best stories from around the world.

Find out more at www.boldwoodbooks.com

Join our reader community for brilliant books, competitions and offers!

Follow us
@BoldwoodBooks
@TheBoldBookClub

Sign up to our weekly deals newsletter

https://bit.ly/BoldwoodBNewsletter

Printed in Dunstable, United Kingdom